ARISTEIA

Book Two

A LITTLE REBELLION

BY WAYNE BASTA

Library of Congress Cataloging-in-Publication Data

Basta, Wayne

Aristeia: revolutionary right / Wayne Basta

Library of Congress Control Number: 2012939004

ISBN 978-0-9854400-4-6

10 9 8 7 6 5 4 3 2 1

First Edition

To Mom and Dad

"I like a little rebellion now and then...The spirit of resistance to government is so valuable that I wish it to be always kept alive. It will often be exercised when wrong, but better so than not to be exercised at all."

--Thomas Jefferson

PROLOGUE

Admiral Katerina Sartori awoke early, as was her habit. She liked giving herself ample time to perform her morning routine before she had to begin the day. The summons to appear before the joint chiefs of the Alliance military had been unexpected, but it was no reason to break her routine.

The summons had included no indication of what the meeting was to be about. She held no illusions that it was merely to wish her well on her retirement. The changing of command ceremony releasing her from her former position as commanding officer of the 2nd Fleet had taken place a week before. Fleet Admiral Holiday had already sent the customary letter congratulating her on a job well done. It was unlikely he would be calling her now to say the same in person.

Katerina had been looking forward to returning to Terra. More than a year had passed since she had last seen her grandchildren, and it would be nice to be on the same planet as her children again. This meeting suggested that she wouldn't be seeing them as soon as she had hoped.

The waiting room outside the chiefs' conference room was well appointed. A nervous junior lieutenant asked if she needed anything while she waited. Declining the offer, she contented herself with admiring the view of Braz through the station's wide window. She considered it a tactical weakness to have such a large, vulnerable window at the heart of Alliance command, but it was a nice view.

While she waited, the junior lieutenant kept looking up from his desk anxiously. The Academy must still be talking about her as if she were some kind of legend. She supposed it was because her victory over the Dotran at Ailleroc had been the last major naval engagement of the war. In truth, it had been the last major battle in sixteen years. Either way, the manner in which they talked about her made new officers idealize her. It just made her uncomfortable.

After only a few minutes, the lieutenant informed her that the chiefs were ready. She thanked the young man and went into the conference room. Seated around an oval table were the chiefs of the Alliance military: Fleet Admiral Grant Holiday of the navy, General Gret Joroka of the marines, and General Jose Garcia of the army. The room was devoid of the customary aides that should have been accompanying these leaders.

Katerina saluted when she entered, and Admiral Holiday returned the gesture. The lieutenant who had showed her in closed the door behind her. Her curiosity was piqued as she considered the implications of the lack of aides. Whatever this meeting was about, it would involve only the three highest ranking members of the military and her. No good could come of that.

"Admiral Sartori, forgive us for calling you here on such short notice. I have no doubt you were looking forward to your retirement. Unfortunately, we are going to have to ask you to postpone your plans," Admiral Holiday said by way of greeting.

At least they weren't beating around the bush, Katerina thought. She would be officially retired as of tomorrow. Since she had spent the better part of forty years in uniform, it was unlikely they would forcibly require her to return to service, but that they wanted her for anything had her concerned.

"The Alliance will always have my service," Katerina replied automatically.

"Thank you, Katerina," Holiday said. "I wouldn't ask if it wasn't important."

Turning to a computer terminal beside him, he activated a holo projector in the table. An image of a prison facility appeared, hovering over the table. One of the outer walls of the compound had collapsed, and there were other signs of destruction around the compound.

"Two days ago, we received a packet ship from our forces on Sulas. One of our detention centers was savagely attacked by insurgents. They succeeded in freeing over seven hundred highly dangerous dissidents and terrorists. The insurgents attacked the prison with starships and a highly effective and dangerous commando unit. They killed half the prison guards and also managed to shoot down half a dozen of our fighters before escaping into hyperspace."

Despite the seriousness of the news, Sartori found herself impressed. That a civilian group could manage to pull off such a feat was quite an accomplishment. She'd never have thought that a group existed within the Alliance that could pull something like this off. That troubled her.

Holiday continued, "The attack was led by two of our own: Major Maarkean Ocaitchi and Corporal Zeric Dustlighter. Our forces intercepted communications between the two during the attack."

The image of the prison shifted to the faces of a Terran and a Braz. Next to each man was a brief military biography. She did not recognize either of them, but something jumped out from the Braz's biography.

"Major Ocaitchi served under me," Katerina said. "He was in the Enterprise's air group during the battle of Ailleroc."

With a sound of disgust, General Joroka said, "Corporal Dustlighter also served during the war. It seems their loyalties have since changed.

"Up until five years ago, Major Ocaitchi had an exemplary record. After retiring from active duty, he continued to serve in the Reserves for many years and had recently been promoted to squadron commander. Then his sister got involved with some subversive groups. She must have been the one to turn him, because shortly before she was due to be arrested, they both disappeared from the planet.

"Dustlighter left the military years ago, and every indication is that he spent that time in a life of crime."

"Why did they attack the detention center?" Katerina asked.

"The prison held several high-profile subversives. This is not common knowledge, but several months ago, the governments of each of the planets in the Kreogh region held a meeting. The result of this meeting was a set of demands that they transmitted to the Alliance government. Several of the members of this illegal gathering were arrested on Sulas. We believe Major Ocaitchi was attempting to free them."

This news came as more of a shock than the prison break. She had heard nothing about this meeting or demands being made to the Alliance government. As far as she had been aware, all of the planets in the Kreogh region were peaceful and loyal.

"Unfortunately, this is not the worst of the news," Holiday continued. "There are indications that the Dotrans are covertly pulling the strings. One of the attendees at the conference, a Kowwok named Lahkaba, was a former member of their military. We believe he may have been involved in the attack on the prison as well. This suggests the Dotran may be attempting to destabilize the region so they can retake control."

If the news before had been unsettling, this was even more so. While the Alliance had been at peace with the Dotrans for years, Katerina had no doubt their former enemies were capable of plotting something like this. They had been embarrassingly defeated during the war, by her in several cases, and would no doubt be eager for revenge.

Holiday went on, "Congress has decreed that all governments that participated in this meeting are to be unseated.

They have already authorized local Alliance governors to assume control until new elections can be held. Unfortunately, that message was dispatched before we learned about the attack on Sulas. Things appear to have escalated. On station in the sector, we only have Task Group 42 along with a few squadrons from Task Group 43, plus small army garrisons on each world. These may not be sufficient to handle any attempts to rebel.

"We're preparing the 3rd Marine Expeditionary Force to assert Alliance authority in the sector and to show the Dotrans they won't get it back without a fight. You have experience in the region and the respect of friend and foe alike. We'd like to appoint you as colonial sector commander, which will include a promotion to the rank of fleet admiral. You'll have command over the 3rd MEF, all of the army garrisons and the entire 4th Fleet. With you in command, we're hoping the bloodshed can be minimized."

Katerina had no doubt about that. She had seen more than enough bloodshed in her time. A younger and less experienced commander would be more likely to retaliate with unnecessary violence. That would only lead to pointless deaths and exacerbate the situation.

The chiefs' decision to send her made strategic sense, but returning to the uniform right as she was about to put it aside gave her pause. This would not be a short-term assignment. It was a three-month journey just to get to the Kreogh Sector, plus the time preparing, the time there, and the journey home. Taking this command would push her retirement back at least a year—more likely, two or three.

Had her husband still been alive, she was sure she would have declined. As much as she missed her children and grandchildren, she would still be spending a good portion of her retirement alone. One last mission did hold some appeal for her.

Making her decision, Katerina asked, "When will the task force be ready?"

"Hopefully within the next two months. We've recalled some ships and are prioritizing others in maintenance. We have an intelligence unit preparing to depart in the next few days. We hope to be able to infiltrate the subversive elements and gather intel before your arrival."

"Excellent," Katerina replied. "We'll need to know everything we can about them. This operation won't be as straightforward as the war with the Dotran."

She took a harder look at the two men whose faces were still displayed on the hologram. What would cause Alliance officers to betray their oaths of allegiance? she wondered. Whatever the reason, she would make sure they paid the price for their treason.

CHAPTER 1

Lahkaba stared out into the darkness as the vehicle carried him forward. They were many kilometers from the nearest city, so there was no city glow to brighten the night. Neither of Sulas' moons was currently visible, which made the darkness even more oppressive.

He found something poetic in that. Being surrounded by darkness, unable to see beyond the car's headlights, matched how he felt. The victory on Enro had inspired him—for the first time, he had felt things were about to change—but that feeling had only lasted until he had returned to Sulas.

The news about the uprising had reached Sulas days before Lahkaba and the rest of the delegates had. This fact was unavoidable and not unexpected. He expected similar uprisings or protests to spring up across Sulas, either as a direct response to their own legislature being disbanded or after hearing news about Enro's uprising. Despite his general distaste for the ancient Kowwok religion, he had made several silent prayers to the Great One that he wouldn't find the entire planet in a violent upheaval.

Much to his dismay, his prayers had apparently been answered. As far as he could tell, there hadn't been a single incident. The general population believed that the uprising on Enro had failed. The planetary news network repeated this as fact, which was also not unexpected. This news had kept any homegrown protests from spreading beyond a few isolated incidents.

What had surprised Lahkaba was the person who kept calling for people not to protest: Hans Kantor, former speaker of the Sulas legislature. He could be seen on every news source, official and unofficial, calling for people not to respond. The man had apparently peacefully capitulated when the Alliance had disbanded the legislature.

Hans Kantor had been a leading public figure on Sulas since the end of the Great War. He had helped bridge the gap between the Alliance and non-Alliance populations. It had been his efforts that had led to non-Alliance species gaining voting rights in the planetary government.

He had also done nothing to stop the baseless arrests and imprisonments in Olan prison, nor had he seriously campaigned for the extension for full Alliance citizenship, though those things were also beyond his authority. Governor Howell, the Alliance-appointed governor, had final authority. He had overturned or ignored most of the efforts of the legislature.

While Lahkaba was merely disappointed by Kantor's acceptance of the disbandment, Lei-mey, his Ronid associate, was livid. Her first reaction had been to suggest treating Kantor as the enemy. She even went so far as to suggest sending Zeric after him. Lahkaba found that amusing, but he kept it to himself.

They were currently on their way to meet with Kantor and all of the former legislature members. As this was in clear violation of the Alliance decree, Lahkaba took it as a good sign. Lei-mey, however, planned to use it as an opportunity to tell Kantor exactly what she thought. That was not unusual, either.

Lights appeared in the darkness. They grew, and soon Lahkaba could make out the shape of a house, though he couldn't make out any more details beyond that. The vehicle came to a stop just inside the glow from the windows.

Lahkaba, along with Lei-mey and a Terran named Pasha Alon, climbed out of the vehicle. The remaining two delegates, who had traveled with him from Enro, followed. They were Ayla Doorna, a Braz female, and Muhammed Kumar, a

Terran male. Unlike the others, these last two had not participated directly in the battle on Enro, but that was more due to their advanced age than to a lack of conviction.

A squeak broke the silence of the dark night, and Lahkaba turned to see a grey-haired Terran opening a screen door. Hans Kantor smiled down at them from the porch, the light from behind casting him in an eerie shadow. Silently, Lahkaba mouthed another prayer to the Great One that this wasn't an omen of Kantor's intentions. Then, remembering the backhanded way in which his previous prayer had been answered, he immediately regretted it.

"My friends, welcome home," Kantor said, greeting them with a smile. "Please come in; the night air is chilly at this time of year."

Lahkaba glanced at the others and saw them shivering, Lei-mey more so than the others. His white fur did an excellent job of regulating his temperature and insulating him from outside fluctuations. It felt quite pleasant to him.

The group followed Kantor into the house. The door and walls were made from local wood instead of synthetic materials. Once inside, they went down a short hall lined with pictures. Lahkaba recognized Kantor and his wife in several of them, along with a wide variety of other Terrans, whom he assumed to be members of Kantor's family.

Kantor showed them into a large room that was currently filled to overflowing with others. Almost every member of the former legislature was present, standing or sitting around the room. How all of these people had managed to gather without attracting Alliance attention, Lahkaba didn't know. The thought that this might be an Alliance trap to arrest them all at once had occurred to him more than once. But the risk was necessary.

Almost as one, the group started to greet Lahkaba and the others. It had been six months since he had seen most of them. After returning to Sulas from the first Kreogh Sector Congress meeting, he had immediately been forced to go into hiding. From there, he had helped with the prison break on Olan and then been on the run with Maarkean.

The pleasantries were kept short, and Kantor called everyone to attention after only a few minutes. With this many people, it took a few more for everyone to get settled and quiet. All eyes turned toward Kantor, and the air buzzed with anticipation.

"Thank you all for coming. I've called this meeting as a private citizen, inviting friends together. We are not meeting as the Sulas legislature. But as friends, we owe it to those who recently returned from Enro to hear their side of the story before we jump to any conclusions about their actions," Kantor began.

Lahkaba cocked his head to the side at the introduction. Legally speaking, it was a necessary declaration. The Alliance had outlawed the legislature but had not, so far, banned gatherings at private residences. The rest of Kantor's remarks were evasive and revealed nothing about his true intentions.

"So I invite Lahkaba to step forward and give a report to the rest of us about what happened."

That startled Lahkaba. Lei-mey had traditionally been the speaker for the delegation. He had not even been among them when they had departed Sulas before the last meeting, so he had only a vague idea of what had occurred on Sulas recently.

Looking at the others, though, he started to think it might be a good idea for him to speak. Ayla and Muhammed were highly regarded by the legislature, but neither gave very good speeches. Pasha had been raised to the delegation after his involvement in the Olan prison break, which meant the members probably supported that action, but he also had no experience with public speaking. And Lei-mey, based on the look on her face, probably wouldn't play nice.

So Lahkaba began. "As you all know, after I returned to Sulas from the first Kreogh Sector Congress meeting, I went into hiding to avoid an arrest warrant. After Lei-mey was arrested, I met a former Alliance naval officer named Maarkean Ocaitchi and a former marine, Zeric Dustlighter. They convinced me and several others, Pasha included, to stage a prison break of everyone held illegally in Olan Detention Center.

"The break-out went well, and we fled with the refugees to the planet of Irod." Though Irod was technically a moon, it had been decided at the last Congress meeting to keep the location secret. Irod existed in navigational charts merely as PX-1997, one of many barely charted worlds in an uninhabited system.

"From there, I left to join Maarkean and Zeric as they continued to fight the oppressive rule of the Alliance." That wasn't exactly true, either. Maarkean had originally wanted nothing beyond getting his sister, Saracasi, out of prison. But his friend had since become fully committed to fighting the Alliance, so Lahkaba doubted he'd mind this slight fib.

"When I learned of the second Kreogh Sector Congress meeting, Maarkean took me to Enro to participate. While there, the order from the Alliance unseating the planetary governments arrived. Prime Minister Corte, leader of the Enro parliament, requested that all of the congressional delegates join the Enroians in opposing the order. Maarkean offered to lead the defense of Perth, where their parliament met. He convinced us that if we let the Enroians make this stand alone, it would be in vain.

"Together, the planets of the Kreogh sector are strong. We showed that in the victory over the Alliance on Enro. The city held, and the Alliance commander surrendered. Enro is now free from Alliance occupation, but they will not remain that way unless we all band together."

Lahkaba watched the crowd as he spoke. While he considered himself capable, he would never call himself a moving public speaker. Yet, he noticed many heads nodding as he spoke. It became clear that many in the legislature were inspired by the events on Enro.

A bit of Lei-mey must have slipped into his head, because Lahkaba found himself continuing, "When I arrived back here to find that Sulas' leadership had simply rolled over to the Alliance, I was ashamed. The people of Enro rose up to defend their government. People here on Sulas are ready to do the same. But this body has not picked up that call. Instead, we meet in secret and call for citizens to remain calm."

Many faces turned sour at his accusation, but far more looked ashamed. Lahkaba went on, "We represent the people of this planet. It is our responsibility to protect their rights. One of their rights is to pick their leaders. By allowing the Alliance to disband us without a fight, we have robbed the people of that right."

An uncomfortable silence hung in the air, and Kantor stood up behind Lahkaba. "Thank you, Lahkaba. That was very illuminating."

Kantor fixed Lahkaba with a look that made it clear his time speaking was done. Reluctantly, he moved from the center of the group, yielding the floor back to Kantor. It was still unclear to him where Kantor stood and what would happen next.

"It is clear that many of you support our delegate's decision to participate in the rebellion on Enro," Kantor began, casting a stern look across the room. "While I don't disagree with the principle, the sudden escalation to violence is troubling. As I warned after the events at Olan, violence will only lead to more violence. The attack on the prison corrected a grave injustice, but now we stand on the precipice of war because of it.

"Would you have us incite the people to rise up like the Enroians? The Alliance already has troops occupying several cities. It is not a matter of defending a single city from a small force. Here on Sulas, there are many more Alliance forces on the ground, along with warships in orbit. An uprising will lead to the deaths of thousands, maybe tens or hundreds of thousands."

Shooting up from her seat, Lei-mey angrily retorted, "You want us to just accept this as you've done? Go on the media and tell the people to bow down to tyranny?"

Kantor stiffened, and Lahkaba expected a shouting match to begin. Those two had never gotten along very well. "No. I regret my earlier announcements. We had incomplete information, and I did not want a massacre to occur, as I believed had happened on Enro. I would still like to avoid violence and death. Anyone's death."

Lei-mey appeared ready to continue, but Lahkaba reached up and put a hand on her arm. She turned her head to look down at him, and he looked into her multi-faceted eyes. Her mandibles rubbed together and she pursed her lips as she considered him. From past experience, he knew that to be a sign that she was thinking something over.

Lei-mey turned back to Kantor and spoke in a calmer voice. "What do you propose instead?"

Taking a deep breath, Kantor took Lei-mey's tone as a peace offering and continued in his usual calm voice. "A spontaneous uprising will result in many people dead. Lahkaba was correct about one thing: we need to remain united with the other worlds of the Kreogh sector. We cannot win a fight alone. I assume a date was set for another meeting?"

"It was. Each delegation is to meet with their government and decide whether or not to ignore the Alliance's order to disband. And then to send delegates along with military aid to a secret location to be used to start training an army to oppose the Alliance's order."

"Then I propose exactly that," Kantor said, his voice gaining enthusiasm. "We continue our work with the other worlds of the sector. Only with their help can we succeed."

Most of the people nodded in agreement with Kantor. For some reason, Lahkaba felt like he had just lost, despite getting one of the things he had been advocating.

Zeric Dustlighter looked out over the city of Perth. It had been a while since the uncontrolled fires had all been put out, but he still remembered what it looked like when they were marring the city with smoke and flame. Even without the fires, the city still looked scarred from the earlier battle, even though it had been almost a month since the last shot had been fired.

Despite the craziness of the battle that had caused all of the damage, Zeric found himself thinking fondly of those days. Normally, he would have chosen sitting in a comfortable hotel room over getting shot at, but after sitting around with nothing to do for a month, he was getting restless.

At first, he had helped with the clean up. But the predominately Ronid population of Enro had shown their legendary efficiency. It had not taken them long to complete all of the work that unskilled labor could manage. The process of rebuilding would take longer but would now require trained hands.

If it had been his choice, he wouldn't still be here. Defending the city of Perth from an Alliance assault force had been a noble act that he didn't regret, even though they had commissioned him into their hastily formed militia. But he had no desire to continue to support them. His time here so far had already laced his reddish-brown hair with more grey than he was comfortable with. Now that the battle was done and all of the Alliance forces had surrendered, he felt ready to move on.

But Maarkean had felt obliged to help prepare the city for the next Alliance attack. The Alliance would undoubtedly retaliate with a strike force to reclaim the planet. Zeric didn't disagree that it would happen. He just didn't see it as his problem.

While he could sympathize with the Enroians, Zeric felt that his talents were wasted here. If he was really going to commit himself to this rebellion—and it was a rebellion, despite what others might try to call it—he should be out taking the fight to the Alliance. Defensive battles were already half lost.

He had been unable to convince anyone else of that. Gu'od and Gamaly were content to wait. The Enroian government had made good on their promise to pay for the shielded personnel carrier (SPC) and the weapons Zeric and the others had provided them. Using their share, the two Liw'kel had even taken some time to have a mini-vacation in one of the planet's other, more intact cities.

Even though Maarkean insisted that they should continue to serve the Enroians, the Enroians weren't that interested in receiving their help. Technically, Maarkean was still the official commander of the militia, but it had been weeks since he had had any duties. When Maarkean had nothing to do, there was even less for Zeric.

With luck, that was all about to change. Maarkean and Lohcja had been summoned to a meeting with the Enroian cabinet. Zeric was glad that he hadn't been included, but he was very curious to learn the results.

A sound from the door caught his attention, and he turned to see Gu'od, Gamaly, and Saracasi coming in. Like her brother, Saracasi bore a purple screfa tattoo on her pale skin, identifying her clan. The purple matched her eyes and contrasted nicely with her long braid of red hair. Gu'od and Gamaly were both Liw'kel, him a light tan and her a powder blue. The antennae on their head were thicker and shorter than the narrow stalks of Enro's Ronid population.

Startled to see all of them arrive at once, Zeric was glad he had bothered to get dressed this morning. A man with room service and nowhere to go didn't really need pants.

"You could have knocked," Zeric said.

"And miss the chance to catch you in your underwear?" Gamaly asked with a playful smile.

"You just need to ask for that," Zeric said with a grin, before casting a glance at Gu'od. "And get me a promise that he won't kill me."

"I could never make that promise," Gu'od said, his facial expression his normal variety of neutral.

"But seriously, what's up?" Zeric asked, ignoring the implied threat like he had all of the ones before it.

"Got a message from Maarkean," Saracasi said as she took a seat. "He's on his way back here."

"Already?" Zeric asked, surprised. "That was a quick meeting."

Saracasi shrugged. "Guess so. He wanted to meet with us. Guess he has a plan now."

"Finally," Zeric said, rubbing his hands together.

They sat around for another fifteen minutes waiting for Maarkean. During that time, Solyss Novastar, Eri'dos Ar'cher, and Fracsid Relis arrived. The three transport captains made the room feel overly full, and Zeric considered seeing if the hotel had a conference room they could use. But everyone had been told to come here instead of Maarkean's room or someplace else, and Zeric assumed that had been done for a reason.

When Maarkean finally arrived, followed into the room by Lohcja Cargon, Zeric immediately picked up on his friend's irritation. Normally emotionally reserved, Maarkean's eyes were on fire and his cheeks were flushed. Instead of a cool, determined gait, he strode into the room quickly without acknowledging anyone.

Zeric turned to Lohcja, who stopped beside him, and gave the green Ronid a curious look. Lohcja ignored him, instead focusing his attention on the floor. Zeric found this behavior even more unexpected. He had seen Maarkean angry, but he had never seen Lohcja look ashamed.

"The Enro cabinet has decided our services will no longer be required," Maarkean said without preamble.

The group exclaimed in surprise and outrage. Zeric was surprised by the news, too, but something caught his attention he didn't think anyone else had noticed. "You said 'our.'"

Maarkean looked at Zeric and nodded. "Indeed, I did. The cabinet said that a Ronid world should be protected by Ronids. We're not Ronids."

"That's preposterous," Gamaly said. "There's quite a sizable Liw'kel population living here, along with not a few other species."

"Who's taking command? Chief Kamalas?" Gu'od said, staying much calmer than his wife.

Maarkean shook his head and said, his tone still laced with sarcasm, "No. Apparently, only a member of the warrior caste should lead their army."

"Warrior caste?" Zeric asked, confused. Lohcja had mentioned the old Ronid caste system on occasion, but he thought that had disappeared centuries ago.

"You know that guy who's been in the news lately?" Maarkean asked.

Zeric just returned a blank stare, but Saracasi answered, "Shaden Zhet?"

"That's the one. He succeeded in getting himself appointed as the new minister of defense. Apparently his Heritage Party has gained a lot of popularity in the last month."

"Who is this guy, and why do we care?' Zeric asked, not following the conversation.

Saracasi let out an exasperated sigh. "Zhet is the leader of a party that is calling for a return to the old ways of the caste system. He's claiming that had they returned to the caste system after the Kravic occupation ended, Rona would have been strong enough to defend Enro from the Alliance. He also claims that they wouldn't have needed a Braz to step in and defend them."

"Apparently, I am everything that is wrong with Ronid civilization," Maarkean said with a flourish.

"So who is in charge then?" Zeric asked, ignoring the details.

Maarkean looked past him toward Lohcja, who was still looking down at the floor. Everyone in the room followed the look. Had he been in Lohcja's place, Zeric was sure he would have gone pink with embarrassment. Fortunately for Lohcja, Ronid carapace had no ability to change shades like that.

"I'm not actually in charge," Lohcja retorted. "Just in command of the unit they are sending to join the Union army."

"The unit he speaks of is a new battalion," Maarkean explained. "The grand total of Enro's commitment to the united cause is a single battalion."

Saracasi looked at her brother, confused. "Wasn't the Alliance garrisoning this planet with just a single battalion?"

"They were. But this is one of the least defended planets, being so far from Confederate space. The rest of the systems have a much bigger Alliance presence," Zeric answered.

"So we go with Lohcja and join this Union army," Saracasi said, her comment more of a question than a statement. Zeric would have expected her to be the one clamoring to join.

"If it ever forms," Lohcja said quietly. "Another thing Zhet is championing is that Enro can stand on her own."

"Then why is he sending you to join with the rest of the sector?" Fracsid asked. "If he thinks Enro can defend itself, why send troops away?"

"To get rid of Lohcja," Solyss said, nodding in understanding from where he sat next to Fracsid.

Wearing a finely tailored jacket, which stood out amongst the torn and ragged clothing of the other transport captains, Solyss leaned his dark Terran body back in his chair. He started gesturing as he continued. He was the perfect image of a university professor giving a lecture. "Lohcja is a threat to him, just as much as Maarkean was. More so. Because he's a Ronid who fought and gained some notoriety. But unlike Maarkean or Chief Kamalas, he can't just dismiss Lohcja."

"Why not?" Zeric asked, feeling just as confused as Fracsid looked.

"He's a member of the warrior caste. And Zhet claims they are the ones who need to lead the fight. Sending Lohcja away to join the Union hedges their bets in case help is needed and gets rid of a potential rival."

Lohcja made an agitated click with his mandibles. "That is mostly right. But fortunately, Zhet doesn't have that much authority. Prime Minister Corte and most of the cabinet are still fully in support of a united Kreogh sector."

"That's good, right?" Fracsid asked.

Speaking up for the first time in a while, Maarkean's tone once again had his normal, calm, authoritative quality. "Yes, it is. We signed up to see the Alliance's harsh rules repealed. Not just for Enro, but for the entire Kreogh sector."

"You got a plan?" Zeric asked, putting Maarkean on the spot. It had been done to him enough that he wanted to see Maarkean squirm a little.

There was a noticeable pause from Maarkean, and Zeric momentarily felt bad for enjoying it, before Maarkean continued. "We recruit. Find people like us who are capable fighters, and join up with the Union."

Chapter 2

"You know, if you wanted, we could just disappear and take off for parts unknown," Saracasi said, lounging in the operations chair on the flight deck of the *Cutty Sark*, Maarkean's personal ship.

Maarkean turned from the pilot's station and raised an eyebrow. "I thought this rebellion thing was exactly what you wanted me to do."

Nodding, Saracasi continued, though her tone was less confident than she wanted it to be. "It is. It has always been what I wanted you to do. But it's never been what you wanted to do. We have a full fuel tank and some money on hand, and there's no one else on the ship. There's nothing stopping you from disappearing and returning to a quiet life of smuggling."

Leaning forward, she looked her brother in the eye, hoping to find an answer. "So, why don't you?"

Maarkean held her gaze for a moment and then turned back to the computer display. Traveling in hyperspace meant there would not be anything new on the pilot's display, and Saracasi knew he was stalling. She had avoided having this conversation with him until now.

The conviction he had shown in helping the Enroians had surprised her. He had shown signs of coming around to accepting the flaws in the Alliance, but it had been a slow process. While it hadn't been the first time he had taken up arms against his former government—once he had done so to save her, and once he'd done so to pay off a debt—he had never done it out of a conviction that the Alliance was doing anything wrong. Enro had changed him.

As much as she was glad to see this change, it worried her. In truth, the idea of an open rebellion scared her. She had advocated for change within the Alliance for a long time and had even agreed with the people who claimed an uprising might be necessary. But Enro had changed her, too.

Until that battle, she had never killed anyone. Until that battle, she had never really understood what war was and what it did to people. Everything was different now.

"I'd be lying if I said I hadn't considered just disappearing," Maarkean finally said. "But I helped to start something, and I can't just walk away from it. The Alliance needs to know it crossed the line."

Saracasi was once again taken off guard by the determination in her brother's voice. She felt guilty for not being happier about it. She had pushed him for years every time the Alliance had violated its core principles. Now that he agreed, she had her own reasons for wishing it were otherwise—reasons she had not yet shared with anyone, and was not sure she ever could.

The hyperspace timer sounded on her computer, saving her from having to think any further about it. She ran a quick diagnosis of the engine systems before they reverted to real space. The twisted display of colors outside the cockpit window flashed and was replaced by the darkness of space. Before her in the distance lay the brown and blue world of Kol.

"Destination confirmed. Beginning sensor sweep," Saracasi said formally.

Nothing unusual appeared on her scan. There was the usual array of satellites, about a dozen freighters in various orbits, and a few sub-orbital planetary craft. Kol had no space stations or orbital defensive weapons.

The only Alliance presence was a small base on one of the equatorial islands.

Maarkean guided the *Cutty Sark* into a descending orbit while Saracasi idly watched the terrain. There was no central authority on Kol governing space traffic; there technically wasn't even a planetary government, only a joint advisory council consisting of representatives from the major mining companies and a few elected officials from the main population centers on the islands.

This limited amount of order allowed Kol to serve as home to a number of pirate and smuggling gangs. The mining companies loved the smugglers and frequently made use of them to circumvent Alliance taxes and trade restrictions. But they detested the pirates who preyed on their freighters.

The planetary council had tried to get the Alliance to clear out the pirates for years. The council wasn't a fan of more Alliance regulation, but it felt Kol was owed protection for the taxes they had to pay. Every so often, a task force of navy ships would arrive, crush smuggling, and inspect cargo. The pirates were smart enough to go into hiding during these brief interludes, making the planet's pleas look exaggerated.

Lack of planetary authority and limited Alliance presence were the very reasons she and Maarkean were coming here. They had hidden an old mining freighter in an abandoned mining facility in the planet's vast desert several months back. Until the Union officially formed its military, they were in need of a base. Enro had made it clear they would not be welcome there.

As they descended into the atmosphere, one of the suborbital passenger transports caught her attention. The vehicle suddenly changed course to an intercept vector with them. Before she could verify her initial assessment, she lost sensor data due to interference from reentry.

There could be any number of reasons for the transport to change course. Maybe there was bad weather at their destination, or they were having mechanical difficulty, or their course was erratic because they were simply sightseeing instead of going someplace in particular. The sensors identified it as a simple passenger transport with no armament or even shielding. Yet something about it bothered her.

Saracasi increased power to the shields, from the minimal levels for flight to full combat strength. There was no harm in strengthening the shields, aside from the increased energy drain. She debated saying something to Maarkean but didn't want to look foolish.

Immediately upon emerging from the reentry blind spot, she began looking for the transport. Her suspicions appeared to be confirmed when she couldn't locate it. The ship had changed course again while they were blinded. It was now flying a parallel path with them, slightly above and behind them. The odds were still high that the ship had done this for purely innocent reasons, but she decided she couldn't risk that anymore.

"Alter course," Saracasi told Maarkean.

"What?"

"Evasive maneuvers, now!" she said more forcefully.

Reacting instantly, Maarkean swerved the *Cutty Sark* on a sharp turn down and to port. They were low enough that she could see the ground suddenly flip sideways, though the inertial dampeners kept her from feeling anything. It didn't stop her mind from thinking the world was spinning though, and a nauseous feeling filled her stomach.

Once they had completed the turn, and Maarkean leveled them out again, he turned his head toward her. "Now would you mind explaining that?"

Ignoring him, Saracasi studied the sensor data. Just as she had feared, she picked up a new signal. A UBW missile sailed through the space they had once occupied. UBWs, Unguided Ballistic Weapons, were difficult to detect because they lacked tracking systems or correctional engines. They were launched by an initial rocket that burned off quickly and set them on an unalterable path. Not useful in the middle of a dogfight, they were great for catching someone unaware.

Maarkean saw the scene play out on the sensor readout. At exactly the place they would have been had they not changed course, the missile detonated, filling the sky with a bright explosion.

Nodding appreciatively, he said, "Good catch. Did you see where it was launched from?"

In response to his question, the passenger transport changed course again and began accelerating toward them. The craft made a turn that was far sharper than she would have expected, and Saracasi began an active sensor scan. This time, the sensors registered significant weapon signatures and far greater energy output from the engines than a passenger shuttle should have. The transponder signal it had been emitting was clearly a decoy.

Two flashes appeared along the hull of the craft, and two more missiles appeared on the sensors. This time they were traditional self-guided missiles, which wouldn't be so easily avoided. Maarkean took the *Cutty Sark* into a sharp dive toward Kol's surface, while Saracasi got up and moved to the aft weapons console.

Slipping into the seat, she mentally kicked herself for not powering the weapons up when she had increased shield strength. She had been too worried about looking paranoid. For most people, it would have been an overly cautious action. But when you were wanted dead by both powerful intergalactic governments and crime lords, a little paranoia was called for.

The weapon console took an eternity to power up. By the time she had enough power to begin firing a defensive pattern toward the missiles, Maarkean had already brought them to only a couple dozen meters above the desert floor. They flew straight for several seconds, giving Saracasi a better firing position. Her steady stream of fire managed to take out one of the missiles, but the other one kept coming.

A second before the missile would have impacted them, Maarkean pulled the ship up, causing the missile to miss. However, its proximity sensor triggered and detonated the missile. The compression wave from the explosion lifted the ship higher, almost causing Maarkean to lose control. Warning alarms triggered, and the operations console was filled with flashing red lights.

Saracasi scanned the air for their attacker but saw no sign of him. The weapons console's sensor data was limited, so she got up again to move to operations. She also needed to see how much damage they had taken. Their shields were far less effective against missile attacks than they were against energy weapons.

A quick glance at the ship's status display showed no immediate concerns; there was definite damage, but they were still flying. She checked the passive sensors but failed to locate their attacker. An active scan would have a better chance of revealing him, but it would also announce their location. Since they were not being fired on, there was a chance he had lost track of them.

"I've got no reading on him," Saracasi informed Maarkean.

Maarkean grunted. "How's the ship holding up? My controls are sluggish, and I'm having trouble holding a course."

This time, Saracasi took a closer look at the sensor display. Many of the reports indicated damaged relays and superficial hull damage. Due to the damage to the diagnostic systems, it took her a moment to fully grasp the extent of the problem.

"Port RCS cluster is gone, and there's a tear in the hull on the lower port wing. It's causing drag, which is probably what's causing the drift."

A curse escaped Maarkean's lips. This ship was his baby. She was only slightly less important to him than his sister was. The damage would also seriously hamper their ability to maneuver in a dogfight.

"Should we set down?" Saracasi asked.

"Out here in the middle of nowhere? That's probably exactly what he wants. I doubt I lost him that easily. If he wanted us dead, we'd still be fighting," Maarkean replied as he strained to keep the ship flying level.

"We're only about a hundred kilometers from Bravo HQ. Think you can get us there?" Saracasi asked, considering their options.

"That was an ambush. He knew we'd come back to Kol, he must know we'd go there."

"Well," Saracasi argued, "it's either there, or the closest active mining camp seven hundred kilometers in the opposite direction."

Maarkean growled under his breath. "I don't think we'll make it that far. Keep an eye out. We're going to have to risk going to Bravo."

With a sigh, Zeric got out of bed in order to answer the door chime. He couldn't recall ever having slept in a bed that comfortable; even the hotel suite he had been staying in on Enro had an inferior mattress. The fact that this bed was aboard a small courier ship made no difference.

Opening his cabin's door, Zeric saw a short Braz with a light blue screfa. Kard Ulis wore a dark green set of coveralls that had bits of equipment and tools sticking out of the many pockets. The coveralls were pretty standard fare on a ship, but the belt he wore was not. With two hip holsters holding a set of pistols, Kard was actually less armed than was normal for him. Any time he left the ship, he had another pair of pistols in a special holster hidden under his jacket.

"What is it, Kard?" Zeric asked.

"Captain says we're about to come out of hyperspace, Lieutenant," Kard said, trying to sound formal.

"I'm not a lieutenant," Zeric grumbled as he followed Kard toward the *Chimopori*'s flight deck.

While he had technically been a lieutenant with the Enro militia for a short time, and most military traditions held that a person's highest rank stayed with them even when they resigned, Zeric tried to ignore that. He had no interest in being an officer. If this lieutenant nonsense stuck with him, he might end up getting stuck as one in this new military they were trying to help the congress form.

The *Chimopori*'s flight deck was far more spacious than the one on *Cutty Sark*. The helm and operations stations were up front underneath the cockpit window, where they were located on most ships. On the back wall, to either side of the door, were additional control stations. These three additional terminals were configurable instead of having predefined controls. This gave them a lot of flexibility, but with many of the controls being touchpad based, they lacked any tactile feel. Zeric knew many pilots and gunners who would hate using controls like that.

Despite the number of control terminals, there was still plenty of room for people to stand around. Well, "plenty" might be pushing it, Zeric decided. But there was definitely some room, whereas the *Cutty Sark* only had space for one person to stand, and they would be blocking the door.

Seated at the helm and operations controls were the Notha pilot, Isaxo Mahon, and the ship's owner, Solyss Novastar. Gu'od and Gamaly Dos'redna, Zeric's two Liw'kel companions, were sitting at two unused control stations. At the remaining back station, currently configured as a weapons console, was the terrifying light-red-skinned Liw'kel, Asheerah Aru.

When Zeric had entered, Asheerah had been casting unusual looks toward Gu'od. Though she wore coveralls similar to Kard's, Zeric still imagined her in her mismatching armor. Solyss refused to allow her to wear her armor onboard ship, though the more conventional clothing did nothing to change her demeanor. Yet, the looks she had been giving Gu'od were surprisingly alluring.

For his part, Gu'od was looking forward, seemingly oblivious. Gamaly, on the other hand, had one of the darkest expressions he had ever seen mar her blue-skinned face. There was definitely something interesting going on there that Zeric wanted to watch, but only if he could do it from a safe distance.

Turning his attention away from the Liw'kel women, Zeric looked out of the forward window. They had evidently already exited hyperspace, because before them lay the dark green world of Mirthod. Even the oceans had a slight green tinge to them from orbit, as Mirthod boasted one of the most diverse and active biospheres of life on any world in the known galaxy. Compared to other places, even those that had produced sentient life, the vast number of unique life forms down there was remarkable.

"Ah, Mirthod, how I don't miss you," Zeric said.

"I hear it's quite a place," Solyss said. "Though I don't really agree with their primary industry."

"Why not? It's a great way to test your strength. Facing the wilds of this planet separates the weak from the strong," Asheerah said, casting another seductive look toward Gu'od as she spoke.

Mirthod's primary industry was the export of the unique life forms that lived there. The deadliest creatures that inhabited the wilderness were sought after by scientists and rich collectors alike. Many breakthroughs in disease prevention had been discovered here. There was also a large hunting community that felt surviving the wilds was the ultimate test of skill.

"Yeah, well, I don't plan on going anywhere near the jungle if I can manage it," Zeric said. "What we need won't be found there, but in the cities."

They had come to Mirthod for two reasons, both involving finding potentially experienced recruits for the new military. While many of those individuals would be experts at hunting in the wilds, Zeric had no intention of trying to find them out there.

"When we land, Gu'od and I will head into the city," Zeric said. "We'll go meet with Ice Company while the rest of you check out the cantinas and other hangouts."

"Ice Company?" Solyss said. He whistled. "That's who you used to work for? The stories I've heard are quite impressive. And disturbing. They are supposed to be quite vicious."

"Those are just stories," Zeric said, though his voice lacked confidence. "They were exaggerated to make people scared."

"If you say so," Solyss said, unconvinced.

Turning away from the flight deck, Zeric headed down the ship's main corridor, followed by Gamaly and Gu'od. Once the door sealed behind them, Gamaly fixed Zeric with a pointed stare. He wasn't going to enjoy this.

"I still think I should go with you," Gamaly began. "The last time you saw them, they tried to kill you."

"'Kill' is such a loaded word," Zeric said, trying to sound confident.

"You're not worried about Ymp?"

"Of course not," Zeric lied.

He was indeed worried about Ymp Ki-Li, the leader of Ice Company. When last they had met, the Camari woman had stranded him in the middle of a barely habitable moon. Ymp should be worried about seeing him. Yet, despite that, Zeric did not want to face the woman. She was the type to hold a grudge, and she would hold it against Zeric that he hadn't died when she'd wanted him to.

"Ice Company is full of experienced fighters," Zeric continued. "If we can recruit them as a whole, it would give us an immediate experienced unit. So, despite our past, I'm the one who needs to go, and I need to go without an entourage."

"Yeah, but I doubt they'll sign up out of a sense of patriotic pride. They may be based on Mirthod, but they have no sense of loyalty there. And we don't have any money to pay mercenaries," Gamaly argued.

"Then we have our work cut out for us," Gu'od said with a smile. "I will ensure he comes back safely."

"I'm not worried about him," Gamaly said, firmly. "Who's going to watch out for you?"

"Thanks," Zeric grumbled, but he stepped away in order to give his friends a moment alone.

When they stepped off of *Chimopori* a short time later, Zeric was immediately hit by the intense humidity. It had been a few years since he had spent any amount of time on Mirthod, and he had forgotten how much he hated the weather. Some of the towns in the north or south were more pleasant, but almost the entire planet was significantly warmer and more humid than what he would consider ideal.

"I should have changed into shorts," Zeric said, already sweating.

"It'll be cold inside," Gu'od said. He stood with a slight smile on his face.

"No, it will be tolerable inside. Only weirdoes like you enjoy this."

"It's normally so dry everywhere. This is nice."

"Bah," Zeric said grumpily. "Let's get this over with before I die of heat stroke."

They left the starport and got into a cab. As they rode through the city, Zeric looked at the dingy buildings and wondered for the first time why they were so decrepit. The resources Mirthod had to trade were very valuable—it was the only reason he could think anyone would want to live in this awful climate. Despite that, most of the people and the buildings he passed looked like they were dirt poor.

Why had he never noticed that before? He had spent quite a bit of time on Mirthod when he had worked with Ice. Most of the cities were like Scipost. The mercenary company had been hired to provide protection to many very wealthy individuals and companies that worked here.

The cab continued on while Zeric pondered. They arrived at one of the more opulent buildings, at least in this district. With a clean exterior, free from any of the most resilient plant species, the building stood out next to its neighbors. Most buildings in the area were more akin to warehouses. While this one was not much different in design, it was not dark and covered with graffiti.

Gu'od paid the cab driver while Zeric stared at the building, trying to summon up some courage. At one point, he had been friends with many of the people inside. It had been years since he had been here, and the life of a mercenary was not a safe one. He had no idea if any of them would still be alive.

"You want to stand out here and enjoy the weather or go inside?" Gu'od asked after the cab drove off.

"All right, all right," Zeric grumbled.

They walked up to the building's entrance and stepped inside. The area immediately beyond the door still resembled a warehouse. There was a cavernous ceiling and mostly empty space from one wall to the other. Along one wall stood a thick concrete barricade and a series of targeting dummies. At the other end of the room was a padded mat and a collection of training melee weapons.

Beyond this room, Zeric knew the warehouse held Ice Company's barracks, mess, and armory. That would be where the majority of the members would be located. But they were not alone in the open training area.

On the training mat, a small group sparred. Two were in the center, swinging at each other using padded sticks. Surrounding them were four others, one of whom appeared to be giving instructions to the fighters.

The fight ceased as soon as the group noticed Zeric and Gu'od approaching them. The one who had been giving instructions, a Terran with sandy-colored hair and broad shoulders, turned to face them. Everyone wore a cautious expression, and Zeric picked up that they were each ready to attack if provoked, but none appeared openly hostile.

None of the people in the group looked familiar to Zeric. That could either be a good or a bad thing. Having a friend to speak to would have been helpful, but it was just as likely anyone he had called a friend would not return the favor.

The Terran spoke first. "My name is Sigfa Neith. Can I help you gentlemen? In need of the services of Ice, perhaps?"

"You could say that," Zeric said. "We're looking for Ymp Ki-Li."

The expressions from the group suddenly grew dark. Zeric didn't know what to make of them. Some appeared hostile at the mention of Ymp's name, but others, Sigfa included, had another look.

"You won't find Ymp here anymore," Sigfa said ambiguously.

"Did she die?" Zeric asked. He wasn't sure if he would be relieved or saddened by the news.

"No, she's very much alive. Just no longer with Ice."

"Who's in charge, then?" Zeric asked.

"I am," a voice said from behind Zeric.

Turning, Zeric felt his stomach twist as he recognized the voice. Walking toward him from the door that led to the company's barracks was a tall Braz with a confident walk and a look of contempt for Zeric. His eyes were a brilliant yellow, his skin was relatively dark for a Braz, and the dark red screfa adorning both sides of the man's face gave him a menacing presence.

"Firek," Zeric said flatly.

"Zeric. I'd heard you weren't dead."

"No thanks to you."

Firek Lawrej had been a low-ranked member of Ice when Zeric had last been with them. When he had joined, he'd been brash, reckless, and cruel. Zeric had counseled against accepting him, but he had brought with him several new clients at a time when the company had been in need of new work, so Ymp had brought him onboard.

Apparently, that had ended just as badly for Ymp as it had for Zeric. Zeric's refusal to go along with the desires of their new clients had gotten him stranded on a moon. It had been Ymp's order, but Firek had been the one pushing for it.

"What brings you back here? The Alliance hot on your trail, and you're looking for some protection?"

"Not really. I take it you've heard about the rebellion, then."

Firek nodded. "We have. Quite ironic for you to be involved with them. After being banished because you refused to violate Alliance law."

"I wasn't trying to uphold Alliance law, asshole," Zeric said, his temper rising. "I was trying to uphold some basic level of decency."

There were not many things that made Zeric mad. Firek was one of them. The Braz had no honor or moral compass. Just because they were mercenaries did not mean they were free to act like thugs.

"So you say. But you come here now for what, revenge?"

"No," Zeric said, trying to ignore his feelings for Firek. "I came here to talk to the members of Ice. The planets of this sector have banded together to oppose the Alliance's oppression. They are preparing to form an army. Maarkean Ocaitchi and I are planning to form an elite special forces unit to aid them. I could think of no one with more fighting experience than the members of Ice. I was hoping to convince Ymp to join me."

Firek smiled. "I doubt you'll find many Ice members who are sympathetic to your rebellion. Ymp was expelled for thinking like you. Our clients wouldn't like our associating with your sort."

Firek looked at Gu'od when he said the last part. The glance was the first acknowledgement of Gu'od's presence. Zeric realized that his friend was the only non-Terran or Braz in the room.

When he had been with Ice, the company had been made up of members from every known species. It was home to people who knew how to fight; that was the only qualification for entry. Was it just a coincidence that the only members in the room were Terrans and Braz?

Zeric was suddenly glad he had his pistol at his side. Aside from the foam practice weapons, none of the Ice members were armed. Of course, that did not mean much, as there was undoubtedly an entire company on the other side of the wall, along with an entire armory of weaponry.

"Well, had I known you were in charge, I wouldn't have bothered coming down here," Zeric said, and then, knowing he shouldn't, he added, "Asses like you wouldn't be welcome, anyway."

Zeric started to back away toward the door, but Firek stopped him by saying, "I don't doubt that. But you won't be rejoining them. You're too valuable to just let go. Detain them."

The two mercenaries who had been sparring with the swords charged toward Zeric and Gu'od. Zeric reached down for his pistol but knew he wouldn't have it out in time. Fortunately, he was given some extra time.

Gu'od stepped forward and intercepted the two mercenaries. With a flurry of blows, he disarmed the two and took them to the ground.

Still surprised at his friend's reflexes, Zeric managed to get his pistol out and pointed it at Firek. That stopped the others from advancing any further.

"I think we'll be going now," he said, looking around at the others. "But if any of you change your mind, seek me out. Ask for the Rogues. Anyone who is not an ass is welcome to join the fight."

Carefully, Zeric and Gu'od backed toward the door. Once outside, they made their way quickly down the street. Zeric did not expect them to be followed, at least not right away. Firek wouldn't want to get into a firefight in the middle of the busy street. But he had no doubt he'd see the Braz again.

Once they were several blocks away from the Ice compound, Gu'od spoke. "That could have gone better."

"And I thought it would be dicey with Ymp still in charge," Zeric complained. "Well, there goes the easy solution. Guess we'll have to recruit the hard way."

"Are we ever able to do things the easy way?" Gu'od joked.

"It would have been nice."

"Who are the Rogues?" Gu'od asked.

"Oh, that's the name I came up with for us. Since we're recruiting from mercenaries, smugglers, and other rogue figures. Thought it was clever," Zeric said, a satisfied smile on his face.

Gu'od just gave him a small shake of the head.

CHAPTER 3

During the entire journey to the abandoned mining outpost known as Bravo HQ, Saracasi continued to scan the skies, both with sensors and her eyes. The flight deck's window did not provide a very wide field of view, but she didn't feel comfortable relying on the sensors. The sensors had told her their attacker was an unarmed passenger ship; obviously, they weren't completely reliable.

Maarkean kept the *Cutty Sark* flying low, using the desert's natural gullies and ravines to hide in when they were wide enough. Under ideal conditions, it would have been difficult flying, but with the damage they had sustained, Saracasi thought it should have been impossible. Had she been flying, she was positive they would just be a smoking crater now.

Even though the journey only took ten minutes, it felt to her like an eternity. When the main warehouse finally became visible on the horizon, she let out a loud sigh of relief. Engaged in the task of flying, Maarkean failed to make a quip about her nerves, which only served to reinforce the difficulty he was having.

The ship began to slow, and Maarkean brought the landing thrusters online. Almost immediately, a pair of the thrusters failed, and Saracasi had to do a quick override to keep the entire system from shutting down. Had they been carrying a full load of cargo, the remaining thrusters would not have been enough to keep them from crashing. With a shudder that ran through the entire ship, the *Cutty Sark* settled down into the desert sand.

Saracasi fervently hoped that it wasn't for the last time. Maarkean was protective of the ship, but so was she.

Once the engines shut down, Saracasi half expected another missile to come shooting down at them out of the sky. If that happened, there would be nothing they could do about it. The damaged thrusters had barely gotten them down safely; there was no way they could launch the ship without repair.

When they didn't die in a horrible explosion, she felt a momentary hope that they might get through this in one piece. As if in a deliberate attempt to quash that feeling, Maarkean stood up from the helm. He drew his favorite pistol, and checked the power levels."Grab a weapon and stay behind me."

Saracasi swallowed and nodded. Following Maarkean out of the flight deck, she retrieved a blaster from her quarters and then proceeded down to the cargo deck.

With a quick word of warning, Maarkean activated the cargo ramp. The blinding sun of Kol began streaming into the dark cargo bay. A hot, dry wind blew a cloud of sand through the opening and forced Saracasi to cough and squeeze her eyes shut. Spotting an ambush would prove especially difficult if she couldn't even see.

Fortunately, the wind died down quickly, and she was left with just the heat to contend with. There was a short distance of sand and dry, cracked ground between her and the main doors of the large warehouse. No signs were visible that anyone had been there recently, but with the wind and sand, an entire platoon of troops could have just walked past, and she'd have no idea.

Carefully, she followed Maarkean down the ramp, scanning in all directions for signs of a trap. Each step along the way, she expected something to happen, and she actually felt a little disappointed when nothing did. Her fear started to be overridden with impatience. The sooner their attacker made his move, the sooner she could be done with worrying about it.

At the door, Maarkean directed her toward the control panel while he continued to scan behind them. She moved to the panel and was surprised to find the door operational. Typically, when they arrived here after a long absence, the solar panel that powered the door became covered by sand and stopped providing power. The fact that the panel was functional suggested someone had been here since their last visit.

There were other smugglers and pirates who might use this abandoned outpost as a safe harbor. The door being active did not necessarily mean they were walking into a trap. But it did compound her level of concern.

With another sigh, Saracasi activated the door controls and then turned to train her weapon toward the opening doors. To her surprise, the doors did not reveal a dark interior. Lights were lit and the room was abuzz with activity. Along with their abandoned YM-82 freighter, there were two additional ships: a Bauer-class courier and another smaller mining freighter whose class she couldn't identify.

As the door opened, a few dozen pairs of eyes turned toward them. A dark brown Kowwok standing near the courier ship shouted something Saracasi couldn't decipher over the sound of the door. When the Kowwok drew a pistol and started moving toward them, his intentions became clear.

Much to her relief, no one started firing. On an intellectual level, she knew the smart tactic would have been for her and Maarkean to start firing while the people inside were surprised. Now that several of them had grabbed weapons and moved toward them, the element of surprise was lost.

"Who are you? Explain your purpose here," the Kowwok ordered once the grinding from the door ceased.

"We're travelers," Maarkean answered evasively. "Our ship was attacked and we had to set down. We've used this place as a refuge before. We had no idea you were here."

The Kowwok slipped past Maarkean to take a look at the *Cutty Sark* for himself. For the first time, Saracasi glanced back and really saw the condition of the ship. The port lower wing was warped and the last half meter, where the RCS assembly had once been, was missing from the tip. Smoke drifted off of the hull—not a problem that spaceships normally had to contend with. Once again, she wondered how they had managed to land.

The Kowwok must have agreed with her thought, because he said, "How did you even make it here? The Great One must be watching over you."

"Maybe," Maarkean said.

"What's the other guy look like?" the Kowwok said, forcing a smile as he tried to relieve the initial tension.

"Got away clear," Maarkean answered truthfully. "He ambushed us, which is why we came in guns drawn. We were expecting him to beat us here and lay a trap."

The Kowwok shared a glance with some of the others and then holstered his pistol. "Captain Htaretter of the *Bright Blade* at your service."

"Maarkean Ocaitchi. And my sister Saracasi," Maarkean answered, holstering his weapon as well.

Inwardly, Saracasi cringed when her brother mentioned their names. He was too trusting sometimes, she thought. They were both wanted by the Alliance, and if their attacker was some kind of bounty hunter, as she suspected, there was now a price on their heads.

"Well, you came to the right place," Htaretter said. "Welcome to UDF Inc.'s new headquarters. I'm currently getting my ship upgraded. I have no doubt they can fix yours right up."

"UDF Inc.?" Saracasi said. The name sounded familiar to her, but she couldn't place it. None of the major ship or component manufacturers were named UDF.

"Yep, the owner and chief shipwright is a prodigy. He only set up shop recently, and he's already ahead of schedule," Htaretter said, looking enthusiastically toward Maarkean. "You'll love what this guy can do to your ship."

"UDF, UDF," Saracasi quietly to herself, then let out a squeal of excitement as it clicked. "Chava! Chavatwor. UDF was his company."

Htaretter looked at her curiously. "It still is. You know Chavatwor?"

Nodding vigorously, Saracasi turned to Maarkean. "He was the shipwright I met on Sulas that I told you about."

"Well, then, I think it's time I met this Chavatwor. We may be in need of his services," Maarkean said, curiosity evident in his voice.

Htaretter led the pair of them into the warehouse. Much had changed about the building since her last visit. Instead of standing empty, the giant storage room was mostly filled with cranes, grav-lifts, welding equipment, and many other pieces of machinery. The walls were lined with crates of equipment, half-assembled engine components, deuterium storage cylinders, and more.

Now that she had the time to look closer, some of the workers looked vaguely familiar to her. As they walked through the warehouse-turned-shipyard, the workers would stop, look, and point at her and Maarkean. Saracasi got the impression that, although Htaretter didn't recognize them, others did.

At the far end of the building, Htaretter brought them to a computer table where another Kowwok and a shorter Notha were having a vigorous discussion. She immediately recognized the Kowwok's lighter brown fur streaked with white; this was Chavatwor. The Notha was La'ari Mahon, another escapee from Olan. The sight of them made her smile broadly.

When he noticed the new arrivals, Chavatwor first waved them off, saying he was busy, but then he stopped. He turned and took another look. That's when he rushed toward Saracasi and lifted her up in a tight bear hug.

Her understanding of Kowwok greeting customs notwithstanding, she wished her friend was less enthusiastic. The hug left her struggling to breathe and with a ball of fur in her mouth. When he finally released her, he turned to Maarkean and proceeded to do the same to her brother, despite their never having met.

Accustomed to Lahkaba's similar habit, Maarkean took the hug in stride, though he did cast her a slightly distressed look. She just shrugged in reply. After a moment, Chavatwor released Maarkean and then looked from one of them to the other.

"I'm sorry for my enthusiasm," he began. "I assume you are Saracasi's brother, Maarkean? The man who saved us from that terrible prison?"

"I am her brother," Maarkean replied, failing to acknowledge his role in the prison break. Saracasi knew that he was no longer ashamed of what he had done, but her brother had always been slow to take credit for things.

"Well, I am truly pleased to meet you. You have returned to reclaim your freighter?"

"Something like that," Saracasi answered. "What are you doing here? Last I saw, you were left on Irod."

Chavatwor smiled and gestured at Htaretter. "Captain Htaretter was one of the traders who visited there. He agreed to take me back to Sulas in exchange for some repair work. When I got there, I decided it wasn't safe to return to my business. So Htaretter helped me transport everything here from my old shop."

"But how did you find this place?" Maarkean asked, with some concern.

"Saracasi told me about it," Chavatwor said innocently. "Wasn't this where we were originally supposed to escape to, before we had to change plans for Irod?"

Saracasi nodded, remembering telling Chavatwor about this place. "It was. But it's so remote. Why did you want to set up here?"

"I was hoping to find you, actually. I figured my skills might come in handy. When I found the freighter, I knew you'd be back at some point."

The knowledge that Chavatwor had come here in order to help them was overshadowed by the realization that others could have made the same deductions. There might be more bounty hunters out there. Or even the Alliance itself.

"We were attacked by what we think was a bounty hunter on our way here," Saracasi told Chavatwor.

"You may all be in danger if the Alliance learns we've been here," Maarkean added. "Our ship took some damage, or we'd leave now."

"Nonsense," Chavatwor replied dismissively. "I've already registered my business with the Kol Business Council. I've laid claim to the land and structures. In fact, I've already gotten a contract with two of the biggest mining companies to upgrade some of their freighters. Seems they feel it's worth the expense to increase their shield capacity."

Chavatwor continued talking while walking away, toward the warehouse door they had come in through. "They wouldn't let the Alliance learn of this place—they have too much already invested. We'll take a look at that ship of yours, though. I'd be happy to provide what help I can, free of charge, of course. I owe you my freedom, after all."

Chavatwor led them out of the building and then started inspecting the damage to the *Cutty Sark*. He made several disapproving noises as he looked, exchanging some words with La'ari who had followed them. Then he looked up toward Maarkean."I should be able to have her working, good as new—better, even—in two weeks."

The estimate surprised Saracasi. The damage was serious, but she thought she could get it patched up in a couple of days. Chavatwor would undoubtedly be more thorough than she would be, but she saw no reason it should take that long.

However, Maarkean gave Chavatwor a relieved smile. She would have thought two weeks would be too long for him, but instead he said, "That's amazing. And very generous."

"Nonse—" Chavatwor started to say. He was cut off by the sound of stun blasts ripping through the air.

Saracasi let out a startled yelp as she saw her brother collapse. Reacting without thinking, she traced where the bolts had been fired from. On the edge of the plateau stood a towering armored figure.

Drawing her pistol, she fired indiscriminately toward the figure. Her pistol had been set to stun, and the bolts cascaded across the armored suit. The bolts had no noticeable effect, but that didn't stop her from firing.

Suddenly, Saracasi was falling to the ground, and she realized that Chavatwor had pulled her down. Several stun bolts passed through the air where she had just been standing. The wind knocked out of her, she remained still for a moment.

In that time, the armored figure sprinted forward, firing at anyone still standing. Several of the workers who were not quick enough dropped to the ground, stunned. Htaretter and a few others managed to get their weapons out and return fire. Like hers, their stun bolts had no noticeable effect. By the time everyone realized the futility of firing stun bolts at him, the figure had reached Maarkean. He picked him up and threw him over his shoulder.

Switching her blaster to full power might allow her to penetrate the armor, but it would also make it far more likely she'd hit Maarkean. She glanced around for another weapon and noticed the tool belt around Chavatwor's waist. An idea struck her. Dropping her gun, she grabbed a plasma fuser and slipped it up her sleeve.

Shaking herself out from under Chavatwor, Saracasi dashed toward the figure. "Hey! You want me instead!"

The armored figure paused and turned to look at her. "The bounty's higher for him. But you're welcome to come, too."

By holding her hands up, she managed to keep the plasma fuser from falling out of her sleeve. She approached slowly, trying to look nonthreatening. "I can't let you take my brother alone. If that means I have to go with you, so be it."

The figure considered her, clearly trying to ascertain what her angle was. Seeing no weapon, he must have decided she wasn't a threat, because he turned away and continued toward the edge of the plateau. Deciding she wouldn't get a better chance, Saracasi dashed forward.

Before she could reach him, the figure turned and tried again to shoot her. Fortunately, she was close enough that he wasn't able to get a good angle. After his first shot missed, he changed tactics; he moved his gun arm to sweep her up against him. She struggled until she was pulled right up against him.

"You could have gotten away; I might not have come back for you. But I won't mind collecting both bounties."

He turned the weapon in his hand so that the muzzle was pressed into her back, giving her no more room to squirm. Before he pulled the trigger, she let the plasma fuser slip down her sleeve and into her hand. The nozzle ended up pressed into his hip. With a wicked grin, she thumbed the activation switch.

A scream erupted from the figure as the superheated plasma penetrated his armor and his leg. He immediately dropped Maarkean and started to collapse, his leg no longer able to bear his weight. Before Saracasi could gloat, his blaster went off and her world faded to black.

CHAPTER 4

Solyss Novastar looked out of place in the cantina. Priding himself on maintaining a respectable look, he always wore the latest fashions and paid careful attention to his grooming. After all, even though he wasn't on Terra, he still represented the Novastar family name. They had been on the front lines of the resistance during the Kravic Occupation and had been among the leaders in rebuilding Terran society after the Withdrawal. A man of his pedigree couldn't be seen dressed like a slob.

Yet, despite his efforts, it was difficult to remain proper in a place like the Dirty Notha. In fact, he had felt bad even coming in here because of the name. He was worried at first that his pilot, Isaxo, who was a Notha, might find it offensive. To his relief, Isaxo hadn't minded, finding the name humorous.

Their time in the Dirty Notha had paid off so far. Sitting before him was a diverse group of miscreants. Isaxo and Gamaly had given pretty impassioned speeches about their treatment at the hands of the Alliance, which had attracted some of them. Kard's guns had attracted a few others, who had grown into a small party of gun enthusiasts.

The bulk of their attention, however, Solyss attributed to himself and Asheerah. Between his family name and rugged good looks, every being interested in men would naturally be attracted to his table. And while Asheerah objected to, as she described it, 'standing there and looking pretty,' she would undoubtedly attract anyone interested in females. Gamaly wasn't hurting them that area, either, he admitted.

Currently sitting before him were a black-and-white furred Kowwok named Baldurok, a black-haired, light-skinned Terran named Davidus Brieni, and a pink-skinned Camari who had declined to identify herself. They had already heard Isaxo's account of the rescue from Olan, and Solyss had just finished retelling his part in the Battle of Perth. Now he was trying to address their questions, most of which he had already heard from each group he had talked to.

"So there's no pay for this?" Baldurok asked, skeptically.

"Not currently. If Congress votes to form a military, you will be fully compensated as a member of the new Kreogh sector military. If not, then Major Ocaitchi will still be continuing the fight, and pay will come as a share of goods taken from Alliance bases," Solyss answered.

Maarkean had not specifically said that, but Solyss had extrapolated those details. It was, after all, what Maarkean had been doing before the Battle of Perth. Besides, he doubted Congress would not form a military. The delegates had left Enro with that intention. Why would they change their minds?

"So we'll be going after the Alliance, not just sitting around defending cities?" Baldurok continued.

"That is the goal. As with all military life, it is dependent on the needs of the service," Solyss answered honestly. "But Maarkean wants to form a group made up of experienced fighters to be the offensive arms. Each planet will recruit its own defensive forces.

"We're looking for experienced fighters, pilots, medics, engineers, star fighter mechanics, starship crewers—anyone with useful skills and the will to fight. It's a cause worth fighting for."

"And this is all Maarkean Ocaitchi's idea?" the Terran, Davidus, asked, his tone accusatory. He had several days' worth of beard growth. His dark hair was speckled with grey, and he had a gaunt expression to his cheeks. His hand had never left his bottle of whiskey, except when the waitress had replaced it with a new one.

"For the most part. He wants to have a fighting force ready to go as soon as Congress casts their vote," Solyss responded.

"So we'll be working directly for him?" Davidus pressed.

Solyss was unsure how to read the man's tone. There was a clear level of eagerness when he said Maarkean's name, but it was different than the typical excitement many had shown. This was not a case of hero worship, he decided. But what it was, he had no idea.

"Probably not directly," Solyss said hesitantly. "Much will depend on what Congress authorizes."

Before the exchange could continue, a commotion drew Solyss' attention. Zeric and Gu'od had just entered the cantina. The pair drew everyone's attention, which seemed to surprise Zeric. Despite Davidus' clear interest in Maarkean, there had been many recruits speaking highly of Zeric as well. Some had even claimed to know him.

A hushed silence followed Zeric and Gu'od as they walked toward Solyss. Quiet whispers were exchanged among both the people who had already signed up and those who were ignoring the gathering. Perhaps he had discounted the effect Zeric might have on their recruiting efforts.

Gu'od exchanged a look with his wife, which put a frown on Asheerah's lips. Solyss' understanding of Liw'kel mating habits was pretty rudimentary, but what he did know suggested that Asheerah's pursuit of Gu'od was not considered impolite the way it would be in Terran society. He couldn't help but feel a touch of jealousy. What man wouldn't want two beautiful Liw'kel fighting over him?

Despite that fact, Gu'od paid absolutely no attention to Asheerah. That was a smart move in Solyss' mind, regardless of cultural differences. So it surprised him when Gu'od turned to look at another Liw'kel woman sitting in a corner of the bar.

The new Liw'kel wore a dark brown robe that made her hard to see in the dim lighting of the cantina. If it weren't for the contrast of her blue skin against the brown fabric, she would be difficult to make out. Asheerah's expression darkened noticeably, and Solyss started to wonder if Gu'od was simply attracted to blue-skinned members of his species. He could sympathize; he preferred darker-skinned Terrans.

Pulling his attention away from the Liw'kel, Solyss stood up to greet Zeric. They had arrived on Mirthod aboard Solyss' ship, and they had no formal ranks. But for recruiting purposes, he decided it would be best to give the impression of yielding to Zeric.

"Zeric, how did your meeting with Ice Company go?" Solyss asked.

"It didn't," Zeric answered grumpily. "It seems Ymp was replaced and their new leader hates me even more."

"I never hated you."

Zeric's eyes went wide at the new voice. Solyss followed Zeric's gaze toward the pink Camari who sat at his table. She turned her head to face Zeric, though one of her eye stalks still faced Solyss.

"Ymp?" Zeric asked, almost as a cough.

"Trust me, I'm just as surprised to see you," Ymp said coldly. "Your friends here have been telling me some pretty exciting stories about your exploits. You've been busy since our last meeting."

"You mean since you dumped me on an almost airless moon to die?" Zeric demanded, though his voice lacked the necessary force for the accusation.

"That wasn't my choice. It was that or lose the company to Firek," Ymp said, though Solyss couldn't detect any hint of apology in her tone.

"Yeah, that worked out well for you," Zeric said sarcastically.

If Camari could squint in anger, Solyss would have expected Ymp to do so as she said, "It bought me a few more years."

"So, what, you decided to pretend to sign up and wait for me to arrive?" Zeric said accusingly. "Planning to capture me, take me back to Ice, and get your position back?"

"It occurred to me. I expect you're probably worth something to the Alliance garrison here if Firek doesn't want you." Ymp shrugged. "But don't worry, your man Novastar has been very persuasive. I think I actually want to sign up."

A skeptical look crossed Zeric's face, while a feeling of pride filled Solyss' chest. They were making a very persuasive argument, he agreed. Even someone who clearly had some bad blood with Zeric was considering joining.

"Riiiiiight," Zeric said, drawing out the word in a skeptical tone. Zeric continued to give Ymp a suspicious look for a moment before putting his hand on Solyss' shoulder. "Excuse us for a second."

Following Zeric, Solyss moved to the corner of the room. Eyes around the cantina continued to watch Zeric. Good, Solyss thought; the more attention, the better.

"You think we shouldn't accept her as a recruit?" Solyss asked once they were out of earshot.

"Huh?" Zeric said, evidently confused. "No, she doesn't like me, but she's a good fighter."

"Then why did you pull me aside?"

"I just didn't want to talk to Ymp anymore," Zeric answered. "How's your recruiting going? Mine obviously failed."

Solyss smiled and began a detailed accounting of the people who had expressed interest in joining them. Most were down-on-their-luck mercenaries, eager for any work that promised a warm meal. He was particularly proud of the pilots they'd convinced. One even owned a transport ship big enough to carry all of them.

"I guess it's a start," Zeric said, less enthusiastically than Solyss thought he should. "Almost enough to form a platoon."

"But we don't need a traditionally sized platoon," Solyss countered. "This group is supposed to be more equivalent to special forces, right?"

Zeric nodded, and Solyss continued, "So we don't need quantity, but quality."

Turning his head, Zeric scanned the room around them. When he brought his eyes back to Solyss, he had an eyebrow raised and a skeptical expression on his face. Before Solyss could respond, a commotion erupted from the cantina's entrance.

A blond-haired Terran burst into the room. Panting, the man looked around the room hurriedly, pushing past people. When he saw his quarry, he stumbled over to her.

Watching the man stop and speak to Ymp, Zeric frowned. Solyss found the exchange uninteresting. The man was obviously a friend of Ymp's, and while his arrival had been a bit wild, there was nothing concerning about it. Yet Zeric definitely appeared concerned.

"What is it?" Solyss asked.

"I met that man when I went to speak to Ice," Zeric said. "His name's Sigfa something."

"Maybe he came to join you?" Solyss offered.

"Then why is he speaking to Ymp?" Zeric asked and then started over toward them.

Solyss followed. When Zeric reached the table, Sigfa stopped speaking. Silence filled the air between them for a moment, even spreading in a wave to the people nearby. Before the whole cantina was listening in, Ymp spoke.

"Sigfa just came here to give me a warning," she said calmly. "Apparently, Firek and a squad from Ice are coming here to arrest you."

"Arrest me? Are they the police for Scipost now?" Zeric asked skeptically.

"Just as good as," Ymp said. "They've made some powerful friends here, and the real police won't interfere."

Looking to Sigfa, Zeric said, "And you came here to warn me?"

Sigfa glanced at Ymp and then back at Zeric. "I came here to warn her."

Zeric took the comment in stride. "Whatever. When will they get here, and how many are there?"

While Zeric continued to talk with Ymp and Sigfa, Solyss slowly stepped away. He slipped through the crowd over toward Asheerah. The Liw'kel was standing near Kard. Most of their group of recruits were ignoring them now; they were focused on Zeric.

"This is why I always prefer to wear my armor," Asheerah said, a dangerous bite to her voice.

Solyss sighed in reply. Asheerah would prefer to go everywhere well armed and in full combat armor. He understood the necessity of it at times, but it just wasn't civil to traipse through city streets expecting a fight. Asheerah in armor would scare people away, when they had come to Mirthod to attract people.

Even though she had foregone her armor, Asheerah wore a repeating rifle on her back and a pistol at her belt. Solyss would place even money on there being several knives and at least one grenade hidden among her clothing. Those things weren't strictly legal, even on Mirthod, but she never went unarmed by choice.

Sitting at the table beside her, Kard propped his feet up on the table. He drew the two pistols he wore at his hip and twirled them around his fingers. With a cocky grin, he looked up at Solyss. "We going to stay and fight, Boss?"

Despite the young man's swagger, Solyss knew he hadn't been in very many actual firefights. None of them had been in a real battle until Perth. But the success there had done nothing to stem the over-confidence of either Kard or Asheerah.

"Why would we stay and fight?" Solyss demanded. As their captain, it was his duty to rein in their aggressive tendencies. It was the reason he had accepted them as crew in the first place. Both were very capable, but their arrogance and temper would get them killed on their own. It had almost led to them killing each other on more than one occasion.

Solyss went on, "If we have to, we will defend ourselves. But this is a privately owned establishment, and this isn't the Alliance coming for us. We have no quarrel with these mercenaries."

While Solyss spoke, Isaxo walked up to join them. The young Notha was a great pilot, but he couldn't hit anything with a pistol to save his life. Oddly enough, he had a natural ability when wielding a sniper rifle that he claimed to have learned hunting on his native world of Dantyne.

Solyss suffered the same ineptness with pistols as Isaxo, though to a lesser degree. He could hit targets during practice, but usually not if they were moving. Now, fencing was something he could do. Unfortunately, no one fought duels with swords these days.

"That being said," Solyss continued, arriving at why he had moved over to his crew, "we should get ready to defend ourselves. Isaxo, go out to the street and keep an eye out for approaching vehicles or people. Asheerah, Kard, position yourselves so you can cover both exits."

Unslinging her rifle and grinning at the prospect of getting to use it, Asheerah moved to a booth along one wall of the cantina. Kard holstered his pistols and moved to the other side of the building. A few people nearby took notice, but most were either minding their own business or trying to eavesdrop on Zeric.

Solyss loosened the pistol he carried in the concealed holster under his jacket. The small PK-76 did not have the penetrating power of many blasters. It would never do much damage to someone with armor like Asheerah's, for example. But its stun setting was fully rated against all species for multiple hours.

Gu'od and Gamaly had joined Zeric but were staying slightly behind while he continued to try to wrangle information out of Sigfa. The two Liw'kel nodded to him. Surprisingly, Gu'od had no evident weapon on him, though Gamaly had a small carbine on her hip.

A beep interrupted Zeric, who turned to look at Solyss. It took Solyss a second to realize that the beep was his comm. Quickly, he slipped it out of his pocket and saw that the transmission was coming from Isaxo. He accepted the transmission and set the device to speaker.

"You were right, Captain," Isaxo said. "There is a big, ugly transport coming down the street. It looks armored and armed. I would bet this is our friends."

Beside him, Zeric let out a curse. Solyss felt the same urge but contained it, as he always tried to do. Ymp gave Zeric a look that seemed to say 'I told you so.' The rest of the cantina grew agitated, and people started streaming toward the doors.

"Think we should join them?" Zeric asked, looking to Gu'od and Gamaly.

As if in response, Isaxo's voice called again from the comm. "The vehicle has come to a stop and fired toward the crowd. It's just stun fire, but it's cutting off the escape route."

"Well, that answers that," Zeric said. "We can be sure there's more coming down the back street. But let's go check."

Zeric started to go, but Gamaly grabbed his arm. Gu'od headed behind the bar and into the back room. The bartender made no attempt to stop him, but he did reach down below the bar and pull out a projectile shotgun. A moment later, Gu'od came back in, looking relieved and waving to the rest of them to follow him.

"All right, then, let's get out of here," Zeric said enthusiastically. "They obviously thought they'd catch us by surprise and didn't come prepared for a siege."

Solyss nodded in agreement and keyed the comm. "Sax, can you get away?"

"Yeah, I'm a bit down the street with some bystanders. They're ignoring anyone not coming out of the cantina."

"All right, meet us back at the ship," he ordered and shut down the comm.

Waving to Asheerah and Kard to join them, Solyss followed Zeric and Gamaly out of the back of the cantina. They emerged into a dark alley, which immediately made Solyss worry about an ambush. Fortunately, the alley was too narrow for any vehicles to fit down.

The group raced down the alleyway toward the next open street. Before they arrived, a voice called out from behind them. Solyss reached his hand into his jacket and pulled out his pistol. Ice must have made it through the cantina already.

Instead of a group of heavily armed mercenaries, a lone blue-skinned Liw'kel female came rushing down the alley toward them. Solyss recognized her as the one he had noticed Gu'od admiring in the cantina. Gu'od stopped and allowed her to catch up.

"That street will not give you easy access to the starport. You'll have to pass through a chokepoint in the roadways," the Liw'kel said, her voice and breathing normal despite having just run several hundred meters.

"How do you know we're going to the starport?" Solyss asked suspiciously.

"Where else would you be going?" she replied matter-of-factly. "I can show you another way."

"Please do," Gu'od replied immediately.

"Wait, she could be leading us into an ambush," Zeric said, echoing Solyss' thoughts.

"We can trust her," Gamaly said, looking at her husband. The two Liw'kel then began following the woman.

Zeric shrugged and followed his friend. Asheerah made an angry noise and reluctantly started following. Liw'kel had the ability to communicate using their antennae, and Solyss started to suspect that something had been exchanged between Gamaly and Gu'od and not shared with the others.

Catching up to Asheerah, he asked, "What did they say?"

"You heard everything I did," she replied gruffly.

"I did hear everything you did. But we both know there was more said than with words."

With a shrug, Asheerah answered, "Apparently, this woman is a member of the Ni'jar."

CHAPTER 5

The images from the latest riot in Chuthor ran across the vid-screen. Each one proved more horrific than the last. Bodies lay scattered across the street, many of them burned, none of them moving. And these images were the ones the planetary media was allowed to show. Even the Alliance, despite its desire to show what happened to rebels, wouldn't broadcast the worst of it.

Lahkaba felt a swirl of emotions competing inside of him: anger at the Alliance's harsh retaliation to the riot; guilt over the part he had played, even though this time his role had only been as an inspirational figure; most of all, sadness that things had gotten to this point.

Young Kowwoks were taught that violence was a violation of the will of the Great One. Yet Lahkaba had formed an uneasy truce with violence. His family had never followed the pacifistic teachings of the Great One dogmatically, even the older generations; that was one of the reasons they had emigrated to Sulas when his parents were only children. In fact, a significant sect of the Kowwok population now believed that violence was acceptable to the Great One, if your cause was just. Lahkaba was among them. He had joined the Confederate army because of that philosophy, which he had never let go of.

But believing violence a necessary, and acceptable, tool to overthrow the Alliance did not mean believing it to always be the answer. The riots in Chuthor had achieved nothing; they hadn't been anything more than a release of frustration.

There had been no chance the protestors would end the Alliance occupation.

Now there were dozens of people dead. The Alliance had resorted to lethal force too quickly, and the bloodshed that their response had caused would serve to undermine their authority in the long run. But the riot itself had not been their doing, and in the short term, it showed everyone what happened to those who stood up to the Alliance. It also gave Governor Howell an excuse to increase the military occupation.

Turning off the vid-screen, Lahkaba left the viewing room and went to the kitchen of his apartment. It was much smaller than his last home, where his estranged wife Valursca still lived, but it was considerably bigger than the room he had shared with Lohcja on the *Cutty Sark* for the last few months.

He had considered trying to return home, but one call to Valursca had convinced him there was no redeeming that relationship.

Valursca considered herself a true follower of the Great One. She abhorred violence and conflict. When they had gotten married, she had accepted Lahkaba's past as a soldier, believing that anyone could be redeemed for past sins and trusting that that was all behind them. For a time, they had been happy—until Lahkaba had become involved in politics.

He had joined the movement pushing for Sulas to take a stronger stance against the Alliance's harsh rule. When he had joined the delegation to the Kreogh Sector Congress, he had thought he was participating in an effort to avoid violence. Valursca had seen it differently. She had accurately predicted that the congress would prove to be the first step toward bloodshed. He had been optimistic about the congress' chances, and his relationship had suffered for it.

Now, after the prison break here on Sulas, his participation in the raid on Dantyne, and the Battle of Perth, Valursca had been proven right. So Lahkaba remained in a small, out-of-the-way apartment, alone.

Fortunately, he did not have much time to spend here feeling sorry for himself. The last day and a half that he had spent in the apartment, as he tried to keep an even lower profile following the riots, had been the longest time he'd been here. Before that, he had barely had enough time to return here every night to sleep.

Though he had initially been skeptical of Kantor's call to offer no resistance to the Alliance until the congress could form an army, the riots had shown that those efforts were necessary. In the last few weeks, he had personally spoken to dozens of groups, urging them not to confront the Alliance forces yet.

As Lahkaba poured himself a glass of Emerald Valley wine, a knock rang through the apartment. Concern rose to the surface of his thoughts. Only a handful of people knew he was here. None of them would risk coming here unless there was some kind of emergency.

Cautiously, Lahkaba went to the apartment door. He activated the security feed, which revealed Pasha Alon. Breathing a sigh of relief that the Alliance hadn't found him, he opened the door. Pasha quickly slipped inside.

As someone he had stood beside in battle, Lahkaba greeted Pasha with a firm hug. Pasha accepted the hug as reluctantly as most Terrans did. Their entire species had a very odd sense of distance, even among relations.

"Pasha, what brings you here? Time for us to get back out there among the people again?" Lahkaba asked, eagerness at the idea of getting out of the apartment leaking into his voice.

"Something like that," Pasha replied. "I've either got some good news, or I've got really bad news."

His curiosity piqued, Lahkaba invited Pasha to sit while he poured the man a drink. Once Lahkaba had returned from the kitchen and taken a seat himself, Pasha continued. "Yesterday, one of my constituents came to me. I believe she's completely trustworthy. She informed me about a man who had been subtly asking around about where he could find me, you, Lohcja, or Maarkean."

Lahkaba tilted his head to his right, considering the implications. There were a number of reasons someone could be looking for them. The way Pasha had emphasized 'subtly' suggested he was more than just a regular citizen looking to join the movement. People like that rarely knew how to be subtle.

"Turns out this man is an Alliance intelligence officer," Pasha continued. "But this is where it gets interesting. Supposedly, he wants to defect."

That revelation took Lahkaba by surprise. The odds were good that the man simply wanted to infiltrate them. But if that were the case, revealing that he was an intelligence officer was not the best approach.

"Have you met with him?" Lahkaba asked, concerned.

"No, not yet. I wanted to get your thoughts. If he's legit, it would be a great boon to have a source inside their intelligence network."

"It's also a good way for us to walk right into the hands of the Alliance. We've both seen the inside of Olan. I don't want to again."

The two sat in silence for a moment, thinking about their options. Lahkaba was naturally suspicious of any Alliance officer, especially from intelligence. But Maarkean and Zeric had been members of the Alliance military, and they were now supporters.

Caution would be necessary, but they couldn't just ignore the opportunity. Access to Alliance military intelligence—any of it—could prove to be a tremendous boon once the fighting started. Currently, they had no idea how many troops and ships the Alliance had in the sector. They did not believe their forces were very strong, but knowing how strong they were would help them know how quickly retaliation could come.

"All right, let's try to set up a meeting," Lahkaba said. "We'll deal with the consequences, whatever they might be."

As Maarkean awoke, he recognized the now-familiar tingling sensations that lingered in his limbs. The lasting effects from the stun bolt had mostly dissipated, allowing him to move again. Finding himself in a cot in a room made of sandstone walls, he quickly recognized that he had been taken to one of Bravo HQ's old personnel barracks. He was not a prisoner of a bounty hunter, then—whatever had happened, he had been rescued by their new friends.

Why he had been stunned remained a question. The last he could remember, he had been walking through the warehouse-turned-shipyard. He had a vague memory of stepping outside, but he couldn't be sure. Whoever had shot him had taken him completely by surprise.

Standing up from the cot, Maarkean quickly performed some of the Ni'jar stretching movements Gu'od had taught him. He found them a great way to start a day, working out the tight muscles from sleep, or, in this case, stun sleep. Most mornings, he followed them up with some meditation, but he decided to forgo that for now.

Feeling energized and recovered from the stun effects, Maarkean left the room. Even though he was not a prisoner, he was anxious to learn what had happened and make sure Saracasi was all right, too.

The dark, narrow hallway outside led him past several similar rooms. The only light source came from a square-shaped common area at the end of the hall. Seated at one of the available dining tables was a purple-skinned Liw'kel. Unlike his screfa, which was deep violet, her skin was only a dull shade. One arm ended with a cybernetic replacement.

When Maarkean came into the room, the Liw'kel stood up eagerly. Her shoulders slackened slightly when he fully emerged from the hallway's shadows, as if she had been expecting someone else, but a smile quickly came to her face. She walked around the table to meet him.

"Maarkean, I presume?" she asked.

"Yes. What happened?" Maarkean asked. He felt confident he was not a prisoner and that no one among Chavatwor's workers had shot him, but you could never be certain about anything.

"I'm Asirzi Z'ren," the Liw'kel woman answered. "You were taken here after you were stunned by a bounty hunter."

Maarkean nodded. That made sense. This bounty hunter was also likely the same person who had attacked the *Cutty Sark*. He had been stunned, but not taken, which begged the question of what had happened to the bounty hunter.

When he asked, Asirzi replied with a smile. "Thanks mainly to Casi—Saracasi—your sister—" She started stammering, stopped, and picked back up. "We were able to bring him down. She was stunned in the process; she will probably wake in the next hour or so. Chavatwor rigged up a temporary holding cell for the bounty hunter."

Pleased to hear that Saracasi had not been taken, either, Maarkean relaxed slightly. He ignored Asirzi's stammering about her; she was probably just nervous that he'd be mad that Saracasi was stunned. But stunned was always preferable to dead.

"Can you take me to this cell? I'd like to have a word with this bounty hunter."

Casting a quick glance down the hallway Maarkean had emerged from, as if looking for someone, Asirzi nodded. "Of course. Follow me."

They left the barracks building and emerged into the central courtyard. The uniform shade of brown surrounding them was interrupted here by a natural desert oasis. Green fronds surrounded a small spring of water. None of the plants were currently in bloom, so the oasis lacked the grandeur it was capable of achieving.

They crossed the courtyard, swinging around the oasis toward the second largest building. Once the home of a long-gone mining company, it had now been appropriated by Chavatwor. The old Bravo HQ sign had been removed and replaced with a new sign that read, "UDF Inc.: If we can't make it fly, no one can."

Inside, the front atrium held a reception desk, which sat empty. Several offices and conference rooms lined the edges of the atrium. Their glass and metal frames stood out among the sandstone walls, and most appeared to be empty, devoid even of furniture. Asirzi led Maarkean past the offices to a set of stairs. She took the stairs leading down into the structure's basement.

The basement contained a hallway of doors, similar to the sleeping quarters in the barracks, though he doubted that there were beds behind the doors. The place felt just as abandoned as it had been the last time he was here. The only sign of life was the shaggy form of Htaretter seated by a door at the end of the hall.

The Kowwok stood up as they approached. "Glad to see you awake."

"Thanks. How's the bounty hunter?"

"Surprisingly cooperative," Htaretter said with a shrug. "Doc's in there with him now. I've got one of my crew serving as guard, but the guy hasn't been any trouble. So far."

Maarkean nodded. "What are you going to do with him?"

Htaretter shrugged again. "Chavatwor wanted to let you decide. There're no rules against bounty hunting on Kol. And no real central authority to turn him over to, aside from the Alliance, but since they likely sent him, doubt that's a good idea."

Maarkean didn't find it likely that the bounty hunter had been hired directly by the Alliance. They weren't in the habit of hiring bounty hunters. It was likely, however, that the Alliance was offering a reward for his arrest. That would attract the bounty hunters.

"All right, I'm going to talk to him. See if he's working on his own or if we have more to worry about."

Before he could open the door to the converted cell, Asirzi said, "I'm going to go back and wait. So Casi—Saracasi—doesn't wake up without anyone there."

The woman didn't wait for an acknowledgement before turning and starting back down the hallway. Maarkean was starting to find the woman's stammer at his sister's name curious, but he pushed it aside. He needed to focus on the task at hand.

Inside the room, Maarkean found a blond-haired Terran male lying on a cot. Kneeling beside him was a Ronid with a yellow carapace. The Ronid was running a device over the Terran's leg while looking at a handheld data display.

The two of them were behind a series of metal bars that split the room in half. Maarkean guessed that the room had once been a bathroom, as there was half a stall and a urinal behind the bars and a sink behind him near the door. Standing in front of the sink was a blue-scaled Dotran.

The Dotran's presence felt out of place to Maarkean. Htaretter had said one of his crew was in here acting as a guard. But he never would have guessed that a Dotran would serve on a crew with a Kowwok captain. The Dotran held a pistol in his hands and flashed his sharp teeth at Maarkean when he entered, but took no threatening action.

"How's the patient, Doc?" Maarkean asked.

When he spoke, the Ronid doctor jumped slightly. He turned his multifaceted eyes to look at Maarkean. "Ah, good to see you recovered from your stunning. Most people do, but about 0.05% of Braz never wake from a stun shot as powerful as the one you took. That number increases to 0.09% for Braz of your age bracket."

Maarkean sighed at the reminder that he had reached the middle years of his life. He didn't say anything in response, as the doctor began wrapping a bandage around the Terran's leg. The man bore a pained expression on his face as the doctor worked, but said nothing.

"I am Doctor Noti Istru," the Ronid continued. "Your friend here is Jerik Needa. He suffered a severe plasma burn to the left leg. I've regenerated some of the muscle tissue, but it will take some time to heal completely. He is perfectly capable of answering any questions you might have. For a prisoner, he was quite forthcoming in giving me his medical history."

"I've learned it's never beneficial to hide things from your doctor," Jerik said through gritted teeth.

"You would be one of the few, then," Istru said. "I hope you will be as helpful with Major Ocaitchi."

Jerik laughed. "I don't tend to be very open with my marks."

"Even marks you've failed to capture?" Maarkean asked.

With a slight shrug, Jerik said, "'Failure to capture' is the same as 'just haven't finished the job yet.'"

"Admirable," Maarkean said, leaning against the metal bars. "So tell me about this job. Who hired you? How many others are you working with?"

"I work alone. You can rest easy; I was the one who fired on your ship. Until I fail to deliver, no one else will be coming for you."

"A single bounty hunter going after a bounty? I find that unlikely. I'm sure there are plenty more after the Alliance's reward," Maarkean said.

Jerik shrugged again. "Probably. But I wasn't after that. Believe it or not, I actually support your fight against the Alliance. I have no desire to see you turned over to them. My employer wanted you alive."

A frown crept across Maarkean's face. If Jerik wasn't after him for an Alliance bounty, that left only one person he could think of who might want to, and have the resources to, send a bounty hunter after him. To be fair, it was just as likely that someone he didn't know was after him. His name was well known in the sector now.

Taking a chance, Maarkean asked, "So why does Josserand want me alive?"

"Ah, good, you figured it out. I hate breaking confidentiality agreements," Jerik said. "Hell if I know why he wants you. But he did make the 'alive' part very clear."

Josserand Renard had been a thorn in Maarkean's side for years. Maarkean had often taken smuggling jobs from Josserand, despite their mutual dislike of each other. On several occasions, Josserand had tried to buy the *Cutty Sark*, but Maarkean had turned him down each time. After the last rejection, Josserand had decided to just take the ship.

After working a delivery job, Josserand had inserted Zeric, Gu'od, and Gamaly, who were working as simple mercenaries at the time, into the cargo. During the flight to Sulas, the three had commandeered the ship from Maarkean and Saracasi. That was when Josserand's plan had fallen apart, and the ship had been stopped by the Alliance. Maarkean had been forced to work with Zeric to get Saracasi and the others out of prison.

When Maarkean had learned that Josserand had been the one to hire Zeric, he had confronted the man on the *Black Market*, a former Alliance carrier that now served as a home for illicit trading. The scuffle had resulted in getting them both banned from the ship. As Josserand operated his illicit business from there, it had been a bigger blow to him than it had been to Maarkean.

"So he told you to find me here?" Maarkean asked.

"Yeah, gave me a whole rundown of places you've been known to frequent. When word started spreading about you leading a rebellion on Enro, I started to think you'd get harder to find. But when I saw the shipyard these guys turned this place into, I knew you'd be back here eventually."

Despite the fact that Maarkean's arrival here had nothing to do with the shipyard, Jerik was correct. The biggest remaining question was whether Josserand had hired more than one bounty hunter. He would never have told Jerik the truth about that.

Josserand was sneaky, but he was also clever. Hiring multiple bounty hunters might increase the odds of his finding Maarkean, but it would also open the door to multiple hunters competing with each other to be the one to bring him in, which would run the risk of them fighting over Maarkean and accidentally killing him along the way. With independent agents likely out there also trying to get Maarkean in order to collect the Alliance's reward, increasing the competition could backfire.

For a short time, at least, Maarkean didn't think he would have to worry about any more bounty hunters coming from Josserand. He wouldn't want to reveal his secrets about Maarkean's hangouts to many people. In time, more would come, but he felt confident he had a little breathing room.

That just left the question of what to do with Jerik. He doubted Chavatwor wanted to maintain a prison. Turning him over to the Alliance was out, and as Htaretter had indicated, there was no authority on Kol that would take him. That left him with killing the man, turning him loose, or marooning him somewhere.

An idea occurred to him that he almost dismissed immediately. It was a ridiculous thing to consider, but based on what had happened to him over the last few months, it might not be as outrageous as he thought. But could he risk it?

"You said you supported my fight against the Alliance?" Maarkean asked.

Jerik nodded. "I do. My father was a commander in the Alliance navy. He wanted me to follow him, and I tried it for a while. But there was too much hypocrisy. So I turned to the underworld. There, everyone is at least honest about their intentions to screw you."

Maarkean wasn't sure he agreed with Jerik's assessment. Josserand certainly hadn't been honest when he had tried to steal the *Cutty Sark*. But Maarkean also found some elements of truth in what Jerik said. Smuggling had felt more like honest work than working for a shipping company had.

"I'm faced with a dilemma here," Maarkean said. "I don't want to kill you, and I can't trust that you won't go running back to Josserand if I let you go. At best, even if you agree not to come after me again, he'll know sooner that he should send someone else. So that leaves the question of what to do with you."

Jerik locked his green eyes on Maarkean but said nothing. Letting the question hang out there for a moment, Maarkean studied the man. Terrans often called the eyes the "windows to the soul." There was nothing in them that Maarkean could see, but he did recognize that Jerik held his gaze, not being evasive.

"You might want to think about how much you support the fight against the Alliance. Join me, and I can learn to trust you. Otherwise, we'll just have to leave you locked up in here until Josserand sends another bounty hunter. At that point, you'll be free to go, since by then Josserand will have terminated your contract, and you'll no longer have any reason to target us. Besides, we'll need to use the space to put the new guy."

After holding Jerik's gaze for another second, Maarkean turned from the cell bars and strode from the room.

CHAPTER 6

When the strange Liw'kel started to lead them into a sewer hatch, Zeric almost decided to take his chances back at the cantina with Ice. But he trusted Gu'od, and he didn't really want to fight an entire company of mercenaries, so he followed. The sewers stank, but no one was shooting at him.

The trek through the sewers did not take long, though any amount of time down there was too long. They emerged into a dark basement. The Liw'kel told them to remain there and then disappeared up a flight of stairs. There were no chairs or tables in the basement, but there were enough crates for everyone to find a place to sit.

Even though they had walked on a service path and avoided having to step in the muck, the smells clung to Zeric. If they couldn't get to a shower soon, he felt sure Ice would be able to track the stench from anywhere in the city. He really didn't want to die smelling of sewer.

Once the Liw'kel left, Zeric moved close to Gu'od and Gamaly. He fixed Gu'od with the most demanding expression he could muster. The fact that Gamaly did not do the same told him that the pair had already communicated using their secret language. Not for the first time, he wished he could learn it, but the subtleties were completely lost on him.

"So are you going to tell me what this is all about?" Zeric finally said.

With an annoyingly patient expression, Gu'od turned his head toward Zeric. "What do you wish to know?"

Zeric let out a soft growl. "Let's not play cute tonight, shall we? Who's the girl, and where are we?"

"I do not know her name. But she is a member of the Ni'jar. Where we are, I'm also not certain, but it is safe for us here," Gu'od answered, a note of reluctance in his voice.

Zeric had never met another Ni'jar outside of Gu'od. They were a very elusive bunch, for the most part remaining cut off from society. Their main enclave was located on Kel, the Liw'kel homeworld, but he had seen evidence of others on several other worlds he'd been to. Gu'od would occasionally go visit them, though Zeric had never seen anyone else come out.

"So this is what one of your enclaves look like?" Zeric asked.

Shaking his head, Gu'od said, "No. We are likely in the basement of one of their storefronts."

"Storefronts?"

"Yes. Many Ni'jar are isolated, but they still need things. Many enclaves grow much of their food and make as much as they can. But there's still the need for outside things. There will usually be a store that each enclave operates to sell some of their homemade products or extra food."

"Ah," Zeric said, seeing the logic. "I guess we won't get to see one, then?"

"I do not know," Gu'od admitted. "I still do not know why she helped us or what her plans are. It is not like most Ni'jar to get involved in disputes such as ours. Few would not help an individual in need, as would most anyone. But getting involved in a potential firefight is unusual for most people, especially a Ni'jar."

"Why didn't you ask her?" Zeric suggested.

"Nonverbal communication has very limited functions, especially between strangers. You get main ideas, like, 'follow me, go down there,' and emotions. But specifics, such as names, do not translate well," Gu'od explained.

"Well, I just hope you're right about being able to trust her. Just because she's Ni'jar doesn't make her trustworthy.

She's getting involved, after all, so she's already not acting like a typical Ni'jar," Zeric said grumpily.

Solyss and his crew had formed up in a group in another corner of the basement. Off away from them were Ymp and Sigfa. Zeric had not noticed that the pair of them were following until they had left the cantina. It irritated him some, but he supposed that Ymp needed to get away just as much as he did. And Sigfa would probably be on the run now, having betrayed Ice to warn Ymp.

Watching the others sit quietly only increased Zeric's level of anxiety. He hated waiting, and he hated it that he appeared to be the only impatient one in the group, aside from Asheerah, who always looked impatient. He wanted to just walk up the stairs and out of the building.

Supposedly, Solyss had recruited a reasonably sized force. Maybe they could call all of them and form up at the ship. That might give them a decent chance to get past Ice.

With a reluctant sigh, he abandoned that idea. Anyone who had agreed to follow them off Mirthod had done so in order to fight the Alliance. He couldn't reward that commitment by asking them to die fighting a group of thugs. That was why he hadn't tried to stay and fight at the cantina. He couldn't reverse that decision now just because he was impatient.

After about an hour, the Liw'kel woman returned. Two older-looking women followed her down the stairs. One, another Liw'kel woman, had skin the same shade of blue as the first. The other, a Terran, had almost completely grey hair and prominent wrinkles. Zeric guessed her to be at least in her eighties.

The elder Terran stepped forward off the stairs, placing herself at the front of the group. Gu'od moved to stand before her. Not sure why he was doing it, Zeric joined him. Everyone else stood up but remained where they were.

"I must apologize for Sienn'lyn's rash action by involving herself in your affairs," the woman said.

"No need," Zeric said, trying to sound grateful. "She pulled us out of a tight spot. It was appreciated."

Gu'od gave him a sharp look, which Zeric decided to ignore. He'd always wanted to talk to another Ni'jar to see how Gu'od compared. He couldn't pass up this opportunity, and he'd be completely respectful.

"We will be unable to provide you any more assistance in the future. We have already done too much to disturb the Balance. We can only hope that it can be restored," the woman said.

"Master," Gu'od said, his voice obsequious, "the young one's interference was minimal, as I was already involved with this group. There is no need to restore the Balance."

"Your Focus may have led you to leave your Enclave, but it has not done so for Sienn'lyn," the older Liw'kel said, speaking for the first time. "Therefore, the Balance was upset."

Zeric had heard Gu'od speak about Focus and Balance before. He knew Gamaly was his Focus and that all Ni'jar strived to find that which allowed them to achieve Balance in themselves. He always thought of it as some kind of personal spiritual thing. The way they were speaking now made him think he might have misunderstood something.

"This Enclave has remained apart and has not disturbed the Balance in my lifetime," the Terran woman said firmly. "We made it through the last war and will not get involved in the one you are trying to start.

"We apologize again for our interference," she said, looking over all of them. "We will leave you now and allow the Balance to equalize."

Turning back up the stairs, the two elder women started to move up them. The younger Liw'kel, who Zeric didn't think was really young enough to be called 'young one,' remained at the bottom. The elder Liw'kel snapped an order at her to come with them.

"No, Mother," Sienn'lyn said. "You may not agree, but I have found my Focus. Fighting the injustice that these brave people struggle against is what I will devote myself to."

The two women cast dark looks down at the woman, but Zeric was surprised when Gu'od was the one to speak. "The masters are correct, young one. A cause as vast as that which we fight for cannot be the Focus for a true Ni'jar. A Focus must be personal. Do not let your empathy for us sway you from your true path."

Defiantly, Sienn'lyn replied, still looking up at her mother, "A Focus is something only an individual can know. And he may be right. Their cause probably is not mine. But I do know that I must go with them to find it."

"Very well," the Terran woman said reluctantly. "May you find Balance."

The elder Liw'kel lingered for a moment after the Terran left. "If this is your decision, begin your journey quickly."

With that, she was gone. Zeric thought the whole exchange to be unusual, but he saw it as a net gain. Another Ni'jar had joined them. If she was half the fighter that Gu'od was, their combat strength had doubled. Even considering the sewer, it wasn't a bad result.

"We must leave," Gu'od said quickly.

Zeric nodded. "Yeah, they appear to want us to go. But I think we should take a few minutes and figure out our next move."

Coming over to join them, Solyss nodded. "Yeah, I doubt we can just go back to the ship yet. If Ice really wants you and knew to find you at the Dirty Notha, they undoubtedly know where the *Chimopori* is."

"We could just fight them," Asheerah grumbled.

"Maybe Ymp knows someplace," Isaxo suggested, drawing everyone's eyes to the Camari sitting quietly in one corner.

"No," Gu'od interrupted, his voice almost frantic, which Zeric had never heard him do before. "Ice will be here soon. We have to go. Now."

"How would Ice know where to find us?" Solyss asked.

"The Ni'jar told them," Gu'od answered reluctantly.

"What?!" Zeric declared. "Why would they do that?"

"To restore the Balance," Sienn'lyn said. "You faced them before, and I prevented that from occurring. To restore the Balance, they will attempt to return things to the situation as it was before my interference. That way, things can unfold naturally."

"Restore things to the way they were before?" Zeric shouted angrily. "We're trapped in a narrow basement instead of an open cantina. There aren't any potential allies or witnesses around. This is not the same situation."

"Regardless," Gu'od said, "they will be coming, and we must leave before they get here."

Ymp joined the conversation. "I can take you to a friend's company's headquarters. Ice has a lot of freedom in Scipost, but wars between mercenary companies inside city limits are strictly forbidden. From there, you can hire them to escort you to the starport."

Zeric wasn't sure he liked that idea, or if he could afford it. The rule about fighting between mercenary companies hadn't stopped incidents from occurring in the past. But right now, he didn't see a lot of other options.

"All right, let's move. Hopefully we can get there before Ice shows up," Zeric said.

Everyone started heading up the stairs, and he turned to Gu'od and Sienn'lyn. "Then, we can have a talk about this Balance mumbo jumbo of yours."

"You have never been interested before. Why attempt to understand now?" Gu'od asked.

"It's never almost gotten me killed before."

This did not feel like a good place for a covert meeting. Random people roamed past, looking at the shelves of books. Despite every book being available at the touch of a button, Nima's Bookstore and Coffee Shop had a steady stream of customers. Several times, Lahkaba had been forced to turn people away when they tried to use the unoccupied seat beside him.

The meeting that Pasha had arranged for them and the Alliance intelligence agent was still several minutes away. They had been in the store for an hour already. Pasha had recruited several people to arrive at various times and help keep an eye out for Alliance forces.

Going through with this meeting held a lot of risks. Lahkaba considered getting up and walking away at several points. In the end, he remained seated, reading a collection of short mystery stories.

When the designated time arrived, a pale, raven-haired Terran male took the seat next to Lahkaba. Pasha immediately started to tell him that the seat was reserved, as he had been doing, but he stopped when the man fixed him with an intense glare. Pasha then waved a signal to his friends nearby.

Silently, Lahkaba said a prayer to the Great One—a habit he found himself in more frequently as of late—that this meeting would go smoothly, and then he spoke. "As I am sure you know, I am Representative Lahkaba. And this is Representative Alon." He gestured toward Pasha, sitting on his other side.

"I'll admit, I had been hoping to meet Ocaitchi or Dustlighter, but meeting you both is still an honor," the man said. Lahkaba made a note of the fact the man did not offer his name. He couldn't decide if it was a mark against his credibility or an indication of his professional caution.

When neither Lahkaba nor Pasha said anything more, the man continued. "I've sought you out because I've decided I can no longer support the Alliance. I thought about simply resigning, but due to the sensitive nature of the information I have access to, I would be shipped back to Terra and watched closely. I figure I could do more good by offering my services to you before that happens."

"You do realize that by even having this conversation, you've given up any chance of ever going back to Terra as anything other than a prisoner?" Pasha asked. Lahkaba thought it was a little blunt, but it was a necessary question.

The man nodded. "I do. I don't take half measures. What I'm offering you is complete information on Alliance troop deployments, ship movements, and strategic plans. While I myself will need immediate protection within your organization once you collect this data, I will also continue to get occasional updates from friends who are on the fence, not yet ready to abandon their posts completely."

The last offer was unexpected. Continued intelligence information from within the Alliance would be a real coup. Knowing current deployments would be useful, but knowing when reinforcements would inevitably arrive would prove even more valuable.

Assuming, of course, that this man could back up anything he said. So far, without even a name, they had no idea if he actually was with Alliance Intelligence. And they still had no idea whether he was trying to infiltrate them or otherwise set them up.

"What can you tell me about Alliance forces right now?" Lahkaba asked.

"The 4th Fleet is assigned to protect all three Colonial Sectors. I don't know where all of the ships are, but there are ships in each sector. At least TF-421 is guarding Ailleroc, possibly more. There are a few other ships on standard pa-trol sweeps of Kreogh, but when word of the rebellion on Enro arrived, they were recalled to Ailleroc. Right now, all ships are either in transit back to Ailleroc or are in orbit of Sulas."

Lahkaba nodded at the information. It matched what lit-tle they did know about Alliance forces. It would make sense for all ships to be recalled before a counter-offensive could be launched against Enro.

"When is the counter-invasion against Enro planned?" Lahkaba said.

"There isn't one," the man answered hesitantly.

"There isn't one?" Pasha asked, his voice making it clear he did not believe the news.

"Vice Admiral Gorzet is the senior commander in the sec-tor. She does not have the capability of transporting large numbers of troops at this time. The only ground forces she has are the marines aboard her ships and the army units de-fending Ailleroc or other worlds.

"However, once the fleet is recalled, I have heard rumors that she is planning a retaliatory attack. No ground forces, just a bombardment from orbit."

Lahkaba shared a worried glance with Pasha. Orbital bombardment was their biggest concern, militarily. The Alli-ance had more than enough power to decimate every major city on every world in the entire sector if they chose to. Weapons even existed that could eradicate all life on a world.

They clung to the hope that while the Alliance was abu-sive of its power and worth resisting, it was not actually evil. Wiping out all life would render a planet uninhabitable for generations, and bombarding cities into submission would not allow the Alliance to maintain its claim of providing a benevolent democracy. However, it would also be the easiest and quickest way to defeat the resistance.

"We don't need rumors," Lahkaba finally said. The notions disturbed him, but this guy could just be running a misinformation campaign to scare them.

Continuing, Lahkaba looked the man directly in the eyes. "Get what information you can and be ready to go in two days. Pasha will contact you with the meeting place. If everything looks good, you'll come with us. If not . . . "

He left the consequences unsaid, trying to sound menacing, and partly because he didn't know what the consequences would be. He didn't think he could kill this man—not unless it was in self-defense.

The man nodded, seemingly unfazed by the implied threat. "Sounds reasonable. I look forward to our next meeting."

With that, the man nodded to each of them and walked away. Lahkaba watched him depart. He was initially surprised when the man stopped to buy a book, but then he realized that it would keep up his cover of just being an innocent customer.

"What do you think?" Pasha asked once the man was out of earshot.

"I don't know. It sounds too good to be true," Lahkaba sighed.

Nodding in agreement, Pasha said, "My mother always said, if it sounds too good to be true, it probably is."

CHAPTER 7

The reunion with Asirzi did not go at all like Saracasi had imagined. At no point did their eyes lock, nor did they rush into each other's arms. There was no spontaneous, passionate first kiss.

To be fair, Saracasi thought there was a certain romantic quality to waking up to find Asirzi tending to her. Getting stunned didn't really require much in the way of medical attention, but that just made it more romantic.

When Saracasi opened her eyes and saw Asirzi, she was surprised at how beautiful she still thought the Liw'kel was, even though the injuries she had suffered during the Olan prison break were in clear evidence. Her right arm ended in a mechanical replacement, and her right breast lay flat next to her left one.

Despite those deformities, Saracasi still saw the beauty she had first been attracted to. The woman's face was lit by a friendly smile that made everything else seem unimportant.

Unfortunately, her brother's presence ruined things somewhat. Once he knew she was okay, he wanted them to get started on repairing the *Cutty Sark*.

After only some basic conversation with Asirzi, she was sucked into the world of engineering. Her next few days were quickly consumed by repair work and design discussions.

During a discussion about the status of the mining freighter, Chavatwor mentioned his idea of converting the ship into an escort carrier. Maarkean immediately latched onto that idea, so Saracasi and Chavatwor started on a design for the conversion in addition to the repair work.

For Saracasi, Chava's original excessive estimates for the repairs started to make sense—not only did Chavatwor work more thoroughly, but she started to suspect that he had had a few upgrades in mind from the start.

This work, which would prove to take up the next few weeks, was quite enjoyable. She had always found comfort in working on the *Cutty Sark*, and Chavatwor insisted on giving them some upgrades in addition to the other work.

Seeing her home begin to come back to life, better than ever, gave her a nice sense of pride.

The design work on the mining freighter challenged her in ways she had not experienced in years. Living the life of a smuggler provided unique challenges, but they didn't provide much mental exercise. Trying to figure out how to turn an old, beat-up freighter into a combat-capable warship required careful planning and ingenuity.

She much preferred this way of thinking to the make-it-up-as-you-go kind that survival required.

The most pleasant of several interruptions to her work came several days into it, when she finally got to have a true reunion with Asirzi.

One evening, while sitting on the balcony of the headquarters building and going over some calculations, Saracasi noticed Asirzi come out to join her. The two were alone—something she had hoped for since arriving.

Trying to decide what to say, Saracasi was relieved when Asirzi spoke first. "Nice evening."

The night air had a chill to it. Their hemisphere on Kol was currently in the early stages of autumn. That meant the days were tolerable and the nights relatively comfortable.

"It is. Last time I was here, it was well into summer. This is much nicer," Saracasi replied.

"Not as nice as my home on Sulas was. The summers never got very oppressive, and the winters didn't see that much snow. You could almost say it was nice during every season. It's also far too dry here. I miss the humidity the most."

"What made you decide to come here instead of returning to Sulas?" Saracasi asked, putting her datapad down beside her.

Asirzi turned from her position overlooking the balcony to face Saracasi. "There wasn't anything for me back on Sulas. My family returned to Kel several years ago. They saw what was happening. But I was born and raised on Sulas.

"At the time, I didn't want to leave. When Chava originally made plans to return to Sulas after Olan, he offered me work as a sales representative. So when he decided not to stay there after all, I came with him."

Leaning back on the balcony railing, Asirzi tilted her head as she spoke. "What about you? Why didn't you go back to life as a smuggler once you got free?"

Saracasi shrugged. "Smuggling was never my dream. But I probably would have if my brother hadn't come around to the idea of opposing the Alliance."

"Are you going to join this army that's being formed?" Asirzi asked, her voice quiet.

The question gave Saracasi pause. A few months ago, she would have answered with an emphatic 'yes.' She still believed in the cause, and she still wanted to see the Alliance fall. But after Perth, the idea of going back into battle worried her, and not for the obvious reasons.

"I don't know," she finally said. She dropped her eyes to her lap. She felt she could talk to the other woman, and she tried to find the right words to unburden herself of her secret, but she was unable to look at Asirzi as she spoke.

"Opposing the Alliance is something I've believed in for years. I still do. But I don't know if I can fight anymore. I never wanted to bring about change by a war.

"Sometimes I thought it might be necessary, and at the time, I said that would be okay if it was the only way. But now that I've seen war, seen the bodies of the dead, I don't like what it does to me. I still want to see the Alliance defeated. I think the fight–ing is necessary. I just don't know if I should personally do it again."

She wasn't sure if she had made herself clear, and she was worried about how Asirzi would respond. It startled her when she felt an arm go around her shoulder.

She looked to her side to see Asirzi sitting in the chair beside her, putting her one real arm around Saracasi. The Liw'kel woman had a comforting smile on her face.

"I don't think there is anything wrong with that," Asirzi said. "I feel the same way. The Alliance needs to be opposed, and things have happened that make a fight inevitable. I just know that is not something I am capable of doing. The idea of killing someone . . . I don't know if I could live with it, either."

Saracasi felt cold inside, but she nodded in response. She hadn't managed to make Asirzi understand. Her secret was still inside her, and now she couldn't bring herself to further clarify it.

She sighed and put it aside. "What worries me now," she said, "is that I can't leave my brother alone to go fight a fight I pushed him to start."

"So don't," Asirzi said. "You and Chava are working on turning the freighter into a combat ship, right?"

Saracasi nodded, and Asirzi continued, "Stay here and work on that. That's an important thing for the fight, having some warships. Someone has to build them. You'd still be helping your brother; you just wouldn't have to do any of the actual fighting."

The idea appealed to Saracasi. She also got the feeling there was an unsaid second component to Asirzi's suggestion. That added no small amount of appeal for Saracasi.

"Let's just hope I can convince my brother of that as well," she finally replied, smiling at Asirzi.

Getting back to the *Chimopori* proved easier than Solyss had expected. Ymp's mercenary friends offered to escort them to the starport at no charge. They apparently had a deep resentment of Ice because Firek had stolen several of their best clients. Spite always worked as a strong motivator.

Once back on board, Solyss ordered a thorough inspection of all systems and the exterior hull. He wouldn't be surprised if someone had installed a tracking device or bomb while they were cut off. It wouldn't be a nice end to their escape to take off and have a squadron of fighters follow them.

"But it wouldn't do them any good," Zeric argued. "You can't track anything through hyperspace. And Firek has plenty of connections with the port authority, so he can track our departure anyway."

"True, but once we got to Kol, they'd be able to pick up a tracking beacon from anywhere and know right where we are," Solyss countered.

"Only if they know we're going to Kol. We'd be better off getting out of here as quickly as possible, before Firek decides to just turn our location over to the Alliance authorities."

"Maybe. But we're still trying to locate all of our recruits," Solyss insisted.

When the news about Ice approaching had arrived in the cantina, their collection of recruits had scattered along with everyone else. Since they hadn't been planning to make a stand, Solyss thought that had been a practical decision, though it did put some doubts into his mind about the caliber of the recruits.

"We've already located half of them. That's actually quite an accomplishment," Zeric said as he closed the service panel he had been inspecting and leaned against it. "To be honest, I didn't expect to get anywhere near the number of people you did. So getting half of them to actually show up at the transport site is pretty amazing. "

Solyss nodded reluctantly. Optimism told him to hold out hope that more would show up, but practicality agreed with Zeric. The facts about the events on Enro were in a bitter battle with rumor and gossip. That level of uncertainty made it difficult to convince people.

"I guess you're right," Solyss admitted. "We have almost enough people to form a small platoon and even a half squadron of pilots."

"More than we had at Perth," Zeric said with a mischievous grin. "We should be able to take on the entire Alliance now."

Letting out a laugh, Solyss sat down at the engine monitoring station he had just finished inspecting. "We may have to do just that. Especially if the congress doesn't decide to form an army. 'Course, I doubt most of these guys will hang around for long if we can't pay them."

Zeric shrugged. "I've been a pirate before. We'll just be more discriminating."

They sat in silence for a moment. Solyss found Zeric different than he had expected—far less serious and more relaxed than Maarkean. He had a difficult time taking the younger man seriously. Yet Zeric had led the defense of Perth, and while it hadn't been a rousing success, the city had held far longer than he knew it should have.

Solyss knew that some of his discomfort stemmed from social conventions. The Dustlighters clearly did not come from the same family background as the Novastars. Zeric's affection for wearing a ball cap for a hockey team, regardless of the setting, made him look unsophisticated.

Normally, he tried not to hold that kind of thing against people.

It was important to be sensitive to the cultural differences of others. But Zeric was a fellow Terran.

As if to reinforce Solyss' belief in his social inappropriateness, Zeric asked, "You noticed anything weird going on with the Liw'kel?"

Though he had noticed the odd rivalry between Gamaly and Asheerah develop, seemingly over Gu'od, Solyss said, "No." It was none of his business.

"Gu'od has always attracted both women and men when we've gone out for a night of fun," Zeric said. "He's always brushed them off seamlessly. But now . . . he's not exactly encouraging Asheerah, but he's not stopping her either. Even this new girl, Sienn'lyn, seems to be flirting with him. But what's really weird is that I've never seen Gamaly jealous before. She knows Gu'od's devoted to her. She's usually just amused when people try to hit on him."

Solyss shrugged. "Asheerah is quite attractive. And also a capable fighter, like Gu'od. Maybe he sees something appealing there." He tried to make his comments noncommittal, without revealing his own attraction to Asheerah. He had always kept it hidden, as it wasn't proper for a ship's captain to have a relationship with a member of his crew.

Zeric looked skeptical. "I don't buy it. Gamaly's no Asheerah in a fight, but she's no pushover. On a firing range, I'd place bets on her. But none of that matters to Gu."

Solyss detected a deeper concern in Zeric's question. He started to wonder what was at the heart of Zeric's curiosity. Could Zeric have developed an interest in Asheerah, too?

Deciding that line of thinking was both pointless and none of his business, Solyss tried to think of a way to redirect the conversation. It was not his place to get involved in anyone else's personal life. Even if he did have an interest.

"All right, once Isaxo and Kard finish the inspection of the hull, we'll tell Captain Vellious to follow us into orbit. We'll leave with whoever's shown up."

Nodding in agreement, Zeric stood up. "Excellent. Oh, let's give them some coordinates in deep space for a rendezvous point. We'll let them know our final destination from there. Hopefully, that will reduce the chances of Ice or the Alliance finding out."

The practical and cautious suggestion reminded Solyss that there was more to Zeric than he sometimes thought. Though deep-space rendezvous could be difficult, it was much harder for anyone trying to follow them to calculate coordinates for the middle of nowhere. Most jumps had a destination that was relative to nearby objects: planets, stars, moons, etc. The nearest guide points in space were light years away.

"I better get started on some calculations," Solyss said. "Maybe we should send someone to travel with them, just in case."

Zeric looked thoughtful and then nodded enthusiastically. "Good idea. Gu'od and Gamaly can do it."

"Why not you?" Solyss asked suspiciously.

"This way, Gamaly and Asheerah are separated. I wouldn't want to be anywhere nearby when they finally go at each other."

That made sense, Solyss thought, but it also kept Zeric onboard the *Chimopori*. And this time there would be no Gu'od to distract Asheerah.

CHAPTER 8

As the shuttle ramp lowered, the sounds of pomp and ceremony greeted Fleet Admiral Katerina Sartori. She fought down a sigh and tried to maintain a professional expression on her face. Due to her unexpected arrival, the assembled troops had had less than an hour to prepare this ceremony. It would be disrespectful to their efforts to let her weariness with ceremony show.

Decorated with the Alliance flag, the flag of Ailleroc, and pendants from all of the military units represented, the hangar bay looked like a patriotic explosion. A small band stood in one corner, playing the Alliance anthem. To the port side of her shuttle, crewmen stood in rigid attention. Across from them were rows of marines in their dark blue dress uniforms.

At the bottom of the shuttle ramp stood three individuals, two in dark green naval dress uniforms and one in a rich-looking civilian business suit. With a smile toward the assembled troops, Katerina walked down the shuttle's ramp and stopped before the three individuals. The civilian, a Terran male in his advanced middle years, gave her a wide, insincere-looking smile. "Admiral Sartori, I am Governor Zhant. Welcome to Ailleroc. It is truly an honor to meet you."

Ignoring the governor and the female Braz vice admiral standing beside him, Sartori turned to the Braz male, who was wearing a commander's uniform. He looked older than the picture in his dossier file. The blue screfa on his right cheek looked faded, but his eyes had a sharpness to them.

"Permission to come aboard, Captain Rusktorl?" Sartori asked, using the traditional title and giving a formal salute.

Even though Sartori outranked Commander Rusktorl by several orders of magnitude, she had just arrived aboard his ship, the carrier ANS *Dominance*. It was proper for her to ask his permission to come aboard before anything else. It also gave her a small bit of satisfaction when Governor Zhant frowned at being ignored.

"Permission granted, Fleet Admiral," Rusktorl said, returning the salute.

Next, Sartori turned to the female Braz. This was Vice Admiral Jasmine Gorzet, the senior military commander. This time, Vice Admiral Gorzet saluted her first. Sartori returned the greeting and then said, "Admiral, you are hereby informed that I am now formally taking command of all forces in the Alliance Colonial Sectors. Task Group 42 will hereby report directly to me until Admiral Garcia returns with the rest of the 4th Fleet."

"Aye, Admiral," Gorzet said, nodding. Sartori thought she saw a look of relief cross the woman's face, but she dismissed the thought. An officer who was relieved to pass responsibility up the chain of command would not be worth much in her mind, and she did not want to prejudge Gorzet too quickly.

Finally, Sartori turned to Governor Zhant. The man looked annoyed at being ignored until now, but she didn't care. It was mismanagement by him and the other governors that had allowed the situation in the sector to get to the point of rebellion. Cleaning up their mess was keeping her from retirement.

"Governor, thank you. It is nice to return to Ailleroc," Sartori said with false sincerity. "I look forward to your report on the state of affairs on the planet. Please inform your army commanders that they will now be reporting to my office aboard *Dominance*."

"Admiral, surely you do not mean to take away my defensive forces while we are in the midst of a rebellion. Who will protect the people from these traitors?" Zhant demanded.

"The people of Ailleroc will be well protected, Governor," Sartori said, her tone reassuring. When Zhant nodded in relief, she continued, making her tone steely. "As you know, Governor, as sector commander, my authority extends to all military forces and exceeds that of planetary governors. I wish that to be the only time I need to mention that fact."

Zhant held her gaze stubbornly for several seconds before breaking eye contact and nodding his acquiescence. Sartori assumed he would cause trouble for her in the future, but for the moment, at least, he accepted her authority. That would have to do for the time being.

"Now, Captain, please show me to where I can get to work. I want an update on the present situation in the sector."

Commander Rusktorl nodded and then spun sharply on his heel. When he turned, the band stopped playing, and if it were possible, the assembled troops came to sharper attention. He spoke to the men with a clear but loud voice. "Commander, Colonial Sectors, arriving."

In unison, the marines and crewman snapped their hands in a salute. Sartori strode purposefully down the aisle between them, holding her head at a confident, yet not elitist, angle. Zhant, Gorzet, and Rusktorl followed her in order of rank. After passing the troops, Sartori slipped through the door exiting the hangar deck and stopped to wait in the corridor for the others.

She heard Rusktorl dismiss the troops behind her. He then took the point position in their group, leading Sartori through the ship's corridors. She knew her way around ships like *Dominance* like the back of her hand, but every ship had some uniqueness to its design, and she did not know which rooms Rusktorl had designated for her use.

The primary CIC would likely be already occupied by Gorzet's staff. Since Gorzet would be the active commander in any battle situation, Sartori had no wish to usurp her. Sector commander was a far more strategic and administrative position than that of task group commander. She regretted that fact somewhat; directing forces in the heat of battle suited her talents better.

When they arrived in a large room, Sartori was pleased to see that her staff had already begun setting everything up for her needs. They had transferred to the *Dominance* before her, from the cramped packet ship on which they had traveled from Braz. Commander Hari Dolan, a dark-skinned Terran male with short, buzz-cut black hair, greeted her with a cup of coffee and a datapad.

Commander Dolan had been Sartori's chief of staff during her time commanding the 2nd Fleet. When she had stepped down, she had recommended him for promotion to commodore and command of a squadron. Upon learning she would not be retiring, he had asked to join her, as had most of her former staff.

She appreciated the loyalty, but she wished Dolan had remained closer to headquarters until his promotion came through. Having him as one of her senior commanders, instead of a bunch of unknowns, would have been reassuring.

Dolan led her, Rusktorl, Gorzet, and Zhant into a conference room off of the main room. The room contained a medium-sized U-shaped table with a holo projector hanging from the ceiling in the center. A junior lieutenant sat at the room's computer terminal, at the top of one side of the U. A major, presumably from Gorzet's staff, stood at the center of the table, looking nervous. He would have the task of bringing Sartori up to speed.

Once everyone was seated, Gorzet nodded to the major, who began speaking. "Admiral Sartori, as you know, all planetary governments in the sector have been suspended by order of the Alliance Congress. This order was done in response to a group calling itself the Kreogh Sector Congress issuing demands to the Alliance."

As the major continued speaking, holographic images started appearing in the open space before him. "During the months-long transit time between here and the core worlds, a terrorist attack occurred on the world of Sulas. A group of radicals, led by former naval officer Maarkean Ocaitchi and former Marine Zeric Dustlighter attacked Olan Detention Center and freed hundreds of convicted criminals."

The hologram showed scenes from the attack on the prison and the faces of Maarkean and Zeric. She had received all of this data before leaving Braz; it was the reason she had been dispatched in the first place.

At the time, that data had already been months out of date, which was why she had chosen to journey to Ailleroc aboard a fast courier instead of waiting for the Marine Expeditionary Force to be assembled.

She would have time to develop a strategy before the marines arrived. Still, the trip had taken her two months.

Shifting, the hologram now showed an Alliance military base. The major went on, "A month later, this same group raided the Alliance supply depot on Dantyne, stealing guns, explosives, and even a combat SPC."

This news startled Sartori. How could a small group of radicals carry off a raid against an Alliance base, even if they were led by a former officer? The prison attack was believable; it was, after all, designed to keep people in, not to stop an outside attack force. But an Alliance military base should have been far more secure.

The raid on Dantyne disappeared from her mind as the major continued, "Two months ago, a rebellion broke out on Enro. We have confirmed reports from the planet's army commander that Maarkean Ocaitchi was responsible for this revolt as well. The rebels succeeded in defeating the army forces and seizing control of the planet."

Sartori felt a frown cross her face, and she saw the major squirm. She forced a neutral expression back onto her face. The poor officer was just the bearer of bad news, not the cause of it—he didn't deserve to face her displeasure.

With an almost inaudible gulp, the man continued. "Resistance activity has increased across the sector as the news of this rebellion has spread. Sulas is under martial law. Taxes have gone uncollected on Mirthod and Kol while smuggling activity has become more blatant. Dantyne forces have been forced into defensive positions, surrendering several facilities to the rebels."

The major shot a hesitant glance toward Zhang before continuing. "Cardine and Ailleroc have remained relatively peaceful, though there are several reports that the planetary governments continue to meet in secret. We believe the self-proclaimed sector congress will be meeting again in the next few weeks, but we have not gotten any hard data on where."

Sartori took a moment to absorb the information. Things had deteriorated much faster than she had expected.

Communication delays were the bane of a military commander. All of the information the major had given, with the exception of details of Ailleroc, was already between three and ten days old. All-out rebellions could have erupted on any number of other worlds, and she would have no idea.

"Governor Zhang, I know you cannot speak for all of the worlds, but for Ailleroc, when are the new elections scheduled to be held?" Sartori asked.

Zhang cast a confused look toward her. "New elections? For what?"

"Ailleroc's planetary government," Sartori replied, thinking that should be obvious.

"They aren't. That body was disbanded," Zhang said indignantly.

"The current body was pending a new election," Sartori replied forcefully. "The current representatives were unseated, but the entire institution was not disbanded. That was included in Congress' order to you, Governor."

"In light of the current spirit of rebellion, I do not think an election would be a good idea. We cannot reward people for defying us," Zhang said stubbornly.

"Having an elected government is not a reward," Sartori argued, shocked at Zhang's attitude. "Commander Dolan, prepare a message for the next packet ship. All planets are to hold fresh elections within three months of receiving the message. Include it with the update about my assumption of command."

"Aye, Admiral," Dolan said from beside her, making a note on his datapad.

"Admiral Gorzet, what information does Admiral Garcia have about the present situation?"

"I dispatched a packet ship to him as soon as word of the events on Enro reached me. That ship should just now be arriving in the Trepon sector. But the admiral likes to patrol with the fleet sometimes, instead of remaining at Spreta Station. It could be several more weeks before the ship finds him. I would estimate three to four months before he can return with the rest of the 4th Fleet."

"The 3rd MEF should be here within that same timeframe," Sartori said, nodding. "The question we must answer is how to proceed until the reinforcements arrive. Admiral, what plans have you already enacted?"

"I have issued a recall of all ships back to Ailleroc," Gorzet answered confidently. "Most of my forces are light ships. If the rebels gained control of any planetary defense weapons, my men would be vulnerable without support from the main body of TF-421. Once they arrive, I was planning on staging a strike against Enro."

Sartori raised an eyebrow. "I was under the impression that our troop transport capacity was limited. Have you commandeered some civilian craft?"

"No, Admiral, I was not planning on bringing ground forces. An orbital bombardment of the captured Alliance bases and the city of Perth should keep the rebellion from spreading until the rest of the fleet can arrive."

Despite herself, Sartori felt her mouth drop. This idiot had been about to do exactly what she had been sent out here to prevent. Had she waited and journeyed with the marines, thousands would be dead, and the entire sector would have just cause to rise up in rebellion.

Controlling herself, Sartori asked, "Admiral Gorzet, are you telling me that you were planning to bombard Alliance civilians from orbit?"

"No, Admiral," Gorzet answered.

Sartori breathed a sigh of relief, thinking she had misunderstood Gorzet's plan. However, her relief died when Gorzet continued speaking. "I was planning on bombarding enemy combatants. By rebelling against legitimate Alliance rule, the citizenry gave up their rights to our protection and became the enemy."

Anger fumed inside Sartori. It was only years of practice that kept her next words from not coming out in a shout. Instead, she said, almost in a whisper, "Commander Dolan, please summon the commander of Taffy 421. Inform him that he will be assuming command of TG-42 because Vice Admiral Gorzet has been relieved from duty due to gross incompetence."

Gorzet stood up. "This is preposterous! On what grounds am I being relieved?"

Keeping her tone low, Sartori cast a dangerous look toward the looming figure of Gorzet. "You were planning to slaughter Alliance citizens. This is not a foreign invasion we are dealing with. And even if it were, we do not bombard civilians. You have clearly lost all perspective. You are dismissed, Vice Admiral."

Looking as if she would like to continue arguing, Gorzet paused for a moment. She looked at Zhang and Rusktorl, but neither man would meet her eye. Finally, she did the first thing Sartori could respect. With a crisp salute, Gorzet said, "I stand relieved." Then she spun sharply on her heel and walked from the meeting room.

The tension in the air remained high after Gorzet's departure. Sartori started taking deep breaths in an effort to keep calm. Zhang, apparently, decided to do everything he could to prevent that from happening.

"That's your response to this rebellion?" he demanded angrily. "Dismissing a senior commander and holding elections?"

"My first response, yes," Sartori replied. "But it won't be the only response. Until the rest of the 4th Fleet and the 3rd MEF arrive, our military options are limited. Our goal is to keep the rebellion from spreading. Once we have the necessary forces, then we can clamp down on those responsible and bring them to justice. But we do not need to slaughter thousands in order to do that."

Zhang nodded to her in acceptance, and Sartori ended the meeting. There was no point in continuing until Rear Admiral Norrax arrived and got up to speed. All of the officers and Zhang departed. After a moment, Sartori was alone, except for Dolan, standing at the door.

"Can I get you anything, Admiral?" Dolan asked.

"The authority to promote you directly to vice admiral," Sartori answered, only half joking.

"I'll get right on that, Admiral," Dolan replied with a grin and then left her alone in the conference room.

With a sigh, Sartori leaned back in her chair, closing her eyes. Things were going to be more difficult here than she had first thought. But it was only a matter of time, and then she could crush the rebels. Until then, she would undermine their reasons for rebelling in the first place.

Chapter 9

Maarkean was getting impatient. The time when he would need to depart for Irod crept closer, but Solyss, Fracsid, and Eri'dos had not yet arrived with the recruits. He would soon face the choice of either waiting for them or going to Irod with nothing to offer.

He didn't have a lot of confidence that the others would have much luck in finding recruits. But anything was a place to start from. It wouldn't be a good sign if their only recruit was a bounty hunter who had been hired to capture him.

Repairs to the *Cutty Sark* were coming along well. He hated letting others do all of the work, but it was becoming increasingly clear that his efforts to help were more of a hindrance. Switching out ruined control circuits and replacing broken components was the extent of his engineering skills. The work Chavatwor and Saracasi were doing went beyond that, yet neither admitted as much to him.

When a ship was spotted approaching the shipyard, Maarkean felt relief. It occurred to him only after he went to greet the ship that it might not be friendly. Another bounty hunter or an Alliance ship was not out of the question.

Fortunately, as the craft got closer, he recognized her as *Chimopori*, Solyss Novastar's ship. The small courier, slightly bigger than the *Cutty Sark*, descended through the cloudless sky. As she came in for a landing, Maarkean noticed another speck fast approaching. His earlier concerns about another bounty hunter resurfaced.

The second ship grew more distinct, and Maarkean identified her as a passenger transport. Jerik's ship had masked itself as a passenger transport, but that had been mostly sensor illusions. This one actually looked like a passenger ship.

Either a second bounty hunter had a much more effective disguise, or Solyss and Zeric had been effective in recruiting at least someone. That, or Zeric had decided to return to his old life as a ship thief.

By the time the passenger transport came in for its final descent, the boarding ramp on *Chimopori* came down, dispersing Zeric and a Camari female. Maarkean assumed this woman to be Ymp, the head of Zeric's former mercenary group. With luck, that might mean that the rest of the company was onboard the transport.

"Maarkean Ocaitchi, allow me to present Ymp Ki-Li," Zeric said with a less-than-enthusiastic tone in his voice.

"Major Ocaitchi," Ymp said, her eye stalks bowing slightly in a Camari sign of respect.

"Ms. Ki-Li," Maarkean replied. He debated whether to insist on just being called Maarkean. Formally, he had no authority; he was just another rebel. But it was his express goal to form a military fighting unit, and a level of formality would be required.

In the end, he shelved that decision for later. "Welcome to Kol. I take it Zeric was successful in convincing you and Ice to join us?"

A sheepish grin crossed Zeric's face. "Not exactly. Though we did pick up a little under forty experienced people. Plus some experienced pilots and others with other skills, Ymp and a few of her more faithful companions among them."

"Excellent," Maarkean said, adding as much enthusiasm as he could to his voice. He was curious about what Zeric wasn't saying, but he could learn that later. "If Eri'dos and Fracsid can do as well, we'll have close to a company in strength, with maybe a few star fighter squadrons."

"Just need guns and some star fighters," Zeric said, his grin genuine again.

"What is this place?" Ymp asked. "Zeric said we were coming to an abandoned outpost. This does not look abandoned."

The main doors to the converted warehouse were open, revealing the buzz of activity inside. People and robots moved about between ships, sparks flew from welding equipment, and a cacophony of noise bounded outward. Several ships filled the available space inside, leaving only a relatively narrow corridor down the center for movement.

In the time Maarkean had been here, work had finished on one freighter and two more had arrived to take its place. Chavatwor had dispatched Htaretter in his newly refurbished *Bright Blade* to pick up another crew of new workers along with a supply shuttle of new equipment. The speed of growth amazed him, but the Kowwok's business sense was exceeded only by his engineering skill.

"This is UDF Inc. Shipyards. Chavatwor arrived and set up shop before I got here," Maarkean explained. "But he's agreed to allow us to use some of the other buildings, at least for a while."

While Maarkean talked with Zeric and Ymp, the rest of the crew from *Chimopori* disembarked. Before long, the people aboard the passenger transport joined them. He soon found himself surrounded by several dozen people, and he had no idea what to say. Everyone here had come to follow him in a fight against the Alliance. What do you say to a group like that?

Gratitude was always appreciated, he decided. That and instructions on what would happen next. Unfortunately, he only knew the next step, not the one after that. People would inevitably assume, or at least hope, he had everything planned out for the next year.

"Welcome, everyone, to Kol." He didn't know that everyone here could be trusted yet, but secrecy regarding their location would not hold for long. "You've all come here for one reason: you are tired of the Alliance's abuses of power.

We're here to stand up to them until they realize our voices cannot be ignored, our rights cannot be suppressed. This won't be an easy or a short struggle. But it is just."

At this, there was a mix of cheers and uncomfortable stares. Apparently, some people had bought into the revolutionary zeal more than others. Maarkean was fine with that. He had gotten involved in this rebellion before he was fully committed to the cause; others could do the same.

"For now, we're going to find everyone a place to stay. Beyond the shipyard behind me are three buildings. One of them has been set aside for our use as a barracks. The rooms are small, but big enough for two people to a room. Right now, there are enough rooms to spread out, but we expect more to arrive in the next few days. So if there is someone you wish to bunk with, go ahead and do so."

Asirzi Z'ren came out of the shipyard and started guiding the group around the side of the building. She had volunteered to help Maarkean with some of the logistics.

The woman did not appear interested in joining his band of rebels, but he found her frequently trying to make herself useful to him. He appreciated the help, but he wondered what her interest in him was.

At first, he had entertained the fantasy that she was attracted to him. Since his wife, Eyris, had died in the same vehicle accident that took his parents, he hadn't been in any form of relationship.

Life as a smuggler hadn't even afforded him the chance for short-term relationships, especially in the last year. And even with one mechanical arm, Asirzi was reasonably attractive.

When he had mentioned this theory to Saracasi, however, she'd bluntly told him that Asirzi had no sexual interest in men. He trusted his sister's judgment on this subject, though he had no idea how she could tell. It was difficult to identify what gender some species were, much less their sexual preference. For some reason, Saracasi appeared particularly annoyed with his ignorance this time.

As the group of recruits began following Asirzi, Maarkean caught sight of a dark-haired Terran male. The man looked familiar. He couldn't believe what he was seeing at first, but his sense of recognition grew stronger the more he looked. He just had to ignore the unkempt hair and the multiple-days-old growth of facial hair.

"Dav?" Maarkean asked.

The Terran stopped moving with the others and turned to face him. "Maark."

Maarkean stood there, flabbergasted. Davidus Brieni had been a member of his flight school group, and they had joined the same squadron. They had flown countless missions together against the Confederacy along the way. And they had hated each other.

Well, hate might be too strong of a word, Maarkean decided. During their early career, they had competed for assignments and promotions.

They had always been neck and neck. Davidus had been the first promoted to lieutenant and the first made a flight leader. He had taken no small amount of pleasure in rubbing that fact in Maarkean's face.

"You know each other?" Zeric asked, surprised.

Maarkean nodded. "Everyone, Major Davidus Brieni, Alliance navy pilot."

"That's Commander Brieni, Major," Davidus said, in the arrogant tone Maarkean remembered so well. "And it's ex-Alliance navy pilot, just like you."

"You never mentioned that during the interview," Solyss said with an accusatory tone.

Davidus shrugged dismissively. "Had I mentioned I was a navy officer and an old friend of Maarkean's, would you have brought me here?"

"'Friend' might be pushing the meaning of the word," Maarkean said, frowning.

"Maybe. But the point stands. Would you have trusted Alliance military?"

"Yes," Zeric answered, causing Davidus to raise a questioning eyebrow. "I'm former Alliance. Maarkean, as you apparently know, is, too. I expect there are some others here among that group."

Zeric looked to Solyss as if for confirmation, and the Terran nodded. "A few of them were former marines or army. There is one who flew for the Confederate navy."

Davidus frowned at that last comment, and Maarkean resisted the urge to do the same. He had come to trust Lahkaba, a former member of the Confederate military, but he found it hard to feel happy about working with any others. Old enmities were hard to let go of. Which raised the question of why Davidus had decided to come here.

"Regardless of that," Maarkean said, "why are you here, Dav? There was no one more committed to the Alliance than you."

"I could say the same thing about you," Davidus retorted. "There were lots of things I could question about you, but your patriotism was never one of them. Yet here you are, leading a rebellion against the Alliance."

"I'm not leading a rebellion," Maarkean said. "Elected officials from every world in the sector are. I'm just helping to form a fighting force to aid them."

"Of course you are," Davidus said, skepticism in his voice. "And that's why you're recruiting people by telling them that if this congress does not form an army, you'll go rogue?"

Shocked, Maarkean turned to look at Solyss and Zeric. They had discussed that possibility, but he thought they hadn't come to a firm plan. Apparently, he was the only one who had thought that.

For their part, Zeric had the good sense to look ashamed, though Solyss looked confused by Maarkean's scrutiny. The man clearly believed that the fight would continue with or without Congress' support. Solyss had sought him out before he had even decided to actively oppose the Alliance. Solyss was definitely committed to this fight.

With a reluctant sigh, Maarkean nodded. "According to the Alliance, the congress is a rogue terrorist group. I'm called a traitor and a subversive. I think the only chance for success requires Congress, or some kind of similar group, to be leading a united front of all the planets in the sector. But someone needs to stand up to the Alliance, and if we have to do it on our own for a time, well, I was already doing that."

Not that he had meant to be doing that, Maarkean said to himself. Most of his close friends knew that, but it wouldn't be good to go around advertising that now. He needed people to believe in the cause, not to think he was here by accident.

Davidus smiled. "Good. Then you're not being used as some kind of figurehead. I couldn't follow someone like that. But knowing you're committed to this makes me confident it's worth fighting for."

There was a compliment buried in what Davidus said. They had always respected each other, but had rarely let pleasantries get past their antagonism. Maarkean found himself touched by the sentiment.

Then Davidus reminded him of why they hadn't gotten along well. "Because you're going to need me if you hope to win. You never were a good teacher, and this mishmash of rabble is going to need a lot of training."

Maarkean just shook his head. He didn't like Davidus much, but it looked like he had found his flight instructor.

A few weeks later, Zeric had to face reality. It wasn't as if he had wanted anyone else to be in charge. Gu'od, Gamaly,

Maarkean, Saracasi, Lahkaba, and Lohcja were the only ones he really trusted. Maarkean, Lahkaba, and Lohcja had been gone for a while; presumably, Maarkean had met the other two on Irod, where they were hoping to get an official answer from the congress. Saracasi was bright but didn't know a thing about working with mercenaries or organizing a ground unit. And Gu'od and Gamaly had both just given him a pointed look when he suggested one of them do it.

So in the end, Zeric found himself in charge of the collection of mercenaries, renegades, smugglers, scoundrels, thieves, and other scumbags they had recruited. But he had no idea what to do with them. Until Maarkean returned with the official word from the congress, they had agreed to not take any formal action.

Most of the group had brought their own personal weapons. As they stood now, they could probably overthrow the limited Alliance presence on Kol. There would have been little point in doing that, however. The cities and mining companies had already stopped paying custom duties to the Alliance authorities, and the planetary governor did not have enough troops to force the issue. For all practical purposes, Kol was free from Alliance rule.

Aside from the Alliance, Kol still suffered from a severe smuggling and piracy problem. Technically, by refusing to pay the custom duties, every single ship coming in and out of Kol was now a smuggler, but the companies didn't care much about that. The pirates, however, were a different matter.

Maarkean and Zeric had discussed going after the pirates as their first action. Clearing out the pirates would go a long way to convincing the locals, and in turn the people around the sector, that they were better off without the Alliance. Even though most companies had stopped paying their taxes, it was generally assumed most were just holding onto that money so that they could hand it over if an Alliance task force showed up to press the issue.

Even if Zeric wanted to start the piracy campaign, he didn't feel it would be a good idea to go into combat with this rabble. Most of them had some fighting experience. Some had former military training or time with organized mercenary bands. But by and large, they were more a disorderly band of thugs than a coherent military unit.

To deal with the problem of organizing the Rogues, as he liked to call them, before they were officially organized, he fell back on the old marine standby: physical training, or PT. Holding regular PT sessions provided routine. Being in the middle of the desert saved them from the usual problem of drunkenness, and exhaustion saved them from fighting among themselves.

Most of the group, while in relatively good shape, were far from their peak. Zeric counted himself among that group and pushed himself hard. Serving as an example to the others was only a small part of his motivation. If any of the group got unruly and decided to challenge him, he wanted to have a good chance of winning. Or, at the very least, out-running them.

The desert environment provided an additional challenge to overcome. The dry, hot air played havoc for the Camari and, to a lesser extent, the Liw'kel. But the Dotran thrived. For their part, the Notha and Kowwok surprised him with their adaption. With their fur coats, Zeric would have assumed they'd suffer from the heat. Instead, the fur proved to be an effective insulator and kept them at a stable temperature. They fared even better than the Terrans and Braz.

On a whim, Zeric convinced Gu'od to begin instructing the group in martial arts techniques. His friend had resisted at first, citing the need for proper spiritual guidance for Ni'jar techniques to be effective. In the end, he had relented when Zeric suggested that he would just ask Sienn'lyn to do it.

Gu'od had taken Sienn'lyn on as an apprentice of sorts, claiming to be responsible for her ouster from her enclave on Mirthod. Based on the continued interest the girl and

Asheerah continued to show in him, Zeric was suspicious. The daily PT had even taken on a sense of competition between those two and Gamaly. Under different circumstances, Zeric might have found it sexy. Now he just worried about Gu'od.

To his surprise, Ymp proved herself to be a valuable asset. He had expected conflict from the former mercenary commander. Instead, Ymp helped keep order among the group and made no public arguments with him. There were some private ones, which only served to reinforce her public support.

Conscious of the need for a solid officer and NCO core when they were formally organized, Zeric tried to get to know everyone. It started out easy enough; the first batch of marine recruits was less than forty people. When Fracsid and Eri'dos arrived, that number swelled to well over one hundred. That didn't include the pilots and crewers, or the almost one hundred workers Chavatwor already had working for him. He had never been very good with names before, and he felt like a heel every time he couldn't remember the name of one of the new people.

Fortunately, not all of them were his sole responsibility. Davidus had agreed to Maarkean's offer to serve as flight instructor. A few dozen of the recruits had more experience in a cockpit or aboard a starship than they did carrying a gun. They participated in some of the PT, but Davidus had them helping with the work on the mining freighter about half the time.

After a few weeks, Zeric had started to form a picture of how the group would be organized. A Liw'kel with very dark red skin, named Deja'z'reth Adat'to, had former experience in the Liw'kel army as a drill instructor. He had proved himself to be invaluable with training, and Zeric thought him a good candidate to continue that role.

Sigfa Neith, a former Ice member and Ymp's associate, had shown good leadership potential. He, along with

Asheerah and a blue-carapaced Ronid named Calek Orion, would make good platoon leaders. Some of the mercenaries had brought armored combat space suits, similar to what Asheerah fancied wearing, and Zeric had an idea about forming a space assault platoon.

He had, once again, attempted to convince Gu'od or Gamaly to serve as the group's second in command. Gu'od had refused, claiming that as a Ni'jar he could fight and advise, but not lead. Zeric thought the notion ridiculous, but he did manage to convince Gu'od to serve as the group's first sergeant.

Gamaly's reluctance came as more of a surprise. She turned down any offer or suggestion he made. He never got a genuine answer about why; she only said it wouldn't be right to commit herself to a role she wouldn't be able to fill for long. Zeric wondered if her reluctance had something to do with the Liw'kel women who were all over Gu'od. He would never have thought there was anything there for her to worry about.

In the end, circumstances forced him to accept the inevitable. The only person remotely qualified to serve as a second was Ymp. Despite her assistance of late, he wondered how well she would continue to handle their role reversal.

Aside from Gu'od and Gamaly, he mentioned none of this to anyone. He had no idea how long Maarkean would be on Irod. The journey there was only a few days, and there had already been ample time to make the round trip several times.

But politicians always took forever to do anything. Even rebel ones. So Zeric waited, hoping Maarkean would return with good news before his band of misfits got tired of exercising in the desert.

Lahkaba considered himself a patient person. It was a necessary quality in politics. Most times, he could sit quietly while someone else droned on about an insignificant matter without showing any signs of agitation or annoyance.

Or that's what he told himself he did. In truth, he didn't know how everyone else perceived him, but he did know that he didn't have a reputation for impatience. He was counting on that helping him have an impact now.

"Two weeks we have been here and for two weeks we have avoided the main reason we're here," he grumbled to Maarkean as they walked toward the building the people of Irod had given them to use as a meeting place.

"You've been telling me you don't want to bring the idea of an army up for vote unless you're sure it will pass. What's changed?" Maarkean asked.

"I'm fed up. That's what's changed," Lahkaba growled. He then calmed himself and spoke again with a more normal tone. "But also, I've gotten a message from Sulas. There was another riot turned massacre. If we don't act soon, the people of Sulas aren't going to wait for us. And I don't think a spontaneous uprising is going to go as well there as it did on Enro."

Maarkean nodded appreciatively as they walked. Then he said, "I've been reviewing the data our Alliance spy has given us. I might have found something that could help you."

Kaars Aerinstar, former Alliance intelligence officer, had finally revealed his name to Lahkaba once they had departed from Sulas. He had brought with him mountains of reports: supply lists, troop transfer requests, discipline charges, battle plans, requisition forms, and more. It was a treasure trove of data, but also a giant mess.

Once Maarkean had arrived on Irod, he and Lahkaba had begun going over the data. Most of it turned out to be useless—typical bureaucratic paperwork. Kaars insisted that intelligence was gleaned by pulling fragments from many different sources. Lahkaba hadn't disagreed, but he had feared that it would require a sophisticated computer program and a team of highly trained analysts.

Now, Maarkean explained that while he had looked over supply reports, a pattern had started to form. Packet ships from Braz would arrive at regular intervals, bringing updates and orders from headquarters. Every time, the packet ship would then be dispatched to the Trepon sector. A standard courier would occasionally be sent to Loisa, but the fast packet ship would always go to Trepon.

"When I crossed that with some of the supply reports, I noticed a large shipment being dispatched to Trepon as well. Every indication shows that a fairly substantial portion of the Alliance's capabilities are located in Trepon, not Kreogh," Maarkean concluded. "We're probably only dealing with a handful of ships for this entire sector. Trepon is almost as far away as the core worlds of the Alliance. Messages about Enro will just be arriving there in another few days. So, the upshot is, we still have three to five months before any reinforcements get here."

Lahkaba considered the news. He wanted to push the congress to finally act, but he doubted the news about the massacre on Sulas would help. Some of the delegates would fear that any military action would bring similar consequences to their worlds. But he also knew that if he didn't push for a vote on the military, Lei-mey would. And she had antagonized enough members that they might vote it down just out of spite.

Lahkaba mused, "It sounds like an opportunity that we don't want to pass up. I might be able to use that. But Ailleroc and Cardine are still both very hesitant to take this kind of action. They only tentatively supported Enro's decision to fight. Kol and Mirthod take their lead from those two. Only Dantyne, Sulas, and Enro are sure to vote yes. That's still a pretty weak position."

"They won't be swayed by this data? Or the news from Sulas?" Maarkean asked skeptically.

Lahkaba shook his head. "They're too afraid of retaliation. Ailleroc has the strongest Alliance presence and the largest population of Braz and Terrans. Cardine, despite a primarily Camari population, rivals Sulas economically and has relatively limited Alliance interference. Siding openly with a rebellion, should we lose, will jeopardize that freedom."

"So what do we do? Just hope they'll come around?" Maarkean asked. "You're pretty persuasive."

With a grunt, Lahkaba said, "Thank you, but I have a more realistic understanding of my abilities. We need to find something they want."

"You mean bribe them?" Maarkean asked, unease clear in his voice.

"Don't look at me like that," Lahkaba said. "It may be a stereotype that politicians will just do whatever the highest bidder says, but it has a basis in fact. Politicians are people, and people do things that benefit them. It's not as coarse as offering bribes. We just need to find something that will benefit the people of Cardine or Ailleroc enough that it would make declaring war on the Alliance worthwhile."

Lahkaba pondered his options. Idealistic appeals would only go so far. The desire to be free of the Alliance had gotten the people to form this congress. But forming a congress to air grievances was a far cry from forming an army to fight for those grievances to be addressed.

"What about placing one of them in charge of this military?" Maarkean pondered.

Tilting his head to the side, Lahkaba considered Maarkean. "What do you mean? I always assumed you would be in charge of the military. The people see you as an inspiration."

"Thank you, but I have a more realistic understanding of my abilities," Maarkean said with a wry grin, before continuing with a more serious tone, "Isn't one of their delegates a general?"

Lahkaba nodded. "Celris Numba. Retired from the Camar Army."

"Perfect. Then he'll have far more experience with ground forces than I do. He'd do a better job organizing and planning that than I would. I can still be involved. Maybe head up this group of Rogues, as Zeric keeps calling them. I'll do more good from a starship or star fighter than I could leading ground forces."

The idea had merit, Lahkaba thought. Offering the people of Cardine a leadership role in the military would increase their prestige in the sector. Making the leader a non-Braz and non-Terran would also sway anyone who would have had issues with Maarkean for those reasons.

But he was also hesitant. He did not know much about Celris Numba, aside from the fact that he had been in the Camar military. The Camari was older than many of the other delegates. He had not been a part of the Cardine delegation until after Enro, which suggested they had some interest in seeing an army formed.

He had assumed Maarkean would be at the head of the military. Several others had as well. Despite his friend's claim to the contrary, many people had confidence in his abilities. He was a symbol of resistance, and not having him at the head might undermine confidence.

On the other hand, it wouldn't matter how much confidence Maarkean could inspire if they never formed a military in the first place. They had a rare opportunity where the Alliance was weak. If they could seize control of the sector before reinforcements arrived, it would put them in a much better bargaining position.

"All right," Lahkaba finally said. "I'll make that suggestion, and we'll see how the cards fall."

"An honor to meet you, General Numba," Maarkean said with a slight bow.

The Camari standing before him returned the bow with a nod of his eye stalks. Camari skin grew darker with age, and Numba's was a very deep, dark red. Numba reached his hand out, and Maarkean hesitantly shook, concerned about how hard to grip, since Numba's fingers felt more akin to squishy tentacles than fingers.

"And you as well, Major General," Numba replied. "You have been an inspiration to us all."

"Thank you, sir," Maarkean said as the pair started walking away from the congressional chambers.

The debate Lahkaba had sparked had dragged on for far longer than Maarkean would have thought possible. In the end, they had agreed to form a united military force with the intention of ousting any Alliance forces that prevented them from restoring each planet's duly elected government. The details still needed to be worked out, but Numba had been designated as the military's leader.

Several delegates had argued for Maarkean to fill that role. Ailleroc, after realizing that the motion for forming a military would pass, had backed Maarkean. Unsurprisingly, Zhet from Enro had supported Numba, along with several other non-Alliance native-species members. In the end, a compromise had been reached, and Maarkean had been assigned as the leader of all naval and marine forces. He would have preferred a naval rank title over the marine one, but he was just glad a decision had been made.

"It seems we have a lot to do," Numba said idly.

"Yes, sir," Maarkean said, trying to slip back into a subordinate role. He had spent most of his adult life in the Alliance navy but had now been on the run for several years. Answering to no one had gotten comfortable and familiar.

"I understand you already have a small force of volunteers assembled and a shipyard willing to work with us?" Numba asked.

Maarkean nodded. "Yes. Chavatwor was a refugee from the prison on Olan. He has moved his old shipyard to Kol and is prepared to begin work retrofitting civilian transports into gunships and even has begun plans to design us our own capital ships."

"Capital ships? Sounds expensive," Numba said.

"Maybe. Lahkaba has all of the figures and estimates. He'll see what the congress can afford," Maarkean answered.

"Hmm," Numba said. "You will need to run things like that through me from now on. I plan on presenting a budget to the congress for all military needs. That way our finances are decided by us military experts instead of the politicians."

"Of course, sir," Maarkean replied. Numba's request—order, rather—made sense. It would not do to start undermining his new commander right out of the gate. "I'll get those figures to you. Chavatwor is charging a very reasonable fee for his service. He estimates he can retrofit a mining freighter into an escort carrier and build three squadrons of fighters and two frigates in under a year. He'll need to get some more experienced workers and some more equipment as well."

"A pretty tall order," Numba said. "We won't win this war in space. Most of our space resources will need to go to troop transports. Moving troops to the planets where they are needed will be the most important job for the navy."

Maarkean frowned. Dismissing the need for a combat navy was a major underestimation in his mind, especially if Numba was planning to have a concentrated, mobile army rather than homegrown armies on each world.

"Sir, troop transports will be vulnerable to the Alliance if we don't have a navy of our own."

"Of course," Numba said with a grunt. "We will need combat ships. We just can't afford to devote the time and resources to building an entire fleet. But send me your recommendations, and I'll include some of them in my request to congress."

"Yes, sir," Maarkean said, starting to wish he and Lahkaba had not rushed into recommending Numba as military leader. He tried to dismiss that thought; maybe he just wasn't used to taking orders anymore. But he couldn't help but think about the problems that arose with rushing into things without thinking them through.

"When would you like to meet to begin strategic planning?"

"That won't be necessary," Numba replied. "I'll handle that. You should return to your troops on Kol and get them trained up. I'll send any prospective candidates to join you there."

"Sir, if I'm not to be involved in the strategic planning, how can I coordinate our strikes effectively?"

"Coordinate strikes?" Numba said, surprise in his voice. "It's a little early to be thinking about that. You have no ships, I have no troops. We need to get things organized first; then we can decide what to do with them."

The statement made sense to Maarkean. Just because the congress had decided to raise an army did not mean one would just appear overnight. He might be letting his eagerness get the better of his judgment. Perhaps it really was best that Numba was in charge.

"Of course," Maarkean said. "Once the congress has decided on ship funds, I'll return to Kol and get Chavatwor started."

"Good, good," Numba said and started to walk away. "Carry on, Major General."

Maarkean remained where he was, watching the old Camari depart. He felt relief and comfort at odds with a sense of regret and unease. What happened next would be out of his hands. But that was not unusual.

CHAPTER 10

When the *Cutty Sark* landed on Kol, she was greeted by an eager crowd of recruits and shipyard workers. Stepping off the ship into the crowd, Maarkean looked uncomfortable. Saracasi sympathized with her brother, but she knew he should start to expect this. Everyone was curious about what had transpired during the congress' meeting. Instead of answering everyone's questions, he brushed off the crowd, calling for a meeting with just a few people.

In a room in Chavatwor's headquarters building, Saracasi joined Zeric, Gu'od, Gamaly, Solyss, Chavatwor, and Davidus. She wasn't sure if Zeric or Chavatwor looked more eager. Chavatwor had a major construction project on the line. His ideas and plans for ship upgrades, a new fighter design, and plans for a new type of capital ship were all he could talk about recently. This project combined his two loves: designing starships and opposing the Alliance.

As for Zeric, Saracasi wasn't sure what he was anticipating. The man had been running the core of recruits ragged. She didn't enjoy daily PT and combat training, which was why she had only joined them a few times. But she had gotten to know several of the pilot recruits when they came to help work on the freighter. They thought Zeric was enjoying himself.

"Congress voted to form an army for the United Worlds of the Kreogh Sector," Maarkean said without preamble.

The tension in the room evaporated. Saracasi felt a wave of satisfaction. The people would not abandon Enro and just roll over for the Alliance. Now, if the Alliance would just bow to the pressure and back down from its undemocratic actions before actual bloodshed occurred.

"I assume you are in command?" Solyss said with a congratulatory smile.

"No, General Celris Numba of Cardine has been placed in command," Maarkean answered.

The response around the room was decidedly more mixed than it had been for the news about the formation of the army. Solyss looked shocked, Gamaly frowned, Chavatwor looked curious, Gu'od nodded, and Zeric smiled. Saracasi was not sure how she felt about the news.

Knowing nothing about General Numba, she had no opinion there, but she knew her brother's reservations about leading. She thought he'd do a good job, and she knew that at least part of him had been disappointed at being relieved of command on Enro.

"That's great!" Zeric said, covering up Solyss' initial objection. "Now you can join the rest of us in the fight, instead of sitting behind a desk."

Maarkean smiled slightly. "Not quite. I have been given command of the military's naval and marine forces, with the rank of major general."

Solyss brightened somewhat, while Zeric frowned. "Better you than me."

"Don't be so sure. I've been given authority to form the ranks of the marines and navy as I deem necessary," Maarkean said, giving Zeric a pointed look.

Saracasi tried to hide a smile as she watched Zeric's eyes grow large with only slightly exaggerated fear. Gamaly showed no restraint and laughed at the man's expression. Zeric ignored her, remaining focused on Maarkean. "You wouldn't?"

"I don't know," Maarkean said with mock sincerity. "Brigadier Dustlighter has a nice ring to it."

Everyone enjoyed a few minutes of mirth before Chavatwor asked a question that brought things back to a more serious tone. "Which ships would you like me to get started on first?"

The question caused Maarkean to frown. "That's where we start to run into problems."

Attention turned back to Maarkean. Saracasi didn't like where she thought this might be going. As her brother started explaining, what he said just confirmed her displeasure.

"Congress has voted to suspend all payments of Alliance taxes. Instead, each world will send half of what it was supposed to have collected to the congress, and the other half can be kept by the planet and used as they deem necessary, or cut and kept by the people and companies.

"The majority of this income Congress has designated for planetary defensive infrastructure, equipment and weapons for the army, troop transports, paying for Congress' expenses, etc. A fraction has been designated for use to form a navy and marines."

This brought a frown to everyone's faces. Chavatwor asked the obvious question. "How small of a fraction?"

"Well, let's just say, if we used all of it, we'd be able to pay for about half of your new frigate design," Maarkean said, annoyance creeping into his voice.

Saracasi's shoulders slumped. Chavatwor had been incredibly excited by the idea of designing a ship from scratch, and some of that enthusiasm had rubbed off on her. Designing a craft that would be perfectly suited to their needs would have been an exciting challenge to overcome.

"Lahkaba is going to try to get us some more funding, and he has promised we won't be left out when they purchase weapons, but General Numba is focusing most of the military resources on the army. Which makes sense. There is no way we can build up a strong enough navy quickly enough to be able to defend the worlds from space. We'll have to rely on ground defenses once we clear out Alliance forces. Which will be a job for the army," Maarkean explained. Saracasi got the sense her brother wasn't completely sold on the plan, though he did speak respectfully.

Taking a deep breath, Maarkean continued, "Since the general is planning on making a mobile army, instead of a solely defensive force, our marines will primarily be used for special actions. Therefore, we won't need several divisions of them. For now, we'll aim to form a single, highly trained battalion."

With a smile and nod, he looked at Zeric. "As such, you can avoid becoming a general for now, Colonel Dustlighter."

Zeric frowned for a second but then nodded. "I knew a few colonels I respected."

"But I reserve the right to promote you," Maarkean said, getting one more frown out of Zeric. Then he turned to Davidus. "Dav, if you're willing, I'd like to put you in command of our star fighter group. And we'll be lucky if it can really be group size. I don't know where we'll get fighters yet, but we have four captured ones from Enro that have been promised to us."

"Of course," Davidus replied.

Maarkean nodded in acknowledgement and turned to Solyss. "About the only thing we can afford to do ship-wise is to retrofit some of the transports that have been volunteered, such as the *Chimopori*, *Unending Justice*, and *Durandal II*. I'd like you to command the squadron of new gunships."

"It would be an honor," Solyss said, giving a slight bow.

"What are we going to do about ships?" Saracasi asked. "Can we afford to finish the conversion of the freighter?"

"Yes, though she won't be as well equipped as I would like. We'll be able to pay for the replacement life support system, convert the cargo bays to hangar decks, and hopefully add a few defensive weapons. But we won't be able to afford a heavy battery, shield upgrades, or a new hyperdrive," Maarkean said, looking at Chavatwor.

The Kowwok engineer nodded, looking thoughtful. "If you could acquire any of those components, I would be happy to install them at a reasonable rate."

Maarkean smiled gratefully. "I was hoping you'd say that. Because Zeric and his Rogues are going to help us with our ship and funding shortage."

"I am?" Zeric asked, confused.

"You're going to steal some for us."

"Okay, cool," Zeric said with a shrug. "From where?"

"Ailleroc."

"Isn't that the headquarters for Alliance forces in the sector? Most heavily populated and defended planet?" Zeric asked.

"Yes."

"Just wanted to be sure we were talking about the same Ailleroc."

The meeting continued for another half an hour as Maarkean laid out his plans and intelligence data on the Alliance that he gotten from another former Alliance officer. During the meeting, Saracasi felt a small touch of disappointment that Maarkean had not singled her out for an important role in this new military.

She hadn't yet talked to him about her desire to stay out of the fighting, and she hadn't really made a final decision. But it would have been nice to have been offered a role.

When the meeting broke up, she waited while everyone else left so that she could have a word with her brother. He was always treating her like she was still a child. She might not want to join the fight, but he didn't know that. It was time he recognized that she was a grown woman and a competent engineer. She couldn't just follow him around or hide on the *Cutty Sark*.

She was prepared to lay into him, but her speech was cut off when Maarkean began, "I know what you're going to say. But I wanted to give you a choice, instead of railroading you into a role like I did with the others."

Suspicious, Saracasi managed to ask, "And what was I going to say?"

"That you deserve to have a part in this rebel army. That I can't treat you like a child and try to protect you anymore."

Saracasi frowned, unsure if he was genuine or just anticipating her argument. In the end, she decided it didn't matter. So long as he gave her a chance to participate, it didn't matter why he did it.

"All right," she said. "So what's my role going to be?"

"You have a choice. I need someone to oversee the retrofitting of all the ships and work with Chavatwor. He's been incredibly generous, but he has his business to look out for before seeing to our needs. I need someone who speaks his language.

"Or you can take command of the *Cutty Sark*. With the upgrades she's already received, she'll make a good gunboat. She'll remain my personal transport if I ever need to go to Irod or meet with General Numba, but we'll need her in the fight as well."

The second offer surprised Saracasi. She knew how much the *Cutty Sark* meant to Maarkean. That ship had been the thing that allowed him to keep flying after resigning from the navy to raise her. In some ways, she thought it had taken the place of his wife as well.

Maarkean offering her the chance to take command of the *Cutty Sark*, potentially in combat, touched her. She knew there was some selfishness to the offer: better her than a stranger. And needing to fly him around would be a perfect excuse not to send her into combat. But it did show his confidence in her. Those selfish reasons wouldn't be enough for him to make the offer if he didn't really believe she could do it.

Despite the import of that offer, she found herself drawn to the first choice. Commanding the *Cutty Sark* would mean being directly involved in combat, something she still did not trust herself to handle. Being an engineer would mean helping the cause without having to kill. It would also allow her to do what she loved: work on ships.

"I'll be your chief engineer," she finally answered.

Though he looked like he was trying to hide it, relief was evident on Maarkean's face. She knew how hard it must have been for him to make the offer to send his little sister into combat. This way, everyone would be happy.

As tired as Zeric was getting of PT and training exercises in the Kol desert, he was disappointed that their mission to Ailleroc occurred as soon as it did. The conversion of the mining freighter proved to be nearly complete; Chavatwor had started work on it before Maarkean had even arrived. The upgrades to the transports only took two weeks, despite his wish that it would take a few more.

As a marine grunt, he had always preferred missions to training. Training was monotonous and boring, while combat was exciting. Even though some of the recruits were close to his age, or older, and had fought in the same war, he could tell that most of them still thought as he once had.

Now, however, war and age had tempered his own enthusiasm to a point where he now saw combat as something to be avoided whenever possible. And now that he was the one in charge of and responsible for all of these lives, he looked at training in a different light. Training could make the difference between victory and defeat, life and death. As much raw combat experience as his Rogues had, they did not have much experience working together.

Although the decision on when to go was not technically up to him, he knew Maarkean would listen if he told him the Rogues weren't ready. But despite his newfound desire for more and more training, he couldn't justify making that claim. The recruits had trained hard. There had been complaints and grumbling, but he supposed they had weeded out anyone not really dedicated to the cause back on Mirthod. In a way, it was a blessing in disguise that Ice had disrupted their recruiting.

The morning of the departure, Zeric stood before the mirror in his room. As an officer, he had one of the few remaining single-occupancy rooms. He supposed there were some perks to being in charge.

Chavatwor had used some of his business contacts to find a clothing retailer on Kol who would take Maarkean's credit voucher instead of hard cash. A collection of uniforms had arrived the day before, and Zeric now stood in a black-and-grey camouflage battle dress uniform, or BDU. It looked a little out of place here in the desert, but it was the perfect gear for where they were going.

Zeric started toward the door but then stopped. It might not be strictly appropriate, but he had named his group the Rogues, after all. With a nod to his own logic, he grabbed his Ba'aar Razors hockey team cap from atop the dresser. The logo was red, but the cap was mostly black. A satisfied smile on his face, he pulled the cap onto his head.

Making his way through the combined shipyard and military camp, Zeric found the marines already formed up. For the moment, they were organized into a single company with three platoons. Sigfa Neith, Calek Orion, and Asheerah each stood before one of the platoons. Asheerah's was the smallest. All had cases at their feet, holding their space combat armor.

Standing a slight distance in front of the marines were Ymp Ki-Li and Gu'od. At the sight of Zeric, Gu'od turned and bellowed a call to attention. It seemed his friend was enjoying his role as gruff first sergeant. The marines came to attention, though in a more disorderly fashion than Zeric thought reasonable given the weeks of training.

He approached closer and Ymp snapped off a perfect salute, which said something considering how uncomfortable it was for a Camari to hold their fingers in a straight locked position. Zeric quickly returned the salute, and Ymp dropped her arm back to her side. He surveyed the assembled group and felt a mix of apprehension and pride. It was a weird contradiction.

"All right, Rogues, listen up," Zeric said, hoping that he was raising his voice only as much as he needed to in order to be heard. He hated being yelled at.

"This isn't going to be an easy op. I won't pretend otherwise. But if we're successful, we'll have shown the Alliance that nowhere in this sector are they safe, because the entire sector is united against them. We're going to grow our navy from an old mining freighter and a few couriers to real warships.

"In order to do that, we need to be quick, coordinated, and disciplined. We need to show the Alliance that we're not pirates, we're not thugs. We may be Rogues, but we're also professional marines. Keep weapons on stun if at all possible, stick to the mission, and watch each other's backs."

Zeric felt belittling saying things he thought should be obvious, but he knew from experience that the obvious things were not generally obvious to everyone. Going into a combat situation with weapons set to stun was one of his orders that was less than obvious. Stun setting had several drawbacks: less range, less accuracy, easier to defend against. But it would also preserve lives.

"All right, get to your ships," Zeric said. He never knew how to end speeches.

Beside him, Ymp called out, "Company dismissed. Report to your assigned transports."

The orderly ranks immediately vanished as the marines grabbed their gear and started wandering around the makeshift landing field. This part could go smoother, Zeric thought, but as long as everyone made it where they needed to go, he would be satisfied. There were only five transports and a freighter. He didn't think it would be that hard to find the one you were supposed to be on.

As the disorderly scattering continued, Solyss Novastar walked up to join him, Ymp, and Gu'od. Zeric noticed Solyss watching with a frown as Asheerah and her entire platoon headed toward the massive mining freighter. Zeric could sympathize. He wouldn't like it if Gu'od and Gamaly were going off on another ship.

"Major Novastar," Zeric said with a grin. Unlike himself, Novastar puffed up slightly when his rank was mentioned. The man appeared proud of it, despite the fact that they were just an amateurish, illegal group of rebels.

"Colonel," Solyss said and then nodded to Ymp. "Major, have you talked to him yet?"

Ymp pursed her large, wide lips. "No."

"Talked to me about what?" Zeric asked, confused.

Ymp and Solyss exchanged a look. Solyss apparently lost the confrontation because he spoke. "We think you should talk to General Ocaitchi about the mission."

"What about the mission?"

"It is inappropriate for a general to fly into combat," Solyss stated. "The *Cutty Sark* is going into one of the most dangerous places."

Zeric frowned. As much as he hated going into combat, he knew he would hate sitting on the sidelines even more. He suspected Maarkean would feel the same way.

However, he also agreed with Solyss. A general's place was behind the lines, directing things and making the important strategic decisions. From the flight deck of a gunship in the middle of battle, he wouldn't be able to keep track of everything. And someone needed to do that.

"Why are you telling me this?" Zeric asked, resistant.

"As you are the next senior officer, it would be inappropriate for us to go over your head," Ymp said, which surprised Zeric. As a mercenary, he hadn't expected her to take to military protocols well. Many of the other mercenaries hadn't.

"What about Commander Brieni?" Zeric asked. Unlike himself, Davidus insisted on remaining formal at all times. While Solyss appeared proud of his rank, Davidus, on the other hand, was defensive and demanding about respecting it.

Another look crossed between Ymp and Solyss. This time Gu'od spoke. "They thought Maarkean would listen to you."

Zeric sighed. He didn't consider himself observant, but even he knew that there was tension between Maarkean and Davidus. Oddly, this tension was balanced by respect. He actually thought Maarkean would be more inclined to listen to Davidus.

"Do you have someone to take his place flying the *Cutty Sark*?" Zeric asked.

"Sienn'lyn," Gu'od answered immediately.

"Your new apprentice?" Zeric asked skeptically.

"She's actually quite a good pilot," Solyss said, his voice approving. "Rivals Isaxo. While that's no comparison to the general, she's one of the best we have. The next best is Jerik Needa, but I doubt General Ocaitchi would feel comfortable giving his ship to a bounty hunter that tried to capture him."

With a snort, Zeric nodded. He had been surprised when he had first heard the news that Maarkean had recruited the bounty hunter. Though, upon reflection, he shouldn't have. Zeric now worked for Maarkean, and he had tried to steal the *Cutty Sark*. Twice.

"All right," Zeric said finally. "Go find Sienn and bring her to the *Cutty Sark*. I'll talk to Maark."

Solyss nodded gratefully to Zeric and then popped off a formal salute before turning and heading toward his own ship. Gu'od just nodded before going to find Sienn'lyn. Ymp remained behind.

Zeric raised an eyebrow at her. "I don't suppose you're going to try to tell me I should sit this one out, too?"

Ymp gave one of her wide, disconcerting smiles. "Of course not. Colonels are supposed to get their hands dirty. Plus, if you die, I get your job. And since you have a tendency to screw things up, those odds aren't bad."

The sudden reversion from her new formal, military persona to her old condescending attitude toward him took him off guard. She compounded the confusion by snapping off a salute before departing. Zeric was left to just shake his head.

Left alone now, Zeric had no reason not to head to the *Cutty Sark* himself. It would be awkward if Gu'od arrived with Sienn'lyn before he talked to Maarkean, though it might make things easier on him.

Walking down the dusty field, Zeric examined the mining freighter that had just recently emerged from the protective warehouse. From the outside, the ship looked much like he remembered it. Few of the weapons Chavatwor hoped to add had been installed yet. The hull was still a rusty brown color, which gave it a nice camouflage look against the desert background.

The differences were centered around the cargo pods. Originally, the three pods each had one massive door that lowered and exposed a cavernous interior. Those doors had been replaced, and the pods cut in half. The bottom half of each pod had a new door that lifted up into the ship, instead of lowering outward.

Not visible from the outside, the upper half of the pods had been merged together into one massive space that served as a maintenance and storage deck. Before, each pod had been completely independent and large enough that a ship the size of the *Cutty Sark* could have fit inside. Now, the lower parts were still big enough for six fighter-size craft, but not tall enough for a ship like the *Cutty Sark*.

Moving past the freighter turned carrier, Zeric came to the courier transports turned gunships. He wasn't sure 'gunship' really qualified as the appropriate designation. Each courier now carried the equivalent firepower as an Alliance gunship, but their main cargo bays had been converted to barracks.

When Zeric reached the *Cutty Sark*, the once-open cargo area was a jumble of people, storage lockers, and bunks. One corner of the bay had been converted into a multiple-person washroom. The bay was crowded with Sigfa Neith's 1st Platoon's 1st Squad as they set themselves up for the journey.

Zeric squeezed his way through the marines. A couple made sloppy attempts to salute him, though most appeared oblivious to his presence. Zeric just nodded in reply, moving as quickly as he could toward the stairs at the back of the bay. Once up the stairs, he emerged onto a much less crowded crew deck.

The common room was currently empty, though there was a marine in the small kitchen suite already at work on the midday meal. Between the crew, the marine squad, and others, the *Cutty Sark* would be carrying almost twenty people on a nine-day journey to Ailleroc and then, hopefully, bringing all of them back. The return trip would not need to be done in formation with the freighter, so it would be a few days shorter. All told, Zeric would be spending almost three weeks onboard.

He moved quickly down the narrow corridor and deposited his gear in one of the four crew cabins. He would not have to share this room with anyone else.

Again, being an officer had its advantages. From there, he took the few remaining steps to the ship's flight deck.

Zeric wasn't sure why the command area was called a cockpit for fighters, whereas it was a flight deck on ships like this, the bridge on big ships like the freighter, and the CIC (Combat Information Center) on big warships. He just chalked it up to naval tradition—the same way a ship's commander was always addressed as "Captain," when he might carry the rank of major or commander, or even be a civilian.

Sitting in the pilot's chair, which seemed like the natural place for him, Maarkean was going through pre-flight. Next to him sat Gamaly, running checks on the operations console. Behind them, and to Zeric's right, at the weapon's console, sat a raven-haired Terran named Almes. The man was one of the marines, but he had some experience operating ship-based weaponry, so Maarkean had drafted him.

"All your marines onboard?" Maarkean asked when he noticed Zeric.

Zeric shrugged. "You'd have to ask Sigfa."

Maarkean nodded absently in reply, going back to his pre-flight routine. Zeric considered how to approach this topic without being inappropriate. If he could get Maarkean alone, it wouldn't matter. And even having Gamaly there was fine. But it wouldn't do to undermine Maarkean in front of one of the recruits.

An idea struck him. "Almes, go down and ask Lieutenant Neith what the status of the squad is."

"Aye, Colonel," Almes said, giving a sloppy salute as he stood.

Once the man disappeared down the short corridor, Zeric turned back to Maarkean. "You shouldn't be here."

"You're right, I should be relaxing on a beach somewhere sipping on a drink with one of those little umbrellas. You Terrans have some weird creations, but some of them are real genius."

Zeric frowned but pressed on. "Seriously, General, your place is directing this operation, not flying a ship into combat."

"We're not a large military. Everyone has to do what they are best at. I'm a better flier than a general. I'll do the general thing because I have to, but I can't just sit around and expect others to do all of the work," Maarkean argued, still paying more attention to his checklist.

"And what happens if the *Cutty Sark* gets shot down? Losing you in our first operation would completely undermine the entire effort."

Maarkean stopped, seeming to consider Zeric's words. But after a second, he shook his head. "Then I just won't get shot down."

With a disappointed noise, Gamaly said, "Zeric's right, and you know it."

This caused Maarkean to stop and Zeric to give her a look of shock. It wasn't often that Gamaly agreed with him, at least in front of others. Lately, she had actually been quite passive, not involving herself directly in any of the planning discussions.

"Maybe," Maarkean said, a note of reluctance in his tone. "But the point remains, we need highly qualified pilots if this is going to succeed."

"And we have them. The whole point of this operation is that we need ships for our group of pilots to fly. There's no lacking for talent. That girl we picked up on Mirthod, for instance. She is quite a good pilot," Gamaly said.

The suggestion further confused Zeric. With all of the attention Gu'od was paying to Sienn'lyn lately, she was the last one he would expect Gamaly to suggest. Whatever was going on there, he didn't know if he wanted to get involved, despite his curiosity and concern.

Putting that out of his mind, Zeric turned back to Maarkean. "Plus, I'll be here, so you know this ship is coming back."

Maarkean turned around and gave Zeric a penetrating look. "Really? You mean this isn't part of your long-term plan to steal my ship?"

"What? No, of course not. You know me. I don't have long-term plans," Zeric said defensively.

"Good point," Maarkean said, then sighed. "Very well. Dav said much the same thing to me earlier."

With clear reluctance, Maarkean stood up from the pilot's seat. He slipped past Zeric without another word and went into his personal quarters to pack.

A few minutes later, Almes appeared down the corridor. He was followed by Gu'od and Sienn'lyn. Almes came to a stop before Zeric and gave another sloppy salute.

"The LT says everyone is aboard and secure, sir."

"Thank you, Private," Zeric said, squeezing himself against the bulkhead as much as possible to allow Almes and then Sienn'lyn to get past him. They each took a seat at their respective stations, Sienn'lyn looking very uncertain.

"You sure General Ocaitchi is fine with me flying his ship?" she asked.

Zeric chuckled. "I am most definitely sure he is not fine with it."

Gamaly cast him a dirty look and then gave a more comforting look to Sienn'lyn. "The general decided he would be more useful aboard the carrier. Gu spoke very highly of your skills, and the general agreed you would be the best choice to replace him as pilot."

"And the general is a wise man," Almes said, turning to face the Liw'kel women. "Now I get to spend some quality time with two beautiful ladies."

The young man gave what he must have thought was a charming or seductive smile. Zeric almost burst out laughing at the cold expressions Gamaly and Sienn'lyn both returned. The looks did nothing to deter the man, however; he continued to leer.

"All right," Zeric finally said, regretting being the one needing to say this. "Not appropriate, Private."

"Yes, sir," Almes replied, though the wink he gave Sienn'lyn before turning around suggested he didn't really mean it.

The sound of a door opening drew Zeric's attention. Behind him, Maarkean emerged from his quarters. He nodded to Gu'od and Zeric but said nothing. With one last forlorn look at the flight controls, he turned and headed toward the hatch down to the cargo deck.

CHAPTER 11

When Saracasi had agreed to become Maarkean's chief engineer, she had been under the impression that meant working at Chavatwor's shipyard. She had just assumed that she could stay behind, building and repairing ships, while others went into the fight. That had been true as long as the troops were still there. But now that everyone was preparing to go into battle, she discovered that "everyone" included her.

It wasn't that she disagreed with the logic behind her going along on this raid. The converted freighter had not been tested yet, and many things could go wrong. Someone also had to make sure the ships they captured were worthwhile.

Apparently, the only way to truly avoid combat would be to just resign and go to work for Chavatwor full time. That might be something to consider, but she couldn't do it today. Her brother had done too good a job of instilling a sense of duty in her. She had made this commitment and was needed now. So she would carry out the mission, even with a feeling of dread in the pit of her stomach.

Saracasi climbed the last steps onto the freighter's bridge. For the most part, it looked the same as when she had first seen it. The stairs opened up facing the aft section, which held several centrally placed computer display tables along with workstations lining the walls. Most of the work they had done there had been programming changes to the software. It had been a relatively small matter, reprogramming the asteroid tracking system to become a tactical combat display.

Behind her, on the other side of the stair's safety railing, were the ship's main operational controls. Ceno Gotit, the Camari pilot who had flown this ship off Sulas during their escape from Olan, sat at the helm controls. That gave her a small sense of reassurance and a little bit of concern. The last time he had flown, she had been forced to run the length of the ship several times trying to fix the hyperdrive before an Alliance fleet captured them.

The only visible change to the bridge was evident when you looked at the bow section. Originally, the freighter had contained several massive windows. While they were heavily reinforced windows that could withstand some moderate asteroid impacts, they were still a significant weak spot on the ship. Chavatwor's crews had replaced them with a dual layer of hull plating, giving the bridge an extra layer of protection.

Saracasi moved toward the aft section of the bridge, which her brother and Davidus kept referring to as the Combat Information Center, or CIC. She understood the purpose of a CIC and bridge being separate rooms on most ships; they served two separate functions, after all. But here there was no functional dividing line, and it felt unnecessary.

Along the aft wall was the main engineering control station; she sat down there. Most of the ship's functions were carried out by dedicated terminals elsewhere on the bridge or in engineering itself, but this terminal gave her a complete picture of their statuses, and if everything functioned properly, she could access most every function from here.

"What's our status, Major?" Davidus asked, stepping up behind her.

It took Saracasi a moment to realize that he was speaking to her. Maarkean had always been the "Major Ocaitchi" in her family. It felt odd being addressed with that title. "Everything looks good so far. As I feared, all of the extra systems are starting to tax the reactor. It's stable now, but if we do manage to install any of those big guns, it might be too much."

"That's a problem for another time, Major. We're good to launch now?" Davidus stated, a reprimand clear in his formal tone.

Saracasi frowned slightly. She knew her brother and Davidus had never really gotten along. But she had found Dav friendly on the few occasions she had met him. Now she started to see what Maarkean saw—he was very formal and strict. A hard-ass, as some of the crew recruits had already started to say.

"Aye, Captain. All systems report green," Saracasi replied, keeping her voice formal.

"Excellent," Davidus said and then turned toward the bridge stations at the front. "Ops, bring navigation and flight systems online. Helm, begin pre-flight. Flight Ops, signal the fleet commander that we are ready to depart."

"Commander, we're receiving a signal from the *Cutty Sark*," the Ronid at the flight operations station said. Flight Ops handled all ship-to-ship communication, primarily relaying information to the carrier fighter squadron, once they had one.

Saracasi cringed as she expected Davidus to reprimand him. Naval tradition dictated that the commander of a ship be referred to as "captain," and Davidus was even more a stickler for tradition than he was for protocol. Surprisingly, Davidus' tone was mild, only a slight rebuke evident.

"Put it through, Crewman."

"They say that General Ocaitchi is en route to us and we should be prepared for him to come aboard."

"Thank you, Crewman," Davidus said and turned to a Braz standing near him. "Ensign, see to preparing quarters for the general."

Quietly, Saracasi chided herself. She didn't know either of the crew that Davidus had just spoken to, and while everyone now wore a standard blue ship utility uniform, she hadn't learned all of the rank symbols.

Even though they were using the Alliance rank structure, the decision had been made to avoid Alliance symbols, along with Camari or Dotran. This had necessitated new ones being created. Even though she preferred to think of herself as an engineer first, she was an officer now, and she should learn the symbols and people's names.

"Major," Davidus said, turning back toward her. "Would you care to escort the general aboard?"

"Of course, Captain," Saracasi said. Davidus did not seem at all surprised or concerned about the news that Maarkean was coming aboard, but that didn't stop her from being curious.

Once again, Saracasi crossed the bridge and headed down the stairs to the main deck. She took her time, glad she didn't need to run the length of the ship while they were taking fire. That would probably come later.

After moving about a quarter of the ship's length, Saracasi reached the main intersection. To her right and left, the corridor branched off, leading to the ship's weapon batteries. She continued forward into a heavily modified section.

Originally, this passageway had simply been a narrow corridor that ran the length of the cargo pods to the aft engineering section. While the passage was not any wider than it had been, there were now doors leading off of it. Behind the walls had once been unused space at the top of the cargo pods. This space had been converted into living quarters for the ship's new contingent of pilots.

The main elevator that led down to the former cargo pods was still located halfway down the spine of the ship. A new access point had been installed on the crew deck below her, but that only led to the hangar and maintenance deck. She would need to ride the elevator all the way to the bottom, as the ship was still accessed from the ground via the launch bay.

The elevator deposited her into the central launch bay. The massive bay door stood open, exposing the deck to the sandy winds of Kol. Keeping the ship clean and free of sand was proving to be an unending task. Already, the sand had gotten into the lift that would be used to move ships between the hangar deck and the launch bay.

She didn't have long to wait before Maarkean appeared and stepped into the hangar. Even though they were alone down here, she expected him to follow the naval tradition of asking for permission to come aboard. To her dismay, he barely acknowledged her before stepping onto the elevator she had just left.

Quickly following, she frowned at her brother. "You don't look happy."

With a grunt, Maarkean replied, "Zeric decided to ambush me with an uncomfortable new reality. As a general, I shouldn't be flying into combat."

"He's right," Saracasi said simply. The irony amused her. Here she was trying to avoid going into any kind of combat, while her brother was annoyed at being forced to avoid direct action. It made her embarrassed at the annoyance she felt.

"Not you, too," Maarkean groaned.

Saracasi shrugged. "I'm your sister. I'm always going to take the side that will annoy you the most."

That got a small chuckle out of him, and she continued, "But you also think it's right; otherwise, you wouldn't be here."

The elevator doors opened, revealing the main corridor. Their conversation ceased for the remaining walk up to the bridge. They passed a few crewmen, and Saracasi tried to stand straight and tall, with a serious expression, even though she was walking with her brother. To everyone else, he was the general.

"General on deck," Davidus announced as soon as Maarkean and Saracasi stepped off the stairs. The entire bridge and CIC crews snapped to attention. Maarkean acknowledged them with a quick, "As you were," before continuing to join Davidus.

Saracasi retook her engineering station, but she was close enough to the two senior officers to overhear their conversation.

"You won this one, Dav," Maarkean said quietly.

"Whatever do you mean, sir?" Davidus asked, his tone surprisingly mocking, despite his normal formalness.

Saracasi smiled at the annoyed look Maarkean gave Davidus before he continued, his tone more level. "Are we ready to depart, Captain?"

"Aye, sir. The ship stands ready."

"Excellent. Before we do, it's high time we gave her a name."

The matter of naming the carrier had been one of some controversy. Davidus felt that changing the name of a ship was bad luck. When they had looked up the ship's original name, they had been disappointed with the lack of creativity of her previous owners. It was named *Asteroid Mining Freighter 12*, which had left them referring to her simply as "the freighter" for most conversations. While Davidus, even though he admitted it was stupid, advocated for keeping the name, everyone else wanted something more grand.

Maarkean had accepted submissions from everyone, both military and shipyard workers. He had so far kept quiet about his decision, intending to announce the winner in an address before they launched. It felt more fitting that he would do this while on board, instead of from the *Cutty Sark*.

Davidus directed the crewman at Flight Ops to give Maarkean a channel to the entire fleet, and Saracasi watched as her brother picked up a microphone, giving a small sigh before activating it.

"Attention to the fleet, this is General Ocaitchi."

Eyes around the bridge and CIC turned to face him as he spoke, and Saracasi could imagine people on all of the other ships stopping to listen. It still surprised her how much reverence everyone had for her brother. She held a lot of respect for him, but he was still just her brother.

"We are preparing to conduct our first operation as a formal military. The duly elected representatives from every planet in this sector have appointed us as their guardians. The Alliance has our homes under occupation. We lack the resources to remove them by force, but after this mission, we will be closer to having the strength to do just that.

"Though the odds are against us, and the situation may look grim, our ideals and our commitment will see us through. That is why I have chosen a name for our new flagship carrier that matches that determination. This name was submitted by Major Novastar, and it carries with it a long history.

"Many years ago, during the Kravic occupation of all of our homeworlds, a distant relative of Major Novastar's, Mace Novastar, formed a team of freedom fighters to oppose the occupation. Though intergalactic space flight was new to Terrans, they captured a Kravic warship and began a fight for their freedom. They named their ship *Defiant Glory*, symbolizing the glorious cause of their struggle.

"That is why I have chosen that name to represent us. Though the Alliance is not as cruel or as powerful as the Kravic, they do control our worlds without our permission. Together, we will use the new *Defiant Glory* to fight back."

A spontaneous eruption of applause on the bridge cut Maarkean off. He appeared surprised by it, but Saracasi found herself caught up in the emotion of the moment. She had never thought of her brother as an inspirational speaker. Yet his words had caught even her.

Beside her, Davidus appeared to be the only one not swayed by the speech. Just loud enough for Saracasi to hear him, he said, "But that *Defiant Glory* was destroyed twenty years before the Kravic left. It had nothing to do with their departure."

Her spirits dampened a bit when she heard that, even though she knew he was probably only saying it to get to her. Would they end up the same way?

Lahkaba grumbled as he took his seat next to Lei-mey. The Congress meeting had run late the night before, and they had decided not to reconvene until the afternoon today. But then an emergency summons had gone out first thing in the morning, calling them all in.

What was worse, the meetings were held on Galactic Standard time rather than local time, and despite last night's meeting ending well into GS night, it had been almost noon local time. Lahkaba hated going to bed with the sun bright in the sky, especially when Irod had such a short period of bright days.

"Any idea what this meeting is about?" he asked after settling himself into his chair.

Lei-mey, looking far more awake than Lahkaba did, shrugged. "No idea. The Mirthod delegation called it."

Lahkaba frowned as he thought. The Mirthod delegation had been relatively quiet during the previous meetings. Next to Irod, their planet had one of the smallest populations and industrial sectors. That they would call for an emergency meeting now was curious.

It was possible they were only doing it for the attention. As one of the least populated planets, they probably felt their concerns would not be everyone else's concerns. Maybe they thought calling an emergency session would get them noticed.

Lahkaba could sympathize with their position. There were many issues he felt were important that he wished he could bring up. But he knew they were only important to small populations on each world. Many things important to Kowwoks were probably best addressed by the government of Sulas. But right now, they were fighting for their right to have a government, and those issues could wait.

The rest of the delegates trickled in over the next fifteen minutes. Even though Lahkaba did not expect today's agenda to qualify as an emergency, he expected a quicker response to that kind of summons. Most of the other delegates appeared to feel as he did, though, and were not taking the call too seriously.

When everyone had assembled, Faide Darkthorne, former prisoner on Sulas, new representative for Irod, stood up. As the host planet, Irod had been offered the chance to chair the meetings. Faide called the meeting to order and turned the floor over to the Mirthod delegation.

Zoeko Lide, a gold-scaled Dotran, stood up to speak. At over two meters, Zoeko was easily the tallest figure in the room. She had bulk to match her height, but that did nothing to distract from the graceful beauty her gold scales provided. She seemed to fit the stereotype of the elegant beauty of Dotran Golds. Personally, Lahkaba thought those stereotypes were perpetuated by the Golds on Dotra in order to justify their dominant position in society.

"My fellow delegates," Zoeko began, a slight hiss accenting her voice, "I come before you with two gifts from the people of Mirthod.

"The first is our contingent of warriors to serve in the grand Union army. We have recruited and brought forth Ice Company, the most experienced and well-trained mercenary company on Mirthod. With these elite warriors fighting for us, we are sure to win."

Lahkaba frowned slightly before he caught himself. Maarkean had told him about Zeric's encounter with Ice on

Mirthod. It sounded like a petty personal issue, but they had insinuated that they were going to turn Zeric over to the Alliance. Though that was probably motivated by profit rather than patriotic sympathy, it didn't really speak to their loyalty to Mirthod or the Union. They were mercenaries, after all.

He was considering voicing these concerns to the congress when he noticed Zeko looking at him. As a Kowwok, an intense look from a Dotran always made him uncomfortable. Despite that, it made him think that Zoeko was aware of the incident with Zeric and expected him to raise an objection.

That idea gave Lahkaba pause. When a Dotran wanted you to do something, it probably wasn't good for you. He considered his choice. Dismissing Ice because they were mercenaries would disqualify a lot of their recruits. Since they had signed up for the army, they were not likely to cross paths with Zeric any time soon.

Calmly, Lahkaba remained quiet. Both Pasha and Lei-mey looked at him, clearly surprised by his silence. They were aware of the incident as well.

As if nothing had happened, Zoeko continued, "While these warriors will be a great benefit for our cause, they were not the reason for this impromptu meeting. The second gift Mirthod wishes to make might be seen as controversial. But it will give our worlds the freedom we cannot get from the Alliance. I have brought a visitor with me to present some of the details to this body. With the chairperson's permission?"

Faide nodded his consent to Zoeko, who in turn nodded to another delegate at her table. The delegate stood up and went to the room's exit. As he walked, Lahkaba tried to anticipate what was about to happen. If hiring an infamous mercenary band was the opening act, the main show should be entertaining.

When the delegate returned, followed by a blue-scaled Dotran in a crisp uniform. Lahkaba couldn't keep the shock off his face. The uniform was that of the Dotran Confederate Navy. It had been years since Lahkaba had seen one, and he had hoped to never see one again.

The mood in the room shifted from uninterested speculation to high tension. With the exception of Owrik from Dantyne, everyone here had been an adult during the Alliance/Dotran war. All of their worlds had been the battleground, and they had seen the devastation firsthand. Like him, some had been on the side of the Confederacy; others had been with the Alliance. Most, however, had simply been civilians.

As the Confederate officer walked in, Zoeko began speaking. "Allow me to present Lieutenant Commander Bryel Prytoker, liaison officer sent to us from the Dotran Confederacy. He is here to present their offer of a treaty."

Lahkaba couldn't help but stare at the pronouncement. He didn't notice the pandemonium that erupted around him as everyone started talking at once. A Confederate officer here could not be a good thing. The Dotran were untrustworthy, and if the Alliance thought that this whole rebellion was orchestrated by the Confederacy...

Faide banged a gavel, getting everyone's attention. Once everyone had quieted down, he leveled a pointed gaze toward Zoeko. "When you asked to bring someone in, we assumed it would be someone from Mirthod. This is most irregular."

"Please, Mr. Chairman, I only wish to have the chance to speak," the Dotran officer, Bryel, said, his hissing accent thicker than Zoeko's.

With a reluctant nod, Faide gave his consent, and Bryel turned toward the rest of the delegates. "I come before you to offer the friendship of the Dotran Confederacy. Many of you once lived in peace under our governance before the Alliance viciously subjugated you. We want to offer our aid in helping you have that freedom again."

Lahkaba stifled a laugh. There were many conflicting theories as to the cause of the Colonial War, but it had been a Dotran fleet at Kol that had fired the first shot. He found the notion of Dotran friendship and freedom even more ridiculous. His family had moved to Sulas to get away from the harsh Dotran subjugation on their own homeworld. Even though he had fought for the Confederacy, he had fought for Kowwa and his home on Sulas, not for Dotra.

To his embarrassment and relief, Valinther, one of the corporate representatives from Kol, said what he was feeling. "This is an insult, Zoeko! We all have problems with the Alliance, but we aren't traitors. Bringing in the Confederacy, who brutally subjugated my people, as a potential ally? This is a blatant insult to myself, Lahkaba, and every other Kowwok we all collectively represent."

Lahkaba wished Valinther hadn't mentioned his name, but he didn't disagree. His relationship had been cordial with Zoeko so far, but he knew Valinther had had several heated exchanges with her. She was not as arrogant and haughty as most Golds he had met, which he attributed to her being raised on Mirthod, far from the Confederacy. But that didn't stop a Dotran from being a Dotran.

"Now, wait a minute," Wilchu Num, a Camari from Cardine, said. "I think we should hear him out. The Confederacy could be a valuable ally."

Several more voices spoke up at once, and Lahkaba realized it was going to be another long day.

CHAPTER 12

Zeric was pleased that their descent through the atmosphere of Ailleroc went smoothly. Despite this being a full assault on a heavily fortified enemy stronghold, they had so far been unchallenged. If only their departure would go this smoothly.

But then, Zeric admitted, they would have failed in their mission. This was not a covert operation. They were here to steal supplies and make a lot of noise. The Alliance needed to know they were here.

"Two minutes to target," Sienn'lyn said from the *Cutty Sark*'s controls.

"All right, I'm headed down. Gamaly, Almes, stay with Sienn and the ship," Zeric ordered.

He was halfway down the corridor before he realized that Gamaly had not argued with him. She normally did not like being told to stay behind any more than he did. Not that it happened much; she was an excellent shot.

Pushing that aside, Zeric opened the door to the cargo bay. Below him, looking nervous, were the nine members of Sigfa Neith's platoon's 1st Squad, plus Gu'od and Sigfa himself. They all wore dark combat clothing and had rifles. Their portion of this mission would involve speed, so they carried very little gear beyond that.

"One minute, Lieutenant," Zeric called down to Sigfa, his voice as calm as he could manage.

"You heard the colonel—line up and stand ready!" Sigfa shouted.

According to Ymp, the blond-haired Terran had seen quite a bit of action while with Ice. Yet to Zeric, he just looked young. There were many faces in the squad who clearly had been toddlers during the Colonial War, but there were also a few grizzled old faces like him. One of them should have been in command of the platoon, but none of them had shown the same levelheadedness as Sigfa.

Zeric came down the stairs and stood in the rear beside Gu'od. His Liw'kel friend looked out of place in a military uniform. He was an exceptional fighter, and there was no one Zeric would prefer to have by his side in almost any situation, but the uniform just didn't fit him.

With the inertial dampeners functioning, there was no indication that the ship was slowing. The final sixty seconds stretched on, causing Zeric to wonder if they had changed course for some reason. Their only warning came when Gamaly triggered an alarm, seconds before a shudder went through the floor as the ship touched ground. At the same time, the forward cargo ramp came down.

Running forward after the other marines, Zeric saw the tops of *Durandal II* and *Unending Justice* sticking up over the roofs of the nearby low-level buildings. The rest of 1st Platoon would be storming the Alliance base from other directions. Second Platoon, along with Ymp, were aboard *Chimopori* and *Bright Blade* and should be simultaneously hitting another base on another continent.

They charged through an area of open field and came up to the wall of a large building. Zeric was reminded of a similar building on Dantyne, though the night sky was showing the first light of dawn now, instead of full night as it had then. Behind them, the *Cutty Sark* stood between them and the exterior wall to the Alliance base.

"Secure the perimeter!" Sigfa ordered, and two teams of three marines headed toward either corner of the building. A final team of three moved toward a large door above a loading dock. They immediately ignited a plasma cutter and began work on the locking mechanism.

"Second Squad, report," Sigfa said, speaking into his headset.

On his ear piece, Zeric heard the reply from Sergeant Obod Ocif. "Two AA weapons taken out. Moving into position near the mess."

"Third Squad," Sigfa called next.

"Encountering resistance emerging from the barracks," Scarcit Darcrest replied, the sounds of blaster fire coming over her comm.

Sigfa looked toward the direction of 3rd Squad and fidgeted slightly. Zeric could sympathize. He had even less to do right at this moment than the younger man did—at least until they got the door to the armory open.

"Send a fire team from 2nd to assist 3rd Squad," Zeric said quietly, so that just Sigfa could hear him. Technically, he could issue orders straight out, but he wanted everyone to get used to them coming from Sigfa.

The man nodded and relayed the order. Zeric stopped listening, switching his comm unit over to 2nd Platoon's channel. There, he was pleased to hear similar reports coming in. So far, there were no reports of casualties or signs of Alliance response.

That would come, though. They had succeeded in taking the Alliance off guard. Now they just needed to keep them occupied for the next half hour without getting themselves trapped, captured, or killed.

Saracasi was uncomfortable. Without the helmet attached, her spacesuit's cooling system was inactive. It was also becoming heavy in the full gravity of the ship.

But she had elected to be on the bridge during their insertion, and since time would be a factor, she had to be suited up ahead of time. The rest of the marines, pilots, and engineers were down on the *Defiant Glory*'s launch deck, ready to storm out as soon as the ship touched down. Part of her hoped she could just remain on the bridge, but she mainly wanted to be on hand if there were any problems.

Despite the upgrades and repairs, *Defiant Glory* had experienced a few problems during the journey from Kol. A couple power failures across the ship and a faulty CO_2 sensor had given her a few sleepless nights. She had no idea what would happen when the shields were brought to full power and the weapons came online.

The hyperdrive had performed admirably, however, and they had arrived at Ailleroc on schedule. After a rendezvous with the other ships on the outer edge of the system, they had made a short jump to the fifth planet in the system.

Roc 5 was a lifeless hunk of rock. The planet contained no remarkable or valuable resources and was too far from the system's sun for any kind of worthwhile terraforming efforts. It was, for all intents and purposes, a useless planet.

Except for the collection of decommissioned Alliance warships that were stored there. With an orbit that kept half the planet permanently facing away from the star Roc, it was protected from stellar radiation. Without an atmosphere to cause corrosion, any ships stored on her surface were essentially in a state of suspended animation.

That was why the Alliance had decided to use it as a decommission depot. None of the ships below were fully operational, and all were at least twenty years old. But the Alliance could restore them to full combat capacity in a matter of weeks, instead of the months or years it would take to build new vessels.

The information they had received from Kaars Aerinstar via Lahkaba stated that the depot was lightly defended. It relied on the proximity of the fleet at Ailleroc. While four months from now would have been a better time for the raid, when the two planets were at their furthest point from each other, they were still more than thirty light minutes apart.

"We're being scanned by the facility," the operations officer reported.

"Ignore it," Maarkean ordered. "Hold course for the orbital satellite."

Saracasi watched the tactical display as it displayed the situation around Roc 5. The tactical hologram showed the distorted sphere of Roc 5 and the ship depot on the "northern" part of the planet. A representation of *Defiant Glory* moved toward the planet, on a course toward the lone remaining symbol: that of a polar satellite. The ship depot, by virtue of always facing away from Roc, and therefore away from the closer orbiting Ailleroc, relied on a high polar satellite to relay communication.

"Coming into weapons range," Davidus reported. He had taken over the role of Tactical Action Officer, TAO, yielding battle command to Maarkean.

"Lock on and fire when ready," Maarkean ordered.

Forcing herself to break away from the tactical display, Saracasi turned back to the engineering system. She watched the reactor's power output increase as the weapons charged up. The power levels crept into the yellow warning zone for total output as they discharged their deadly pulses of energy. Relief settled over her as the levels stabilized in the yellow zone before dropping to optimal levels when the weapons ceased firing.

"We have a kill," Davidus reported, his voice revealing more excitement than he normally did.

"Nice work," Maarkean said flatly. "Helm, come about; bring us toward the base."

Ceno, at the helm, acknowledged, and Saracasi watched as the symbol for the ship shifted on the tactical display. With the main bridge windows removed, there was no sense of motion within the ship. It was a bit disconcerting. Most of her experience with space travel had been aboard the *Cutty Sark*, which had viewports. Space was dark, but there were plenty of stars to provide a sense of direction.

As they altered course, she started to think about going down to the launch bay. She had been concerned about the weapons, which had never been tested, but things looked like they were well in hand.

That was when the alarm sounded.

"We are taking fire from the surface," Davidus reported. "Two ground-to-orbit G1-A Mk 7 blaster cannons."

Saracasi switched her screen to a shield power display. "Ten percent of shields have been depleted. Beginning recharge sequence."

She diverted more reactor power to the bow shield generators. The shields weren't a huge power hog when maintaining their protective barrier, but when energy needed to be channeled to rebuild the defensive layer, while still maintaining the rest of the generators, it became energy hungry. When they started firing the weapons, which she anticipated happening any second, that was when she feared the ship's reactor might overload and shutdown.

"Return fire. Starboard main cannon," Maarkean ordered, casting Saracasi a quick glance. She had hounded her brother about the dangers repeatedly during the journey, every time they experienced any power failure. *Defiant Glory* would make an excellent carrier, but she wasn't a battleship.

Saracasi watched as the reactor power spiked when the weapons were activated and then saw the shields, which had crept back up in strength some, drop to 85% and then 80% as they took a few more hits. Fortunately, all the hits were occurring on the forward generators, which left the other five sets only drawing maintenance levels of power.

"Direct hits against their shields," Davidus reported. "Not enough to get through. We need more firepower."

Both he and Maarkean glanced back toward Saracasi. So far, they had been using only one main cannon. The ship had two high-power blaster cannons, along with four defensive weapon batteries.

With a frown, Saracasi said, "I can shut down the shield regeneration and reduce power to the untargeted shield facings. That should keep us from reaching dangerous levels."

Maarkean nodded. "Helm, rotate us on our axis 90 by 90. Hold position and distance from the base. Bring the rest of the weapons online, cut power to dorsal shields, cut regeneration of bow shields."

The *Defiant Glory* rotated from a position with the bow facing the Alliance depot to one where her ventral side faced it, essentially hovering above the base at several dozen kilometers. This gave them a larger profile, making themselves an easier target, but brought a fresh shield facing to bear and allowed the bow and aft turrets a line of attack.

Once the maneuver was complete, Maarkean ordered all batteries to fire, and the power drain on the reactor spiked to its highest point. The defensive batteries were less powerful than the two main cannons, but combined they were enough to penetrate the depot's limited shields. Saracasi felt a surge of relief when Davidus declared the ground weapons destroyed.

"Helm, bring us down to the depot," Maarkean said and then stepped away from the tactical display to Saracasi. "How'd we fare?"

Saracasi nodded with satisfaction. "Ventral shields depleted below 50%, but the reactor held. I think she could have handled the defensive batteries all operating simultaneously and still maintained shield regeneration. Those main cannons are gluttons, though. You sure you want to install more?"

"As you saw, they may be power hungry, but we need more to break through shields," Maarkean said quietly. "But it will really come down to whether you find any more down there for me."

"Right," Saracasi said. "You shouldn't have any problem getting the shields back to full strength before we're ready to depart. I should get down to the launch bay."

Picking up her helmet and gloves, Saracasi got the sense her brother wanted to give her a hug, which she appreciated but was glad he had the decorum not to do. Even without him being the general, she hated when he did stuff like that. Instead, he merely gave her a nod, but the look in his eyes said it all.

She returned the nod and headed down the stairs off the bridge.

As Zeric set down another crate of weapons he had just helped carry aboard the *Cutty Sark*, he looked down at his watch. Twenty-five minutes had gone by since they had touched down. The Alliance forces were putting up a fight, but most of the troops had been cut off from the armory, which 1st Squad was still in the process of clearing out.

"All right, Lieutenant," Zeric called to Sigfa. "Call them in. I'm ordering all ships to lift off in three minutes."

Sigfa nodded and then started calling out orders. Zeric switched his comm unit to the company channel. "Major Ki-Li, time to go. Three minutes."

He got an acknowledgement from Ymp, and then Zeric watched as the members of 1st Squad stopped grabbing crates and started setting timers on explosive packs. What they couldn't haul away, the Alliance would not be able to use either. The fire team finished arming the explosives in under a minute and started making their way back to the *Cutty Sark*.

Once they started toward the ship, the two marines stationed at either corner holding back the Alliance forces turned and started high-tailing it back to the ship. They were only a few dozen meters away, but Alliance forces had been pushing closer. Zeric hoped they could get back.

Just as he thought they would make it, blaster fire appeared from around the edge of the armory building. One of the marines in the rear of the retreat was hit by a blast from the left side. Zeric and the marines standing at the ramp of the *Cutty Sark* started returning fire, but not before another marine went down.

"Rogues, covering fire!" Zeric shouted. "Gu, let's go!"

Without waiting for an acknowledgement, Zeric dashed out into the open. Firing wildly from the hip as he ran, he dove for the ground when he got near the first marine. Regrettably, he couldn't remember the name of the young Notha who was writhing on the ground in pain. As Zeric started to stand up so that he could grab the Notha, blaster bolts flying over his head forced him back down again.

Zeric glanced to his side and saw Gu'od pinned down next to the other injured marine. There was nothing between them and the Alliance, or between them and the *Cutty Sark*, except for open field. With a grunt, Zeric grabbed the marine's uniform collar and started trying to slide the two of them back toward the ship.

Blaster bolts whizzed over his head, and Zeric felt dirt spray over him from near misses. Fortunately for him, but unfortunately for the marine, the marine provided a bit of cover for him. Switching sides wouldn't do either of them any good, though.

Suddenly, the air filled with a high-pitched whine. The sounds of small arms blaster fire disappeared just as the air filled with a high concentration of blaster bolts. Zeric glanced back and saw a barrage of fire emerging from the two newly installed defensive blaster suppression cannons hanging on the *Cutty Sark*'s wing cargo pods.

Glancing up, he gauged that the height of the barrage gave him sufficient space to stand. Getting up, Zeric reached down and pulled the marine onto his shoulders in a fireman's carry. As he suspected would be the case, Gu'od was already well ahead of him.

With a grunt, Zeric pushed himself toward the waiting boarding ramp. Sigfa was pulling the other marines back from the edge, giving Zeric and Gu'od plenty of room to come aboard. By the time Zeric heard the Alliance again trying to return fire, he was safely on the ship. Relief washed through his aching muscles as he set the marine down onto the deck.

A red-haired Terran female pushed through the surrounding marines beside the injured Notha. Zeric recognized the squad's medic, Tamarynn Farr, as she began the triage process. The one downside to this whole operation was that the nearest real doctor was aboard the *Defiant Glory*, and it wouldn't be easy to get any of their injured over there. If either of the two marines were badly injured, it might be another week before they could get real medical treatment.

Taking a deep breath, Zeric activated his comm and pushed through the gathered marines, heading toward the aft stairs. "All ships launch."

As he climbed the stairs, Zeric gratefully listened to the reports that everyone had made it back to their ships. There were several other injuries, but so far no one had died and no one had been left behind. Now they just needed to escape from the undoubtedly waiting Alliance fleet. But that part of the operation was Solyss' problem.

Chapter 13

"Admiral Sartori," the steady voice of Commander Dolan repeated over the *Dominance*'s comm.

The first thing Katerina noticed was that her aide's voice was unusually loud. It was not like him to express much emotion, especially in front of her. He repeated his call, and she realized it must not have been the first time he had tried to wake her. At her age, waking up was becoming as difficult as going to sleep.

"Yes, Commander," Katerina said, trying to sound completely awake, though she suspected she wasn't successful.

"We've gotten a report of attacks on our supply bases on the surface," Dolan said, his voice even.

"I'll be right there," Katerina said, starting for the door. After a moment, she remembered that she was in her pajamas. Since the *Dominance* was not supposed to be anywhere near a combat zone, she had not seen any need to sleep with her uniform ready. That policy might need to change.

Taking a quick moment to dress herself, Katerina left her quarters while still wrapping her hair into a quick bun. It wasn't pretty, but it would keep her hair out of her eyes. Her uniform had been firmly pressed the night before and was wrinkle free.

Stepping into her command center, Katerina was not surprised to see Dolan looking like he always did. Her chief of staff undoubtedly had been awake since the previous morning, but you couldn't tell from his appearance. Completely professional, she thought.

"Twenty minutes ago, we received a flash warning from our supply bases, Fort Holder and Fort Watcher. They reported multiple heavily armed transports had broken through their perimeters and deployed ground forces before they were able to activate their defenses," Dolan reported.

"Response?" Katerina asked as she examined the holographic display showing the bases on Ailleroc. They were on separate continents, but only about a quarter of the planet's circumference apart. Currently, *Dominance* and the rest of the main fleet were on the other side of the planet.

"Two fighters from other bases were dispatched to ascertain the situation. One was shot at by the landed transports. With no back up, the pilots backed off. They were able to confirm the existence of five transports at the two bases.

"Admiral Norrax has ordered the fleet to accelerate in its orbit. We'll be over the bases in five minutes," Dolan continued

Katerina nodded and studied the tactical display. Despite having a vast advantage in firepower over five transports, no matter how well armed, the Alliance's fleet faced an unfortunate disadvantage. As long as the transports were inside the Alliance bases, they couldn't fire on them from orbit without the risk of hitting their own people. Once the transports launched, they would still run the risk of errant fire hitting the dense civilian populations nearby.

After she had dismissed Admiral Gorzet for her heavy-handed response plan, Katerina couldn't turn around and bombard their most loyal planet in an attempt to shoot down what might just be opportunistic thieves, rather than rebels. A defensive screen with the capital ships and an attack force of fighters would be their best strategy. If the raiders dispersed, some might get away, but she should be able to capture or shoot down several of them.

She was pleased when she saw the ships began to break formation. Their trajectories suggested that she and Admiral

Norrax had decided on the same strategy. It gave her a bit of confidence in her decision to promote him.

A warning flash caught Katarina's eye on the display. She watched as Dolan read a report and then spoke to his liaison on Admiral Norrax's staff. The warning winked off.

Without having to be asked, Dolan answered her question. "We just received a notice that contact has been lost with our base on Roc 5. Admiral Norrax decided it was likely a communication failure in the orbital satellite. It is overdue for some maintenance."

Katerina nodded and continued to watch the dance of ships on the holo display. New signals appeared as the five transports launched from the Alliance bases. They flew low, heading toward the nearest cities before accelerating on an orbital trajectory. Several squadrons and gunships were on intercept courses, but it did not look like they would reach the transports before they got into the upper atmosphere.

So much the better, she decided. Once in higher orbit, the transports could more easily be engaged by the capital ships. They would undoubtedly prove difficult to hit, but she had a lot of fields of fire that could converge.

As she watched, something started nagging at the back of her head. She looked back toward the display that had flashed the message about the communication loss with Roc 5. The time stamp on the message indicated that the last comm signal had come through about five minutes before.

She brought up information about Roc 5 on her terminal. The first thing she looked for was the distance to the planet from Ailleroc: about thirty-two light minutes. That meant the communication satellite had failed just about thirty-seven minutes ago, which was just a few minutes before the attack on the planetary bases had occurred.

Was it just a coincidence? Roc 5 housed decades-old decommissioned ships. Essentially, junk kept around in case of another major war. An idea started to coalesce. Those ships were junk to her, with her state-of-the–art fleet. To a rebel force, however, they would be a treasure trove, even in their decommissioned state.

"Signal Admiral Norrax," Katerina said, confident in her analysis. "This is a distraction. The real raid is occurring on Roc 5. Redeploy the fleet; we need to get ships there before the rebels get away with any of our ships."

Saracasi hopped along in the low gravity of Roc 5. She was leading a team of three technicians, one pilot, and a marine toward their third potential ship. The last two they had checked out had not had functional hyperdrives. With no way to get the ship back to Kol without its own hyperdrive, they had been forced to move on.

This next ship, an old frigate whose class she couldn't identify, looked much weaker than the previous two. Both of those cruisers had been fairly well preserved, but without a functional hyperdrive, they were essentially useless. This ship had an unusually high power signature, which suggested that its systems had a back-up power battery able to bring it to life.

While Saracasi moved between decommissioned capital ships, she listened to the radio chatter as small fighter-sized craft were picked up by the *Defiant Glory*'s tractor beams and loaded into her launch bay. That part of the operation was going much better than hers. Picking out fighters that would be transported aboard the carrier required little discrimination. Anything in range of the tractor beam was fair game.

There were three other teams like hers that were assessing the capital ships. It was a long shot, but if they could get away with a few ships, it would greatly increase their overall fleet combat strength. They just needed to find ones that would fly.

With a hop, Saracasi floated the last few meters to join Sheanna Coramont, a raven-haired Terran woman with some experience working on starships, just as she finished opening the sealed airlock of the frigate. Her team's marine, a Ronid named Mogren Talac, edged forward, preceding the rest of them inside.

Aside from the attack on the *Defiant Glory* during their landing, they had not encountered any resistance. Asheerah's platoon had secured the facility's main building by cutting the control lines to the defense grid and the power systems. That had sealed the Alliance forces inside and cut them off from doing anything to affect the raiders.

Following the marine through the airlock, Saracasi waited inside until everyone was through. They sealed the outer door, but all remained in their space suits. Until they ascertained the status of the hyperdrive, they wouldn't bother activating the ship's life support system.

Moving as quickly as was possible, Saracasi took her best guess on where engineering would be. Neither Maarkean or Davidus had been able to identify the class of frigate she was on, so neither had any idea on the ship's layout. She used her hand scanner to track the unusual power source, which she guessed would be the reserve battery.

Following the signal, she emerged a few minutes later into the ship's main power room. The reactor's status display panel blinked, meaning the diagnostic computer should at least be operational. Gingerly, she brought the computer up, her bulky gloves making the task unnecessarily difficult.

A wide smile spread across her face as she read the display. She turned and beamed back toward the others. "We've got a live one."

"*Defiant Glory*, this is Team Four leader. We've found a frigate with a functional hyperdrive. Proceeding to begin power-up sequence," Saracasi reported over the comm line as she started to activate the life support system.

"Acknowledged, Team Four," Davidus' voice replied. "You have ten minutes to ascertain if it can be salvaged. If not, you are to head back to the ship with all haste."

"Yeah, yeah. I can read the time," Saracasi said under her breath. Davidus had been making a point of announcing time until departure to everyone on a regular basis. She supposed it was useful to keep everyone on track, but it got annoying after a while.

Lights came on in the room and the other computer terminals lit up. Air was starting to fill the empty space, but it would be a few minutes before it reached a breathable concentration and a survivable pressure. It would be many minutes more than that before the temperature inside the ship got above freezing.

Saracasi moved to the main diagnostic terminal while the others each took a terminal. Something on the ship's display immediately leaped out at her as unusual. Unlike almost all ships, this one did not have a standard deuterium-fueled fusion reactor. The unusual power readings she'd followed turned out to be a magnetic field that functioned as a containment field for several pods full of anti-matter.

Anti-matter power reactors were not unheard of, but she had never seen one equipped on a ship of this size. Typically used to power battle carriers or large cities, their power output was completely unnecessary for most smaller ships, as well as taking up a lot of valuable mass.

The more she studied the schematics, the more confused she became. Power distribution systems were quite unusual. The numbers of conduits leading to the shield and hyperdrive were three times what was typically necessary. Most frigates had a small docking bay, suitable for two fighters or recon vessel resupply shuttles, but the anti-matter reactor must have taken over the space necessary for that. Despite the extra power, the ship also had far fewer guns than most frigates.

Trying to put aside her confusion over the design, Saracasi focused on functional systems. Weapon systems were not operational; it appeared their capacitors were fried. Probably a result of the high power of the reactor. That was the downside to anti-matter reactors: their output was much harder to fine tune. This meant a lot more power, but that could be bad if you didn't need it all and didn't have any place for it to go.

Assuming that the unusual design still left the hyperdrive working the way she would expect, everything seemed to be functional. The diagnostics reported that everything was in the green, at least. Surely they were programmed for this specific ship's requirements. Even though it was an odd design, then, its own software said it would fly.

"I don't understand half of what these systems do," Tadashio, a light tan-and-brown Kowwok, said when Saracasi asked the others for their assessment.

"Me either," Saisee Traze, a light pink Camari, agreed. "But it looks like they are functional."

"They are unusual, but everything came on," Sheanna said, adding her assent.

"That about sums it up," Saracasi agreed and activated her comm. "*Defiant Glory*, this is Team Four. We have power to the ship, and everything looks good. We should be able to fly her."

"Good to hear," Davidus said in reply. "Because it looks like our time has run out. An Alliance battle carrier just jumped out of hyperspace. ETA, fifteen minutes."

Chapter 14

Solyss, leading the raid for supplies on Ailleroc, had been glad when the marines finally got back on board the *Chimopori*. They had been forced to fire on an Alliance fighter that had come to investigate the raid, which told him more would be on the way. Sitting on the ground had meant he couldn't raise his shields, and he had felt particularly vulnerable.

Now that they were airborne, however, he started to regret his earlier eagerness to be there. Sitting at the ship's operations terminal, he had a full view of the Alliance fleet taking up positions in orbit around them, the squadrons of fighters coming at them from multiple angles.

But he'd gone into this mission knowing the odds would be against them. They had to keep the Alliance busy while General Ocaitchi raided the decommissioned ship depot on Roc 5. If he went down in this fight, it would be a small price to pay—a few modified transports in exchange for a ready-to-go war fleet. But he had no intention of letting that become necessary.

"All ships, this is *Chimopori*. Alter course toward orbit. We're going to try to punch through near the gunship squadron," Solyss ordered over the comm. With all the transports upgraded by Chavatwor, they were now the functional equivalent of Alliance gunships. That gave them five to two odds against the Alliance ships, though if they had to fight, it would give the star fighters that were following them time to catch up.

Out of the forward viewport, the landscape of Ailleroc disappeared, replaced with a rapidly lightening sky. It had been near dawn when they had arrived, and they had traveled east after departing. Their goal was to try to keep the Alliance fleet on the day side of Ailleroc—the furthest they could get from Roc 5 and the *Defiant Glory.*

Solyss looked over to his Notha pilot, Isaxo. "You ready for this, kid?"

"Ready as you, grandpa," Isaxo retorted.

Behind them, at one of the two weapons consoles, Kard laughed. At the other console, Ymp kept herself facing away from Solyss.

Solyss gave the Braz a harsh look. He was a little older than most everyone else here, but he wasn't a grandpa. At least he hoped not—it had been a few years since he had talked to his daughter, Miaya.

Turning back to the operations sensors, he watched as they started to close on the Alliance capital ships. He had faith in their cause. They would be victorious.

Without warning, the Alliance ships all changed their heading; they reversed direction and started accelerating away from Ailleroc. The remaining fighters wouldn't get into weapons range before his squadron could jump to hyperspace.

He considered the possibility of a trap, but dismissed it. The only way the Alliance could trap them was with a mine field, which he had no indications existed on that course, or with another fleet emerging from hyperspace. No, their way was most likely clear now. But that meant he had failed in his mission of distraction.

The comm network with the other gunships in his squadron came alive.

"Are you guys seeing this?" Fracsid Relis on *Unending Justice* asked.

"Yeah, we hit the jackpot?" Eri'dos Ar'cher on *Durandal II* added, his usual skepticism evident in his voice.

"Could this be some kind of trap?" Htaretter asked from *Bright Blade*.

Before Solyss had a chance to answer, Zeric said, "No—worse. They're going after the ship depot. We must not be seen as a big enough threat, so they're just letting us go."

"Sounds good to me," Eri'dos said. "Free path of escape."

"But the *Defiant Glory* can't fight off even one of those ships. Not without a fighter wing," Fracsid argued. "We have to go to their aid."

Solyss did a quick calculation with the navigational computer. "Due to the position of the planets, they're going to have to make a jump that will put them several minutes away from the base. They could try to jump into several positions and box in the *Defiant Glory*, but it will take several minutes to set up. If our people are on schedule, they might have time to jump away."

"Might," Fracsid emphasized.

"Better than getting ourselves killed trying to stop the inevitable," Eri'dos countered.

"What do you say, Colonel?' Solyss asked. He was technically in charge of the squadron of gunships, but Zeric outranked him.

"This is your squadron, Major, I'm just a marine. The decision is yours," Zeric replied.

Solyss nodded quietly. It was a mistake for him to have tried to pass off responsibility like that, and Zeric was right to bow out of it. What kind of leader could Solyss be if he passed all the hard choices up the chain of command?

Looking at the navigational projections, Solyss estimated that if they changed course in the next two minutes, they would be able to catch up with the fleet before it jumped. On the other hand, there was no place his squadron could jump to that would allow them to get to the *Defiant Glory* before the Alliance. It was either run or fight here.

Solyss glanced at the others on the flight deck. Kard was nodding with excitement at the desire to fight like his cousin Fracsid had been advocating. Ymp remained impassive, clearly taking a cue from Zeric for the marines to stay out of it. Young Isaxo looked nervous. Solyss could sympathize with Isaxo, but they were fighting a war for their freedom. It was no time to back down.

"All craft, come about along the following heading. We're going to convince the Alliance that it's not a good idea to run away from us," Solyss ordered over the comm and then turned to Isaxo. "Set a pursuit course. Aim for the cruiser, the *Entala*."

Isaxo turned his head toward Solyss, his brow furrowed. "The cruiser? Are you crazy?! We're no match for a cruiser."

"Come on, 'Sax," Kard said from behind them. "Live a little."

"I'd like to live a lot, actually, which is my problem," Isaxo retorted.

"We're not going to try to destroy it. We want to distract them, slow down their jump, even for just a few minutes. Those minutes might be the difference between the *Defiant Glory* getting away and getting surrounded."

"It also might be the difference between us getting away and getting blown to bits," Ymp said, joining the conversation.

"Don't worry. We'll get all your marines to safety," Solyss said as he flashed a confident grin at the Camari.

The lids on Ymp's eyestalks tightened and the stalks lowered closer to her head. Solyss got the distinct impression that she was not impressed by his bravado. But it didn't matter. His results would speak for themselves.

Isaxo turned the ship from its course to leave the gravity well of Ailleroc. The blackness of space was soon replaced by

Ailleroc itself filling the left half of the viewport. The distance to the Alliance ships was far too vast for them to see with the naked eye just yet.

Solyss still felt Ymp's gaze on him, but he heard Kard turn around and lock his chair into position. After another moment, he heard the sound again as Ymp did the same. Having an angry Camari behind him wasn't the most comforting feeling.

On his sensor display, the icons representing their pursuing fighters changed course with them. They would probably reach the cruiser first, but it would not be long before the squadron of fighters caught up. And the other two squadrons would not be far behind them.

Solyss activated the comm again. "All ships, hold fire until my signal. Target all weapons at the main engines."

The distance between them and the Alliance cruiser stopped increasing as Isaxo accelerated. Soon their superior acceleration had exceeded the cruiser's current speed, and the distance started to decrease. After a few minutes, the ship became visible as a speck of light ahead of them. That speck grew slowly into a wide shape.

The *Entala* was an assault cruiser, designed primarily for planetary bombardment. Most of her main weapons were spread across a wide ventral surface. Unlike many ships, she was wider than she was long. *Chimopori* and the other gunships were approaching from directly aft, where the *Entala*'s six powerful engines glowed with their thrust.

Though his ship was well within effective weapons range, Solyss held their fire. Blaster bolts lost their power over long distances in an atmosphere, even the upper levels they were flying through. Distance also increased the odds of missing. Solyss wanted all of their ships' fire to combine. It was the only way they'd have a chance of penetrating the shields before the fighters caught up.

"All right, this is a good speed. Stop accelerating," Solyss said.

"Really? Our relative speed isn't that much more than theirs. And they are still accelerating. We won't slip past them very fast," Isaxo argued.

"We don't want to slip past them," Solyss replied and triggered the comm. "All ships, open fire; concentrate on the central engine housing."

Five converted transports began firing their recently upgraded weapons into the *Entala*. A dozen or so blaster bolts streamed ahead and hit the central junction between the cruiser's three lower and three upper engines. It was well known among pilots that particle wake from a starship's engines distorted and weakened shields. Normally this effect was minimal, as it was not necessary for a ship to fire its engines continuously unless it was accelerating.

But the *Entala* was accelerating, trying to get herself well beyond escape velocity and out of orbit around Ailleroc. This kept her engines firing constantly at full thrust. Solyss was betting that the *Entala* would not consider the transports much of a threat and, therefore, would not slow down.

His view of the cruiser, now filling half of the viewport, started to brighten as the blasters impacted the shields. The protective energy field of the shields crackled with white electric energy as it dissipated the energy from the blaster bolts. Behind this flash of energy, Solyss could still see the glowing engines. After a few seconds, the cruiser crew caught onto what Solyss was attempting, and the engines stopped firing.

The bombardment continued for almost a minute. Isaxo was forced to adjust their orientation as the cruiser started to rotate her aft engines away from them. Just as Solyss started to think they had failed, the scene before him suddenly changed.

Blaster bolts continued to dissipate against the shield, but several began to go completely through the fluctuating energy field. As multiple blaster bolts impacted the engine housing, Solyss smiled. When one of the bolts triggered an unexpected firing of one of the engines, right before exploding, his smiled widened.

"Damn," Isaxo said quietly. "I can't believe that worked."

"I told you it would," Solyss said and then looked down at his sensor readings for the cruiser. "That erratic engine firing changed their course. They hadn't yet achieved escape velocity, and now they are being shifted into a decaying orbit."

"You mean they're going to crash into the planet?" Ymp said, startled.

Solyss nodded. "If they are allowed to continue, they will. But not for several hours. More than enough time if those other ships turn around now and tow them to a higher orbit."

"Well, looks like that worked out pretty well," Isaxo said, leaning back in his chair.

That was when the missile hit.

CHAPTER 15

"I'm losing power to the engines!" Arzesaeth Ernebee called from the helm of the decommissioned Alliance frigate.

Under her breath, Saracasi cursed. The power distribution systems were not designed along any means that made any logical sense. She had tried bringing the ship's systems online following a standard start-up sequence. When that had failed, she had resorted to trial and error.

They had succeeded in bringing the ship to life and beginning their ascent from the surface of Roc 5. While Arzesaeth flew, Saracasi and the others had tried to get more systems working, particularly the shields. That was when the engines had cut out.

"We're starting to lose altitude!" Arzesaeth called again.

"I hear you!" Saracasi snapped. "Sheanna, what happened that time?"

"I don't know," Sheanna said over the comm. She was in engineering with Tadashio. "The power transferred just fine, but the shields collapsed as soon as they started to form. That might have caused a feedback surge, but that doesn't make any sense."

Saracasi tapped her fingers on the control panel, her face tightened into a grimace as she thought. As confusing as the ship's systems were, there was an element of order to them that felt just out of reach. They had either been designed by a genius or a crazy person.

A flash of inspiration occurred to her. The ship was powered by an anti-matter reactor capable of dramatically more energy output than typical fusion reactors. Unlike the *Defiant*

Glory, which had to ration its insufficient power generation across several greedy systems, this ship had power to spare. Almost too much power.

"Bring the shields on, full power," Saracasi said out loud.

Next to her, Saisee bent his eyestalks in question. "But we keep shorting out."

"Exactly," Saracasi said, not explaining. "I'm bringing the engines back online; once I do, throw as much power at the shields as they'll take."

"Okay," Saisee answered skeptically.

Saracasi reinitialized the engines and heard a relieved shout come from Arzesaeth. The ship must have stopped falling back down toward Roc 5. That was a great relief, as Saracasi did not fancy the idea of crashing on an uninhabitable planet. But with an Alliance battle carrier between them and freedom, if her idea for the shields didn't work, it wouldn't matter.

As Saisee brought the shields up, Saracasi watched the display nervously. Most shield systems required some time to build up their protective layer of energy. This was caused by limited reactor power output and the limited amounts of energy that the generators could channel. But the shield bubble for this ship went from non-existent to a full field in a matter of seconds.

What happened next surprised her. Instead of expanding and growing the field, the shield generators stopped. The protective field was far more dense than was typical, but the layers were not expanding. This resulted in a far weaker field than she would have expected.

"The power drain is not reducing," Saisee said, sounding just as confused as Saracasi felt. "With the field density, it is going to require this same amount of power to maintain the field."

"That would explain the anti-matter reactor," Saracasi said.

On the comm, Sheanna added, "But that doesn't explain why it works that way. A dense field will give us better protection, but without multiple layers, they'll fail quicker."

"Well, for now, we don't have to worry about a sustained fight. We'll only need to cross into weapons range of that carrier for a short time," Saracasi stated. "Let's focus on keeping the ship flying and getting the hyperdrive ready to go."

As she worked, Saracasi tried not to think about what her brother must be experiencing onboard the *Defiant Glory*. No more capable of going toe-to-toe with an Alliance battle carrier than any of the rest of them, he would be forced to flee with all the other ships. It would not sit well with him, and she hoped he would not dash into the fray in a vain attempt to rescue her.

The ship broke free of Roc 5's gravity well and continued to move into space. "We're coming into range of the carrier now," Arzesaeth said.

Despite there being nothing to look at, Saracasi turned toward the front of the bridge. The room was buried deep inside the center of the frigate and had no windows. None of the tactical displays or video screens were active. But it felt right looking forward as they attempted to skirt the edge of the carrier's field of fire.

Several tense seconds went by, and Saracasi started to think the carrier would ignore them and continue to fire long-range shots at the fleeing *Defiant Glory*. A sudden warning broke her of that notion. Turning back from the useless view forward, she looked down at the shield status.

Once again, the frigate surprised her. The shields' field level remained the same as it had always been. They had taken two hits from the Alliance carrier's powerful main blaster cannons, but the shields had absorbed and dissipated the energy and then immediately regenerated to their full strength.

She glanced at Saisee, who wore the same astonished expression she felt she must have. The ship kept moving away from the enemy. Another warning alarm sounded, and two more blasts came from the carrier. Again, the shields absorbed the fire without any noticeable damage to the ship.

Just as she was starting to think that the shields were a miracle, the entire field suddenly collapsed. One second the field was stable, and the next the entire field disappeared. Warning messages started appearing on her status board, showing blown power circuits all over the ship.

"We've just lost the entire shield grid," Sheanna said over the comm. "The power conduits have fused. There's no way we're getting those shields back up."

Sheanna's assessment matched her own. Quickly, Saracasi turned away from the engineering board and over to a tactical terminal. She brought up the positions of themselves, Roc 5, the Alliance carrier, the *Defiant Glory*, and the other fleeing ships. They would still be in range for dozens of seconds.

"Arz," Saracasi said. "Go evasive."

"It will take longer to get out of tracking range."

"Better taking longer and becoming harder to hit than going quickly and being an easy target," Saracasi replied. She just hoped Arzesaeth was up to the task. He had said he was a good pilot, but this was the first time she would see him demonstrate it.

On the tactical display, Saracasi watched their course shift erratically. Several shots from the carrier missed them. Being on the outer edge of their effective tracking range helped. If they could get much further away, the odds of being hit would drop precipitously.

The ship suddenly shook as her hull absorbed the energy of a neutron blast. More warnings started to sound.

Behind her, Saisee shouted, "We took a hit to the port aft section. We have a hull breach in what looks to be crew quarters and a storage bay. Emergency bulkheads remain sealed, so we're not in any danger of decompression."

Saracasi nodded. They'd need the atmosphere inside the ship well before they reached Kol, but so far they were still wearing their suits.

"Looks like we're reaching the edge of their effective range," Saracasi said after turning back to the tactical display. "They're shifting targets back to the *Defiant Glory*. Looks like she's loitering on the edge."

"Hyperdrive should be ready to go in just a minute," Sheanna added.

"Then let's get out of here." She let out a slow breath. They were going to make it.

Solyss couldn't focus. Before him, the world of Ailleroc spun around as the *Chimopori* twirled out of control after the missile hit from the Alliance cruiser. Warning alarms blared, the sound pounding into his head. The spinning image of Ailleroc and the earsplitting sounds combined to overwhelm him with nausea.

Solyss struggled to turn his eyes away from the viewport. Without the spinning image, he lost all sense of movement. It took him another moment, but he soon managed to shut down the emergency alarms.

Looking around him, Solyss saw Isaxo fighting with the ship's helm controls. The Notha's face was compressed in a tight look of concentration. Kard was crawling back toward his chair. Ymp remained in hers, but held one of her eyestalks as if in pain. Behind them, the emergency bulkhead door to the flight deck had sealed itself.

Satisfied that everyone on the flight deck would live, at least for the next few minutes, Solyss turned back to the operations display. He had shut down the alarms, but warning lights were still flashing on the ship's status screen. The number of warnings were too many for him to process; he changed the screen to report only high-priority warnings. Several messages vanished, but not as many as he would have hoped.

"We took a direct hit to our ventral port quarter," Solyss said, registering the information as he relayed it to the others. "Engines two and three are offline. Ventral shield generators are down. And . . . oh, no . . . " Solyss' heart dropped as he read the next warning message. "We have a hull breach in the cargo bay. I'm reading no atmosphere."

Turning back toward Ymp, he had no idea what to say next. There had been more than a dozen marines in the cargo bay. To his surprise, Ymp's expression was neutral.

"We should focus on getting the rest of the squadron to safety. My sensors aren't functioning. How many enemy ships are we facing?" Ymp said calmly.

Nodding his understanding, Solyss felt his respect for Ymp go up. She was a professional, and they had a job to do. There were almost sixty other marines out there plus the crews on the other ships to worry about.

"We lost several sensor clusters as well," Solyss reported. "I'm rebooting the system now. We should get a better picture of what's out there, but there will be gaps."

After a moment, the tactical display came back up, showing the locations of nearby ships. "I'm only reading three of our ships, but the last one might be in our blind spot. There are a dozen Alliance fighters swarming over them. They appear to be leaving us alone for the moment."

"That's because we're still tumbling out of control," Isaxo said through gritted teeth.

"Right," Solyss replied, quickly turning his attention back to the operations controls. He shut down the dorsal shield and rerouted its power to the remaining engine. With the extra power, Isaxo was able to correct their spin and stabilize their course with just the one engine.

"We're not going to be any good in a fight with just one engine," Isaxo said, the tension on his face easing slightly.

"No, we're not," Solyss reluctantly agreed. "It's time we made our exit. The hyperdrive, fortunately, is still functional. Isaxo, get us to a safe jumping distance."

"What about the other ships?" Kard asked, concern for his cousin evident on his face.

"Hopefully they can get free from the fighters. We'll just be a liability to them."

As Isaxo flew, Solyss spent the next several minutes plotting a hyperspace course and then trying to get the communication array functional. He also watched the sensor display out of the corner of his eye. To his relief, he saw no Alliance fighters approaching them. The other three gunships he could detect were also attempting to break away from the planet.

The flight deck was quiet while they waited. There was not much to say and nothing the other two could do until they restored atmosphere to the cargo bay and gained access to the rest of the ship.

Finally, Solyss succeeded in opening a comm line to the squadron. "This is *Chimopori*. We have sustained heavy damage and are attempting to get to a safe distance for a hyperspace jump."

"We read you, *Chimopori*," Zeric's voice said over the comm line. "We thought we had lost you as well. All of us have taken some damage from these fighters, but we've held our own and should be able to jump with you."

A dark feeling settled over Solyss. "What do you mean, lost us as well?"

There was a noticeable pause before Zeric replied. "*Unending Justice* was hit in that initial missile barrage. She's a wreck and in an uncontrolled descent down to Ailleroc."

"Frac," Kard said, his voice coming out as a whimper.

A weight pressed down on Solyss' shoulders. First the marines aboard his ship, and now they had lost an entire other ship. All in a vain attempt to stop or delay the Alliance forces. Disgusted, he found some consolation in the fact that *Unending Justice* had carried the least number of marines of any of the gunships.

Just as Solyss shut down the communication equipment, the silence was broken by a loud banging on the door to the flight deck. Kard let out a startled yelp, and everyone turned around to stare at the door. Tentatively, Ymp stood up and moved to the door. She activated the controls, and to everyone's surprise, it slid open. One of the marine sergeants, a Terran named Rielly Stower, stood there, looking just as surprised as they were, but very much alive.

"Oh, thank the Great One," a Kowwok marine behind Rielly exclaimed, followed by several other declarations of excitement and relief. Rielly turned to Ymp and saluted. "Good to see you alive, Major. We thought everyone up here was dead."

"We thought the same thing about you, Sergeant," Ymp replied. "The ship said the cargo bay had lost all atmosphere."

Rielly nodded. "It did. But it started inside the head. The chamber held long enough for us to move into the crew section. When we didn't hear anything from the flight deck and the emergency door sealed, we started to fear you had lost atmosphere, too."

Solyss felt a wide smile spread across his face. They had not lost all of the marines to a horrible decompression. The hand of fate was indeed on their side. They had come close to death, but their righteous cause had saved them. That meant there was still a chance that Fracsid and the crew of *Unending Justice* were still alive.

"You see that, Kard?" Solyss said. "These marines survived. That means there's a chance your cousin did as well. We'll come back and find him."

The young Braz nodded solemnly. Solyss knew the odds were low that Fracsid and his crew would survive an uncontrolled reentry. But hope was an important thing.

CHAPTER 16

Sartori listened as Commander Dolan updated her on the results from the recent rebel raid, his voice neutral. "There were no fatalities aboard, only about a dozen injuries. The *Entala* has been towed to a high stable orbit, and a dry-dock facility is being maneuvered to assist with the repairs. Current estimates say the ship will be out of commission for approximately seven months."

It was not a stellar start to Sartori's mission. Losing the use of her only cruiser, at least until the reinforcements arrived, would seriously limit her tactical options.

"What about the bases?" Sartori asked.

"Two soldiers killed. Couple dozen were stunned and suffered a few minor injuries as a result. Nothing serious," Dolan answered.

That bit of news did not sit right with her. The rebels had gone out of their way to raid several bases, steal equipment, and disable a cruiser, but had made a point of using stun weapons? It did not fit with the terrorist mentality she would have expected. Or it just meant they lacked heavy firepower, which could be the point of this raid.

"How much did they take?"

"Between both armories on the planet," Dolan said as he skimmed his datapad, "several kilos of high explosives, one hundred and fifty assault rifles, four crates of frag grenades, four crates of stun grenades, two dozen heavy repeating rifles, ten space combat suits, six crates of encrypted comm gear, seventeen cases of emergency medical kits, eight portable shield generators."

It was an impressive list of equipment—enough firepower to equip an entire army or marine company, though this amount was small compared to what they would have already had available when they took over Enro. The supply depots at the bases there would have held enough gear for two entire divisions.

"And the ship depot on Roc 5?"

"Fortunately, everything stored there was at least ten years out of date," Dolan said. "Ten SSF-19 interceptors, four AB-11 bombers, five AF-51s, and three SS-72s."

"Those SSF-19s could be a problem. They are old, but there are still many squadrons in service at our bases out here," Sartori said.

"They also were able to power up and fly out a Hazard class frigate, an Essex escort carrier, and an experimental ship identified as FX-21. In addition, they also were able to clear out a storage shed of some uninstalled equipment. The records are a mess, so we don't have a clear idea of what was in there. It looks like at least some heavy ship blaster cannons and other parts."

Sartori had seen a few capital-size ships jump to hyperspace while they were moving to intercept the rebel's freighter. But three capital ships was more than she would have thought possible to re-enable so quickly. The service depot must not have done a proper job of decommissioning the ships.

Something Dolan said triggered a memory, and Sartori tried to figure out what it was. "Wait, FX-21? That was an experimental craft from the early days of the war. Something to do with increasing shield capacity?"

Dolan brought up a summary on his datapad. "Yes, the FX program was an attempt to increase shield capacity on warships by using an anti-matter reactor instead of a standard fusion reactor. The experiment is listed as a failure. The ship's shield proved unstable, failing during every combat scenario. The hyperdrive was also judged to be too danger-ous to use for any long-duration hyperspace travel."

Sartori smiled. "Well, it looks like the ship will at least take some enemies of the Alliance down with her."

It was the only bit of good news to come out of the raid. Everything else gave the rebels better equipment and made the Alliance look weak. It would not make her job easier.

"Anything else, Commander?"

"Yes, Admiral, Governor Zhant is here to see you, and the captured rebel captain is available for interrogation at your convenience."

Sartori frowned. The last thing she wanted to do was talk to the Ailleroc governor, but she could not avoid it forever. He had been resisting her attempts to have new elections called.

"The prisoner first. Then I'll see the governor," Sartori said.

"Aye, Admiral."

Dolan left the room. While he was gone, Sartori consid-ered her options. The raid on Ailleroc could provide her with an excuse to reverse her decision to call the elections. But she still believed that was the best way to undermine the re-bels' position.

Several minutes later, Dolan returned to the conference room followed by four marines and a Braz in a prison jumpsuit and binding cuffs. She did not recognize the clan of the Braz's green screfa. Despite the marines escorting him, he held his head high. There was spirit in him, which might make him difficult to get information from.

"Admiral Sartori, our prisoner, former captain of the transport *Unending Justice*, Fracsid Relis, of clan Lis. He has been implicated in several smuggling operations and is wanted for trafficking stolen goods. That is, before he turned traitor," Dolan said, introducing the Braz.

"Well, I guess I should thank you for rescuing me and my crew. We were in the wrong place at the wrong time. I'm not a traitor," Fracsid said, his defiant stance shifting to an expression of cowardly, boyish innocence.

Sartori remained silent, studying the Braz. His denial of being a rebel stood in contrast to the defiant manner in which he had held himself. Either he wasn't as committed to the rebels' cause as she first suspected, or he was simply falling back on old habits of trying to lie his way out of a problem. Either way, her best approach was to wait.

"So you see, it's all been a misunderstanding. We thought we were following a convoy of fellow transports. I was taken completely by surprise when they started shooting at that ship. I tried to get away but got shot down before I could," Fracsid said, his tone rambling at first, then becoming more pleading. "If I could just be taken to my crew, we'll be on our way. I still need to get my passengers to their destination."

He certainly was making every effort to sell the innocent bystander story. He could probably go on like this for hours. She did not have that much patience. "Captain Relis, you stand here accused of treason against the Alliance. You attacked an Alliance military base and a naval warship. Therefore, you will be treated as an enemy of the state. After you reveal all that you know about your fellow rebels, you will be executed for your crimes."

In an instant, Fracsid's face turned from boyish innocence back to determined defiance. "I see. No trial, then. I guess that proves I was fighting for the right side. You won't get anything from me or my crew. We'll resist you until our last breath."

Sartori smiled, trying to insert as much menace as she could. "We'll see how you respond after a few hours with our intelligence division. Marines, take him away."

Once again, Fracsid held his head high as the marines escorted him from the room. Sartori shook her head and said to Dolan once the Braz was gone, "That is what I was afraid of.

It looks like the rebels have some genuine believers. I had hoped they were just ambitious criminals."

"Shall I authorize the interrogation teams to use all methods for information extraction?" Dolan asked.

Sartori frowned. After the events of the day, torturing the captured rebels was tempting. "Any word from our operative?"

"Just that he has succeeded in planting himself in an important position in their hierarchy. He indicated that, in order to maintain his cover, it would be some time before he would attempt to make contact again. Even if he knew about this raid, he probably had no time to warn us beforehand without breaking cover."

"Very well. We'll give him some more time to make contact," Sartori said impatiently.

She again considered the idea of torturing their prisoners. "Torture is not authorized. Standard techniques only. They can't all be as stubborn as Mr. Relis. One of them will break."

"Aye, Admiral. Shall I send in Governor Zhant?" Dolan asked.

It was tempting to say no, but Sartori sighed. "Very well."

A moment later the arrogant figure of Ailleroc Governor Zhant came into the conference room. He had changed his attitude with her in the weeks since her arrival, though he still seemed to think he had the authority to order her around.

"Admiral," he began immediately, "I must insist on the cancellation of your plans for new elections. After this blatant disregard for Alliance law, we cannot reward the rebels by giving them elections."

Sartori forced herself to wait a moment before responding. It might feel good, but it would not be very productive to snap at the arrogant man. "Governor, elections are not a reward. They are a basic right for all Alliance citizens. We will hold them as planned."

"But after this attack it will embolden the rebels!"

"No, Governor, it will take away their reason to fight. We have managed to capture several prisoners. A public execution will serve to remind the rest of the rebels of the consequences of attacking the Alliance."

"I never realized how much of running an army was paperwork," Lohcja complained as he took a seat.

Across the table, Lahkaba let out a laugh. "I've heard that. But you shouldn't have too much to do. There's no bureaucracy. Yet."

They were sitting in the small, one-room living quarters that served as Lohcja's home here on Irod. The building had been hastily set up when the Sulas refugees had first come to Irod. By now, those that had stayed had moved on and built their own homes. The building was now serving as officer quarters for the new army.

"That's part of the problem. We already have 44,000 recruits and more still to come. General Numba won't release but a handful for the marines or navy, so we're stuck trying to form them into a cohesive fighting force," Lohcja said, rubbing his mandibles together in frustration.

"But there's no organization in place, so General Numba is using the Camari system. And, even though we don't have many people with a lot of military experience, almost all of us have been raised under the Alliance. Their military structure is what we're familiar with."

Concerned, Lahkaba raised an eyebrow. "When we formed the military, we established the Alliance hierarchy as our structure."

"Technically, we're following that," Lohcja said. "But not much in practice. As far as I understand it, the Alliance officers are leaders of groups. Platoons, companies, departments, etc."

Lahkaba nodded. "Right. And they're merit based. Everyone starts out as a basic enlisted soldier and then starts specializing, either into specific jobs, team leadership as NCOs, or group leadership and tactical planning as officers. We're having to skip most of that since we have to create everything from scratch."

"Of course," Lohcja said hesitantly. "But I get the impression that the officer ranks are being filled more on background than on merit."

"I'm not following you."

Across from him, Lohcja's antennae quivered slightly. Lahkaba had come to understand that to mean his friend was uncomfortable with something. Normally, he was pretty laid back and didn't like to say anything controversial.

After a moment, Lohcja finally said. "Well, look at me. I'm a colonel. And for no reason other than the fact that I fought at Perth and am from the warrior caste. Camari military structure and Ronid caste structure aren't much different.

"There are several other officers that Numba has selected for equally ridiculous reasons. Now don't get me wrong, I'm proud of my warrior heritage, but I don't think it qualifies me to be a colonel."

Lahkaba pondered how to respond to his friend's complaint. For the most part, he agreed. The Confederate military operated much the same way; all of the officers were Dotran, and all senior officer positions were reserved for gold- and bronze-scaled Dotran only. The more common blues and greens could become officers, whereas a Kowwok never would, but even the blues and greens never rose far.

In a way, he thought that stratification of the Confederate culture had been one of the reasons they had lost the Colonial War. No matter what other issues the Alliance had, its military was at least designed to be merit-based, moving people to positions where they would be the most effective.

On the other hand, his friend was also underselling himself. He had been with the rebellion from the beginning, risking his career and livelihood to help Lahkaba. He had followed Maarkean all the way to Enro and been an important participant in that battle. Being a member of a particular Ronid caste was not the only reason he deserved an important position in the new army.

Before he could respond, there was a knock at Lohcja's door. The Ronid rose and went to the door, pulling it open. On the other side, Lahkaba recognized Kaars Aerinstar, the former Alliance intelligence officer.

At the sight of the Terran, Lohcja turned back toward Lahkaba. "This is a perfect example of what I mean. Kaars here has been placed as a mere master intelligence sergeant. He was an officer before, commanding an intelligence unit, and gave up his life to bring us his experience and what information he could. Now he's reporting to me, a former cab driver."

Lahkaba frowned. Regardless of the validity of Lohcja's argument, it was not appropriate for him to continue to complain in front of others. He and Lohcja were old friends; Kaars was apparently an enlisted soldier, whom Lahkaba did not really trust.

"I've told you before, sir, I don't mind. I'm just happy to be helping," Kaars said, with what seemed to be genuine sincerity.

"And I've told you, call me Lohcja At least when we're not on duty," Lohcja said, allowing Kaars to come in and closing the door behind him.

"I'm actually here on official business, sir," Kaars stated. "And it is good that Delegate Lahkaba is here, as I am sure the congress will wish to hear what I have to report."

To his credit, Lohcja said no more in his rant against Numba's officer assignments. Instead, he took a seat again and told Kaars to proceed. Lahkaba leaned forward, eager to hear anything Kaars might have been able to learn from his connections in the Alliance military.

"I received an update from my network on the last shuttle to arrive from Sulas. Now, I have to warn you, the data is several days old, even discounting the standard time to travel from Sulas to here. It sat uncollected for almost a week on Sulas before coming here. If I were allowed to get data sent directly here, it would increase our response time by several days," Kaars began.

Lahkaba sighed heavily. This was not the first time Kaars had requested to know exactly where Irod was and to have a more direct connection to his intelligence network. He had a valid point; waiting for trusted transport pilots to pick up reports added significant delays to what he was able to learn. But it also helped to ensure the secrecy of Irod's location.

"We'll see if we can do something about that," Lohcja said.

"Thank you, sir," Kaars said. Both men appeared to miss Lahkaba's frown. "Anyway, I was able to confirm one of my earlier reports, that Admiral Katerina Sartori has arrived and taken command of all Alliance forces. She has been assigned as the Alliance sector commander for all three Colonial sectors. Her authority exceeds that of the planetary governors in some cases."

Lahkaba nodded, not surprised but disappointed in the news. Kaars had brought the rumor to them a few weeks before, but it had not been confirmed. He had hoped it had just been a rumor, but there had already had time to come to terms with the implications.

Kaars continued, "The biggest bit of news is out of Ailleroc. It seems that several planetary bases and the ship depot on Roc 5 were raided by rebels."

This news did surprise Lahkaba. He looked to Lohcja, who looked just as startled. The Ronid said, "But we haven't deployed any forces yet. Was it the Ailleroc locals?"

Shaking his head, Kaars said, "No, sir. It appears that rebels jumped in with a fleet of gunships and an armed mining freighter. They attacked the Alliance bases and one of their cruisers. The Alliance navy destroyed several of the gunships, but in order to escape, the rebels hit the cruiser *Entala* in a surprise attack while her shields were down. They disabled the ship and knocked her out of orbit on a course to impact one of Ailleroc's main cities. The other Alliance ships were forced to let the remaining rebels escape in order to stabilize the ship's orbit before it decayed too much."

"Maark?" Lohcja asked, looking toward Lahkaba.

"It has to be. That sounds like the mining freighter he was planning to repair," Lahkaba answered.

"General Numba is not going to like this," Lohcja said nervously. "He's stated several times that we need to wait for the opportune time to attack."

"If Numba doesn't like it, the Cardine delegation is going to voice that. And I'm sure the Ailleroc delegation won't be happy either. It was an attack on their world without their knowledge," Lahkaba speculated.

"Think they'll bring up the merger with the Confederacy again?" Lohcja asked.

Lahkaba had been successful in delaying any formal discussion about the Dotran Confederacy's offer to extend membership to the worlds of the Kreogh Sector. Their representative, Bryel Prytoker, had, so far, been content to wait and had not made any attempts to meet with individual delegates. Zoeko was a shrewd politician, though, and was probably waiting for a good time to bring it up again. This might qualify.

"Possibly. But there's not a lot of support for the idea. Not even all of the Mirthod delegates seem to like the idea.

Though I suppose they may be able to sway the Cardine delegation. The Camari and Dotran have always been relatively friendly," Lahkaba said, thinking out loud. Turning to Kaars, he asked. "What's the other side of the story? How is the population of Ailleroc responding, and what do they know?"

Kaars shook his head, looking frustrated. "Unfortunately, I don't have very much more than what I gave you. The Alliance is calling it an act of terrorism and saying that the rebels attempted to use the cruiser as a weapon of mass destruction. But unless I can get better sources and get more people on the ground, I can't give you more than that. I'd need to go to Ailleroc myself."

Frustrated, Lahkaba stood up and paced the small room. For once, he started to think that Kaars should be allowed to return to Ailleroc and Sulas and set up a better network. Getting half information that was just Alliance spin was worse than no information sometimes.

"Okay, we should pass this on to Numba and the rest of Congress," Lahkaba finally said. "But take your time. The session starts in an hour. I'll bring this information before them; hopefully I can reveal it before Numba can sway the Cardine delegates. Let's hope we can keep things from looking too bad for Maark or pushing us into the arms of the Confederacy."

CHAPTER 17

Eighteen days. It had taken Saracasi and the decommissioned Alliance frigate eighteen days to get from Roc 5 back to Kol. A journey that, with the hyperdrive functioning normally, should have taken a little over six. For a while there, it looked like they would never make it. Saracasi couldn't wait to land.

Shortly after jumping away from Ailleroc, an overload had surged through the frigate's systems. They had been violently thrown from hyperspace into the middle of nowhere. Fortunately, no one had been injured.

Saracasi had then spent the next week going over every system on the ship. She had finally come to the conclusion that the ship's designers were equal parts genius and mad scientist. If things had worked the way they were supposed to, it would have been an engineering marvel. Unfortunately, almost nothing did.

While the system's conception had been ingenious, it had been built with excessive amounts of caution. Normally, as an engineer, that was something she could appreciate. In this case, the safety features were the reason the hyperdrive failed. The designers had exchanged the chance of catastrophic failure for the chance of stranding the ship light years away from habitable systems. A slow death in exchange for a quick one.

Working with her small crew, which was starting to feel normal, she had been forced to dismantle half of the ship's systems in order to rebuild the hyperdrive and the reactor links powering it. The patch was almost more dangerous than the original design, but it was the only way to get the hyperdrive working for periods longer than a few hours at a time.

They had brought ten days of rations aboard with them. Cutting those in half had extended their time; for the last few days, they had cut back to quarter rations to give themselves as much time as possible. Now that they had returned to Kol, she looked forward to a full, fresh meal.

"We're beginning our descent," Arzesaeth announced from the helm. "Think we can get those shields back for reentry?"

Saracasi exchanged a glance with Sheanna and Saisee. Their looks mirrored her own. "Possibly. But they would likely shut down the engines again."

"Ooookay," Arzesaeth replied. "A rough landing it is."

Arzesaeth exaggerated things a little. The inertial dampeners balanced out most of the sense of motion the ship experienced and reduced it to a slight shaking. But shields would have helped to make the ship more aerodynamic and absorb the intense heat of their deceleration.

"I'm reading lots of intermittent sensor scans and attempts at weapons locks," Tadashio said from the ship's main operations terminal.

"Probably just the cities and mining settlements tracking us as we come overhead," Saracasi said, trying to sound reassuring.

It was not unusual for the settlements to scan incoming ships. Normally, they would only do basic scans of approaching craft to assess the ship's course. If it was not directly toward a settlement, nothing further was done. But the fact that they were being tracked for longer this time suggested that the locals were jumpy, and they had never used weapon tracking systems before.

"Coming up on our final approach toward the base," Arzesaeth said after about fifteen minutes into their bumpy ride.

"Sensor scans increasing," Tadashio said excitedly. "I'm reading multiple weapon emplacements locking onto us."

"Source?" Saracasi asked quickly.

"It's coming from the shipyard. Wait, I'm getting new scans coming from the airspace near us. Multiple bogies are shadowing us."

Saracasi cursed to herself. Unwittingly, she had put them into a position of being vulnerable by assuming that they could safely approach Chavatwor's shipyard. But it had been almost a month since they had originally left for the mission to Ailleroc. A week and a half would have passed since the *Defiant Glory* made it back, assuming that they had managed to escape the Roc system. Anything could have changed.

"Open a channel on the *Defiant Glory*'s frequency," Saracasi ordered, trying to remain calm as she stood at the tactical display. She imagined how her brother would respond in a situation like this. He would not start panicking in front of others. He would remain calm and in control.

"I'm getting a response!" Tadashio replied. "They're saying the fighters are here to escort us in. We're cleared to touch down outside the shipyard."

Saracasi let out a breath in relief. She had started to worry over nothing. On the other hand, it was still possible that they were walking into a trap. A little paranoia never hurt.

"Private Talac," Saracasi ordered, "go down to the airlock. Verify we have friendlies on the other side before unsealing it."

"Aye, Captain," the young marine said, using the customary title for a ship's commander, before dashing off the bridge. Beside her, Sheanna gave her a curious look, which Saracasi chose to ignore.

The next few minutes passed in silence as Arzesaeth landed the ship in the dry sands of Kol. Saracasi and the others went through the initial steps of powering down the ship and securing it from flight, but she held off on the last few steps until she heard from Talac.

"I see General Ocaitchi approaching. I am unsealing the airlock."

Learning that her brother was alive and well lifted some weight from Saracasi's shoulders. She finished the shutdown sequence while Talac escorted Maarkean up to the bridge. By the time he arrived, they were running on backup generators only.

"We thought we'd lost you there for a while," Maarkean said as he stepped onto the bridge. She didn't think it was obvious to the others, but she could see the concern he was suppressing.

"We thought we were lost as well," Saracasi said. "This ship is pretty amazing, but she's also a death trap."

"Oh?" Maarkean asked, looking concerned. Beside him, Davidus was examining the different stations on the bridge.

Saracasi nodded. "It's a pretty unique design. Very much ahead of its time. We almost destroyed the hyperdrive, but after several days of work, we were able to get it working enough to limp back here. That did give me several days crawling around inside of her, and I'm starting to think some of her problems might be fixable. I need to talk to Chava."

"That can wait," Maarkean said, after looking at each of the five crewmembers. "Get yourselves cleaned up and get something to eat and a good night's sleep. Nice work, all of you. You can give me your full report tomorrow, Major."

"Aye, General," Saracasi said, along with the others.

The others started to move off the bridge, eager to find a place with working showers and hot food. An unexpected twinge of regret struck her when Maarkean used her formal rank. She had started getting used to being called "Captain."

Davidus followed the crewmembers off the bridge, giving Saracasi and Maarkean a moment alone. Once they were out of sight, her brother took her into a hug. As was common among Braz, he had never been very expressive, especially in public, but the hug reminded her of the last time she had come to Kol to meet him, after he had broken her out of prison on Sulas.

"I really did think I had lost you, kid," Maarkean said after releasing her.

"You can't get rid of me that easily," she replied with a smile.

"No, I suppose I can't. But it did make me glad you chose to be an engineer. There won't be many other times like this where you'll be in danger," Maarkean said.

"Yeah, I can't wait to start taking this ship apart with Chava so we can figure out how best to put her back together," Saracasi replied.

Strangely, as much as she meant what she said, knowing that that would be all she would be doing made her a little sad. But, she reminded herself, this mission had been more exciting than she had anticipated because a lot of it involved crawling around fixing a starship. She had not had to shoot anyone. As long as she worked with Chavatwor, she wouldn't have to do that again.

After her reunion with Maarkean, Saracasi departed from the captured frigate, intending to find her quarters. Life support had been functional aboard, but the sanitation systems had been in need of maintenance. As such, she hadn't showered in three weeks.

On the way, her mind began to drift away from her responsibilities, something she had not allowed herself to do while on board. Every waking minute trapped in deep space without a functioning hyperdrive had been spent trying to remedy that problem. Worry about never getting to see Asirzi again had only been a distraction, one she couldn't afford.

Now that she was safe, Asirzi quickly came to the forefront of her mind. Prior to the mission, she and Asirzi had been spending most of their free time together, sharing meals, talking, and getting to know each other. Despite the obvious attraction she felt they shared, neither of the women had yet made an attempt to move their relationship into the physical realm.

Saracasi had started to regret that when she thought she might die in deep space. She almost skipped the shower in her desire to find Asirzi, but she decided against that when she got a whiff of herself in a narrow hallway. Even though she had been looking forward to a nice long shower, she rushed through and left her quarters again within fifteen minutes.

Finding Asirzi proved relatively simple. She had an office inside the UDF HQ building where she worked on contract negotiations for Chavatwor. When Saracasi arrived, the Liw'kel woman flashed her a broad smile, but gestured to the earpiece she wore, indicating she was on a comm call.

Saracasi nodded and paced impatiently outside Asirzi's office. An agonizing number of minutes went by while she waited. It began to feel as if she had waited in the hall for longer than she had been stranded aboard the frigate.

When Asirzi finally emerged from her office, it was in a rush, only checking her enthusiasm once she caught sight of another employee walking down the hall. She gestured for Saracasi to follow her back to her office and closed the door behind them.

"I was so worried that I'd never see you again," she began, but Saracasi stepped up and kissed her, cutting her off. Saracasi wasn't sure where she'd found the courage to do that, but when Asirzi didn't pull away, she was glad she had.

The two women stood there together, lingering at the end of the kiss, for what Saracasi hoped could be forever. When Asirzi pulled back, they both wore wide, silly grins on their faces.

"I was worried I wouldn't get to see you again, either," Saracasi finally said, breaking the silence.

A knock on the door interrupted the moment, and they quickly stepped away from each other. Asirzi straightened her clothes while Saracasi moved back toward the door. She put her hand on the handle and winked at Asirzi.

"You're working. We can finish this later."

She opened the door and slipped past the person on the other side.

CHAPTER 18

Zeric regretted asking about the ship almost as soon as he'd done it. Across the table from him, Saracasi had launched into a long, detailed explanation about the unique design of the frigate she had captured. She had been working on it and talking about it almost non-stop for the last month. He had only asked about it because he had never seen a ship like it. He didn't really care.

Beside him, Gu'od nodded politely as Saracasi talked. To him, the Liw'kel seemed genuinely interested. Maybe he was, Zeric thought. He didn't understand his friend sometimes.

For instance, Asirzi, sitting next to Saracasi, was giving Gu'od some very overtly flirtatious looks. Despite the mechanical arm, the girl was quite attractive. Even with Gamaly sitting beside him, Zeric didn't understand how Gu'od could fail to notice.

Maybe Gu'od had just gotten used to people falling all over him. Every Liw'kel female they had met lately had practically thrown themselves at him. Gamaly and Asheerah still couldn't be in the same room with each other. Strangely, Gamaly did not appear to take any notice of Asirzi, aside from a small frown. It was the same polite, but distant, attitude she had shown toward Sienn'lyn.

What really made Zeric wonder, was that he had been under the impression that Asirzi and Saracasi were together. In between casting Gu'od suggestive looks, Asirzi would turn to smile at Saracasi, and he felt sure the pair of them had started holding hands under the table as soon as they had finished eating. He supposed Asirzi could be interested in both men and women, but Saracasi didn't show any signs of being bothered by the flirtation, either. It was as if he was the only one who was aware of what was going on.

"You have no idea what I just said, do you?" Saracasi asked.

The fact that he was now the center of attention keyed Zeric in more than the words themselves. Saracasi had stopped talking and was looking at him expectantly. Gu'od's expression had changed to a slight smile, the one he got any time Zeric embarrassed himself. Gamaly just frowned at him.

"Um, no. No, I don't."

To his relief, Saracasi just shrugged. "That's okay. I was rambling, anyway. I can tell the rest of you aren't as interested in the ship as I am."

"Too bad Chava doesn't seem to ever be as self-aware," Asirzi said with a sigh, which got a small laugh from Saracasi.

Zeric hadn't spent much time with the Kowwok shipwright, so he had no idea what the two women were referring to. All of his time lately was spent training marines. Another batch of new recruits had arrived on a transport from Irod a few days before. Also aboard had been Lahkaba and a few other delegates from the congress, but he hadn't had any time to catch up with him. This meal was the first one he hadn't eaten while working.

"We should get going," Gamaly said, standing up.

Gu'od did the same, and from across the table, Asirzi batted her eyelashes and puckered her lips as if blowing a kiss. Unexpectedly, Gu'od looked embarrassed, while Gamaly's frown was replaced by a small smile. After the two Liw'kel walked away, Saracasi and Asirzi let out quiet giggles.

"Okay, what was that all about?" Zeric said, finally confused enough to ask. "I didn't think you were interested in men. Why are you flirting with Gu? You're not the only one, either. Sienn'lyn and Asheerah are all over him."

Asirzi smiled and just shook her head, giving a little laugh—clearly at his expense. Saracasi joined her for a moment but then took pity on his bewildered expression.

"It's a Liw'kel thing."

"Yeah, I gathered that," Zeric said, knowing he sounded testy.

"When Liw'kel women get pregnant, other women around them try to steal their mate. It's an evolutionary thing. Apparently, the pregnancy proved the male was fertile and more desirable. And it was up to the pregnant female to keep the male. It's evolved to a social thing, where nowadays the male proves his loyalty to his mate by not giving into the offers of sex from every female he meets," Saracasi explained.

Zeric felt like his eyes should be popping out of his head in shock. "So every Liw'kel female is going to try to sleep with Gu, and he has to prove his love by refusing? Damn, that's harsh."

He suddenly felt sorry for his friend. Previously, he had been jealous of all the attention Gu'od was getting. But now that he knew it was a test that he had to resist, he appreciated his friend's willpower. Then the implication of what Saracasi had said fully sank in.

"Wait, you mean Gamaly's pregnant?" he asked suddenly, turning in his seat to watch Gamaly walk out of the small cafeteria.

"Yes. They're probably off to get a checkup from Dr. Istru," Saracasi confirmed.

"But she doesn't look pregnant. Why did they tell you and not me?" Zeric asked, hurt creeping into his voice.

"They haven't told anyone," Asirzi said. "Liw'kel, women and men, give off a telltale flicker with their antennae after a baby is conceived. It's a hormonal thing. Liw'kel can pick that up, so we all know. I told Saracasi. I didn't want her to get jealous when I tried to flirt with Gu'od. I don't think I did a very convincing job, although it was quite fun."

Zeric ignored the two women as he mulled over the revelation. Gu'od and Gamaly were going to have a baby? Now? In the middle of a war? On the other hand, he considered, would it have been any better when they were just criminals?

Was that why Gamaly had refused any formal position in the marines? Were they going to disappear—go buy a house somewhere and live a normal life? A thousand questions raced through his head.

While he pondered, something interesting must have happened, because he noticed that Asirzi and Saracasi had stopped laughing. They were intently looking at the video screen on the wall of the cafeteria. All conversation in the room had stopped, and everyone was watching.

Turning in his seat, Zeric looked up at the monitor. The text display indicated that a packet ship had just arrived with an important announcement from the Alliance. Another moment went by before the screen changed as the message was transmitted over Kol's planetary data network.

The scene changed to reveal an older Terran female wearing an Alliance admiral's uniform. Short, with silver-grey hair, the woman looked more like a grandmother than a warrior. But Zeric instantly recognized her and knew both were true of her.

"Attention, Alliance citizens. I am Fleet Admiral Katerina Sartori, newly appointed commander of Alliance forces in the Kreogh, Trepon, and Loisa sectors. I have been sent here by the Alliance high command to address the rising levels of terrorism among the colonies. As many of you are aware, I was last here during the Colonial War with the Dotran in which my fleet defeated the Confederacy.

"What you may not be aware of is that the Alliance Congress recognizes that they over-reacted to the earlier demands made by the legally elected representatives of this sector. In calling for the dismissal of all planetary governing bodies, they went too far. As such, I am calling for new elections to return these bodies to power on their respective worlds. Democracy will return to the Kreogh sector.

"Now, while the Alliance will uphold democracy, it will not stand for rebellion among its citizenry. The recent assaults against Alliance personnel on Sulas, Dantyne, Enro, and Ailleroc will not go unpunished. We have in custody some of the terrorists who recently attacked Alliance bases on Ailleroc. We also have one of the culprits from the first attack on Sulas."

The scene shifted, and what appeared caused Zeric to gasp. The screen showed Fracsid Relis, his crew, and some of the marines who had been aboard his ship. But what shocked Zeric was the Terran who stood with them—Jairyd Kil'dare. Jairyd had been one of the small group that had helped him and Maarkean break into Olan Detention Center on Sulas months previously. Jairyd had not returned from that mission, and everyone had assumed that he was dead.

Admiral Sartori returned to the screen and resumed speaking. "These individuals are currently being held as terrorists and traitors. As such, they will be executed in thirty days from the transmission of this message. However, if the following orders are carried out, they will instead have their rights restored and be granted full trials. While I have no doubt as to their guilt, the courts may decide to grant them leniency and sentence them to prison instead of death.

"First, the body known as the Kreogh Sector Congress must disband. All its members must publically refute their previous calls for rebellion. Second, Alliance personnel held prisoner on Enro are to be released. All individuals involved in the rebellion there are to turn themselves over to Colonel Cage and await trial. Third, all involved in the attack on Olan prison and all escaped prisoners are to turn themselves in to stand trial for their actions. As those groups comprise a large number of individuals, only the leaders must comply before my deadline.

"Maarkean Ocaitchi, Zeric Dustlighter, Lahkaba, Halin Corte, and Lei-mey Darshawn must all turn themselves in within one month. If all of these orders have been carried out, martial law will be lifted from the cities where it is being enforced on Cardine, Sulas, and Ailleroc. All prisoners will be subject to full and fair trials by a jury of their peers.

"If these orders are not carried out, the prisoners we have in custody will be executed as traitors. All individuals involved in attacks against Alliance personnel will receive the same treatment when, and I mean when, they are apprehended."

The intense gaze Sartori gave on the monitor as she spoke reinforced the conviction of her words. Zeric felt himself cringing slightly. Sartori certainly had a presence, even in a recorded message.

"It is my hope that the misunderstandings that have occurred can be resolved amicably. The Alliance stands for peace and democracy. Let us return to that state and work out any disagreements like a civilized society."

With that, the image terminated and was replaced by another bit of text. The text was a link to where a copy of the message would be stored on the network, along with a complete list of prisoners that must turn themselves in to Alliance authority.

Around him, the cafeteria remained quiet for a moment. All eyes were slowly turning toward Zeric. To himself, he cursed that Admiral Sartori knew who he was. Outwardly, he tried to project confidence. He tried to think of something defiant and reassuring to say.

"It looks like the Alliance has become desperate enough to resort to threats. They obviously can't back up those words and are hoping we'll just roll over for them," Zeric said.

Several people in the room nodded in response, and the noise level started to climb again as they all started talking about the message amongst themselves. Grateful that attention had drifted off of him, Zeric leaned in close to Saracasi. "We need to go find your brother."

Maarkean hurried across the desert compound on Kol toward the large headquarters building. For the last week, he had been aboard the *Defiant Glory*, working with Davidus and the pilot recruits on training exercises in their newly captured fighters. They had returned a few minutes ago, and it was only then that he learned that several members of the Kreogh Sector Congress had been on Kol waiting for him for several days.

The training session had progressed moderately well, though now he wished he had not extended it an extra day. Almost all of their recruited pilots had been as good as their word in having some experience, though not much combat experience. Surprisingly, the former bounty hunter Jerik Needa, who had tried to collect him as a mark just a few months before, was shaping up to be a good candidate for a squadron leader.

As Maarkean stepped inside the large headquarters building, he found the congressional delegates in the foyer waiting for him. Lei-mey sat calmly in one corner by herself. The Notha named Owrik stood beside Lahkaba, talking quietly. The last delegate, the Kowwok Valinther from Kol, was kneeling at a shrine that occupied one corner of the room.

The shrine was an offering to the Great One, the supreme being in the Kowwok's dominant religion. Chavatwor had set it up after taking up residence here, and some of the Kowwoks would occasionally visit it. Valinther was either praying or meditating, or whatever it was Kowwoks did to the Great One. Curiously, Lahkaba seemed to be watching Valinther with a deep frown on his face.

Maarkean had heard his friend mutter an exclamation to the Great One on occasion. It was common to most Kowwok. They had never discussed religion, a topic generally avoided in public across the Alliance, but he had always assumed Lahkaba to be a follower of the Great One like Chavatwor, Htaretter, and, apparently, Valinther. The frown suggested otherwise.

Putting aside his thoughts about Kowwok belief systems, Maarkean put a smile on his face and said, "Allow me to apologize for my tardiness in meeting with you. I have been on a training exercise and was only just informed of your arrival."

All of the delegates turned toward him as he spoke, Valinther standing up from the shrine and moving to join the others. Maarkean braced for the firm squeeze of a hug from Lahkaba, which was his usual form of greeting, but he merely inclined his head. The others greeted him in similar fashion, a cold and distant atmosphere coming from them.

"General Ocaitchi, is there a place we can speak in private?" Lahkaba said formally.

Curious, Maarkean studied the Kowwok for a second before replying, "Of course. Follow me."

He led them down a flight of stairs to the basement level that Chavatwor had entirely given over for the military to use. There was one room, which occasionally served as a conference room, that was large enough to hold them all. Once inside, they all took seats around the small table before anyone spoke again.

"Major General," Lahkaba said, speaking stiffly again, "on behalf of the United Kreogh Sector Congress, we are here to formally censure you for your unauthorized actions on the world of Ailleroc. Your attack against Alliance facilities was not cleared with General Numba or the Ailleroc delegation. Congress wishes you to know that they do not approve of your independent actions."

Maarkean frowned. Censure by the congress for taking action against the Alliance? The loss of Fracsid and the marines had been hard enough to deal with.

He debated his response, but he held his tongue for the moment, mainly out of respect to Lahkaba. He wasn't sure what he could say that he wouldn't regret later. These delegates were here to deliver a message; they weren't necessarily the ones who had drafted it.

His patience paid off, because after a moment, Lahkaba said, "Now that that is out of the way, allow me to say that I thought the whole idea of a formal censure was ridiculous."

Maarkean smiled with relief. "It sounded a little forced. But why did they have you deliver it?"

"We managed to convince the others that it would be better received by people you know," Owrik said, sitting in his chair at an uncomfortable angle. The cheap chairs that had been placed in the room had not been designed to accommodate Notha tails.

"Regretfully, we won that point only in exchange for an affirmative vote," Lei-mey grumbled.

"It's a meaningless gesture anyway," Valinther added. "It carries no actual weight."

Silently, Maarkean disagreed. Even without any formal consequences or punishment, to be censured by the congress meant something to him. It meant that he had failed them. Either that, or they weren't the stellar body of democratic virtue that he hoped they were.

"General Numba wanted to replace you and planned to send orders relieving you of command. Fortunately, most of the delegates really did support your actions. We reminded the general, in no uncertain terms, that he may be your superior officer in grand strategy, but all matters in regard to naval and marine operations were entirely under your jurisdiction.

"A raid against an Alliance base on an uninhabitable moon qualified," Lahkaba explained. "The censure vote was mostly to appease his ego and that of the Ailleroc delegates. I do wish you had notified us beforehand so we could have headed this off in advance."

Maarkean nodded. "If it wasn't a ten-day round trip to Irod, I probably would have."

"But this is not the main reason we are here," Valinther said tersely.

Curious, Maarkean looked at the Kowwok, who continued, "The Confederacy has sent a representative to meet with Congress."

This news left Maarkean feeling like he had been punched in the stomach. He had gotten over thinking of Kowwoks or Dotran individuals as enemies, but the Dotran Confederation itself would forever remain an enemy in his mind. They had waged a war of aggression across this sector of space, trying to claim every world for themselves. He no longer considered the Alliance blameless in that war, but the Dotran had started it. And they had killed many of his friends.

"For what purpose?" Maarkean asked, trying to keep his voice level.

Lahkaba cast a weary look toward the others before answering. "They have offered us membership in the Confederacy in exchange for their protection against the Alliance."

"Of course," Maarkean fumed. "That way they can gain control of what they failed to in the last war."

"I expect they see our rebellion as a perfect opportunity to grab up some star systems without effort," Lei-mey said.

"Oh, it will take effort. Us siding with the Dotran will cause the Alliance to respond with the full might of their military. I'm sure that war would dwarf the last one," Maarkean said forcefully. "I assume you told them to get packing?"

Lahkaba bowed his head, an embarrassed look on his face. "No. I have managed to delay any discussion of the offer for the time being. But I cannot stall for much longer. Some of the delegates are considering it. They seem to think that with the Dotran on our side, the Alliance will back down.

"We've been trying to convince the others that we don't need the Confederacy," he continued. "In a way, your adventure on Ailleroc both helped and hurt our efforts. Your success against them showed that you can win at least some fights. Of course, until we arrived here, we only had Alliance propaganda, which suggested that you had suffered more losses than the Alliance. Returning with a full report will help."

Maarkean nodded sheepishly. He probably should have sent a report to Congress after returning to Kol. The PR war was not something he was used to dealing with. The Alliance certainly had been quick to cast the engagement in as positive a light as they could.

"So what is your plan?" he asked.

"Even with the ships you have captured, your naval forces are far inferior to the Alliance," Lahkaba began. "The Confederacy offers us a full-strength, powerful navy, but with some unacceptable terms. But there are other powers out there."

Curious, Maarkean tried to figure out where Lahkaba was going. He spoke with a self-satisfied smile, which Maarkean took to mean that the Kowwok thought his idea was especially clever.

"There's also the *Black Market.*"

When Lahkaba said no more, Maarkean realized that must have been the climax he had been building to. Not wanting to dampen his friend's enthusiasm, Maarkean said, "The *Black Market* is now a criminal marketplace, not a warship. It's unlikely the Fox has kept it in peak military order. And I doubt he'd be willing to let us borrow it."

"He did let you go the last time you were onboard. He sent Novastar to meet us, and you said he expressed sympathy with our cause," Lahkaba argued.

"Sympathy is a far cry from letting us use his livelihood to wage war with."

"But it doesn't hurt to ask," Lahkaba pressed.

Maarkean sighed. He knew how much the romanticism of the *Black Market* had appealed to Lahkaba. A powerful warship, stolen and used as a criminal hub. But that very romanticism was blinding him to the reality that the Fox was a crime lord with a lot of power. He didn't offer help out of the goodness of his heart.

"Regardless of whether the Fox would be willing to side with us, how do you think that would sway the Congress to believe that we don't need the Confederacy?" Maarkean asked, changing tactics.

"Why are they even considering it? I thought the purpose of this rebellion was to convince the Alliance to change their ways, not to completely separate from the Alliance."

"It's too late for the Alliance to simply apologize and let things go back to normal," Lei-mey said, her usual level of passion in her voice. "They have shown that they do not believe in their own principles."

"So why not simply declare independence?" Maarkean asked.

As if in response to his question, Zeric and Saracasi barged into the room, both looking flushed. Maarkean stood up, prepared to chastise them for interrupting, but Zeric spoke first.

"There's something you need to see."

Giving his friend and sister the benefit of the doubt, Maarkean sat back down as Zeric went to the room's video monitor. Zeric accessed the planetary network and brought up a video recording.

"This was just transmitted to the planet by a packet ship. We assume the same message has been sent to every world in the sector."

Zeric activated the message, and Maarkean watched as Admiral Sartori appeared and laid out her plans for dealing with the people in the sector. When she mentioned her prisoners, Maarkean was shocked and relieved to see Jairyd and Fracsid alive. The emotion was temporary, however, as she laid out her intentions to execute them.

"This is bad," Lei-mey said when the recording ended. "Very, very bad."

Confused, Maarkean looked at her. "While I agree that her plan to execute our people is bad, at least they are alive. For the last year, we all thought Jairyd was already dead."

"I don't mean that," Lei-mey snapped and then moderated her tone. "Although you are correct. I am quite happy to see Jairyd alive."

"That admiral is a crafty one," Owrik said quietly, adding to Maarkean's belief that he had missed something.

Lahkaba must have noticed, because he explained, "She appears to be offering us everything we claim we want. Returning power to each planet's representative body and offering fair trials to everyone. But what she is really doing is nothing at all."

"If we turn ourselves in and accept new elections, we will be admitting that the Alliance had the right to disband the governments in the first place," Lei-mey added. "If the Alliance had not disbanded them, there would be no need for elections. And by requiring Congress members to turn themselves in, when the only crime they committed was meeting together, she's saying that we don't have a right to meet as a sector and send a united list of desires. We will, essentially, be required to repudiate everything we have done. All the while, she gets to appear to the public like she is bowing to the will of the people. It's a subtle distinction, but an important one."

"Some of the delegates may wish to take this deal," Owrik said, casting a glance at Valinther. "Most of them were not on the list of people required to surrender themselves. With the prospect of open warfare growing, many of them are beginning to forget why we started this fight in the first place. People were imprisoned without trial. Our rights were being curtailed one by one."

The room was quiet for a moment as the new information sank in. Maarkean glanced over to Saracasi, who had nodded in agreement with everything the delegates had said. She understood political nuances and maneuvering far better than he did.

While all of that sounded bad, his main concern was the people slated for execution. By the expression on Zeric's face, he guessed that the Terran agreed with him. As callous as Zeric could be sometimes, he knew that the man felt responsible for those marines.

"Perhaps we should take Maarkean's suggestion," Lahkaba said quietly.

Turning his head, Maarkean wondered what suggestion he was referring to. Fortunately, Lahkaba explained. "You asked why we didn't just declare independence. It would solve several problems. If we declare our worlds independent of the Alliance, we can cast the Alliance's actions as a war of aggression, instead of a war for stability.

"It won't make much of a difference, but it might matter to some. It will also allow us to appear to keep the door open to the Confederacy. Not that we want to join them, but if we're independent, we can buy some time before they come at us in force, at least."

Lei-mey and Owrik nodded in agreement, though Valinther did not look as convinced. Lei-mey said, "Then we should return to Irod and convince the Congress to do this.

They will not have received this news yet. It will be best if we can be the first to deliver it."

"And we'll see about rescuing those prisoners before Admiral Sartori's deadline hits. It's a five-day journey there by packet ship. That gives us twenty-five days to get to Ailleroc and rescue them," Maarkean said.

"Are you sure you wish to conduct another raid on Ailleroc so soon after being censured?" Lei-mey asked.

Maarkean narrowed his eyes as he replied. He didn't like the idea of leaving those people to die simply to avoid a black mark on his name. "Those people deserve our every effort to rescue them."

"Very well," Lei-mey said, bowing her head.

Since her friend was one of the ones to be rescued, Maarkean would have expected more enthusiasm from her. But her feelings on the matter were of little consequence. He would go with or without Congress' approval.

"I believe I should continue with my plans to meet with the Fox," Lahkaba said. "Gaining the support of such a powerful ship will only help our efforts. Maark, I think it would help if you would return to Irod with the others and try to drum up support. You can also explain your rescue plans so that the Ailleroc delegation is not taken by surprise again."

Maarkean frowned at that. Apparently, Lahkaba would not be easily swayed from his plans for the *Black Market*. But he should have known that. Lahkaba did not give up easily.

"No, I'll go to the *Black Market*," he said.

"Aren't you banned?" Zeric asked.

"I'll figure something out. The Fox is more likely to listen to a criminal than a politician. No offense, Lah," Maarkean said.

The Kowwok did indeed look slightly offended but inclined his head. "You're probably right."

Giving Lahkaba an appreciative look, Maarkean turned to Zeric. "Zeric, you'll lead the operation to rescue the prisoners. I'm sure Solyss will be happy to provide transport. Have him select one other gunship, but no more. You'll need to try to be stealthy."

Zeric nodded, and Lahkaba added, "Also, Kaars Aerinstar, our Alliance turncoat, has recently gone to Ailleroc to gather some intelligence for General Numba. I'll tell you how to get in contact with him. He can probably be of assistance."

Things were going to get interesting, Maarkean thought. Assuming the Fox didn't vent him into space.

CHAPTER 19

The cool night air whisked through Solyss' close-cropped hair. With a shudder from the chill, he pulled his jacket tighter around him. It would be warmer to wait on the ship, but a cool breeze was a nice relief from the hot ones he experienced on Kol.

They were waiting in the clearing of a relatively untouched forest on Ailleroc. Beside him, Zeric paced around. Asheerah and two of her marines stood at the *Chimopori*'s boarding ramp. Hidden by a patch of trees, in another small clearing, Solyss could just make out the lights of the *Durandal II*.

When he had last departed, he did not think he would return to Ailleroc so soon. The nature of their escape during the last raid should have made returning an unacceptably risky move. But he had left people behind before, and now it was time to correct that.

He had genuinely believed that Fracsid and his entire crew had died during the raid, his reassurances to Kard notwithstanding. Hope had been necessary to keep his crewmember going. Now, Solyss wished he had believed in that hope himself. He might have made an effort to save the downed ship and avoided coming back here.

Davidus Brieni had convinced Zeric to allow him to come along on the mission, claiming he would have some contacts and would be able to learn where the prisoners were being kept. In Solyss' mind, Zeric had agreed too quickly to the request. Personally, he still did not completely trust the former

Alliance navy man. His signing on with them on Mirthod felt like too much of a coincidence.

He tried to ignore those suspicions. General Ocaitchi trusted Davidus and that should be good enough for him. The man so far had done nothing suspicious, aside from insisting on meeting his contacts alone—if he were going to betray them, that would be an ideal time.

Having Davidus along also raised uncomfortable questions of who was in charge. The general had clearly placed Zeric in command of the overall mission. Solyss approved of this decision. He trusted Zeric's tactical decisions, and he knew to defer to Solyss with regard to how to handle the squadron. But Davidus outranked Solyss and was also a naval officer. Without any military regulations in place yet, where his authority ended was not clear.

A new set of lights among the trees caught Solyss' attention. Zeric turned and nodded to Asheerah, who directed her marines to fan out to flanking positions around the approaching lights. Solyss resisted the temptation to draw his own pistol, instead straightening his uniform and standing taller.

Beside him, Zeric looked up at him and tried to straighten up some. Solyss was almost a head taller than the other Terran. With Zeric still wearing his old hockey team cap, Solyss thought he made the more impressive figure. Which made sense. As much as he respected Zeric, he was not a Novastar.

The lights moved through the trees into the clearing, revealing two Terran males carrying flashlights. Solyss was relieved to see that one of them was Davidus Brieni. He didn't know the other but assumed him to be Kaars Aerinstar, the turncoat Alliance intelligence officer Delegate Lahkaba had instructed them to meet.

Kaars was the first to speak. "You took a big risk coming here, Colonel. Contacting me almost tipped off the Alliance."

Zeric frowned and said, "The situation requires some risk. What have you two managed to learn?"

"It seems all of this might have been a waste of time," Davidus said, sounding dejected. "The prisoners aren't on Ailleroc."

The revelation worried Solyss. Ailleroc was the most fortified planet in the sector for the Alliance, even discounting their previous raid. If the Alliance did not think the prisoners were secure here, where had they been taken?

Solyss asked that question and got an unexpected response from Kaars: "Sulas."

"Sulas? Why?" Zeric asked.

"Apparently, after the prison break from Olan Detention Center, Governor Howell began construction of an orbital prison for future detainees. It's guarded continuously by a corvette and has no permanently docked shuttles. Once you're on there, there's no way off," Kaars explained.

"None? They have to get prisoners there somehow. What about rotating out guards and supplies?" Solyss asked.

"That's the nasty part," Kaars said grimly. "There are no guards. Periodic delivery shuttles arrive with supplies for the prisoners. These are inspected by the guarding corvette before they are allowed to dock. After the supplies are delivered, they are jettisoned and then blown up by the corvette. Prisoners are delivered the same way. As for taking prisoners off, that won't happen often, I expect."

Davidus' shoulders slumped and he shook his head. "It doesn't look like there's any way to get to them, Colonel. Not without a full-out assault. As soon as Chavatwor finishes bringing those captured frigates back to life, we'll have the firepower to take on a corvette. For now, it's best to wait."

Solyss wanted to argue with Davidus for giving up so easily, but in truth he couldn't find a point to argue. A corvette would tear through their gunboats. It was also likely that the corvette would simply destroy the prison if they attempted a rescue. Having no guards on board gave the Alliance that option.

He looked at Zeric, hoping the man saw a flaw that he didn't, but he was disappointed. With reluctance, he nodded to Davidus. For his part, Davidus looked just as disappointed.

"Major, return to base and report to General Ocaitchi. I'll remain behind with *Durandal* and see if there is anything else I or Kaars can learn before we head back. Maybe we can find out when and where they're to be executed and intercept them then," Davidus ordered. Solyss nodded in reply, not bothering to argue that the mission was still under Zeric's command.

With a nod, Kaars and Davidus turned away and headed back into the dark, toward *Durandal*. Once they were gone, Asheerah and the two marines stepped back into the lights of the ship. The five of them then went aboard, sealing the boarding ramp behind them.

Inside, the rest of the ship's passengers and crew had gathered, eager to learn what had transpired. Solyss was not looking forward to breaking the news to Kard. He would not take it well.

Fortunately, Zeric began explaining the situation. The rest of the marines looked disappointed, but they accepted the news stoically. Isaxo patted Kard on the back comfortingly, but the young Braz shook his head defiantly.

"There has to be a way. Breaking into Olan seemed impossible, but you and General Ocaitchi found a way," Kard said pleadingly to Zeric. "If we're tricky, we can approach and dock and get them off. Isaxo's a great pilot. He can avoid getting us shot down by the corvette."

"I appreciate the confidence, Kard," Isaxo said. "But a corvette is designed specifically to blow up maneuverable ships. Ships more maneuverable than us. And it sounds like they'd just blow up the station and kill everyone onboard if we even tried."

"Commander Brieni is right," Zeric said. "We can wait and try with some more firepower."

An idea started to tickle the back of Solyss' mind. Something Kaars had explained about the way the station was supplied. Then it hit him.

"The corvette is the problem," Solyss said, his excitement building as he spoke. "So we need to take out the corvette."

Zeric raised an eyebrow at him. "Exactly, hence the need for more firepower."

"No, not like that. Kaars said that the supply ship was inspected by the corvette before it docked with the station. You were a ship thief. Can't we sneak aboard that supply ship, then board and steal the corvette?"

A skeptical look crossed Zeric's face but was soon replaced by a wide smile. "Sure, that should be relatively easy. Security probably won't be incredibly high on an automated food transport, especially since the corvette will inspect it."

Turning to Asheerah, he said, "Lieutenant, think your marines can handle overpowering the crew of an entire corvette?"

Asheerah gave him a deadly smile. "Of course, sir."

Solyss felt confidence start to return.

Lahkaba sat uncomfortably, listening to the recording of Admiral Sartori for the second time as it was played to the congress on Irod.

It had been nice getting out of these meetings for a few days while on Kol. Traveling to the *Black Market* and negotiating an alliance with the Fox would have been a grand adventure. He regretted it that Maarkean had gone without him.

But it had been necessary. Based on the reactions from his fellow delegates as Lei-mey played the message, they were going to need a lot of convincing not to cave or go running to the Confederacy. Negotiating with a crime lord probably would end up being easier.

Once the message finished, Lei-mey stood back up. "By now, this message has been heard on all of our worlds. We have a mere twenty days remaining until the proposed election and twenty-one before the execution. We must act quickly to get our message out to ignore these elections and continue to resist. The Alliance cannot get us to surrender so easily."

From the Ailleroc table, the Terran Lionell Mandrake stood up. "I must disagree with your assessment. This body exists under the authority of our legally elected governments. We cannot disrupt the election process. We should all return home and allow democracy to resume. If the new legislatures decide to reconvene this congress, only then should we continue."

Shooting up from her chair, Zoeko Lide from Mirthod glared at Lionell. "New legislatures? The old ones were never dismissed—not legally. If we accept these elections, we're admitting the Alliance has the power to dismiss us. I will not stand for this."

For what seemed the first time, Lahkaba found himself agreeing with the gold Dotran. He knew it would not last long, but he held out hope that this meant they could find common ground.

As expected, Zoeko continued. "Now is the time to take up Lieutenant Commander Prytoker's offer. If we accept now, Confederate warships can be here defending us in as little as four months."

"But at what price?" Lei-mey said, joining the debate. "The Alliance offers us peace in exchange for admitting that we were wrong and bowing to their authority. The Confederacy offers us the chance to exchange one master for another, at the cost of a sector-wide war."

Lahkaba felt the tension in the room begin to mount as each delegate intensified the passion with which they spoke. There was no order to the process, with everyone lashing out, but at least they were taking turns and not trying to talk over each other. Yet.

"The Alliance has offered us an olive branch and a chance for a peaceful resolution," Lionell countered. "I agree this solution is not ideal, but it is better than handing ourselves over the Confederacy."

"I will never support surrendering to the authority of any slimy, dirty snakes," Valinther added coldly.

From her table, Zoeko let out a dangerous hiss. She started to rise again, glaring at Valinther. Lahkaba could feel things beginning to deteriorate. Fortunately, Faide banged his gavel from the central table.

"Order! We will not devolve into bickering and slurs. The Alliance governors may act that way, but that is what we are here to combat," Faide said, speaking sharply, something not common to the mild-mannered Notha.

Sensing that it was now or never, Lahkaba slowly stood up and said quietly, "Mr. Chairman, I request the floor."

All eyes in the room turned toward Lahkaba and then back to Faide. The elder Notha nodded his head and retook his seat. For a moment, Lahkaba said nothing, instead slowly looking around the room at each delegate in turn.

"Why are we here?" he began. "I ask you, seriously. What was our purpose for coming together? Did we do this for personal glory? Because we wanted to see our worlds become part of the Confederacy? Because we thought it would be easy?

"I don't know about you, but I know why I am here. I am here because the Alliance, the government that is supposed to stand for freedom and democracy, has betrayed us. It has locked us up because of what species we are. It has placed restrictions on who we may trade with, so that the corporations that control it are the only ones who benefit. It has threatened any who speak out against it with prison and death.

"We came together in order to speak out. To try to reverse this tragic turn of events. We thought a united voice would get through and remind the Alliance about the principles it stands for. But it didn't listen. Instead of a peaceful protest, it saw rebellion and dissent. So it tried to take away our fundamental rights to elected government.

"At that point we were faced with a choice. Bow down before their power. Or stand up and fight for our rights as people. Our right to choose our own leaders. Our right to not be imprisoned because of our species. Our right to make a living and live our lives. Our right to speak and say what we wish.

"And we chose to stand up. On Enro, we—together— chose to fight. Then we went back to the people we represented and asked if they supported our decision. And they said yes. A tremendous outpouring of public support led to the rapid formation of a military to defend their rights."

Lahkaba paused and took another survey of the room. He was pleased to see Lionell looking slightly ashamed, though Zoeko still glared across the room at Valinther. Those two were not going to play nice any time soon.

"Now, the Alliance has offered to forgive our resistance. In exchange, they ask us to admit that every abuse of power, every curbing of our rights, that they have done is acceptable. Most of us here recognize this offer for the hollow offer it is.

"But some of us want to counter it by turning around and offering up our freedom to another abusive power. The Confederacy may seem like a viable alternative, but things will be just as bad under them.

"We cannot let our personal disagreements stand in the way of why we are here. We are here representing the rights and needs of millions of people. It is up to us to represent them. It is up to us to realize that now is not the time to surrender to the Alliance. Or to offer ourselves up to the Confederacy. Now is the time for us to stand up and strike out on our own."

A mumble of surprise flowed through the room as delegates started to see where Lahkaba was going with his speech. Not wanting to give anyone else a chance to say anything, he hastily continued.

"There may be more people in the Alliance. They may have more money, more ships, and more industry. But we have more resources. We have eight minimally developed worlds. We have a lot of space to grow up in. It's time we declare ourselves free from the Alliance. It is time we declared our independence as a community of planets."

Silence greeted him. It stretched on, and Lahkaba started to think the rest of the delegates were trying to decide if he was insane. No one said anything to support him, but neither did anyone disagree with him.

Finally, after nearly a minute of silence, Owrik spoke. "Can we survive on our own? Won't the Alliance's response become much more severe if it no longer views us as citizens and instead views us as the enemy?"

Lahkaba started to respond but was beaten to it by Valinther. "I would say the Alliance already views us as the enemy. We tried to remind them that we were its citizens, the people they are supposed to protect. But they didn't get the message."

Lahkaba added, "General Ocaitchi is already working on a plan to increase our navy so that we can defend against the Alliance. That was the purpose behind the raid on Ailleroc. He is also working to free our people that have been taken prisoner by the Alliance. General Numba is building up a grand army so that we can, if necessary, force the Alliance to withdraw from our homes. We can do these things. We just need to decide to do them."

Lionell stood up from his seat again, and Lahkaba braced himself to counter the Terran's argument. The people from Ailleroc were the ones most loyal to the Alliance and had been the most resistant to previous rebellious efforts.

"I do not feel that I have the authority to decide this matter for the people of Ailleroc." His tone was mild and quiet. "Only they can decide if they want to completely separate themselves from the Alliance."

Nodding in agreement, Lahkaba said, "You make a good point. So let us use this election the Alliance has called. We will add a question to the ballot. Do you support independence from the Alliance? We will all return home and let them know to vote—not for a replacement government, but to keep the one they previously elected and reject the outsiders who tried to dismiss us."

Several delegates started banging their tables and speaking excitedly. But instead of angry arguments, it was the sound of fervent support.

Chapter 20

Maarkean hated being aboard a ship without being behind the helm controls. Standing on the flight deck of the *Bright Blade*, he watched as Htaretter maneuvered his ship toward the massive form of the *Black Market*. Even though he knew he would never have been allowed to dock if he had flown himself here aboard the *Cutty Sark*, it was still difficult to give up control.

"I appreciate your willingness to do this, Htaretter. You're risking your rights to the ship, maybe even your life," Maarkean said gratefully.

"Any time, General," Htaretter said, bowing his furry head slightly. "I never come here, anyway. Plus, after we win the war, I plan on sticking to a purely legitimate business."

Maarkean smiled. "Of course."

The long, curved shape of the Victory-class battle carrier grew to fill the entire viewport. Htaretter lined the ship up with the port launch deck that ran almost the entire length of the larger ship. As they got closer, Maarkean started to make out the point defense blaster turrets tracking them as they came in for docking.

The threat was clear, but it was also a good sign. The Fox had not neglected maintenance on at least some of the weapons. Compared to an active Alliance carrier, this one would undoubtedly be at a disadvantage. But if the Fox had kept the shields and even half the weapons in good working order, she would still be a threat to every other capital ship.

And that was not counting all of the smaller ships she could carry. The *Defiant Glory*, after the full conversion, could carry a maximum of twenty-four fighters that were about the size of the SSF-19s they had stolen. But that would take up every spare meter. It could only launch and receive twelve quickly, and ideal capacity was around fifteen to eighteen. But the *Black Market* could comfortably carry fifty in each hangar bay. If she stored ships directly on the launch deck, she could move two hundred fighters.

Fortunately, the Alliance never carried so many. The battle carrier at Ailleroc probably had no more than ninety fighters. Of course, that was still almost four times the number his small fleet had access to, and that did not include the escort carriers the Alliance had.

"Once we dock, Gu and I will step outside and wait for the Fox to decide what to do with us," Maarkean said. "If he agrees to meet with us, then the rest of you can go about your task. Gamaly, you think you can get everything on Chavatwor's shopping list?"

Standing behind him, Gamaly nodded her head. "Should be able to find everything here, or at least someone who knows where to pick it up. Might take some time, but it's better if I don't go meet my contacts with strangers in tow." With a look toward Gu'od, she added, "But I would prefer going with you."

A frown crossed Gu'od's face and his antennae began twitching rapidly but remained quiet. Maarkean could follow the gist of what he was communicating with the antennae, but not all of the nuances. Gu'od was clearly not happy that Gamaly had even come on this mission and did not want her put in direct danger confronting the Fox. Gamaly's reply was irritated and defensive, explaining she felt more than capable of doing this.

For everyone else on the flight deck, Gamaly's words hung in the air, unaddressed. They were oblivious to the subtle Liw'kel conversation. Maarkean felt embarrassed, not for the first time, that he could understand even the basics of their private spat.

Hoping his response wouldn't piss Gamaly off too much, or look like he was taking Gu'od's side, Maarkean said, "It would be better if I met the Fox alone. I'm only taking Gu because he refused to stay behind on Kol, and since he's banned, too, I doubt the Fox will just let him wander around and go shopping."

Gamaly frowned again but nodded. Maarkean turned to watch as Htaretter set them down on the *Black Market*'s launch deck. A moment went by before a shudder flowed through the ship as a tractor beam enveloped them. Then, the scene of the open launch deck was replaced by the tight walls of the airlock as the ship was lowered into the docking bay.

Without a word, Maarkean turned and left the flight deck. Unlike the *Cutty Sark*, the *Bright Blade* had only a single deck. Much longer, but narrower, the ship could carry more cargo. Located at the rear of the ship, near the engine room, the crew quarters were separated from the flight deck by the cargo bay.

Maarkean moved through the empty cargo bay and stood beside the starboard loading door. It would be another few minutes before the *Black Market*'s crew lowered them to a free space in the hangar. Gamaly and Gu'od followed him into the bay, and stood a short distance away from him. There was a nervous energy to their stance that he found unusual for them.

Maarkean waited patiently for them to say what they wanted to say. The fact that they had waited until he was away from Htaretter's crew suggested it was something important. After a moment, Gu'od cleared his throat.

"We wanted to let you know that very soon, we will not be able to continue helping you and the rebellion. We will need to step aside," Gu'od said, and then looked at Gamaly before continuing. "We are going to have a baby."

Maarkean let a wide smile spread across his face. He had known about this for a while, just like all of the Liw'kel back at camp knew. Gu'od and Gamaly seemed to forget that he could understand their antennae language. They were so used to non-Liw'kel being oblivious to anything said that way.

"Congratulations!" he declared, extending a hand to Gu'od.

Gu'od gave one of his rare smiles as he shook back. Maarkean then offered a hug to Gamaly, who looked relieved to have it out in the open. The business with all of the Liw'kel women pursuing Gu'od had been odd. The man who had taught Maarkean to understand their language, including the signal for a pregnant woman, had not mentioned that tradition.

"I certainly understand your intention to step back," Maarkean said, returning to a more serious tone. "Family is important. When are you due?"

"Not for several more months," Gamaly answered. "But it will become obvious to non-Liw'kel soon, and I will not be able to keep up physically, either."

"What do you plan to do?" Maarkean asked. He fought the temptation to try to convince Gu'od to remain with them. But he should be with Gamaly during this, not off fighting and possibly dying in a war.

"For the time being, we will remain at Chava's shipyard, helping with training and what else we can. We have become attached to Dr. Istru and wish him to deliver the baby. After that, I do not know. Depends on if we can win before then," Gamaly said, adding a confident smile to the last of her words.

Maarkean nodded. He could think of no better present for his friends' baby than a return to peace. But, in truth, it was far more likely the Alliance would crush them in the next few months. That would restore peace, though.

"I will miss having your counsel," Maarkean said, speaking mainly to Gu'od.

Gu'od inclined his head. "I have enjoyed working with you. Your grasp of the Ni'jar ways has allowed you to find your Focus. You are a completely different man than the one I met a year ago. You know your purpose. There is little more I can teach you."

"I highly doubt that," Maarkean replied with certainty.

They passed the next few minutes in silence. When Htaretter signaled that they were down, they opened the bay door. Maarkean and Gu'od stepped out on the *Black Market*'s deck.

The hangar was alive with activity. Robots and people moved around delivering cargo, spying on each other, and making deals. In all the confusion, Maarkean would have thought it would be easy to overlook him and Gu'od. But he knew better.

It did not take long before four armed guards showed up and surrounded the pair of them.

Maarkean had elected to wear his blue naval uniform, instead of his customary duster. He had also left behind his gun holster, and the blue uniform provided few places to conceal a weapon.

"Maarkean Ocaitchi, Gu'od Dos'redna, you are banned from visiting this ship. You were warned of the consequences before. Your lives are forfeit," said one of the guards, a Notha, holding his rifle steady.

It was a bit more of an extreme stance than he had expected. But Maarkean pressed forward. "We understood the conditions of our banishment. And we do not wish to challenge the Fox's decision. We merely wish to talk to him. If he chooses, we'll turn around and depart. But we hope he will be willing to listen to what we have to say."

"The Fox does not talk to anyone unless he wishes it. You made a mistake coming here," the guard said, his voice flat.

Maarkean was starting to think that things might go poorly when the guard's expression changed. He tilted his head slightly, and his eyes dropped. The guard must have been receiving instructions over a small comm device hidden under his fur, because his attitude changed.

"We've been instructed to escort you to a conference room. We do not guarantee you'll be allowed to return, but the Fox will hear you out," the guard said.

Nodding, Maarkean gestured for the guard to show them the way. He had not really expected any other reaction. The implied threat that they still might be executed seemed unnecessary, though.

The guard led him and Gu'od off the hangar deck and into the main corridors of the ship. They took a lift up a few decks to a much less crowded level. This must be a section of the ship the Fox reserved for private meetings, Maarkean thought.

They were shown into an empty conference room. A round, C-shaped table dominated the room. The opening of the C faced a holographic projector and a set of video monitors.

Maarkean and Gu'od took seats on the outside of the table, and the four guards stepped outside. He was about to ask Gu'od how long he thought they would have to wait when the holoprojector came to life. In the empty center of the table, a three-dimensional projection of an orange-furred creature appeared, sitting in a chair. He recognized the creature as a fox, the persona the man behind the hologram had assumed.

Unless there was a whole unknown species out there that looked exactly like a wild animal from Terra, Maarkean knew that the image was a construction, rather than a direct live holo transmission. Idly, he wondered if this meant the Fox was really a Terran, or used the animal to make people think he was. Either way, it didn't matter.

"Thank you for agreeing to meet with us," Maarkean said, trying to sound polite but not obsequious.

"Normally, I would have just thrown you out an airlock. Though, in truth, no one has done what you did. A few have tried to sneak back aboard. No one has come aboard openly requesting dialogue. I may still have you vented to space to keep anyone else from trying it. But I was curious to learn what you have to say first," the Fox said, the hologram's mouth moving in a perfection reproduction of someone saying the words. It was not a cheap generation.

"Let's hope we can convince you it was worth your time," Maarkean said. "We have come here on behalf of the United Congress of the Kreogh Sector in the hopes of making an alliance with you."

"An alliance? To what purpose?" the Fox asked, clearly intrigued. Or, at least, the animation made it look like he was intrigued.

"We are prepared to offer you a legitimate place within the sector after the conflict with the Alliance is over. You will be able to operate out in the open, free from any trade or legal restrictions. You will be able to fuel and seek maintenance on any world in the sector, without undergoing inspection or submitting to anything but safety-based regulations," Maarkean said, knowing this was the easy part. The Fox showed no obvious reaction, and he continued

"In exchange, we would ask for your assistance in the struggle against the Alliance. We would use the *Black Market* in transport, defensive, and deterrent capacities, not direct offensive missions."

When he finished speaking, the words hung in the air for a moment. The Fox did not move or respond. He started to think there had been a communication glitch and the hologram was frozen. But then the Fox leaned back in his chair, his ears twitching.

"So, you wish to use my ship to fight the Alliance. In exchange, you'll offer me basically what I have now, with the added chance to dock at legitimate shipyards. While I do not dismiss the benefit of that, allowing my ship to be used in a war with the Alliance makes it very likely I won't have a ship available at the conclusion of this war."

"I won't pretend that that is not a possibility. But ships like this one are not easy to destroy. Any battle damage you suffer will be repaired at our expense. When the war is over, this ship will be in pristine condition," Maarkean replied.

"A tempting offer. But I must decline," the Fox said. "I have managed to maintain the ship for several years already in my present circumstances. And my clientele prefer anonymity. Being able to station myself near a populated planet might increase traffic some, and free me from the cat-and-mouse game I have had to play with the Alliance, but it would also drive away most of my business. Even if trade is allowed here, there's nothing stopping the legal authorities from stopping ships once they leave here."

Maarkean took a breath while deciding how to proceed. So far, the Fox appeared intrigued and friendly, even if he had said no. He could press forward and try to sway him, but that might end up annoying the crime lord. And the threat of being airlocked still hung in the air.

But if he had played things safe, Saracasi would have been arrested and executed a long time ago. "I know you agree with our fight against the Alliance. Having this ship on our side will allow us to actually pose a threat to the Alliance fleet. It's that threat, that deterrence, that we need more than actual combat. If the Alliance has to worry about this ship showing up, they'll be less likely to commit their ships. That will allow us to keep most of the fighting on the ground, where we have the numerical advantage."

The Fox paused for a moment, seeming to consider the information, but then shook his head. "No, even that would disrupt my business irrevocably. I am sorry, but the *Black Market* is a trade ship now, not a warship. But you are correct—I do sympathize with your struggle. I will lift my banishment on you and your compatriots. You and all who support you are free to journey here to trade or hide out or even to recruit. But that is as far as I am willing to go."

The last words were delivered with a tone that made it clear the negotiations were over. Maarkean had failed, but he had not had a lot of hope for success. Lahkaba would be disappointed, but at least they would be allowed to trade here. Many of the things on Gamaly's list from Chavatwor would not be easy to find elsewhere.

Bowing his head, Maarkean said, "Thank you. I regret we won't be able to work closer together, but being able to return here for trade will be helpful."

The Fox nodded his head in response and then the projection vanished.

Getting aboard the Alliance cargo ship on their way to stealing the Alliance corvette proved easier than Zeric had expected. Security at the ground processing facility had been light, and they had almost been able to walk right aboard.

It helped that the cargo pod was launched from a public starport and contained no onboard navigation, communication, or environmental systems. Stowaways would have no way to breathe, assuming they wanted to make a one-way trip to an Alliance corvette and then prison.

The lack of air necessitated that all of their strike team wear pressure suits. Asheerah and her entire squad were fully geared in pressurized combat armor. Zeric had never liked combat armor; it restricted movement too much, making the wearer a target. Right now, however, he was wearing a cheap emergency pressure suit, which he was discovering was even less comfortable and flexible than the combat armor would have been.

They had elected to bring everyone from the *Chimopori* on this raid, which made the cargo pod rather cramped.

Lacking sensors or information of any kind, Zeric had no idea how close they were to docking with the corvette. He checked the time and guessed that they should be getting close. Or he might just be getting impatient.

Struggling to move in the inflated pressure suit, Zeric floated in the zero-gravity ship over to Asheerah. She stood by the door, locked to the floor by magnetic boots, her custom helmet obscuring her face and making her head look huge as it provided room above her head for her antennae. The rest of her team had equally misshapen armor that conformed to their physiology. By comparison, Zeric's helmet was just an inflated bubble, designed to accommodate any species who wore it.

Activating the suit's short-range comm unit, Zeric linked up with Asheerah and Solyss. "Okay, we'll be docking soon. Lieutenant, you'll take one fire team aft and head toward engineering. I'll take the other and seize the bridge. Major, you and Isaxo will come with me. Keep weapons set to stun."

"Sir, stun is an inferior setting. It does not always put someone down and can be easily dispersed," Asheerah responded, her voice frustrated.

For the first time, Zeric started to really appreciate the differences between Asheerah and Gamaly. The two Liw'kel women were fierce fighters, and the interest they both expressed in Gu'od made them seem similar. But in most cases, Gamaly would be the one telling him to use stun. She was tough, but she was no bloodthirsty killer. Asheerah, on the other hand, did not seem to have the same moral resistance to killing.

"Doesn't matter, Marine," Zeric said, trying to make his voice firm. He didn't want there to be any ambiguity on this point. "We kill only when we have to. We are not thugs; we're marines. We use stun until stun proves ineffective. Is that understood?"

"Yes, sir," Asheerah said, a note of defiance still in her tone.

Zeric wished he could see the woman's face. His own expression was there for the world to see through his clear helmet bubble. Beside him, Solyss frowned slightly, but at what Zeric wasn't sure.

Pushing the issue would be pointless right now. Asheerah had agreed. He just had to hope she meant it. He had to assume she would follow orders until she didn't.

A shudder moved through the deck of the cargo pod, distracting Zeric. One of the few systems the cargo pod had were inertial dampeners, those being cheaper than the hassle of carefully packing the container. The dampeners prevented all sense of movement but would not mask the physical vibrations of the ship coming into contact with something. In this case, the impact meant they had docked with the corvette.

Everyone inside stood up, the artificial gravity field from the corvette now enveloping them. Isaxo and Kard fumbled slightly in their awkward suits, just as Zeric had. The armored marines took up flanking positions around the door. Whomever opened the door would be met with a concentrated barrage.

Minutes went by, making Zeric want to fidget. The approach had been boring but unexciting for him. During the trip there was nothing he could do to help or hinder their progress. But now, his planning could end up getting all of these people killed. Now, it was up to him to prevent that from happening.

After an eternity of waiting, the cargo door started to lower. Light and air rushed into the ship. The sudden surge of air rocked Zeric. Behind him, Isaxo stumbled and fell under the wind. Fortunately, the sound of the wind covered any noise the Notha made collapsing.

When the door finished lowering, Zeric saw a team of four backlit by the light inside the corvette's cargo bay. He didn't get a good look at them before Asheerah's team unleashed a barrage of stun bolts. The four Alliance crewmen collapsed where they had been standing.

Within a second of the Alliance personnel dropping, the armored marines surged forward into the corvette. The cargo bay they had docked with was not much bigger than the cargo pod itself. The room had only one exit, and the marines took up position leading forward, just like they had aboard the cargo pod.

Zeric followed them, stepping over the collapsed crewmen. Curiously, none of the crew had been armed. With luck, that meant this ship was not ready for intruders. But Zeric didn't expect his luck to hold out that long.

As soon as everyone was off the cargo pod, Zeric started to strip off his environmental suit. It would be a hindrance in battle, and they would need to use them to get Fracsid and his crew off the prison station. They had a few spares, but not many.

"All right, Marines, let's go," Zeric said, glad to be free of the suit.

Asheerah triggered the door and then led four marines out the door. No sounds of gun fire followed them and Zeric breathed a sigh of relief. They might make it off this deck without running into more trouble.

He led the second team through the area, heading in the opposite direction as Asheerah's team. One of the marines, a Camari named Sergeant Yuly, edged in front of him. Zeric understood the impact that a commander leading a charge into battle could have on morale. But he was just as happy to not be in front. Yuly was wearing armor, after all.

After only about a dozen meters, the corridor ended in a set of stairs leading down. They passed two sealed doors that indicated they led to one of the ship's weapon batteries. The corvette was essentially a cylindrical hexagon, and they had docked on the dorsal face of the hexagon.

Zeric had never been aboard a corvette of this class, but the design was simple enough that he had a good idea of where to go. The stairs should lead down into the top of three main decks. Another small cargo and maintenance deck would be on the ventral surface, giving the ship five decks. Their destination was the ship's bridge, most likely located on the middle deck toward the ship's center.

Yuly led them down the narrow stairs and into a slightly wider corridor. A short way down, Zeric saw an intersection and several more doors leading off. Fortune remained with them, as the stairs continued down to the next deck. He had been worried they might have to go search for the next access point.

Continuing down, they encountered the crew. Two Terrans froze as Yuly and Zeric came to the middle landing. Remembering what had happened the last time he had hesitated to fire while attempting to steal a ship, he immediately fired his rifle at them. His first shot missed, but the second connected, dropping one of the crew. Yuly dropped the second.

The sounds of the shots would undoubtedly carry down the ship's corridors, so Zeric picked up the pace. He dashed down the corridor, passing the unconscious crew, and came to a four-way intersection. The path to his right was empty, but he caught a glimpse of a figure disappearing around a bend to the left.

"Sergeant, we have a bogie escaping. Two marines pursue and detain," Zeric ordered. "The rest of you, we continue to the bridge."

Yuly nodded his armored helmet and then gestured to two of the other marines, who ran down the corridor. Zeric continued running, hoping the bridge was located where he thought. It was possible the ship's control center was behind them, but that would place it toward the more vulnerable bow of the ship.

Zeric was the first to reach the bulkhead at the end of the corridor. Two branches spun off, and he chose to go left, to the ship's starboard side. Unlike the previous passage, this corridor curved. He went only a short distance before finding a door to his right labeled 'Bridge.'

With a sigh of relief, Zeric paused to allow the rest of the team to catch up. As he did, he examined the door. The activation switch for the door contained a card reader, which was not unexpected. He cursed himself for not having checked the crew they had already taken out for access cards, but he was saved when Solyss came running up holding one.

This next step would be where the marines' armor might become a hindrance. The ship's bridge was likely to be small, and the armor made the marines quite bulky. Once they got inside, they would not be able to maneuver well. Zeric and Solyss could dive for cover. The armored marines would only be able to manage a controlled fall.

Giving a nod to Solyss, Zeric readied himself for the confrontation. Solyss slid the access card and the bridge's door slid open. Yuly and another marine advanced first. The last would remain in the corridor to cover them. Zeric followed behind the marines, leaving Solyss and Isaxo to bring up the rear.

The bridge was a circular room with a tactical display at its center. There were three banks of control terminals around the room's perimeter, each manned by one or two crew. A Braz figure stood tall at the central tactical display. The marines started shouting at everyone to put their hands up, and the crew looked at the Braz for instructions.

Zeric strode in, aiming his rifle at the Braz. "Your ship has been commandeered by the United Worlds of the Kreogh Sector. Surrender and none of your crew will be harmed."

"I don't surrender to rebels," the Braz sneered and then dove toward the tactical display.

Zeric fired his rifle and saw the stun bolt impact the Braz. The blast dispersed over the officer's uniform. He had apparently opted to line his personal uniform with a stun-dampening material.

The two marines kept their guns aimed at the crew, trying to keep them from following their commander's act of defiance. Zeric cursed and switched his rifle from stun to full power.

While he did so, the officer activated a switch on the display and opened his mouth to speak. But he didn't even get out one word before Solyss came into the room and fired his pistol three times. The last shot hit the Braz in the chest. Clearly, Solyss' weapon was already set to full power. The captain's finger came off the button—a transmitter, presumably—and he collapsed to the floor.

Zeric turned to look at Solyss, impressed. He had judged the other man to be a little soft—definitely committed to the rebellion, but only so long as he fought from aboard his ship. It turned out his fancy suits and prim nature hid a capable fighter.

The rest of the Alliance crew raised their hands above their heads after the officer fell. None of them were armed, so Zeric decided to not stun them. Carrying unconscious bodies was difficult and time-consuming.

"Sergeant, contact Asheerah and find out her team's status," Zeric ordered. He then looked over the bridge's control terminals.

It took him a moment, but he soon found the damage control station. The terminal showed the status of each section of the ship. It was designed to be used to coordinate repairs and to quickly seal off areas of the ship that had been exposed to space.

"LT reports she has secured the engine room," Yuly said.

"Good, let her know we're about to begin clean-up operations," Zeric said.

He then activated the damage control terminal and started sealing off each section of the ship. It would be possible for the corvette's crew to eventually bypass his control and open up each section. But he didn't plan on giving them that much time.

Chapter 21

Solyss had thought he would feel more regret after killing someone. Despite participating in ground assaults in the past, he had never taken anyone down before. He had never been a very good shot, either, so he was surprised when one of his blasts did hit the man.

Yet, he did not feel guilty. The man he'd killed had been an enemy. Shooting him had been necessary. He didn't feel satisfied for doing it. He only felt numb.

The Alliance personnel had already been escorted off the bridge by the marines, leaving Solyss there with just Kard, Zeric, and Isaxo. Now they faced the difficult task of learning to operate an Alliance corvette without any experience. Until now, he had assumed it would be simple.

"Well, this is supposed to be the helm," Isaxo said from one of the computer terminals. "But the controls don't look right."

"That's because it's not a light transport," Zeric said with a grin. "The bigger the ship, the more complicated the controls. You'd think it would get easier, because big ships are slow and less maneuverable. But they're also more massive. Didn't you fly the *Defiant Glory* out the last time we escaped Sulas with a bunch of prisoners?"

Isaxo shook his head. "No, that was Ceno. I manned Ops."

"Oh," Zeric said. "I could have sworn that was you."

"It can't be that different," Isaxo said, turning back to the controls.

Solyss did not envy the Notha his task, but despite the differences, the basic concepts in navigation would still be the same. Solyss and Kard, who would be learning the other controls, would not have it as easy. The user interface for the military controls was drastically different than it was for their civilian counterparts.

"Okay, first we need to find the controls for that cargo pod so we can get the marines over there and rescue the prisoners," Zeric said.

"I think that's here," Kard said from a terminal in the same bank as Isaxo's.

After inspecting the controls, Zeric took a seat at the terminal and called down for Asheerah to load two marines into the cargo pod for their insertion. Sergeant Yuly would lead them. The rest of the strike force would remain on the corvette, guarding the Alliance captives.

Solyss turned away, leaving that operation for Zeric to deal with. He and Kard still needed to learn the rest of the ship's controls.

They spent the next half hour studying each system and learning where things were. They discovered that if they ran into any trouble, they might have problems controlling the ship. It was designed to be run by a standard shift of about ten crew, with battle stations for more than thirty.

When Zeric announced that the cargo pod had docked with the prison, Solyss stopped to listen. He glanced at Kard, who wore an anxious expression. They would finally learn if all of this had been for nothing.

"Colonel, we have a secure seal," Yuly's voice said over his combat suit's comm. "There are several people waiting for us. Wait one."

Silence filled the comm line. The sergeant had not sounded worried, which suggested the people he had seen were friendlies, rather than an unexpected contingent of Alliance guards. The silence dragged on for a seemingly unrelenting period before Yuly spoke again.

"We have found Lieutenant Relis, his crew, and marines from 2nd Platoon. There is also Jairyd Kil'dare and two dozen other prisoners here. Please advise."

From the pod controls, Solyss heard Zeric swear before turning around to face him. "I was afraid of this. That's going to require at least three round trips between the prison and the corvette. What do you think?"

Solyss nodded. The cargo pod might be able to fit more than that, but they had only acquired enough pressure suits to move thirteen people. They had assumed that the Alliance was only confining confirmed rebels here, not regular prisoners.

Moving people back and forth would take a significant amount of time. In theory, the corvette should be the only ship assigned to monitor the prison station. But that wouldn't stop other Alliance ships in orbit from noticing the unusual activity.

Shaking his head, Solyss made up his mind. "That doesn't matter. You and General Ocaitchi showed us that we can't leave people behind in an Alliance prison. We get everyone, or we get no one. I'm willing to risk it, and I believe my crew is as well."

Zeric frowned at his words, but Solyss assumed it was just modesty. He knew Isaxo, who had been in one of the prisons in Olan, would not wish to see others remain captives just so he could get away. It was considerate of Zeric to worry about risking the rest of their lives. It was a sign of a good commander.

With a sigh, which Solyss assumed indicated relief that the others would support his decision, Zeric said into the comm, "Sergeant, get as many people as you can over here as fast as possible. Asheerah, I assume you've been listening?"

"Yes."

"Okay, this ship is bound to have emergency pressure suits aboard. Find as many as you can and bring them down to the cargo docking port. Let's try to do this in two loads instead of three."

Finding the necessary pressure suits proved simple, making Solyss wonder why he had not done this before. In every section of the ship, emergency stations contained pressure suits, fire extinguishers, ration packs, and medical gear. The Alliance did not spare any expense in properly outfitting their warships.

By the time the cargo pod had re-docked, Asheerah was able to deliver more than enough of them to the pod. Zeric re-launched as soon as everyone was off, cutting their turnaround time to only ten minutes. But it still had been over an hour since they had seized control of the corvette.

Solyss continued to study the corvette's controls, and when one of the terminals started beeping, he was able to tell right away that it came from the communication system. Since all of their communication with the cargo pod was being done via their personal comm gear, he got a sinking feeling as he realized that the corvette itself was being hailed. The call could be anything from a routine update to an Alliance strike force demanding their surrender.

Stepping up to the comm terminal, Solyss looked for the recipient information. His shoulders tightened slightly as he read the ID code as belonging to the Alliance corvette *Dagger*. He relayed this information to Zeric, who cursed.

"Well, you need to answer it. Find out what they want. Pretend to be a clueless comm tech," Zeric said.

Solyss nodded nervously. Lying had never been one of his best skills, but Zeric was in the middle of piloting the cargo pod back to the prison station and could not take over, so it was up to him. With a gulp, he picked up the headset and opened the channel.

"This is *Gallant*, we read you."

"*Gallant, Dagger* actual requests to speak to *Gallant* actual."

Solyss frowned. Despite the formation of their rebel military, he was still not very well versed in military lingo. Any training they had done had focused on combat tactics more than anything else. He relayed the message to Zeric, who cursed again.

"That means their captain wants to speak to ours. I'm pretty sure he's dead now."

"So what do I tell them? I can't pretend to be him, they might know each other," Solyss said. Deception was not his style.

"Tell him to wait one and you'll put the request through."

Repeating that message over the comm, Solyss racked his brain for a strategy. They could try to delay the other ship for only so long. He just had to hope the commander of the *Dagger* was patient.

After far too short a time, the comm panel beeped again. Solyss responded quicker this time, hoping his promptness would alleviate some suspicion. "*Dagger, Gallant* actual is unavailable at present. Can I take a message?"

The response sounded inappropriate as he said it, but he wasn't sure of how else to delay. The comm operator replied, "*Gallant, Dagger* actual requests to know why the cargo pod was allowed to return to *Gallant* after docking at Prison Station 01 and why it is returning there."

"Umm . . . there was a mix up during the inspection, and cargo accidently got left aboard."

A new voice came on to the comm, this one more commanding. "*Gallant*, authenticate ID code AG-9745-K."

"Oh, crap," Solyss said, which was more of a curse than he normally would allow himself to use. He turned to Zeric. "Colonel, we have a problem. They are requesting us to authenticate an ID code."

Zeric, never circumspect about cursing, let out one of the worst ones Solyss had ever heard him use. "That means we're done for. They suspect something's wrong."

"How long until the cargo pod gets back?" Solyss asked.

"At least half an hour. They just docked and they need to get twenty-plus civilians into the pressure suits and then back here," Zeric growled.

Solyss turned to Kard, who was the closest to the sensor station. The Braz brought up a holographic tactical picture on the central table. On it, the other Alliance corvette was highlighted. Its projected orbit was already starting to shift.

"Well, it looks like we have to fight," Solyss said somberly. "What are your orders, Colonel?"

Zeric shook his head emphatically. "We've been here before, Major. Space combat is your area. I can steal a ship, but I don't know the first thing about fighting with them. You've done some tactical training with Maark and Davidus, haven't you?"

Solyss nodded, and Zeric continued, "Well, then the ship is yours, Major. Err . . . Captain."

Taking a deep breath, Solyss tried to recall some of the combat scenarios he had run through with General Ocaitchi and Commander Brieni. Most had been about fighter squadron tactics. Solyss' gunboat squadron was not used much differently than standard star fighters. Most details involving capital ships had dealt with how to take them down, not how to fight with them.

He would just have to think about this like it was a fight between gunships. Corvettes were bigger, but not on the scale of cruisers or carriers. It would just be a more complicated gunship fight.

"Okay," Solyss began, trying to summon his usual confidence. "Isaxo, position us between the *Dagger* and the station. Kard, bring our shields up and then monitor the operations console. Asheerah, I need you and as many marines as you can spare from guard duty up here ASAP."

As his crew acknowledged his orders, Solyss turned back to the comm terminal. He wasn't good at lying, but he decided he should continue to try it. The longer he could postpone open hostilities, the better.

"*Dagger*, we are experiencing some comm malfunctions. Please repeat your last transmission," Solyss said as calmly as he could manage. He fell back on the old trick of periodically taking his finger off the transmit key to simulate a broken comm system.

"*Gallant*, you are hereby ordered to report to Ciread Starport for maintenance. We will take over guard of Prison Station 01, effective immediately."

"Acknowledged, *Dagger*. Pleased stand by while I inform the captain," Solyss said, continuing to interrupt the transmission.

Solyss stepped away from the comm terminal and to the central tactical display. Some of the functions were useless now after having shot them, but the main display still functioned. He zoomed in on the approaching *Dagger* and the estimated time to interception. It was way below Zeric's best guess for getting the cargo pod back.

He tried to switch the terminal to display technical specifications about corvettes, but this failed to function. Turning, he asked Kard, "What can you tell me about our defenses?"

Kard studied his displays and said, "We have two Mark II Neutron Blaster Cannons, two batteries of three PKI-78 Plasma Beam Turrets, and two batteries of three MKPD Flak Turrets. We're protected by a shield with an SER of 100."

The armament was impressive, even if he didn't quite understand all of that. He knew that MKPD stood for Mass Kinetic Point-Defense. These turrets were the corvette's best anti-fighter weapons. Shields were less effective in preventing kinetic damage from projectiles. Capital ships, with more powerful engines and power cores, could afford to equip heavy armor that helped to balance that out. But fighters were designed to be light and easily maneuverable.

Plasma beams were excellent for shooting down missiles and were still effective against close-range fighters. Their beams tended to dissipate over long distances, more so here in the relatively low orbit of the prison station. But they were still deadly weapons.

The two neutron blasters gave the ship its best punch. Most neutron blasters were simply abbreviated to the generic blaster, even though some were based on different technology. There was little difference between those weapons and the pistol at his side, aside from the power scale.

The shields provided slightly more of a relief. He did not fully understand what determined a shield's SER—Shield Effectiveness Rating—but he knew that bigger was better. A rating of 100 was double that of the *Chimopori*'s upgraded shields. He hoped that translated to a lot more protection.

"If I remember correctly, the weapons are dispersed around the hull, split to give 360-degree coverage?" Solyss asked.

Kard nodded. "Yeah, looks that way. Each set of weapons is set so that they each have almost 180-degree firing arcs. We can fire all weapons together along a forward arc, and about half at a time on any other arc."

As Solyss digested this information, Asheerah and two marines came onto the bridge. He directed them toward the weapon consoles and filled them in on the situation. He also ordered Kard to raise their shields and charge the weapons. It would be a clear sign to the *Dagger*, but that bridge had already been burned.

By the time he was done, the tactical display showed *Dagger* starting to edge into weapons range. Of course, since they had been flying a stationary orbit, they had been in weapons range for quite a while, but now they were at a point where, should the *Dagger* fire, the ship might not have enough time to maneuver out of the way.

"*Gallant*, this is *Dagger*. You are ordered to lower your shield and move away from Prison Station 01 immediately. You will not be given another warning," the comm in Solyss' ear said.

"Okay, people, they're about to get angry. Get ready," Solyss said. "Colonel, what's the cargo pod's status?"

"Yuly reports they're loading the last of the prisoners aboard now. Should be ready to go in one minute," Zeric said tensely.

"Isaxo, once they launch, do whatever you have to to keep us between the *Dagger* and that cargo pod. They have no shields and limited maneuverability," Solyss ordered.

Isaxo nodded, stretching his arms at the helm controls. His tail flicked nervously out of the left side of his chair. If they made it through this, he would need to have a Notha-appropriate chair installed.

"They're firing!" Asheerah announced from the weapons console. Solyss turned back toward tactical display, watching as the blaster bolts traveled across the space between them.

"Evasive maneuvers!" Solyss ordered just before Isaxo started shifting their orbit. The RCS thrusters were not powerful enough to move them quickly, and one of the two blasts hit the *Gallant* along the port aft section.

"Shields holding. Dorsal field at 95% effectiveness," Kard reported.

"They're firing again. But not at us," Asheerah added.

"Sax!" Solyss said, as Isaxo once again shifted the ship. This time, he maneuvered them into the path of the incoming blaster fire.

"Dorsal shields down to 86%. Reading minimal armor damage."

"Rotate us on our axis, try to keep a different shield facing to them," Solyss ordered. "Ash, fire whatever batteries have line of sight."

Asheerah growled a response as a smile spread across her face. She still wore most of her armor, but had removed the gloves and helmet in order to work the weapons console. Shooting was one of her favorite pastimes, and the bigger the gun, the better.

Blasts started traveling across the tactical display toward the *Dagger* in exchange for the ones coming toward them. Solyss' biggest hope was that the other corvette would stop accelerating toward them in order to maneuver away from the attack. Any delay they could cause might give them the time they needed.

The fact that corvettes were made primarily to attack fighters worked both in their favor and against them. Neither ship was a huge threat to the other, which meant that, unfortunately, the *Dagger* had little incentive to change course. And since Solyss needed to protect the cargo pod, something the *Dagger* would be very good at destroying, he was at a disadvantage.

"Rotation is helping," Kard said. "Each shield facing is weakened to about 80%, but the *Dagger*'s bow shields are at 60%."

"Concentrate fire on their dorsal main neutron blaster," Solyss said. "If they are going to come straight at us, let's try to do some damage."

Asheerah acknowledged, and the random fire from the marines shifted to focus on the *Dagger*'s dorsal section. As long as the corvette continued approaching bow first, their shields would deteriorate more quickly than the *Gallant*'s.

"The cargo pod is getting close. We need to stop rotation so I can pull them in," Zeric said.

"Halt rotation, Isaxo. Transfer all shield regeneration energy to port."

Solyss watched as the cargo pod slowed and started to line up with the *Gallant*'s starboard cargo port. Their port shields started to weaken more quickly, but so were the *Dagger*'s.

The next minute, everything happened at once.

"We just lost our number two Flak battery!" one of the marines called.

"We've got the cargo pod!" Zeric whooped.

"Shields below 50%!" Kard said and then cheered. "The *Dagger*'s dorsal neutron blaster has stopped firing! It looks to be disabled."

"Isaxo, fire main engines, get that station between us and the *Dagger*!" Solyss ordered.

The *Gallant* started moving from its orbit for the first time in the engagement. Isaxo pushed the ship away from Sulas, angling to swing underneath the prison station. He then changed vectors again, heading on a parallel course to the *Dagger*, with the station between them.

"Ash, retarget that station. Let's not give the Alliance the chance to put anyone else onboard."

The *Gallant*'s guns started firing again, blasting through the prison station. With no shields, thin support structure and no power plant beyond solar arrays, the weapons fire made quick work of decimating the station. It started to disintegrate rapidly, becoming a giant ball of debris that would be a danger to the pursuing *Dagger*.

Solyss leaned back toward the comm station, and began transmitting on a broad frequency. "People of Sulas, twice now the Alliance has imprisoned your citizens without cause. And now, both times, General Ocaitchi and Colonel Dustlighter have freed them. Never again should you allow this to happen. The first time cost the Alliance a few guards. This time, we've taken one of their warships. If they attempt to do this again, take more than that from them. Show that the blood we've shed freeing your people is not in vain."

CHAPTER 22

Wandering aimlessly though the corridors of the *Black Market*, Maarkean found himself standing before the doors to the Ready Room. The converted bar had once been where he would meet with his old employer, Josserand Renard. He had hated coming here. He hated Josserand; working for him had never been pleasant, and he had only done so when desperate.

Also, the room had always reminded him of his past. Ready rooms on other Alliance carriers had been homes-away-from-home for him. Coming here had reminded him of what he had lost when he had rescued Saracasi and fled from Braz.

This time was different. He went inside the small bar and felt no regret.

As Maarkean entered the Ready Room, he saw Josserand's old table sitting empty as if it were still reserved for him. Josserand had been banned from the *Black Market* the same time Maarkean had, and it was doubtful the Fox had lifted that ban as well. Either it was a coincidence, or Josserand still had some influence among the ship's residents.

Hanging above the table was a twenty-year-old picture. In it stood a group of young and eager Alliance pilots, freshly graduated from flight school. They were arrogant about their abilities and ready to take on the Confederacy. More than half of them were now dead.

Among the few in the picture who still lived was Maarkean. He had been a completely different person then, unwaveringly faithful to the Alliance. The war had dulled his spirits as he had watched his friends die, but it had not dulled his patriotism. That had faded slowly over the years.

The last time he had been here, the picture had annoyed him, which was undoubtedly why Josserand had chosen to hang it here. Then, he had still held a tenuous faith in the Alliance. Now, he had a new goal in life: to oppose the Alliance.

Taking a seat at the table, Maarkean placed an order for soup from one of the bar's waiters. The soup arrived quickly, and he started eating. Almost as soon as he did so, a Terran male approached him and sat down. The man had dark brown skin and some grey streaks in his black hair. He was just large enough to not appear weak, without being mistaken for a brainless brawny thug. His moderate, but not lavish, suit added to that impression.

After taking a bite, Maarkean looked up at the man. "Can I help you?"

"I never expected to see you here again," the man said.

Raising a hairless eyebrow, Maarkean asked, "Do we know each other?"

The man gave him a wide smile. "No. I'm Kueth Kahl-Amar. We have a mutual friend. He left about the same time as you did."

"Last I heard, all of his friends were supposed to go with him," Maarkean said, mentally cursing himself.

He had decided to tour the *Black Market* while Gamaly and Htaretter went about trying to acquire the items Chavatwor and Zeric had requested. With Josserand kicked off the ship, he had assumed it would be safe for him to do so alone. Apparently, some of Josserand's minions had managed to stay behind.

Kueth shrugged. "The Fox isn't as thorough as he once was. He's gotten rather lax and risk-averse in his old age. As I believed you discovered when he turned down the opportunity to ally with you and the new Union."

Leaning forward, Kueth lowered his tone slightly. "That is a trait our mutual friend doesn't share. He fully understands the potential value of a good relationship with the Union."

Maarkean frowned. That hadn't been the direction he had thought this conversation would take. His last interactions with Josserand had not been friendly, and then Maarkean had turned the bounty hunter Josserand had sent after him into a rebel. Josserand couldn't have been happy about that.

"Based on the last message our friend sent me, I somehow doubt that," Maarkean said forcefully.

"You mean the bounty?" Kueth said dismissively. "That has already been rescinded. It was a mistake which our friend admits. He also regrets trying to steal your ship. But, based on the upgrades you've had done to her, can you blame him? She was supposed to make a nice addition to his others."

The note about other ships piqued Maarkean's interest. He had wondered why Josserand had always been so interested in his ship. It seemed he had been interested in a lot of ships, rather than the *Cutty Sark* in particular.

"Riiiiiight," Maarkean said skeptically.

"I don't expect you to believe me. I am only here to deliver a message. Come to a meeting with our friend and see for yourself."

"So instead of getting captured by a bounty hunter, he expects me to just hand myself over to him?" Maarkean said, amused. "Why exactly would I do that?"

Kueth smiled. "Because if you do, our friend will give you the opportunity to gain control of this ship and a full complement of star fighters to go with her."

The offer left Maarkean momentarily speechless. Kueth's very presence onboard the *Black Market* suggested that Josserand still had some power here. Did he have enough power to sway the Fox to reconsider? Since he was still banned, Maarkean doubted that. But was he powerful enough to take the ship for himself?

That possibility alarmed him. That the *Black Market* was in the hands of a civilian was bad enough. In the hands of Josserand, it would be scary. But if he could gain control of the ship for the Union navy, that would be ten times better than an alliance with the Fox ever would have been.

"I don't expect you to decide now," Kueth said, standing up. "If you would like to pursue this opportunity, meet our friend at these coordinates. Bring as many marines and ships as you need to feel comfortable. I promise this meeting will remain civil."

Kueth set a datapad down on the table. He then picked up the check that the waiter had left, put down the necessary amount of credits, and left the bar.

The crowd was agitated. The local meeting hall in Lahkaba's hometown of Chuthor, Sulas, was filled to the brim. An electric tension filled the air amongst his constituents.

Lahkaba had participated in a number of open town hall meetings since becoming a politician. Most had been mild affairs. Even though he had campaigned against Alliance policies, he hadn't taken any really controversial positions. Pushing for the inmates at Olan Detention Center to get independent reviews wasn't very controversial, even among Sulas' most loyal Alliance citizens.

This time, things were a bit different. Some of his most hardcore supporters were looking cautiously at the issue of independence. And the vocal Alliance loyalists were being especially vocal.

"Now, I'm not a fan of the Alliance's harsh restrictions, especially disbanding the legislature," a Terran man said. "But declaring independence feels a little extreme. We haven't tried to work things out."

"Tried to work things out? They imprisoned my son for five years without trial!" a dark-yellow-carapaced Ronid woman exclaimed from across the room. Several others in the room nodded or cheered in support of the woman.

"I'll admit the Alliance was a little over-vigilant in its detention policies, but your son must have done something suspicious," a middle-aged Braz male said. "They only had our best intentions at heart. Olan was there to keep us all safe. That is its entire purpose."

The Ronid woman looked furious, her mandibles coming together to form a point and her antennae quivering slightly. Several others in the crowd, most of them non-Terran or Braz, glared as well, and Lahkaba sensed the tension in the room creep up. Most people had been very happy to see Olan shut down.

"Hold on a second," the first Terran man said defensively. "Our Braz friend here may be overstating the Alliance's benevolence somewhat. But he's right about one thing. The Alliance fleet is the only thing standing between us and being overrun by the Confederacy!"

Several people, a few of them who had supported the Ronid woman, voiced their agreement with the man. An elderly Terran woman spoke up from the back of the room, her voice slightly hysterical.

"And from the Kravic! If it weren't for the Alliance fleet in the Trepon sector fighting back the Kravic, they would have taken us all as slaves again. That's why the Confederates ended the war, so they could join the Alliance and fight the real enemy. If we secede, we'll be vulnerable! They've already scouted us out. Check any report from a tracking station and you'll see their ghost ships!"

Lahkaba sighed. *Why did these meetings always bring out the crazies?*

The Kravic had vanished several hundred years ago, but there were still nutcases who regularly claimed that they had been kidnapped by their ghost ships and that the government was covering up a shadow war with them. Fortunately, the woman served as a distraction to the growing tension. Many people were shaking their heads in disbelief at the woman and had stopped staring angrily at the Braz man, though he still looked defiant.

Taking advantage of the momentary lull, Lahkaba stood up and gestured for everyone's attention. The room quieted down slowly as everyone sat back down. He had not said much during this meeting. After sharing the Sector Congress' proposal for independence with his constituents, he had opened the floor to hear their thoughts. Now, he knew how hard it would be to convince them.

"I know this idea of independence sounds scary. We were an independent world once, and it didn't end well. People came from all of the homeworlds to settle here. There were conflicts between them. Eventually, they all turned to their homeworlds to bring bigger powers into the sector to fight over who would control us. And the Alliance won.

"I will be the first to say that this was far preferable to the Confederacy winning. While the Alliance has lost its way and forgotten what freedom and democracy mean, the Confederacy never knew. So, even though I initially fought on the Confederate side, I was grateful they lost the war."

Pausing, Lahkaba looked over the room. There were several other Kowwoks here. They were his strongest supporters. But he was relieved to see the few Dotran nodding in agreement, too. Those few who still lived on Sulas had come to believe in democracy, he thought.

"But even though the Alliance is better than the Confederacy, that doesn't mean I can live under the Alliance's rule. We do not have just two choices before us. Together, we control our own destiny. It does not have to be Alliance or Confederacy. We can stand up and make our own decisions.

"In collaboration with the other planets in the sector, we are strong enough to defend ourselves. The reason the Alliance and the Confederacy want to rule us so badly is because of the resources we have on our unspoiled worlds. The homeworlds have nearly depleted theirs. They are crowded. And their closest colonies are not as pleasant to live on as Sulas is.

"The Alliance has lost its way, and it has lost my support. I have faith in you and your ability to form a just society on your own. A society that will welcome everyone, regardless of species. We can form a true, free democracy."

Around him, many of the people were nodding in agreement, but not as many as he would have liked. Some, like the Braz, would probably never be swayed. They were Alliance loyalists. Others looked like they agreed with him, but they also looked scared.

Disagreeing with the Alliance, voicing disagreement, even rebelling were all things most people supported. But truly taking that final step and cutting the cord with the Alliance—that was harder. Everyone knew how powerful the Alliance was, and the Terran had spoken everyone's worse fears. Could they defeat the might of the Alliance? And if they did, what would happen next?

As if in response to Lahkaba's thoughts, a young Kowwok came into the meeting hall. Lahkaba recognized him as one of volunteers who had worked on his campaign. The boy's name escaped him and he tried to think of it as the boy moved to the front of the room.

"Mr. Lahkaba?" the Kowwok boy asked. "I just saw a news feed I think you'll want to see. It's very important."

Frowning, Lahkaba studied the boy. He didn't like the idea of being ambushed with new information in the middle of a town meeting. It could be worthless trash that just distracted everyone. Even if it were important, he would prefer to have time to digest whatever it was.

After a moment, though, he gave the boy a nod. Even though he couldn't remember his name, he remembered the enthusiasm the boy had had during the campaign. He decided he owed the boy his trust, on this at least.

Moving over the wall display monitor that was currently off, the boy activated it and brought up the planetary network. He quickly navigated to one of the major news sites and brought up a news bulletin. The monitor began displaying a video of a local news anchor.

"Breaking news this hour. Chuthor News 1 has just intercepted a broadcast from planetary orbit. Let's listen."

The video changed to show a dark-skinned male Terran that Lahkaba immediately recognized as Solyss Novastar.

"People of Sulas, twice now the Alliance has imprisoned your citizens without cause. And now, both times, General Ocaitchi and Colonel Dustlighter have freed them. Never again should you allow this to happen. The first time cost the Alliance a few guards. This time, we've taken one of their warships. If they attempt to do this again, take more than that from them. Show that the blood we've shed freeing your people is not in vain."

The view switched back to the news anchor, who continued, "Our preliminary reports say that the speaker is Solyss Novastar, from the wealthy Terran Novastar family, but now a major in the Union navy commanded by General Maarkean Ocaitchi. In the background, our analysts have identified Zeric Dustlighter, a colonel in the same force. You'll recall that just a year ago, it was General Ocaitchi and Colonel Dustlighter who freed the prisoners in Olan Detention Center and started the current levels of unrest.

"We have verified that the transmission originated from what appeared to be the Alliance corvette, *Gallant*, just as it was breaking planetary orbit. We can also verify that the orbital prison station recently built at Governor Howell's order has been destroyed. We cannot verify the statement that the Union rebel navy seized control of the corvette, or that they freed all of the prisoners before the station was destroyed. We will let you know more as things develop."

The new feed ended, and the room was left in silence. Lahkaba wasn't sure if he should curse or thank Solyss. A major public action like this might cause Governor Howell to cancel the upcoming elections, even against Admiral Sartori's orders. But if he played it right, it should help sway the public.

Turning back toward the crowd, Lahkaba grabbed their attention before anyone could recover from the shock of the news story. "I can confirm that news story. When I last left General Ocaitchi, he was planning an operation to free several prisoners held by the Alliance. In addition to this newly captured corvette, the general has also acquired several other Alliance warships and converted them to our cause.

"Make no mistake, his navy is not yet as powerful as the Alliance's. Not yet. But Enro was freed from Alliance control with only four armed transports, one of them commanded by that man, Solyss Novastar. This fight will not be easy. But we can win it. We just need to decide what it is we are fighting for.

"Vote tomorrow for independence. Let the Alliance know that we will not stand for our governments being disbanded, and our citizens arrested without cause. Tell General Ocaitchi that you support his efforts to defend your families!"

CHAPTER 23

Once they had safely left the other Alliance corvette behind and gotten out of range of Sulas' ground-based weapons, Zeric saw to the captured Alliance crew. With the rescued prisoners, they now had equal numbers, but the corvette had not been designed to comfortably accommodate this many people. In truth, it had not been designed to comfortably accommodate its own crew.

Before making the jump to hyperspace, Zeric decided their best choice was to leave the Alliance crew behind. Putting some in emergency pressure suits in the cargo pod and some in escape pods, they sent the Alliance crewmembers on a course back toward Sulas. He felt reasonably confident they would be found soon, as the Alliance would undoubtedly still be tracking them.

He spent most of the next day helping Solyss get the ship and passengers organized, doing whatever he could do to keep busy. The longer he was busy, the longer he could postpone confronting Jairyd. He had gotten a glimpse of the man, and it had only served to heighten his guilt.

Jairyd Kil'dare definitely looked the worse for wear after his time in Alliance custody. While it appeared that his time isolated aboard the prison station had let him heal, his face was still a testament to the treatment he had received. Since he was the only rebel they had captured at first, the Alliance had undoubtedly taken out all of their frustration on the man.

Finally, at the end of their first day in hyperspace, Zeric could find no more excuses and went to find Jairyd. He found him, along with Fracsid and several other ex-prisoners, in the crew mess. Everyone was in the middle of eating, and Zeric almost turned and left. They all appeared to be thoroughly enjoying the opportunity for a freshly cooked meal.

Walking over to the table, Zeric looked down at Jairyd, trying to express his regret in his face. "Jairyd, it's good to see you alive."

"It's good to be seen. And to be known to be alive," Jairyd said, setting his fork down. "Fracsid here has filled me in on some of what I missed while imprisoned. I can't say I mind being a martyr. I just wish it hadn't hurt so much."

Zeric smiled uncomfortably. "Had we known you were alive, we would have tried to find you."

Even as he said it, he knew the words sounded hollow. They had barely given Jairyd a second thought after the escape from Sulas. He had regretted losing the man, but he had easily convinced himself that the man was dead.

"I'm sure. You were probably too busy planning a rebellion against the Alliance," Jairyd said flatly.

"Um, something like that," Zeric replied.

"Tell me. When we planned the operation, you and Maarkean didn't seem that interested in rebellion. As I recall, you were just trying to bust your friends out of prison. So how is it that you ended up leading an uprising on Enro?" Jairyd asked, his tone not quite casual.

"Timing?" Zeric answered with a half smile. "We were there for the Sector Congress meeting when the Alliance disbanded all of the governments. We just helped the people of Enro defend themselves."

"And now you and Maarkean lead the rebel army?" Jairyd asked skeptically.

Zeric shook his head. "No, General Numba of Cardine heads up the army. Maarkean is in charge of the navy. I just head a battalion of marines."

"I see," Jairyd said. "So what is next for me?"

"That's up to you," Zeric said. "We're headed back to base. You're free to sign up and join us or go where you like. You're a free man now."

"Oh, I plan to join the fight. Those bastards need to pay for what they did to me."

Crawling underneath the SSF-19, Saracasi tried to keep the sands of Kol from filling her coveralls. She wasn't very successful and once again regretted that the inside shipyard wasn't bigger. With the *Defiant Glory* still being repaired after the battle at Roc 5, and the other captured capital ships taking up the rest of the shipyard's floor space and the landing field outside, many of the smaller fighters had been moved to a newly cleared area behind the headquarters buildings. Cleared, apparently, only of the brush and the surface layer of sand.

Brushing the sand off her hands, Saracasi reached up and opened the fighter's lower access panel. The sand was a distraction, but, then again, the only reason she was out here fixing fighters was to distract herself from their captured frigate, the FX-21. That ship had become something of an obsession for her.

The potential behind the design was unbelievable. If she could figure out how to get past the flaws, the ship would be revolutionary. Its shield would be more powerful than a ship twice its size, and the hyperdrive would be able to be run at speeds approaching that of packet ships. It was just a matter of getting past the, admittedly fatal, flaws.

La'ari had given up, declaring that there was a reason the ship had been abandoned twenty years ago and no one had come back to the design. There was just too much of a jump from the power output of a top-end fusion reactor to that of an anti-matter reactor. The frigate's systems could not handle the power without overloading. That was why anti-matter reactors were only used for things that required an ungodly amount of power, like large cities or the most powerful warships.

Chavatwor hadn't given up, but she suspected her friend had his doubts. There was no puzzle the professorial Kowwok didn't like, but he was responsible for getting all of the ships at his shipyard working, which included many non-military vessels that paid most of his bills. As much as she suspected his engineering mind wanted to fully tackle this question, he was also a businessman.

So Saracasi had spent most of her time working on the problem. Technically, as the chief engineer for the navy, she was also responsible for every ship in the yard. But most things were relatively routine matters, and between their military volunteers and the quality of Chavatwor's workers, she did not have to spend that much of her time overseeing things. She had therefore spent all of the rest of her time working on the frigate.

That was, until Asirzi put her foot down the night before. It had been a long time since Saracasi had been in any kind of romantic relationship, and she had forgotten that she couldn't just think about herself. She was happy with Asirzi. She enjoyed their time together immensely. She just suffered from the same problem as Chavatwor—engineering problems could completely consume her—and she didn't have his maturity in dealing with it.

When she had met the Kowwok, she thought him an absent-minded professor. He was kindly and easily distracted. When they had discussed ships while in and escaping from Olan, he had acted like he was in another world. But then, he hadn't had any other responsibilities. Now, he had a whole shipyard that depended on him. When he worked on engineering questions, he got lost, but he never let his other duties slack.

Saracasi had let her relationship with Asirzi slide a little. To be truthful, she had also probably been too lax with her responsibilities as the chief engineer. Asirzi had pointed this out to her, in a hurt tone that managed to penetrate her working mind.

After that, Saracasi had decided to put the frigate aside. She had promised Asirzi her full attention this evening, and had devoted her working time today to anything but the frigate. As part of that, she had taken some of the repair work on the fleet's star fighters, which was how she ended up on her back in the sand.

Fully engrossed now with a different engineering task—that of repairing the fighter—Saracasi did not hear the footsteps approaching. So when the voice called out, she banged her head on the fighter's hull, startled.

"Repairs again? I need this fighter operational. You told me yesterday that it would be ready to go today!" the voice said, agitated.

Once again sliding through the sand, Saracasi pulled herself out from under the fighter. A man towered over her, his features lost in the bright sun behind him. She held up her hand to block the sun and sighed as she recognized the Terran.

Jerik Needa, former bounty hunter turned rebel pilot, stood above her. He had an annoyed expression on his face which clearly showed his contempt for the regular flight mechanics. Since these flight mechanics were under her command, Saracasi frowned back up at him in response.

"Oh, uh, Major Ocaitchi, sorry, ma'am, I didn't know it was you down there."

"Of course, not, Lieutenant, why should you?" she said, struggling to keep her voice professional. She did not agree with her brother and Davidus' decision to make the bounty hunter an officer, even if he was a good pilot.

As she pulled herself up, she saw a collection of pilots behind him. She recognized Arzesaeth Ernebee, who had been on her crew that had stolen the frigate, and Sienn'lyn

Ifu, another Liw'kel Ni'jar whom Gu'od had recruited. The rest of the pilots she had seen but didn't know by name.

Jerik remained quiet, clearly not sure how to respond. Authority was something he responded well to, though he demanded strict obedience out of his pilots. As such, when he was around superior officers and subordinates, he always seemed to be torn. Saracasi kind of enjoyed his predicament, after how she assumed he had intended to treat her mechanic.

"I won't let you or any other pilot go up in one of these fighters unless I'm sure it's safe," Saracasi said, trying to sound like an officer. She felt sand clinging to her hair, ruining the effect, and was glad she only had hair on her head. This would be hell for a Notha or Kowwok.

"Of course not. I wouldn't want my pilots to, either," Jerik said, sounding agreeable.

"Good. I'll let you know when they're cleared for flight. Dismissed," Saracasi said, holding Jerik's look with an intent one of her own.

Jerik saluted her, and then turned back to the group of pilots. The man's arrogant attitude annoyed her. That annoyance evaporated as she watched him depart. Jerik walked with a distinct limp—a limp that she had caused by cutting into him with a plasma cutter.

She suddenly regretted how she had just treated him. Doctor Istru had repaired Jerik's leg, but it still caused him some trouble, especially over the uneven sandy terrain. She knew the injury had been necessary, and like many worse things she had done, she did not regret doing it. He had been trying to make off with her brother to collect a bounty.

Yet, it was another example of the terrible things this war was doing to people. She was reminded of this cost every night with Asirzi. The woman had still not gotten her breast replaced and had a mechanical arm. She and Jerik were just a few of many casualties in this war.

After finishing up her work on the fighter, Saracasi started back toward the main living quarters. The Kol sun had started to edge toward the horizon. It wasn't quite midday galactic time, but Chavatwor operated his shipyard on local time and she had started to adapt. It would be good to get a shower and then spend the evening with Asirzi, not thinking about engineering problems.

As she walked, the sky suddenly grew dark very quickly. She glanced up and was startled to see a large ship flying slowly overhead. Her mouth dropped as she recognized the shape of an Alliance naval ship.

Panic threatened to set in as she ran the rest of the way to the shipyard. Fighting against her poor fitness, she struggled to take deep calming breaths. Panic wouldn't do anyone any good.

When she reached the headquarters building, the small courtyard had filled with mechanics and soldiers staring up at the ship as it maneuvered toward the landing field beyond the shipyard. Saracasi fought the urge to join them, as well as the urge to turn and run the other direction. But with her brother and Davidus still gone, she was the senior naval officer present. And with Zeric gone, Ymp was the senior marine. It would be up to them to keep things calm.

She threw her tool bag toward one of her mechanics and told him to get everyone inside. Then she rushed through the ground to get to the other side of the shipyard, where the corvette appeared to be landing. Work inside the shipyard continued, the workers having no view of the landing ship. She said nothing as she ran. Until she knew what the ship wanted, there was no reason to start a panic.

Corvettes were not typically troop transports. And the fact that they hadn't started firing on the shipyard was a good sign. She held out hope that they weren't all about to become Alliance prisoners. Or the latest war casualties.

Getting through the shipyard, Saracasi was relieved to find Ymp Ki-Li and a contingent of marines waiting on the other side. Ymp nodded to her and handed her a sidearm. Saracasi shook her head. If this was an Alliance assault, she would just get in the way. She had never been a stellar shot with a pistol.

"What's the situation, Major?" Saracasi asked.

"The corvette hailed us a moment ago. Claims to be under the control of Colonel Dustlighter. But I find that to be suspicious," Ymp replied, her eye stalks split, one on the corvette, and one on Saracasi. The Camari ability to do that still creeped her out some.

"Well, we're not dead yet. Let's hope they're telling the truth."

"Let's hope, but it could just be a trap," Ymp said. "And if that's the case, I'm sure there are more ships in orbit ready to obliterate us from afar. My marines are ready to defend the shipyard, but if that's what we face . . . "

She left the rest unsaid. Saracasi regretted that they did not have the orbital tracking system installed yet. Chavatwor had agreed to let them set up a complete sensor network and had devoted some of his workers to setting up a powerful defense shield. But it had always taken a backseat to the work on all the ships.

"I'll go forward and meet whoever comes out," Saracasi said. "That way, if they decide to shoot me, you'll be ready to come save my ass."

Ymp chuckled. "Try not to get shot, though. Dry sand is terrible for wounds."

Leaving the Camari woman and the other marines behind, Saracasi walked forward into the space between them and the corvette. Though it wasn't as big as the *Defiant Glory*, or even the other three captured Alliance warships, the corvette towered above her several stories. The sight of it and the guns along its hull was pretty intimidating.

She stopped about a dozen meters in front of an airlock on the lowest deck. Several minutes went by and nothing happened. Eventually, the airlock opened and figures emerged from within the corvette.

Saracasi let out her breath in relief when she recognized Zeric leading the group. Behind him, Solyss and Fracsid emerged. Not only was the corvette not an enemy, but Zeric's mission to rescue Fracsid had been successful. As people continued to stream out of the corvette, she realized that their rescue must have been very successful.

"Colonel, welcome back," Saracasi said, deciding she should salute Zeric. He frowned at the gesture but returned it.

"Thanks, Casi," he replied, emphasizing his use of her nickname. "We had to take a detour to Sulas, but we found Frac and his crew safely inside a brand new Alliance orbital prison. Along with several other residents. We'll just say that history decided to repeat itself, and Sulas is once again without a large collection of innocent prisoners."

Saracasi nodded, impressed. The number of prisoners was miniscule compared to those that had been imprisoned at Olan—she guessed that there were less than forty total—but it was far more than the dozen or so crewmen they had thought were captured by the Alliance.

Clapping a hand on Solyss' shoulder, Zeric nodded his head to the man. "Solyss here managed to make use of our brand new Alliance warship to fight off another one and get us safely off the planet. He's a good captain."

Solyss looked slightly embarrassed, and Saracasi smiled at him. Inside, she felt a slight twinge of jealousy. The encounter sounded like it had been an exciting affair. Part of her regretted that she hadn't been able to be there. Participating in a battle of capital ships would have been quite intriguing.

"He's also good in a fight," Zeric continued. "When we stormed the bridge, the old captain almost got an emergency broadcast off. My stun blast didn't work, but Solyss stepped up and calmly shot the man. Though I suppose that's a bad precedent to set for the changing of command."

All of them chuckled. For a moment, Saracasi felt only a bit of envy that Solyss had distinguished himself in battle. Then she harshly reminded herself that he had had to kill a man in cold blood. She quickly set aside all her thoughts on the subject and changed the topic of conversation. She didn't want to dwell on a problem she couldn't solve.

Chapter 24

"That is quite an impressive feat," Maarkean said, his voice revealing his astonishment at the tale he had just heard. "If there wasn't an Alliance corvette sitting on the landing field, I'm not sure I'd believe it."

He was sitting in the old Bravo HQ building's conference room with Solyss, Zeric, and Saracasi. It had only been an hour since he had returned to Kol aboard *Bright Blade*, but after seeing the Alliance corvette during landing, he hadn't wanted to wait to get briefed on what had happened. It had turned out to be quite a tale.

Solyss gave him a solemn incline of his head, while Zeric smiled a self-satisfied smile. The two men were evidently proud of their accomplishment, and for good reason.

The sheer completeness of their victory worried Maarkean somewhat, as the universe had a tendency to balance itself out over time. An uncontested victory like this was sure to bring on a corresponding dip in fortune somewhere down the line. He wasn't pessimistic enough to think that meant they were doomed, but he would need to be cautious with their future missions to prevent that dip from being too severe.

"How are our rescued people doing?" Maarkean asked, moving the discussion forward into more somber topics.

"Pretty good, all things considered," Zeric said. "Dr. Istru checked them all out to return to duty. Jairyd—well, he took quite a beating over the last few months. It will take a long time for him to fully heal, but he's been living like that and says he's good to go. Wants to sign up and join the fight."

"It's good to see that captivity did not dampen his spirits," Maarkean said. He and Jairyd had not gotten along well during their first meeting. They had seen the Alliance through different lens then. Now that his own opinion about the Alliance had shifted, he had a new appreciation for the man's attitude. "We'll have to find a place for him."

"And Fracsid, too," Saracasi said. "He lost his ship, but he still wants to fight."

Maarkean nodded at his sister's comment. She had always had a soft spot for the smuggler, finding his attitude amusing rather than annoying like Maarkean did. She had a valid point though—without a ship, Fracsid's primary means of contributing to this war was gone. He had an idea for how to address that, though he wasn't sure he liked it.

"Speaking of lost ships, what's the condition of the *Chimopori*?" he asked.

"Safe, in a long-term storage facility on Sulas," Solyss said, a hint of regret in his voice. "Zeric certified it as a place he wouldn't choose to break into so I feel fairly confident she will remain undisturbed until I can go back to claim her."

Solyss then cleared his throat and looked up at Maarkean. "Regarding Lieutenant Relis, I suggest you consider him as an officer to serve on, or possibly to command, the captured corvette."

Maarkean tilted his head to the side as he considered the suggestion. Was Solyss making this suggestion out of a belief in Fracsid's command potential, or because he felt guilty for getting Fracsid's ship destroyed? Both were likely motivators, but even if Solyss was making the suggestion out of a bit of guilt, it might not be a bad decision. Terrans were just more emotional in their decision making.

"Actually, I have another posting in mind for Fracsid. Besides, the position of CO of the *Gallant* is already yours. You captured her, and you brought her back here safe. She's your ship now," Maarkean said to Solyss.

"Thank you, General," Solyss said, blinking in surprise. He had clearly been confident in handing over command to Fracsid. That made Maarkean feel better about his next decision.

"I'll give Fracsid command of the *Cutty Sark*. Even with the two new crews we recruited on the *Black Market*, with one ship destroyed and one in storage for a time, we need every other combat-capable ship ready with a permanent crew. I'm also transferring command of the gunship squadron to him," Maarkean said, his words resulting in a shocked expression on Saracasi's face.

Giving the ship to Zeric to use during the raid on Ailleroc had been difficult enough. But Zeric had the marines to deal with, and she was a fully functional warship now. She needed to be used as such. He couldn't let her sit around. Fracsid wouldn't have been his first choice, but at the moment, he was the only one. He knew Saracasi would never take the position.

He had seen the doubt in his sister's eyes, even though she tried to hide it. The battle on Perth had rattled her determination to fight. The fact that she had taken the position of chief engineer over command of the *Cutty Sark* so quickly before had been the confirmation.

But he wouldn't complain. She was a good engineer, and he really had no desire to put her in danger. If that meant Fracsid had to command his ship, then that would be a small price to pay. Well, not a small price, but an affordable one.

"Now, it's my turn," Maarkean said and recounted the events on the *Black Market*. After the Fox's refusal of alliance, and the mysterious Mr. Kahl-Amar, they had finished the visit by recruiting two new transport crews and finding most of what had been on their shopping lists. The two new crews would arrive in a few days, though they wouldn't come straight here. Meeting them would probably be Fracsid's first duty as squadron leader.

When he finished his report, he leaned back in his chair and waited for comments. He had already discussed the situation with Gu'od and Gamaly during the return journey. He was pretty sure how he planned to respond, but he wanted to hear from the others before making his final decision.

"It's likely a trap. Josserand is not to be trusted," Saracasi said vehemently. Her tone surprised him. She had always called him overly cautious when dealing with Josserand or other criminals.

Zeric nodded. "As nice as it would be to have a full battle carrier on our side, and even it weren't a trap, I don't see how Renard can pull off what he claims. And if he can, why would he need us? Those coordinates he gave you are months away. It may just be a way of sending you on a pointless journey as payback."

Solyss shook his dead. "I don't know this Josserand, and from the sounds of him, he's not very trustworthy, but it's not something we can just ignore."

"Yes, it is," Saracasi said. "Josserand tried to get us hijacked and sent a bounty hunter after us. Our best response to his request to meet him light years away is to ignore him. Besides, the Fox may not have decided to join us, but he has offered us a safe haven. We can't betray that by trying to steal his ship and give it to Josserand."

"I disagree," Solyss said, his voice remaining quiet. "Those coordinates are in the Trepon sector. If I recall, Congress has been trying to get the worlds in Trepon and Loisa to join in resisting the Alliance. If this Josserand has any sway in Trepon, he may be worth listening to, even if he can't deliver the *Black Market*."

Saracasi looked about ready to continue arguing, but she stopped. Maarkean recognized the expression on her face. She got that look when she was thinking about something. She closed her mouth and leaned back in her chair.

With a shrug, Zeric said. "He makes a good point. But that's a long way off. And Renard doesn't have the most sterling record for honesty."

"No, he doesn't," Maarkean said. "But I got a different sense from the man I met, Kueth. He seemed genuine. Casi, I agree with you. I don't like the idea of betraying the Fox, especially after he didn't throw me out an airlock, but Solyss is correct, a chance at gaining support in Trepon, and potentially a carrier, is not something we can just ignore."

He glanced at his sister, expecting her to frown at his decision, but she still wore the thoughtful look, so he continued. "I was planning on sending one of the gunships to check it out. It would be at least a four-month round trip, but the capture of this corvette gives us more options."

Solyss tilted his head at the mention of the corvette, but Maarkean did not elaborate further. He needed to consider things carefully before making a final decision. Lahkaba and the congress would surely want to give their input on this as well. Seeking out the *Black Market* as an asset had been Lahkaba's idea, after all.

"Now," Maarkean said, changing topics, "what else has been happening around here? Where is Dav?"

"Commander Brieni stayed behind on Ailleroc. He thought he could work with Kaars Aerinstar to work some contacts and gain some intel on the Alliance forces. Ar'cher and the *Durandal* are there as well," Solyss answered immediately, his tone a little skeptical.

"And Kol has voted for independence," Saracasi said, her none nonchalant.

When he turned a startled look toward his sister, she smiled, enjoying taking him off guard. She continued, "Apparently Lahkaba was successful. The vote Admiral Sartori said she would call went through, and each world added a measure to it, asking if the people wanted to secede. Kol's passed. We're still waiting on word from the rest of the sector."

Maarkean let out a heavy sigh. He had not given much thought to Lahkaba's mission to address Admiral Sartori's ultimatum. Rescuing Fracsid and the others had been his way to avoid the whole issue. But now, hearing that at least one planet had voted for independence left him with a feeling of satisfaction. All of the fighting he had done was not for nothing. The people were behind him.

As Katerina listened to Dolan detail the results from the election held on each Colonial world, she considered the implications. While next to her, Governor Zhant ranted and called each of those worlds traitors and rebels, she wondered whether he was correct. Each world had participated in a democratic vote that she had called. And they had voted to secede from the Alliance.

While she agreed with Zhant that the results of the elections were to be doubted, she wondered what it would mean if they weren't. Her mission in the Kreogh sector was to stop rebellious elements and restore order. If the people had voted to remove themselves from the Alliance, as a democratic institution, did it have the authority to ignore that vote?

To be sure, Alliance law did not allow for worlds to simply secede on a whim. But with no mechanic for secession in place, was not a vote of the planet's residents the best option? Her orders were to squash the rebellion, but was it the right thing to do now?

She said none of this out loud, however. It would be inappropriate to voice any doubts about their mission to her subordinates. It was just an academic mental exercise, anyway. She had her orders, and the security of the Alliance was her top priority.

Fortunately for her conscience at least, Dolan's next report washed away any doubt. "Our spy has been able to confirm reports that representatives from the Confederacy have met with the Kreogh Sector Congress. He believes that this independence vote is likely a first step in their plans to incorporate the planets into their territory."

That news reassured Katerina that the will of the people was not what they were fighting against. They were fighting a massive infiltration of Confederate spies and agitators. She would not allow Alliance citizens to fall victim to Confederate rule, no matter how misguided they were. That was what the navy was here for.

"That cannot be allowed to happen!" Governor Zhant fumed.

"Do not worry, Governor, the Confederacy will not win here," Katerina said, making no effort to put any reassurance in her voice. "Commander, what is the status of the 4th Fleet?"

"Admiral Garcia has returned a packet ship indicating that TF-412 and 413 were departing to join us. If they left on schedule, they should be arriving in the next few weeks," Dolan reported.

"That's it? What about the rest of TF-411 and TG-43?" Katerina asked, annoyed about her orders being ignored.

"Admiral Garcia apologizes but says he has standing orders to never let the defense forces in Trepon fall below a certain threshold?" Dolan said, confusion clear in his voice.

Katerina sighed to herself. She thought that order outdated and ridiculous. It had been crafted by scared politicians years ago and was an unnecessary drain on resources. However, she could not blame Garcia for following it. She would not want to be the officer who left the gates of hell unguarded just when the demons decided to emerge.

"Very well. Continue, Commander," Katerina said, not wanting to dwell on the topic. Dolan knew not to ask questions, but Zhant would not feel any restraint.

"Governor Howell requests reinforcements for Sulas. He says that with the loss of two corvettes, one into the hands of the rebels and one damaged, his world is vulnerable. His troops are strained and cannot continue to contain the population without reinforcements."

"Well, he can't have any of mine," Zhant said quickly. "When are the troops from the homeworlds arriving?"

An idea suddenly occurred to Katerina. Could she use this call for independence to her advantage? It would be tricky, but she had a number of angles that she could exploit if she acted now.

"Reinforcements from the homeworlds aren't coming," Katerina lied to Zhant.

"What?!" Zhant exclaimed. "We were promised troops."

"Governor, my mission here was to assess the situation and, if possible, stamp out the rebellion. Failing that, it was to secure the sector from Confederate incursion. The people have voted and they wish to be independent. The first part of the mission has failed. Completing the second will require some sacrifices," Katerina said, trying to sound sincere, but knowing she was not a great liar.

"Commander, prepare a dispatch to Sulas," Katerina continued, turning to ignore Zhant's fuming. "Order our ships to withdraw and return to Ailleroc. Then inform the army commanders to begin pulling back their forces to prepare for evacuation."

"You're retreating?!" Zhant roared. "I will not stand for this. And I expect Governor Howell will not, either." Zhant glared at her for a moment. When she didn't say anything in response, the irate Braz turned and stormed from the conference room.

Still standing there, Dolan tried to mask his confusion but failed.

"It's okay, Commander, you can ask," Katerina said after Zhant was gone.

"Why did you lie to the governor? The MEF should already be en route from Braz," Dolan asked.

"That's right. But the more people who think it's not coming, the better," Katerina said. "Has our spy departed the planet yet?"

"No, Admiral."

"Good. Bring him in for one more meeting. There's some intelligence he needs to provide to the rebels," Katerina said, a small smile crossing her lips as more pieces in her plan started to come together.

Chapter 25

As Solyss walked the corridors of his new ship, he found it hard to keep a smile off his face. He had gone to Sulas to free prisoners, and he had not only succeeded at that but also come away with command of a fully functional capital ship. Fortune truly did favor the bold.

When they had first stormed the ship, he hadn't noticed how clean and beautiful the *Gallant's* interior was. The bulkhead walls were more white than grey. Identification and warning labels added touches of color to the corridor, without making it look gaudy. The ship had an air of power and authority to her.

"We're going to have to make some modifications and cram things in here really tight if you're going to make it to Trepon and back," Saracasi was saying as they walked.

It was an additional honor that General Ocaitchi had chosen him and the *Gallant* to make the mission to Trepon to meet with this Josserand Renard. It showed the general's trust in him. Renard was not to be trusted, and it would be a difficult assignment.

"Oh?" Solyss asked. "Don't these ships fly between sectors all the time?"

"They do," Saracasi agreed. "But not by themselves. Either they're going from one Alliance outpost to another, or they're traveling with the rest of the fleet. Usually the latter. Corvettes are fleet support ships. Unlike frigates, they are designed to protect carriers and cruisers from fighters, not go off on independent missions."

"Then why are we being sent?" Isaxo asked. "Didn't we capture two frigates from Roc 5?"

Saracasi shrugged. "One of them is a complete mess, and I wouldn't want to travel anywhere on its hyperdrive right now. And the other is our only heavy hitter. I assume Maark doesn't want to commit it to a six-month mission outside the sector."

"I think we'll have to clear out the armory," La'ari, Isaxo's engineer sister, said. "That takes up a lot of room and can be used for supplies."

Solyss shook his head emphatically. "No. We'll need those weapons for our marines."

"Marines?" La'ari asked. "This ship has space for a small crew and just a handful of marine guards. They could probably keep their guns in their quarters."

"I plan on taking as many as I can. Marines may be more valuable than food for this mission," Solyss stated. Besides, he thought, Asheerah would never let herself get left behind. Suggesting that could be more lethal than anything the Alliance threw at him.

"We're going to have to sacrifice something," Saracasi insisted. "This ship was designed for one purpose, and we want to use her for another. Something has to give."

Solyss frowned. He didn't like the idea of having to sacrifice something from his new ship. She was perfect just the way she was. Although he wouldn't object to more weapons.

"We could remove one of the shuttles," Saracasi suggested. "You can get by with just one. Capital ships usually don't land all that often, hence the shuttles, but this one's small enough it doesn't make much difference."

"I actually had an idea to replace the shuttles with some fighters," Isaxo said, emphatically disagreeing with Saracasi's suggestion.

Solyss liked this idea. The Notha pilot had talked to him about it earlier. Fighters were the best offensive weapon in any fleet. Carrying a few would be quite the surprise to anyone who wanted to challenge them.

"That won't work," La'ari said, eyeing her brother. "The shuttle bay is not designed for quick launches of fighters. A combat launch or landing would be a clumsy affair."

"I suppose we could reconfigure the docking collars," Saracasi said, musingly.

La'ari tilted her head and then smiled. "Yeah, there are four of them. Could set them up for quick launches and retrievals. Wouldn't be able to carry them into an atmosphere without getting them sheared off though. Wouldn't be able to service them, either."

"But if we remove one shuttle, that leaves space for two ships, if we use those PF-56s Chava just got. They're small," Saracasi added, the two engineers speaking quickly and excitedly.

Solyss sighed. "That sounds excellent. But what about our supply problem? Won't fighters need even more supplies?"

Isaxo's shoulders dropped. He had been excited by the idea of having a flight of fighters to play with.

"Well," Saracasi said, her voice reluctant, "we could always remove the MKPD cannons. One of the batteries was already destroyed and needs to be replaced. Their loading mechanisms and the space used to store the flak cartridges take up a lot of space."

"But that's the ship's primary weapon!" Solyss said, exasperated. "We'd just be a weak capital ship."

"Not necessarily," La'ari explained. "We could use the weapon mounts to install more main neutron blasters. That would still leave a lot of interior space to convert to storage. Fill that with food and fuel, and we can increase your range enough for this mission."

"And probably still add the fighter mounts," Saracasi added.

Solyss paused, considering the engineers' words. From the sound of it, their proposed upgrades would strip away the corvette's primary role as an anti-fighter ship. He didn't like the idea of his brand new ship being completely reconfigured. On the other hand, it might make her better.

"So let me see if I understand," Solyss said. "By removing the flak batteries, you can give me more heavy weapons and the ability to launch fighters and increase our range enough to get to Trepon and back?"

"Maybe," Saracasi said. "We'll have to run some specs. Might still need to strap a fuel canister to the side."

Solyss smiled. "That would be fine. Won't get into too many fights while in hyperspace."

He exchanged a giddy look with Isaxo. Their warship was about to get a whole lot more dangerous.

Lahkaba didn't think this feeling would ever go away. The vote on Sulas had been overwhelmingly in favor of independence. Even though it had been a few weeks since then and he was now back on Irod, he still had a warm feeling of victory.

Even now, sitting in yet another Congress meeting, he still felt the sense of victory. They had shown the people that the Alliance could be opposed. And the people had listened and decided to stand on their own.

The subject matter of today's meeting helped fuel his euphoria. Davidus Brieni and Kaars Aerinstar were in the process of briefing Congress on what intelligence they had gathered while on Ailleroc. While he still had doubts about Kaars, he knew Maarkean trusted Davidus.

The two Terrans outlined rumors that the Alliance reinforcements from the homeworlds were delayed. This added to the news that Admiral Garcia was keeping a good portion of the 4th Fleet in the Trepon sector. Together, it meant the Alliance forces here would not be increasing anytime soon.

Their next bit of news served to reinforce Lahkaba's belief in their impending victory. Reports had been received that Admiral Sartori was recalling all Alliance forces in the sector back to Ailleroc. Supposedly, that included ships and ground forces. If this proved to be true, almost all of their worlds would be free from Alliance occupation.

An inkling of doubt played at the back of his mind, but he tried to ignore it. Even without reinforcements, the Alliance fleet outnumbered their ships by at least five to one. He doubted Sartori was doing this because she truly believed that the will of the people had been voiced. She was most likely doing this to consolidate her forces while she awaited reinforcements.

When Davidus and Kaars finished their report, Faide Darkthorne stood up. "Thank you, gentlemen, for your report. This is indeed monumental news. With the vote for independence, we may have won this war with less bloodshed than we all originally feared would be necessary."

Standing up beside him, Lei-mey called for the floor, and Faide yielded it to her. "Sulas would like to second that assessment and to once again, extend our thanks to General Ocaitchi and Colonel Dustlighter. His forces' rescue of Jairyd Kil'dare and the other hostages allowed our people to vote with a free conscience.

"Now, I call for our armed forces to immediately take this opportunity to clear all Alliance forces from their occupation of Sulas," Lei-mey concluded.

Lahkaba found himself nodding in agreement with Lei-mey. He found her proposals rather direct, which was typical of her, but he couldn't say he disagreed. Maarkean may not like her interfering in military planning, but now was an ideal time to act.

Predictably, Lionell Mandrake from Ailleroc stood up next. "Ailleroc feels the call for an assault on Sulas is taking advantage of a forgotten fact. My world will be seeing the control the Alliance has over us increasing. If we devote our forces to clearing Sulas, what will we do about the fleet encamped over Ailleroc?"

Even though he agreed with Lei-mey, Lahkaba could sympathize with Lionell. Deciding to try to head off an hour of back and forth arguments, Lahkaba stood up. "I believe before we continue with this discussion further, we should ask Generals Ocaitchi and Numba their opinions on the military feasibility of assaults on Sulas and Ailleroc."

Nodding in thanks to him, Numba stood up. "Though Major General Ocaitchi is not present, consulting him will not be necessary as I concur with this plan. My forces are more than ready to face the Alliance army. We can completely remove them from control of Sulas and then be ready to move to protect Ailleroc."

Lahkaba felt better hearing that, even though he would rather wait for an answer from Maarkean as well. They had won every engagement they had had against the Alliance so far. Sartori was not someone they should underestimate, but there was no real reason to think they couldn't take advantage of this opportunity. If they didn't, then what did the vote for independence really mean?

The debate continued for a short time, though there wasn't much opposition, other than from the Ailleroc delegation. After the measure passed, Faide called the meeting closed for the day, and Lahkaba stood up to head home. But before he could leave the congress chamber, Zoeko Lide, the gold Dotran from Mirthod, approached him.

"Lahkaba," Zoeko said formally. "May I have a moment of your time?"

"Of course," Lahkaba answered politely. He had barely spoken more than a few words with Zoeko since she had brought the Confederate officer before Congress.

"I was hoping you might be willing to speak with Commander Prytoker. He would very much like to meet you before returning to the Confederacy," Zoeko said.

Cautious, Lahkaba said, "I thought with this vote for independence we had put this issue behind us?"

Zoeko nodded her scaled head. "Indeed. While I still feel it would have been to our advantage, I am more than willing to accept the people's desire for independence. But just because we have chosen not to be members does not mean we cannot be friends with the Confederacy."

Frowning, Lahkaba considered what Zoeko said. He knew his feelings toward the Confederacy tended to be fairly biased. The treatment of Kowwoks back on the homeworld was a sore spot for him, as was his being conscripted to fight during the Colonial War. But Zoeko had a point—friendship with the Confederacy wouldn't be bad for their sector, even if it was just to help stem off any potential invasions.

Reluctantly, Lahkaba said, "Very well. I will meet with him. But I make no promises I will like anything he has to say."

Lahkaba followed Zoeko from the meeting chamber and across Lost Hope's dark streets. The small city was abuzz with activity, and they had to avoid a few crowds who tried to gain some news from them. News about the day's meeting would spread through the city, despite each delegate's attempts to avoid answering direct questions. On Irod, the responsibility for announcing news fell to Revas Shim and Faide.

When they arrived at the building used for housing by the Mirthod delegation, Lahkaba was surprised to find armed figures standing guard. He recognized the patch they wore on their uniforms as that of Ice Company. The controversial paramilitary organization Mirthod had brought to Irod had, so far, not caused any direct trouble.

Once inside the building, Lahkaba waited for a few moments before Zoeko brought the blue-scaled Bryel Prytoker to meet with him. The Dotran smiled a dangerous-looking smile through his sharp teeth. Lahkaba knew all Dotran smiles looked menacing simply because of those teeth, but he couldn't help but take it as the sign of a predator. For a change, he felt glad the members of Ice were outside. They may have a nasty reputation, but most of their members were Terrans or Braz.

"Thank you for agreeing to meet with me, Delegate Lahkaba," Bryel said with a hiss.

"I am always willing to talk to someone," Lahkaba said, forcing truth into his words. He meant what he said, but this pushed the limits of his willingness.

"I must congratulate you on your sector's decision to seek independence. All peoples should be given the chance to choose their own destiny," Bryel said.

Normally, Lahkaba would have taken those words as hollow platitudes, coming from a Dotran. Yet the way Bryel said them made him think the Dotran meant them. Zoeko, despite their differences, had already proven that it was possible for a Dotran to believe in democracy. Perhaps this one did, as well.

It was probably just wishful thinking, Lahkaba decided. Or this Bryel was better at lying than most. "Thank you. I'm glad that you understand that and why we could not accept your government's offer."

"Of course," Bryel said. "But the Confederacy remains dedicated to ensuring that the worlds of the Kreogh Sector achieve their freedom."

Lahkaba's initial confusion intensified as he found himself not believing Bryel's last statement at all. Either Bryel had been sincere before and was not now, or his ability to lie was not consistent.

"That's good to hear," Lahkaba said slowly. "We have no wish for a conflict with the Confederacy."

"Nor we with you," Bryel asserted. "Should your Union ever need our help, the Confederacy will be there. I hope all champions of freedom can work together."

"I will remember that," Lahkaba said, slightly confused by the last statement.

Inclining his head, Bryel backed toward the room's door. "I hope we will have the opportunity to work together in the future. Until we meet again."

With that, Bryel departed, leaving Lahkaba alone and confused.

CHAPTER 26

As Maarkean set the *Cutty Sark* down on Irod, he felt glad to be at the controls again. Even though he had decided to let Fracsid use her, at least until they could get the *Chimopori* off Sulas, he still didn't really like the idea. Needing to go Irod to update Numba and Congress on their recent activities had given him a perfect excuse to use his ship again. It might not be entirely professional, but he didn't really care.

After powering the engines down, he turned the details of securing the ship over to Fracsid and his crew—there were some benefits to allowing them to accompany him. Leaving the flight deck, Maarkean went down to the cargo ramp, where he found Jairyd waiting for him.

The blond-haired Terran looked better than he had after first being rescued. The Alliance had not been kind to him. Doctor Istru had tended to his wounds, patching him up the best he could with their limited medical resources. Unfortunately, without specialized gear, most of the wounds had already started to heal on their own, giving Jairyd many permanent scars.

Instead of being embarrassed about the scars, Jairyd wore them as a badge of honor. Maarkean could understand that. They were a reminder of what he had suffered and what he was fighting against. But they also fit Jairyd's personality. He had been prepared to die during the Olan prison break. To him, being tortured was probably the next best thing to becoming a martyr.

"You ready?" Maarkean asked, sympathy in his voice. He had not really liked the man when they'd first met, as Jairyd threatening to kill him several times had tinted his opinion, but it now seemed silly to hold onto that animosity. Jairyd had traveled with him to Irod to speak before Congress about his incarceration, and Maarkean never envied anyone having to do that.

"Yes," Jairyd said, his old fiery attitude now showing itself. "I appreciate you supporting me on this. I know you probably would like your navy to be involved in liberating Sulas."

Maarkean smiled slightly. "On the contrary, I would prefer the navy never having to fire another shot. Your idea to lead Sulas in an uprising like Enro's is worth considering. The military is more something that we're building to defend the sector once we're free. Getting there is better achieved locally on each world."

Jairyd nodded his agreement as they walked down the boarding ramp. Maarkean had tried to find Jairyd a place in the marines, but the Terran had immediately expressed an interest in returning to Sulas. When he had learned that there were no plans for an invasion to remove the Alliance, he had proposed staging an organized uprising. An invasion of Numba's army would be easily stopped by Alliance naval forces they still couldn't challenge. A home-grown uprising didn't need that kind of support.

"We'll report to General Numba first," Maarkean said, "then I'll take you to Lahkaba and Lei-mey. I'm sure she'll be happy to see you."

As they walked away from the *Cutty Sark*, Maarkean noticed that the military camp was much more active than it had been the last time he had been here. Several transport ships had been assembled, and the landing area was crowded with troops moving containers of supplies to and from the ships.

As they moved past the docking area, the buzz of activity did not decrease. Platoons of soldiers marched throughout the camp, delivering salutes when they recognized Maarkean or the major general emblem on his uniform. The platoons were an eclectic mix. Some wore full matching combat uniforms and marched in lock step. Others looked more like a mob, wearing an assortment of clothing and carrying weapons in a variety of ways.

The plethora of uniforms and styles made Maarkean glad he had splurged for the coherent uniforms for the marines and navy. Upgrading and repairing all of their ships had been expensive, but since almost their entire fleet had been donated or stolen, it had been cheaper than buying new. Their success on Roc 5 had even allowed him to buy a squadron of used patrol fighters from a dealer on Kol. Next to those, the uniforms had been a pittance.

When they reached the central command building, a cheaply constructed building that was still far more solid than the tents most of the troops were still staying in, Maarkean stepped out of the way as a green Ronid and a Terran exited the building. He recognized the Ronid and smiled. "Lohcja!" he said.

"Maark, uh, I mean, General. Good to see you!" Lohcja said, what passed for a smile among Ronids on his face. The last time Maarkean had seen him, Lohcja had stayed behind on Enro to join their newly formed military. Lahkaba had told him that Lohcja had arrived on Irod with that force, but Maarkean had not had a chance to meet up with him.

Lohcja's look suddenly shifted. His antennae went completely vertical and his mandibles spread wide. With no eyelids, his eyes remained the same size, but Maarkean could almost imagine them growing bigger with shock. The Ronid stared at the Terran beside Maarkean.

"Jairyd?" Lohcja said. "We heard about the rescue on Sulas, but we didn't know who was actually in that prison. I never thought I'd see you again!"

Jairyd gave Lohcja a big smile. "It's me, in the flesh. Those rumors of my demise at the hands of the Alliance are slightly exaggerated."

The two men stood there awkwardly, the social norms about how to greet each other becoming muddled. Unlike Kowwoks, who would hug anyone they felt warranted it, regardless of that person's feelings on the subject, or Terrans' usual greeting of a handshake, Ronids greeted each other by rubbing antennae. It was not far from a handshake, but for a non-Ronid to reach up and shake an antennae was usually frowned on.

The moment passed when the Terran beside Lohcja stepped forward, extending his hand to Jairyd. "Kaars Aerinstar. Pleased to meet you, Mr. Kildare. You are an inspiration to me."

"Thank you, but call me Jairyd," Jairyd said with an uneven smile before turning back to Lohcja. "So, a colonel, huh? Come far from that taxi gig of yours."

Lohcja shrugged with his antennae. "Pay isn't any better."

He glanced past Maarkean and Jairyd and then said, "I want to catch up, Jair. But I have a lot to do to prepare for the operation. You showed up at the right time. General Numba and Commander Brieni can fill you both in."

With a nod to Kaars, Lohcja strode purposely off toward a collection of waiting troops. The group all wore uniforms similar to Lohcja's, suggesting that they were also officers. Maarkean felt a tinge of pride for Lohcja. He appeared to be fitting into his role here well.

Turning back toward the command building, Maarkean followed Jairyd inside. He wondered what kind of operation Lohcja was referring to, but he was also pleased to hear that Davidus had returned from his covert mission on Ailleroc. Jerik had turned into an adequate flight instructor, but he needed his StarOps CO.

Maarkean found Numba and Davidus in one of the building's planning rooms. The walls were covered with cheap data paper that displayed logistical details about troops and supplies. In the center of the room, the two men stood around a tactical holo display. It currently showed an image of a fairly large city and the land surrounding it. There were icons representing troops that the two were manipulating.

When the door shutting behind him failed to key the two into his arrival, Maarkean said, "Looks like you're planning an invasion."

At the sound of his voice, Davidus and Numba looked up from the holo and turned toward him. Davidus gave a slight nod toward him, while Numba just frowned and said, "This is unexpected, Major General. I was just about to send Commander Brieni back to Kol with your orders."

"My orders?" Maarkean asked, walking over to join them at the display. As he got closer, details on the city became clearer. He recognized the city as Ciread, the capital of Sulas.

"Yes, we'll be conducting an assault on Sulas shortly. I'll need all ships available for transport and fire support," Numba said, his voice matter-of-fact.

"An assault? What kind of assault?" Maarkean asked, concern rising up inside of him.

"The Alliance has pulled out," Davidus said. "There aren't any reinforcements coming, and Admiral Sartori has pulled all her forces back to Ailleroc."

"Sartori has recognized our declaration of independence. We're going to seize this opportunity and take full control of Sulas," Numba interjected, giving Davidus a dark look.

The pronouncement startled Maarkean. He had come here expecting to need to convince Congress and Numba to back Jairyd's plan for a home-grown uprising. The idea of a full invasion had seemed far beyond their capabilities, primarily because of Alliance naval superiority.

"Everything? They've pulled everything out?"

Davidus shook his head. "No, but all of the ships. Sartori ordered the army and marine forces planetside to be evacuated, but Governor Howell refused to comply. They're in a sort of limbo at the moment, torn between the governor and the admiral."

"But they do not concern us," Numba said, his voice confident. "With the ships gone, we can get our forces planetside with minimal risk. Once on the ground, the forces will either flee or face us in battle."

Tilting his head, Maarkean considered the news. It seemed like a golden opportunity. Sartori was crafty and an excellent military commander. Pulling ships out as bait for a trap was within her capabilities. However, it was just as likely that she was withdrawing from a bad position.

So far, all of his victories had come from the Alliance being unprepared and spread thin. A commander like Sartori would recognize this. Pulling forces back to defendable positions until more forces became available would be her best tactic. He didn't buy the idea that Sartori had recognized their declaration of independence. But it was a convenient cover for a retreat.

"You said there aren't any reinforcements coming?" Maarkean asked, looking toward Davidus.

He nodded. "Aye. The rest of the 4th Fleet is remaining in the Trepon Sector, and there has been a delay on the MEF from Braz. That's what Kaars and I were tracking down on Ailleroc."

Maarkean considered this. He trusted Davidus, and if he'd gotten first-hand reports from some old contacts in the Alliance navy about reinforcements being delayed, then they were likely true. Partially, at least. Any intel always had to be treated as potential disinformation.

If true, it meant Sartori only had the ships available that had already been in the sector. And through luck and skill, Novastar had managed to take a cruiser and a corvette out of action. The cruiser would not take long to repair and was still potentially useful in a defensive capacity, but it would not be functional for attack. And the corvette was now completely out of the Alliance's hands."

Another thought occurred to Maarkean. If this proved to be true, he could justify not going to the meeting with Josserand. With the Alliance pulled back, they had less of an immediate need for the *Black Market*. Even if Josserand wasn't planning a trap for him, whatever help he had in mind wouldn't come without a price.

Beside him, Jairyd nodded enthusiastically. "This is great news. I was preparing to offer to lead an uprising on Sulas. But this is better. We can sweep the Alliance off our worlds with ease."

Maarkean found himself frowning. Removing the Alliance would not be that easy, and the chance that the whole Alliance withdrawal was nothing more than a ruse could not be discounted. The plan would not be as simple as landing and declaring victory.

Jairyd's enthusiasm filled him with sudden apprehension. He had been supportive of Jairyd's plans for an uprising, but he hadn't really thought much of the chance for success. Neither had Jairyd, now that he thought about it. Jairyd had shown more enthusiasm at this news than he had at his own plan.

Had he liked the idea simply because Jairyd hadn't been very enthusiastic? Was his sudden spark of doubt just prejudice against Jairyd? He didn't like to think of himself as petty, but he was self-aware enough to accept that he could be. Saracasi liked to point it out anytime he was.

Accepting that he may be being petty, Maarkean nevertheless voiced his concerns. "What about the planetary defense guns? Those weapons can be used to repel any invasion. We've been able to move around unmolested by them so far because it's been single ships mingling with civilian traffic. We send an invasion force to Sulas, and the Alliance forces there won't hold back."

"Those won't be a concern," Numba said, dismissively. "The Alliance forces have been ordered to withdraw."

"It's a good point," Davidus said. "We had been assuming the Alliance forces won't be there or won't use them. But they could, and we'd be vulnerable."

Numba frowned at Davidus, apparently annoyed at the man not agreeing with him. After a moment, he sighed and shook his head. "Very well. It would be foolish not to plan for that contingency."

"I could lead a team of locals and seize them all," Jairyd said quickly. "It will be just like the attack on Olan. Completely unexpected."

Maarkean shook his head. "No, we'll need professionals for this. I can have Zeric take in the Rogues. We don't have enough forces to hit them all simultaneously, but all we need to do is take out the guns that can hit whichever vector we'll be approaching the planet from."

"I will get them some additional forces," Numba said. "Best to get them all at once. But do not worry, Mr. Kildare. We will have a place for you in this endeavor. A man of your talents should be utilized fully. I will see to it you have a place as one of my senior commanders."

Numba then looked over the rest of them. "Now is the time for us to truly take our victory. The Alliance has made a grave error. By the time they finally get their act together, the sector will be ours."

Chapter 27

Saracasi looked over the crowded room. Every officer in the navy and marines had crammed into the small conference room inside the old Bravo HQ building on Kol. Maarkean had called the meeting immediately after returning from Irod, but he hadn't seen fit to tell her, or anyone else, what it was about.

Knowing her brother, she assumed it would be something big. Reports had come in from each planet about the recent independence vote. Things looked positive that the measure had passed everywhere. But she didn't think Maarkean would call an officer's meeting to repeat that news, even if it would explain Owrik's presence.

The Dantyne delegate had arrived with Maarkean aboard the *Cutty Sark*, but hadn't spoken to anyone yet. He now wore a naval uniform, which she found odd, but there had been a sandstorm blowing when they had landed. He had likely just needed a change of clothes.

She looked around at the other assembled officers. Zeric sat at the right side of the table near the head. Beside him were the marines: Ymp, Sigfa, Calek, Asheerah, and two newly appointed platoon leaders, Ower Hammersong and Seesz Owwoke. She remembered Seesz from the battle of Enro. He had been with her team that had taken the Alliance command bunker. The only non-officer in the room, Master Drill Sergeant Deja'z'reth Adat'to, also sat with the marines.

Across from Zeric were the star fighter officers, led by Davidus. Beside him sat the squadron leaders. First came Isaxo, brother to Owrik and former pilot for the *Chimopori*.

Erc Zejah, a Braz she didn't know well, sat next to Isaxo, followed by Jerik Needa.

On the back part of the table, sitting around her, were the other fleet officers. Koruma Darknauv was a former Camari naval officer who had been put in command of the *Rogue Spirit*, the escort carrier they had captured at Roc 5. His ship's command staff were with him. Then there were the officers from the *Defiant Glory*: La'ari Mahon, who had volunteered to be her engineer, Verad Clemyo, and Ceno Gotit.

The two frigates they had captured did not yet have formal crews. But prospective officers had been identified and were present, including Sheanna Coramont and Arzesaeth Ernebee, who had been with her for the theft of the FX-21.

Seeing all of these people in uniform, ready and eager to take on the Alliance, was making her start to rethink her decision not to fight when Maarkean came in. As he entered, Zeric sighed almost imperceptibly and then shot up to stand at attention. He then called out, "General on deck!"

Everyone in the room stood. Saracasi felt funny standing like this for her brother, but she understood the symbolism. She just didn't want all of the saluting and attention to go to his head. That's why she made it a point to keep him grounded when they were in private. But they weren't in private now, so she started to stand like everyone rest.

"Keep your seats," Maarkean said immediately after Zeric spoke. It was part of the ritual, she thought. The assembled troops had shown respect, and the commander could downplay the need for it by waving them immediately back to their seats.

"As most of you have undoubtedly heard, all of the planets in the sector voted for independence from the Alliance," Maarkean began. He held up a hand when applause started. "But that's not why we're here today. Congress is planning a formal declaration of our intentions to the Alliance. We can celebrate then."

The brief enthusiasm died down, and Saracasi frowned. If this meeting had nothing to do with the independence vote, then it meant something more serious. She suddenly got a dark feeling inside her stomach.

"Congress and General Numba have decided that now is the time to make a move to liberate Sulas. Our intelligence suggests that the Alliance has pulled back their naval forces and that reinforcements from Trepon and Braz have been delayed or aren't coming. We have a small window of opportunity to clear the planet from Alliance control."

The excited atmosphere returned to the room, this time laced with nervous anticipation. Talk around the base about when they would begin an offensive campaign had been a major topic for months. Up until now, all of their operations had been small engagements to prepare for an eventual confrontation. Now looked to be the time.

Saracasi swallowed and straightened up, trying to hide her suddenly shaking, sweaty hands. She hadn't been able to completely avoid combat even during the small raids. If a major operation was coming, she would likely need to participate. She still wasn't sure if she should. Her dark secret was still unresolved, still gnawing at her, in direct conflict with her unabashed desire to get out there and destroy the enemy.

"General Numba will be leading the army for a full ground assault on Sulas. His objective will be to seize control of all major cities and Alliance bases," Maarkean continued. "In order for him to do that, his troops need to get on the surface safely. That's where we come in.

"Zeric and the Rogues will be going in first, snuck planetside via our gunships. Their objective will be to take control, or if necessary, destroy, four planetary defense weapon batteries. With the navy pulled out, these guns are the primary threat to our troop transports.

"Aside from the freshest set of recruits and Lieutenant Aru's space platoon, they'll be taking everyone. But even then, it won't be enough to cover all four guns. So General Numba will be deploying Ice Company to assist."

At that last announcement, Saracasi saw Zeric exchange a look with Ymp. Neither looked pleased at the idea, and Saracasi could understand why. They had both been betrayed by Ice Company at different times, and then Ice Company had come after the whole group of them on Mirthod on behalf of the Alliance. She still didn't understand why Ice was now employed by the army.

"Maar—uh, General, I'm not sure I like this idea of Ice having our backs," Zeric said, his tone indicating it had been a struggle for him to keep his words polite.

"They won't be watching your backs," Maarkean said and then gave them all a mischievous smile. "They will be under your command. Delegate Lahkaba and Congress have seen fit to promote you to lieutenant general, in command of all marines, mercenaries, and special forces. Ice will be reporting to you, and you can deploy them as you see fit."

Zeric's eyes narrowed as he looked at Maarkean, and Saracasi had to suppress a laugh, despite the seriousness of the briefing. She knew Zeric's reluctance at even becoming an officer. Being made a general would be an insult to him, not a reward.

Despite this, everyone in the room offered congratulations to the new general. Zeric faked a smile in return and then turned a not-so-subtle glare on Maarkean once everyone had quieted down.

Maarkean continued his briefing. "Now, with luck, the marines will have the most difficult task of this entire operation. If they can take the guns and our intel is correct, it should be smooth sailing getting the army planetside. Our biggest potential threat will be ground-based fighter craft, but we should be able to handle that.

"*Defiant Glory* will carry a full load of superiority fighters while *Rogue Spirit* will carry our bombers. Ground support will likely be our primary duty. But I want every ship ready for combat nevertheless. We are dealing with Admiral Katerina Sartori in charge of the Alliance fleet. We have to be prepared for the unexpected."

Several of the older officers who had served in the Alliance military or those few who had been in the Confederacy nodded in agreement. She found the regard they all had for Sartori to be odd. Sartori was the enemy, after all.

"Saracasi," Maarkean said, confusing her for a second that he wasn't using her more familiar name of Casi, "what is the status of the rest of our capital ships?"

"The *Gallant* has been fully repaired and we've begun outfitting her for the mission to Trepon," Saracasi began.

"That operation has been scrubbed for the time being," Maarkean interjected, filling her with some relief. She hadn't liked the idea of sending anyone to meet Josserand anymore than her brother probably had.

"As for the Hazard class frigate," Saracasi went on, "she's been brought up to working status. She's old, but functional."

Maarkean nodded. "Excellent. Delegate Mahon here has resigned from the congress in order to offer his experience to us. He'll be taking command of that frigate. In honor of our mission, I think the name of *Liberator* will suit her well."

The decision to place Owrik in command of the frigate made no sense to her. His only combat experience had been during the battle of Perth. He had handled himself well, but he had only been manning the operations console on the *Cutty Sark*. On the other hand, she admitted, very few of the officers here had any actual combat experience. Those that had were the ones in command.

"And the other one, the FX-21?"

Saracasi shook her head, putting aside the issue of Owrik in favor of her nemesis. "We're making some progress in solving the surge problem. We can keep the shields up for extended periods now. The battle simulations look promising, but we haven't done many real world tests. The hyperdrive is still a mess. She's not fit for a jump as distant as Sulas."

"Very well," Maarkean said. "You will remain behind and continue work on her. Try to get everything functional. Lieutenant Needa will remain behind as well, with a squadron of our fighters. With the bombers aboard, we won't have room for all of our ships."

Profound disappointment and relief washed over Saracasi simultaneously. She had been given a reprieve. At least for now, she would not have to face her inner demons.

"We cannot trust them!" Ymp declared, anger lacing her voice.

"Hey, I don't trust them," Zeric said, holding up his hands defensively.

It was the day after Maarkean's big briefing, and he had just wrapped up a meeting with his marine officers. Ymp and Sigfa had cornered him after everyone else left. Neither felt comfortable with Ice's involvement in this operation.

The blond-haired Terran and the Camari now stood before him defiantly. Sigfa was not someone to take lightly, but Zeric actually felt more comfortable with him here than with just Ymp confronting him. She could get irrational when it came to their old mercenary company.

"I don't think they'll compromise the operation," Sigfa said and then received a dark look from Ymp. "Well, I don't. They have been paid. If they don't do their part, that kills their reputation. And Firek is all about their reputation. However, I wouldn't put it past them to still try to kill either of you."

Zeric sighed. He had voiced those same arguments to Maarkean just a few hours ago. His friend had sympathized, but it was out of his hands. Numba was adamant about using

Ice, and he had the backing of the Cardine and Mirthod delegations on the issue. The best Maarkean could do was ensure that Ice reported to Zeric, which gave him control of their deployment.

"You do not have to worry about me. If Firek tries anything, it will be him who ends up dead. Maybe even if he doesn't," Ymp said, bitterness lacing her bravado.

"Believe me, I agree with both of you," Zeric said. "Well, not about killing Firek. Okay, maybe I do there, too. But we can't do it. We will need their skill and firepower if we're going to take down all four gun batteries before Alliance reinforcements get to us or they blow the transports out of the sky."

Sigfa nodded in agreement. Ymp stared at him for a moment, her eyestalks rigid, but finally shrugged her acceptance.

Zeric continued, "Okay, now see to your troops. We need to be ready to depart in six hours."

"Aye, General," Sigfa and Ymp said in chorus. They saluted before departing.

Inwardly, Zeric groaned at the use of his new title. He had also tried to get out of that one when he had talked to Maarkean. Unfortunately, it seemed there were political maneuverings behind the scenes working against him. General Numba had made many promotions to the first flag rank of brigadier. He had tried to get some of his people promoted higher, to lieutenant and major generals. But Congress had resisted, feeling they only had a need for one general and one major general.

Then Numba had put forth Jairyd as his number two and requested that he be made a major general. With Jairyd's reputation from the Olan prison break and his surprise return to life, Congress would have been swept up had not Lahkaba intervened. Apparently, neither he nor Maarkean liked the idea of Jairyd being the only other general.

Lahkaba had proposed that Jairyd be made a lieutenant general under Numba and that Zeric also be made a lieutenant general. He had been careful to craft the phrasing of the appointments so that Zeric was promoted first and this position superseded Jairyd's. Should a situation ever arise between them, Zeric would be the senior officer.

Having been locked up in a basement and threatened by Jairyd, Zeric thought that the logic made sense. At the same time, Lahkaba had also been one of the ones holding him captive then, so he found it rather ironic. But that didn't mean he liked being made a general.

Leaving the marine command room behind, Zeric went to find Gu'od. He had had only a few brief moments to talk to his friend since the announcement of the mission to Sulas. This next conversation would probably make the previous one look like a friendly chat.

He found Gamaly and Gu'od near their quarters after a short search. As he approached, Gamaly stepped forward, shaking her head emphatically before he had even said hello.

"The answer is no," she declared, her tone suggesting there was no compromise available.

"No? No to what?" Zeric said, trying to sound as innocent as he could.

"You know what," Gamaly snapped. "You're here to ask Gu'od to come with you. But the answer is no."

Zeric cursed under his breath. He knew Gamaly would put up a fight, but he hadn't anticipating being shut down before he could even make his case. Stubbornly, he decided to push on.

"Just hear me out," Zeric said quickly. "This is a pretty big operation, but it won't take long. Just a week to travel to Sulas, a few days there to take the guns out, and then a trip back. Be done in under a month.

"I need someone by my side I can trust completely. I don't like Ice being involved in this. You know Firek wants my head. Once we take the guns, I can order Ice to stay on Sulas to help with the fight, and I can come back with the Rogues, putting many light years between us."

Gamaly's expression held firm, drilling her eyes into Zeric with her stare. Beside her, Gu'od's face drooped. It was clear from Gu'od's expression that he wanted to help. They had had each other's backs for years now, one always looking out for the other.

Instead, Gu'od looked at Gamaly while answering. "I'm afraid Gamaly is correct. My place is by her side. This is one mission you must do on your own."

Zeric suddenly comprehended what he was asking his friend to do. They had been a team for years, but he had never known Gu'od without Gamaly. With her pregnancy, she could not risk this mission. And Gu'od was right, that meant he could not either. His place was indeed by his wife's side, ready to take care of their coming baby.

Guilt threatened to well up inside of him, a feeling he had never liked and tended to ignore. But this time he couldn't. As their friend, it was his place to not put them in a position to have to make this decision. He should never have even asked.

"You're absolutely right," Zeric said. "I can handle this. I've got Ymp watching my back."

Turning to go before he said anything stupid, Zeric was suddenly stopped by Gamaly's hand on his shoulder. He turned back around and saw one of her kind expressions. She had those a lot, but they were rarely directed toward him.

"No, Gu'od will go with you. I am not due for several months. I would go myself if I didn't think I would be more a hindrance than a help. I can get by without him for a month," Gamaly said, her tone soft.

Zeric shook his head. "No, you were right before. I shouldn't have asked."

Gamaly grinned. "Maybe not. But this time we are offering instead."

Relieved, Zeric nodded. "Thank you."

Then Gamaly's look hardened and she stared him directly in the eyes. "But if he doesn't come back, you'd better not, either. Because if you do, what I will do to you will be a thousand times worse than anything else you could ever experience."

CHAPTER 28

Asirzi set a plate of food down in front of Saracasi and then took a seat. They usually ate in the cafeteria with everyone else on the base, but tonight Asirzi had decided to cook for just the two of them. With most of the military personnel off-world, finding time to use the common kitchens had become easier.

After taking a tentative bite, Saracasi was pleased to discover a tangy mix of flavors. They had tried cooking for each other before, but after the last time, they had both agreed that Saracasi should never try it again. It was a relief to learn that Asirzi did not share her deficiency in that area of expertise.

"This is excellent. What is it?" Saracasi asked, taking another bite.

"Rolar casserole," Asirzi answered. "It was my father's best dish and he passed the recipe on to me."

"It is a worthwhile inheritance," Saracasi answered, and then moved into their traditional dinner conversation. "How was your day?"

"Usual," Asirzi replied. "Though it looks like tomorrow will be interesting. Chava has been negotiating with Harland Inc. on an upgrade contract for their orbital lifters. After the work he did for Grenil improving their launch capacity by a couple percent, Harland is eager to get the same upgrades. Chava's trying to hold out on them providing an orbital docking facility as part of the contract."

Saracasi's mind drifted as Asirzi continued to talk about her day and the contracts she helped Chavatwor negotiate.

She tried to listen, but the details about these things tended to bore her. They meant a lot to Asirzi, so she wanted to care, but they just felt pointless to her.

In truth, her mind was still focused on her brother and all the others who had departed a few days ago. They were off to free Sulas from Alliance occupation. They were putting their lives on the line for a cause she believed in. They were doing what she wouldn't.

Guilt and desire fought against relief. She had been ordered to remain behind. She was doing her part by continuing to try to get the FX-21 working. But she also knew that had she asked, Maarkean would have let her come. There was always a need for more engineers among the rag-tag fleet.

Jerik, the bounty hunter and soldier of fortune, had tried to convince Davidus to let him go. If a man who had signed up as a way to get out of a cell was willing to argue to be put on the front lines, what did that say about her? She hadn't even tried. She had just been happy to have a tailor-made excuse to stay out of the fighting.

But even that wasn't true—not really. The truth was that she was eager to fight. It was that truth that haunted her.

"Casi?" The quiet question from Asirzi interrupted her thoughts. Embarrassed, Saracasi looked up from her plate and tried to smile apologetically. "Sorry, my mind must have drifted. What did you say?"

Asirzi gave her a frown of annoyance, and Saracasi started to think she might have just ruined dinner. Then Asirzi's antennae twitched in a motion that indicated sympathy, and Asirzi asked, "You're thinking about your brother, aren't you?"

Saracasi nodded, worried that Asirzi could somehow read her true thoughts, and Asirzi continued, "I know it's hard to be left behind. Even though you don't want to fight anymore, a part of you wants to be there with the rest of them. But I'm glad you got to stay here. And not just so we could continue to be together. If you had gone, I'd be consumed by worry that you wouldn't come back."

Guiltily, Saracasi tried to look like Asirzi had caught her. "I know you would worry. But you're right. I am . . . conflicted."

Asirzi frowned again. "Your brother's right. You really aren't a good liar."

Saracasi looked up defensively but caught herself before speaking. She wasn't exactly lying, but she wasn't admitting the full truth, either.

While she debated her response, Asirzi spoke for her. "That's it, isn't it? That's what's been bothering you these last few months. You don't want to be going with them at all."

Reluctantly, Saracasi shook her head. "It's not quite that." She took a deep breath. Her desire to get her secret off her chest finally won out over her worry about what Asirzi would think. She went on, "Ever since Enro, the idea of going into battle has scared me. For the first time, I saw what war really meant. I saw people die. And I didn't hate it."

She looked up, confronting the shock in Asirzi's eyes. "Those soldiers who died, on both sides, did so for a good cause. It was terrible, but it was necessary. I was supposed to feel terrible. I was supposed to be shocked by the sight of death. But I wasn't. I want to see the Alliance fall, no matter how many of their soldiers have to die. I want to go fight.

"When I realized I felt that way, I decided I needed to stay away from the fighting. If I don't, I . . . I don't know what I'll become. And it's hard, wanting to fight and being afraid to."

A silent tension descended upon their table. Asirzi's antennae moved very little, indicating she was deep in thought. Saracasi started to think it would be better if she just left now, instead of subjecting Asirzi to any more conversation.

Before she could rise, Asirzi said, her voice hesitant, "You were fighting for a good cause. It was a necessary fight. And you didn't kill anyone. You told me that. Maarkean had you go into the fight with your weapons on stun."

Closing her eyes, Saracasi finally confessed what she hadn't revealed to anyone. "I changed the setting on my weapon during the fight. Some of the soldiers were in stun-resistant uniforms, and it was taking too many shots to drop them. During the fight, I shot and killed Alliance soldiers. They attacked. Gu'od went down. I responded. I killed them."

Asirzi's antennae flattened against her head in what Saracasi assumed was shocked horror. Tentatively, Asirzi looked into Saracasi's eyes. "And you felt no regret?"

"No!" Saracasi said adamantly. "I don't feel bad about having fought. And I know, every time I do it, it will just get easier. And then I won't care anymore about who I kill."

Silence returned for a moment before Asirzi spoke again. "When Jerik arrived to take Maarkean, what did you do?"

"I shot him," Saracasi said, confused.

"But it didn't work, did it? Why not?"

"I was set to stun," Saracasi said.

"And then what did you do?"

"I stabbed him in the leg with a plasma cutter."

"So you didn't switch to a lethal weapon setting. And you did stab him in the leg instead of someplace more lethal," Asirzi, her voice sounding as if she had just proven her point.

"If I had used a full power blast, I might have hit Maark. And I stabbed him where I could reach. It wasn't intentionally in the leg," Saracasi argued.

Asirzi looked sad for a moment and then nodded. "You did not ask for my opinion, but I'll give it anyway. I don't think you're a monster, nor in any danger of becoming one. You've always done your best to avoid a fight, or to end it with limited bloodshed. Your brother did at least that much right while raising you.

"But I also see no up side to convincing you to go fight. I don't think you have anything to feel guilty about. War is not for everyone. Me, for instance. I believe in independence, but I know my best way to help is to work with Chavatwor. Maybe that's the best thing for you as well."

Saracasi nodded. "You're right. Once Maarkean returns from this mission, I'll resign and go to work full time for Chavatwor. I can still contribute that way, without worrying about having to fight again."

A sense of regret washed over her at that decision. But she knew that regret was the very reason she needed to do this.

"You ready for this?" Zeric asked. They were waiting in a small conference room in the temporary military compound outside Lost Hope, Irod. Firek and the Ice officers were due to join him and his platoon leaders for a planning session. It would be his first confrontation with Firek since Mirthod. He hoped it went better than that one had.

Beside him, Ymp's eyestalks were low to her head. He had learned that when a Camari was preparing for a fight, their eyestalks were elevated and looking around constantly. But when the time to fight came, they lowered close to their skull, in order to protect the vulnerable organ. Ymp's indicated she thought a fight was inevitable.

"I still say we just kill him," Ymp said.

Zeric shook his head. "I'm the one he wants dead, remember?"

"Yes, but he stole my company. He only wants me alive because he knows it's an endless torment."

Shrugging, Zeric decided not to argue. He knew Ymp hated Firek as much as—well, probably more than—he did. But they were on Irod now, and he couldn't afford for that to get in the way. He had a mission to plan, and he needed Ice, and Firek, in order to do it.

While they waited, Zeric looked impatiently out of the open door. After just enough time to be annoyingly late, officers from Ice started coming through the door. He recognized their uniform, but few of their faces. It seemed most of the people he had known, such as Ymp, had been purged.

Once they were all in, Zeric looked for Firek but didn't see him. Glancing back out of the door, he saw the Terran a short way down the corridor. He was in an intense conversation with Davidus Brieni.

Zeric frowned at the sight of the two talking. He had never really trusted Davidus since he had lied to join the team of recruits. Had he known Firek on Mirthod? What could they possibly be talking about now?

As if he could sense Zeric's curiosity, Firek cast a conspiratorial smile his way. He then ended the conversation with Davidus and came to join the others in the conference room.

Taking a seat with his officers, Firek looked at Zeric and said, sarcasm lacing the title, "Well, General, we're here. What's the plan?"

Putting his curiosity aside, Zeric tried to focus on the task at hand. He had never planned a coordinated planet-wide assault before. To be honest, all of his assaults to date had been more or less made up as he went along. This one had to be different.

"Our objective is four Alliance-controlled weapon batteries. We need to take them all out simultaneously. To do that, we need the combined power of the Rogues and Ice."

Zeric wasn't sure why his nickname for his marines felt appropriate to use right then. All of the mercenaries, like Ice, had been lumped in with the marines. He wanted his people to stand out.

While the officers listened, Zeric laid out the attack plan he and Ymp had developed. He thought it was a pretty weak plan. Multiple ways things could go wrong plagued his thoughts. But no one voiced an objection or made any suggestions. That either meant they liked it or no one could think of anything better.

"In order to carry this out, we're going to team up. One Rogue platoon and two Ice squads to each battery," Zeric concluded.

He looked at Firek, waiting for an objection. Instead, the man gave him a slippery smile. "An excellent plan, General. I look forward to working with you."

Zeric suddenly found himself wishing Firek had argued.

"What do you think about this line that Valinther wrote?" Faide asked.

Lahkaba looked up from the terminal he was working from. They were in the final revision stages of their formal announcement of independence. Every delegate had wanted to add something, and Lahkaba had made the mistake of trying to accommodate them all. Now, the formal signing ceremony was supposed to have started already, and he did not have the final version complete.

Scrolling up to the spot that Faide had indicated, Lahkaba read the line. Nothing unusual jumped out at him at first. After reading it a second time, he caught what Faide must be referring to.

"You mean the reference to the Great One?" Lahkaba asked.

Faide nodded. "I understand the significance to your people, but Kowwoks are only one species among many. There are no references to the Kelsolri of the Liw'kel or the God of the Terrans."

"That's because deity worship has largely fallen out of practice among most societies. A trend I support. My people's fixation on the Great One is one of the reasons they're still under the thumb of the Dotran," Lahkaba said scornfully. "Cut it."

It looked as if Faide was about to argue, which made no sense to Lahkaba, but instead he said, "What about his other request, about the Kreogh Sector being a bastion of free trade? That could open the door to trouble when we need to start regulating trade within our own borders."

Lahkaba considered and then shook his head. "Maybe. But trade is one of the big issues behind this independence movement. And it's one of the few things Valinther and Zoeko agree on. This isn't a legally binding document, just a declaration of our intentions and grievances. It doesn't restrict the actions of whatever formal government we put in place."

Before Faide could say anything else, the door to the room swung open, admitting Lei-mey. She looked annoyed, her small mandibles clicking together. With a scathing look, she took both of them in.

"Are you two done yet? We're all waiting."

"Almost," Lahkaba said, straining to keep patience in his voice.

"You don't have to be so precise. We've already declared independence with the vote. This document is just a formality," Lei-mey argued.

"Maybe," Lahkaba said, reading through the last lines one final time. Satisfied, at least for now, he told the computer to print the document onto the special paper he had prepared.

"It may just be a technicality for you, but for history, this will be what they remember. It will be the thing our children are shown that explains why we broke away from the Alliance. We have to make sure we get it right, so that they understand why we did this," Lahkaba said as the page printed.

Lei-mey grunted but said no more. When the computer finished, Lahkaba gently picked up the document and handed it to Faide. The Notha nodded to him and then carefully took the document, walking gingerly with it back toward the congressional meeting room.

Following in the rear, Lahkaba had to squeeze through the crowd to reach his seat. The room was filled with far more people than just the congressional delegates. Maarkean, Zeric, Numba, and Jairyd stood to one side, all wearing the new dark-blue formal dress uniforms. Behind them were a handful of other officers. All around the room, as many people as could be accommodated had been crammed inside, all of them eager to witness history.

Once Lahkaba and Lei-mey took their seats, Faide banged a gavel at his central table. "I call this session of the 3rd Kreogh Sector Congress to session. Our first order of business is the signing of our official Announcement of Independence, which will shortly be delivered to Alliance authorities on each of our respective worlds."

The elderly Notha picked up the paper, holding it out in front of him, and proceeded to read it out loud.

We, the free people of the Kreogh Sector, do hereby express our grievances with the Democratic Alliance of Terra and Braz. As an institution formed in the spirit of democracy and freedom, this Alliance has failed to uphold its own principles and has wronged the people of the Kreogh Sector in the following ways:

1. *Imprisonment of law-abiding citizens without trial or legal representation.*
2. *Denial of suffrage to legal residents not of Terran or Braz descent.*

3. *Unfair and harsh trade restrictions that infringe on the free enterprise of the sector.*
4. *Denial of representation in the Alliance Congress.*
5. *Illegal abolishment of duly-elected governing bodies without the consent of the people.*

For these reasons, the People of the Kreogh Sector have come together to form a new government through which to guide their own destiny, as is the right of all sentient beings. We come together to form a government devoted to the principles of democracy, free enterprise, universal suffrage, and the welfare of the people of the sector.

We, acting with full consent of the people of the United Worlds of the Kreogh Sector as their representatives do, with this declaration, sever our allegiance to the Democratic Alliance of Terra and Braz, revoke all rights and authority from that body, and order their withdrawal from our territory. We wish for continued peace with our Alliance neighbors, but, together, we pledge our lives and fortunes to seeing this order carried out.

Faide finished the reading, letting the words hang over the crowd for a moment. After a moment, he set the document down and said, "As the current chairman of this body, it gives me no end of pleasure to be the first to have the honor of signing it."

Picking up an old-style pen, Faide affixed his signature to the bottom of the document. There would be an electronic document signing later, but all had agreed that a physical signing was more symbolic. Lahkaba agreed with that assessment. Scanning retinas was far less exciting.

After Faide finished, each delegate took a turn going to the central table and affixing their name. When it came to be Lahkaba's turn, he felt nervous. He had been the primary writer of this document, and now it would be recorded and spread across the entire sector. The concern that he had done a terrible job surged to the surface.

As he reached the table, he exchanged a look with Maarkean, who gave him a supportive nod. Steeling himself, he bent over and signed his name. It felt odd doing it with the ink pen. It was not drastically different than a stylus, but he tended to type most things he wrote.

He went back to his seat, and the ceremony continued for another several minutes. Once the last delegate had signed the document, Faide picked it up and walked over to the military personnel. He handed it over to General Numba.

"General, please deliver this to Governor Howell of Sulas. It is time for him to leave and return to Alliance space."

"With pleasure, Chairman," Numba said gruffly, accepting the document. He then ordered, "Right, face," to his men.

Turning sharply on their heels, the military personnel turned to their right. Numba then led the small group from the room, holding the document before him reverently. For the first time, Lahkaba felt a pang of regret that he wouldn't be joining them.

CHAPTER 29

"Once the dock arrives, I'd like to move all work on the larger ships up there. Much easier to do that kind of work in zero-g," Chavatwor explained.

Saracasi nodded, but at the same time, she tried to think of an excuse not to do it. Chavatwor was right—the bigger ships were more efficient to just repair from orbit. Less fuel expended was taking off and landing, and removing large chunks of the hull was simpler when workers didn't have to compete with gravity.

But she hated zero-g. It was a fun experience for the first few minutes. Then it made her nauseous. When she set something down, it should stay there, not rebound and then drift across the room, or out into the blackness of space.

"That will work, I guess," Saracasi finally reluctantly said.

Chavatwor nodded enthusiastically and then switched the holo display to show a design diagram. Saracasi's interest in their conversation perked up. Logistical discussions were necessary to keep the shipyard running, but they weren't very exciting. Now she was looking at the reactor relays aboard the FX-21, and her mind immediately starting functioning again.

Pointing to a spot on the diagram, Chavatwor began, "I was thinking—"

He was interrupted as Saisee Traze, one of the naval personnel who had been left behind, entered. The short Camari, his eyestalks rigid and his stride urgent, spoke rapidly. "Major! Our early warning satellites just picked up an Alliance fleet dropping out of hyperspace."

Saracasi's first reaction was that this was a joke or a mistake. Either would have been annoying. Hoping to prove it a joke, she turned back to the holodisplay and called up the satellite feeds.

A three-dimensional representation of Kol appeared along with all orbital ship traffic. Like all detection grids, gaps existed the closer one got to the planet's surface. But in this case, what they wanted to see was clearly visible in a high orbit over the planet. Five Alliance warships were moving in formation. As she watched, several more symbols appeared, showing fighters launching from one of the ships—presumably a carrier.

"It must be a coincidence," Chavatwor said, his voice quavering slightly. "A regular patrol. They don't come to Kol often, but they do come."

"A random patrol that shows up just after Sartori calls all naval ships back to Ailleroc *and* after our main fleet departs?" Saracasi said.

She could feel her heart start pumping faster. One of the things she had feared looked like it was about to come true. The Alliance had come here, and they didn't have anything to defend themselves with.

"Saisee," Saracasi said, trying to keep her voice calm. "Go and get Lieutenant Needa and Master Sergeant Adat'to in here. On the double."

The Camari paused for a noticeable second, watching the holographic display. With a shake of his eye stalks, he then turned and ran from the room. In truth, she wasn't sure she could blame him if he were just running as far as he could.

"What's the status of your defense shield?" Saracasi asked.

Chavatwor did not respond immediately, and she had to touch his arm to get his attention. The big Kowwok shook his head wildly. "Not complete. It's been on the low priority list. We only just finished the satellite network."

"Well, it's a good thing you did. It's given us a little over half an hour prep time." She studied the terminal more closely. "Maybe more. They seem to be on a course to bring them to a higher, geosynchronous orbit. From there, they'll be able to just rain destruction down upon us. Or launch bombers."

Saracasi's mind raced. She could see three options before her. And as much as she didn't like having to decide, as the senior officer present, it was her decision to make. She had decided to resign when Maarkean got back, but he wasn't back yet.

The first option was mainly wishful thinking. Chavatwor could be right. The Alliance fleet might not have any interest in them. With the main fleet gone, a casual glance from orbit would just show them to be like any number of other operations in the desert. If they did nothing, the Alliance fleet might just fly on past and leave them alone.

The second choice was to abandon the outpost and disappear to hide in the desert. The warships and equipment would be the Alliance's primary objective. They could get all of the people away and probably save their lives. The desert wasn't an ideal place to run to, but if they brought enough water with them, there were plenty of places to hide. This held some appeal in that it was simple.

Her final option could only be described as crazy. Instead of hiding, they could fight. They had an entire squadron of fighters and a frigate available to them. From what she could tell, the Alliance had brought only a small fleet: an escort carrier, frigate, a corvette, and a few gunships. In theory, their frigate should outclass any one of those ships. If the carrier had brought bombers, then they probably would have superiority in fighter craft.

But to fight was what she needed to avoid the most. The FX-21, while a potentially powerful warship, was just that—potential. They had not tested the weaponry and had only just gotten the shields to a point where they didn't collapse and bring every system offline every ten minutes.

In addition, their fighters would undoubtedly be at least a generation out of date compared to the ones the Alliance flew. While Davidus had been training the pilots well, the Alliance pilots would have years of experience. Jerik might actually have more combat experience, and Sienn'lyn might be the best natural pilot her brother had ever seen, but the rest of the squadron was not much more than raw recruits.

Still debating her options, Saracasi ran out of time as Saisee led Jerik and Deja'z'reth, the remaining marine officer, into the room. Now that there were others present, she knew she couldn't appear indecisive. That was a point both Maarkean and Davidus had hammered into her. A wrong decision was better than no decision in battle. Troops didn't follow wishy-washy.

"An Alliance fleet has just appeared in orbit," Saracasi said, trying to make her voice calm, though she was sure she failed. "It is not certain yet that they are heading for us, but that is the most likely explanation."

"How could they know about us?" Jerik asked, concerned.

"How did you know about us?' Saracasi asked pointedly.

Embarrassed, Jerik said sheepishly, "My employer told me."

"Then if he knows, the Alliance can know. Besides, with all the business Chavatwor has been doing, it was only a matter of time before the Alliance learned about this shipyard. Their timing is just poor," Saracasi said, trying to dismiss the issue.

In truth, she wondered about that as well. Chavatwor had been very selective about his clientele, only choosing those who supported the rebellion against the Alliance. That was Asirzi's primary job in the negotiations—gauging their support for the rebellion. It was possible one of the companies had leaked the location, but she didn't see what benefit they would get for it. All the companies that hired Chava had invested a lot of money into his work. Getting the shipyard blown apart by the Alliance would be a foolish business decision.

"With the main fleet deployed, it is up to us to defend and hold this base," Saracasi said, moving forward. "Jerik, get your fighters prepped and ready to launch. But keep them dirtside. There's still a chance they're just patrolling. No point in giving them our position unless we have to."

Jerik nodded, and Saracasi turned to Deja'z'reth. "Deja, I know you just have raw recruits left, but get them guns and prepare to defend the base. Chavatwor is going to try to get the base shield functional, and your marines need to buy him time if any troop ships come down."

In truth, she did not think the Alliance would send troops down. The small fleet probably carried a platoon between them. Unlike their converted transports, the Alliance gunships did not have room for marines. But the marines needed to be doing something.

"Saisee, get everyone we have aboard the FX. It's time she got to flex her muscles."

It felt weird not having Maarkean at the helm. While this wasn't the first time Zeric had flown into battle aboard the *Cutty Sark* without Maarkean, it still seemed wrong. This ship was just as much a part of Maarkean as Zeric's Razors hat was a part of him.

He watched out of the flight deck's window as Fracsid brought the ship in for a landing. They had been flying low across the surface of Sulas, reminding him of their raid on Olan. This time, though, they wouldn't begin their raid with an air strike and wouldn't end it by freeing prisoners.

Looking out of the sides of the windows, he tried to see the other two gunships that were carrying the rest of his strike team. When all he saw was the dark night sky, he felt relieved. If he could see them, then so could the Alliance.

Fracsid set the *Cutty Sark* down onto the ground with a shudder. Zeric gulped, knowing that now it was his turn to perform. Fracsid had succeeded in getting them through the Alliance detection network. His crazy plan now had to work.

"Good luck, General," Fracsid said, turning in the pilot's seat.

"You, too," Zeric said, exiting the flight deck. Fracsid's next job was a simple one: take Kard and pick up the *Chimopori*. After that, it all depended on if the Alliance fleet stayed away.

He moved down the narrow corridor and through the door leading down to the cargo hold. The entire ship was dark, lit only with dim emergency lighting. The darkness served more to help everyone adapt their eyes to the dark than to hide the ship, as the flight deck had the only window.

Once on the stairs, he looked over the assembled marines, two squads from 1st Platoon. They were crammed into the bay tightly. The rest of the platoon along with their group from Ice Company were coming in two other gunships and would meet them outside, if they made it to the surface safely.

Gu'od approached him through the darkness. "All marines ready, General."

Zeric suppressed a growl. Gu'od loved to call him "general" every chance he got. Instead, he whispered to his friend, "Now the fun begins."

Louder, he called out, "All right, Rogues. Move out!"

The cargo bay door lowered and a putrid stench wafted into the bay. They had landed in a swamp, far from any city or home. On a world that still had ample places to settle, no one wanted to live near a rotting quagmire.

Jogging out of the ship, Zeric followed the marines through the bog. They only had a short hike before encountering the rest of 1st Platoon, led by Sigfa Neith. Even though they were still kilometers away from the Alliance gun battery, everyone remained quiet when they met up.

They had to wait a short time for the detachment from Ice. During the wait, Zeric almost held out hope that they weren't coming. But they did arrive, which was just as well—without them, taking the Alliance gun battery would have been a tall order.

After talking quietly with Sigfa and Firek, who for once said nothing antagonizing, to ascertain everything had gone smoothly on their ends, Zeric ordered them into the swamp. They had a few hours of hiking to go. While he would have preferred not to crawl through a swamp before beginning a major assault, it couldn't be helped.

The planetary defense battery was located far off the beaten path. It existed not to defend any particular city, but merely to give the planet defense coverage from every angle of approach. The other three batteries that Ymp and Ice were assaulting were similarly isolated. With no one living nearby, these would be less well guarded than a battery that was part of a major military base. But it also meant any ship getting close would be more carefully scrutinized.

Two hours of slogging through the swamp left Zeric tired and covered with mud. When they saw the lights of the gun battery start to appear through the dense trees, he called a halt. Checking his watch, he was relieved to see that he could afford to let everyone rest for a while before beginning the assault.

Beside him, Gu'od looked like he always did—powerful and ready to go. Zeric again cursed his friend's excellent physical condition. Training the marines the last few months had put Zeric in the best shape of his life, but he was still exhausted. Gu'od did not appear to be.

When the time on his watch grew uncomfortably close to the time that the fleet would appear in Sulas orbit, Zeric called for everyone to move forward. They crept the rest of the way, approaching the edge of the tree line quietly. Several hundred meters still separated them from the gun batteries, but any further movement would undoubtedly trigger a wide array of perimeter sensors.

"Rocket teams," Zeric said, activating his throat mike for the first time. They had maintained comm silence through the march. But now, a stray comm signal would not matter. They were about to give away their position in a much bigger way.

Several teams of marines moved forward, just to the edge of the tree line. They each carried portable rocket launchers that they had dragged through the swamp. Zeric did not envy them that task. Once every team reported ready on the comm network, Zeric gave the order. "Fire."

The silent night air suddenly filled with the roaring whoosh as a dozen rockets flashed out. They sailed over the short distance to the wall surrounding the gun battery in less than a heartbeat. The sound of their launch seemed insignificant next to the thunder of their explosions.

In the light generated by the Alliance base, Zeric could see several holes appear in the wall. Two defensive towers also collapsed, taking their guns with them. In the span of only a few moments, gunfire began raining down from atop the remaining wall sections of the base. This outpost had not been slacking off in their preparations, Zeric acknowledged. A few rockets would not overwhelm them.

Fortunately, he had prepared for that. He said into his mike, "Masks!"

He pulled a visor down from atop his head, cutting off his vision and ability to hear anything. Completely isolated from outside stimuli, aside from the wetness of his pants and the earpiece he wore, Zeric gave the next order. "Shock and awe!"

After firing their deadly payloads, the rocket teams had reloaded their launchers with a specialized SAA munitions. At his order, they fired their second barrage. This time, instead of exploding in a deadly concussion wave of shrapnel, the SAA missiles detonated in a bright flash.

This bright flash was more than just visible light. It generated a field that blanketed out everything across a wide range of the EM spectrum. Infrared, ultraviolet, radio, and even auditory sensors were completely overloaded. Anyone looking at the device would be completely blinded, as would any sensor equipment attached to automated weapons.

Without being given another order, something that was impossible with their comm gear jammed just as much as the Alliance's, the marines carefully charged forward, blinded not by the SAA but by the protective masks they all wore. Rushing across the uneven and still swampy field toward the base blind was dangerous. But in fifteen seconds, they would all be able to remove their masks and be able to see again. Any Alliance trooper who had been unprotected would be stunned for quite a bit longer.

As he ran, Zeric counted the time down in his head. He got to fifteen, when the blast should burn itself out, and kept going. Even though the SAA charge weakened toward the end, it would still blind him. Reaching twenty, he pulled the mask up and was rewarded by a clear view of the broken wall ahead of him.

Sporadic fire still came from the Alliance position. Either the troopers were firing blind, trying to hit whatever was attacking them, or other troops who had been inside during the SAA attack had emerged, fully capable of seeing and shooting. Whichever it happened to be, Zeric didn't care. Raising his rife to his shoulder, he started firing at any shape he saw on the wall that looked like a threat.

When he reached the wall, Zeric stopped running and pressed himself against it beside several other marines who had beaten him there. He glanced back across the field and saw many more marines still running. Mixed in with the dark ground, he also saw several unmoving shapes. Some marines hadn't made it across uninjured.

Putting the dead or injured marines from his mind, Zeric edged over to the hole nearest him. He peered inside the Alliance base and was disappointed to see a defensive line forming across the short open space. Whomever was in charge of this outpost had not slacked on preparing their troops. He could make out several troopers still evidently stunned by the SAA attack, but just as many were setting up fixed gun mounts.

While he considered how best to push forward, the night air around him suddenly lit up with blaster fire coming from *behind* them. Turning, he saw that the members of Ice Company had not followed the marines across the field. And now they were firing on him.

CHAPTER 30

Maarkean felt the familiar weight of his SK-9 on his right hip. He had never been a fan of gunfights, but the weapon somehow gave him comfort. With the *Cutty Sark* out there being flown by someone else and Saracasi back on Kol, it was nice to have something he was comfortable with nearby.

Standing in the CIC onboard the *Defiant Glory*, he felt exposed. At the central tactical display, he was in the middle of everything. By design, this gave him access to every station. It also meant he was in view of every crewman. It brought home the point that they were all counting on him.

The area around him felt crowded, even though there was ample space. Beside him stood Davidus, Lohcja, and Kaars. Davidus had wanted to fly with the fighters, but for once, they had more qualified pilots than fighters. Maarkean had insisted his skills would be better served commanding the *Defiant Glory*.

Lohcja and Kaars were here as General Numba's official liaisons and intelligence officers. Maarkean had suggested that Numba fly aboard the *Rogue Spirit,* as it would be disastrous if something were to happen to the *Defiant Glory* and take out both senior commanders. Numba had insisted on leaving an officer in his place. Maarkean had been lucky it was Lohcja.

Aside from his fellow officers and the *Defiant Glory's* crew, marines were positioned around the room. Like his pistol, they were there mainly as a precaution. It was better to have marines standing by in case you were boarded than to get boarded and not have them.

"Thirty seconds to exit from hyperspace," Ceno Gotit, the *Defiant Glory*'s Camari helmsman, called from the forward bridge section.

At the marker, Davidus gave him a slight nod and moved to his battle position at the front of the ship. He would oversee direct combat operations for the ship while Maarkean orchestrated the fleet. With luck, neither of them would have much to do.

With a slight shudder, the fleet dropped out of hyperspace. The blank tactical display in front of Maarkean came to life, showing the image of Sulas before them. Slowly, icons started appearing, representing ships and other navigational hazards. From the forward section, he heard Davidus issue orders.

"Ops, begin full sensor sweep. FlightOps, signal the other ships of our arrival. Try to make contact with our gunship squadron."

After a moment, Tadashio, the ship's Kowwok Operations officer replied, "Sensor contact made with all ships from the fleet. Scans of the system have picked up our gunships, right where they are supposed to be. Multiple other contacts in orbit or approaching orbit of Sulas. Identified as highly probable civilian vessels."

As Tadashio reported, Maarkean's tactical computer updated the sensor data. Blue icons appeared around the *Defiant Glory* and a set of six more blue icons were shown approaching them. Those represented the Union's warships and troop transports.

Yellow icons appeared near the planet of Sulas. These were unidentified ships that were not judged to be hostile, but had not been confirmed. As the next few minutes went on, most of the yellow icons changed to green, indicated they had been positively identified as non-threats.

Fracsid's voice came over the comm system as the Flight Operations officer made contact with the gunships. "Glad to see you guys. We're all accounted for and our package has been delivered."

"Signal the fleet," Maarkean ordered, relieved to hear that the insertion of the marines had gone off as planned. "Begin moving into planned orbit. Have the gunships take up guard positions around the transports."

The fleet would approach Sulas along a preplanned path. This would keep them along a vector that allowed only four planet-based defense batteries to have a chance to shoot at them. If Zeric's marines had done their job, those batteries would not be a threat.

"Launch all fighters," Davidus ordered. Maarkean frowned but said nothing. He would have only launched a CAP, Combat Air Patrol, until more were needed. The more fighters they had out, the harder it would be to recover all of them. But the decision was up to Davidus.

As the fleet approached closer to Sulas, Maarkean felt a growing sense of nervousness. He could not explain why. They had arrived to find no Alliance presence, just like they had expected. Their gunships had been in orbit and had delivered the marines. As far as operations went, this one appeared to be coming off without a hitch.

But that was exactly what bothered him. No plan survived contact with the enemy. There were still a lot of steps to go before Sulas was under their control. If the marines didn't get all four batteries, it would be a bumpy ride down to the planet's surface for the troops.

The military commanders could decide to risk launching their defensive fighters and attack them. That was their biggest risk, as their fighters would be outnumbered. But without fleet support, the ground-based fighters would face a tough fight.

Braz civilization had mostly abandoned the belief in an all-powerful personified deity. Instead, most believed in the philosophy of cosmic balance. Maarkean counted himself among them. Things couldn't be this easy without something balancing it out.

Almost as if on cue, the universe balanced things out.

"New contacts!" Tadashio shouted. "Five, no, nine, eighteen ships just jumped out of hyperspace behind us. They are deployed in a wide net around us. Identification program is confirming them as Alliance warships!"

On Maarkean's holo display, eighteen red icons appeared. As the identification program ran, he suddenly felt ill. Eighteen ships were more than the Alliance was supposed to have in the entire sector. They were outnumbered almost two to one.

Across the room he tried to catch Davidus' eye. The intel he had gotten was clearly inaccurate. Either too busy, or too embarrassed, Davidus did not look back. Maarkean contented himself with casting a glare to his side where the intelligence officer, Kaars, stood.

"Looks like your information about the Alliance fleet was wrong," Maarkean snarled at the man.

Kaars, for his part, looked embarrassed. To Maarkean's surprise, Lohcja was the one to voice a defensive response. "Now's not the time for accusations, General."

Lohcja gave him an intense glare, made all the more uncomfortable by his Ronid physique. Reluctantly, Maarkean nodded an agreement. He was right, there would be time for accusations of failed intelligence later. If there was a later.

"All ships," Maarkean said, achieving the fleet wide comm, "prepare to alter course away from Sulas. Prepare for emergency hyperspace jump. Randomize courses. Meet at rendezvous point beta."

Acknowledgements came in from the other ships and he heard Davidus issue the orders to the *Defiant Glory*'s crew. Then another voice came over the fleet-wide comm. "This is General Numba. Belay that last order. All ships continue on course for Sulas, maximum speed."

Maarkean cursed, too late realizing he had failed to keep it under his breath. Calming himself as best he could, he reactivated his comm. "General, we've clearly walked into an Alliance trap. We are outnumbered and outgunned. If we break off now, we can escape with minimal casualties. The deeper we go into the gravity well, the longer our escape will take."

"I understand that, *Major* General," Numba replied. "But with those defense batteries taken out, this is our best chance to get troops onto the surface. This war will be won on the ground."

"We have not yet received the confirmation code from the marines. We don't know if those guns are in our control. We could get trapped between the Alliance fleet and ground weapons," Maarkean countered, hating the idea of arguing with his superior over an open communication line. But he saw no other alternative. "Even if we can get the transports down, without space superiority, they'll be vulnerable to surface bombardment."

"You have your orders. Take the fleet in," Numba replied gruffly, and then severed the comm channel.

Maarkean faced a choice. If he obeyed Numba's orders, he felt certain the fleet would be lost. The army could possibly reach the relative safety of the planet's surface. But his warships would not survive the engagement.

If he disobeyed, the fleet would be torn apart by two commanders. Some ships would flee, others would try to land. The Alliance would then have a far easier time picking them off. It would also mean he would be betraying the Union he had just sworn to protect. Split apart, there was no chance of defeating the Alliance.

Regretting the choice, Maarkean realized he had to hope Numba was right, and that the war could be won on the ground. Because he knew it certainly would not be won up here.

"All ships, belay my last. Continue on course for Sulas," Maarkean ordered.

A thought suddenly occurred to him and a mischievous grin crept onto his face. He was about to lose this battle, but that didn't mean they had to lose the war. "Get me the *Gallant*. I want to speak directly with Captain Novastar."

It had been a mad scramble to get the FX-21 crewed and ready for battle. Volunteers had had to be taken from among Chavatwor's dock workers, many of whom were less than enthusiastic about the idea. But they had done it, and the ship was nearing the completion of her start-up sequence.

Fortunately, preparing the squadron of fighters had been simpler. Jerik had proven himself capable by having already had them at a state of ready alert. It had been a simple matter to get the pilots onboard and the systems checked.

Now, Saracasi stood at the center of the frigate's bridge. Frigates were designed to operate independently, and this one was no exception. As such, she had a central command center, which naval parlance referred to as a bridge. Bigger ships would also have Combat Information Centers which were better equipped for coordinating battles with other vessels. Saracasi would have to coordinate with Jerik's squadron from here.

Around her, the unprepared crew went about finishing the last preparations before launch. No one had formal battle stations, since the ship had no formal crew, and Saracasi spent most of her time trying to ensure every necessary role was filled. Fortunately, she knew how ships worked, and Davidus' lessons on combat operations had been easily integrated into her memory.

She glanced at the countdown timer. In five minutes, the Alliance fleet would pass the point of no return. After that, they would be on no other course than one that would put them directly in geosynchronous orbit of the UDF shipyard.

Once that happened, their three options would drop to two: fight or flee.

As Saracasi ran through her crew assignments again, she realized she had missed something. One of the things Maarkean and Davidus had stressed during training classes was the necessity of a clear chain of command. So far, she had ensured that people were manning the ship's guns, there was an engineering team made up of the best they had, and damage control parties were on hand to respond. But she had neglected a chain of officers.

Looking up, she considered the other two on the bridge. Arzesaeth Ernebee sat at the helm, his dark red carapace looking black in the dim bridge lighting. She knew him to be a fair pilot who had participated in all the training courses Davidus had held. Sheanna Coramont, a dark-haired Terran woman, operated the engineering station. Both had been granted lieutenant's commissions and had been slated to serve as officers aboard one of the fleet's ships.

Saracasi knew Sheanna far better than she did Arzesaeth. As a fellow engineer, though her background in materials was only tangentially linked to starships, she spoke the same language as Saracasi. She felt more comfortable with the other woman.

Then she thought about her brother. He and Davidus almost hated each other, but they respected each other. Like with Zeric, Davidus and Maarkean did not see the world through the same lens. A good commander did not surround themselves with people who thought the same way. That meant there wouldn't be any new ideas.

"Arz," Saracasi said, deciding to be less formal to help ease the mood. "Turn the helm over to Saisee. I need you serving as Tactical Action Officer and XO."

Startled, Arzesaeth turned back, his large mandibles spread wide. He considered her order for a moment, clearly uncertain how to respond. After a second, he said, "Aye, Captain."

He stood up and moved to a position by the weapon and tactical systems. In his place, Saisee slipped into the helm seat. Saracasi knew the Camari had flown the ship during some test runs. He would do fine, she told herself.

"Sheanna," Saracasi continued, keeping her voice light. "You'll be 2nd officer and chief engineer. Get down to engineering. We can't have all officers in one room during battle."

With a nod, Sheanna left the bridge. By the time the rearranging of assignments was complete, the timer had passed zero. With a hopeful glance, Saracasi checked the feed from the satellites. The Alliance fleet had not changed course. Their time was up.

CHAPTER 31

"Captain," said Celay Dar'Su, his Liw'kel operations officer, "we're being signaled by the flagship. Fleet command requests to speak to you."

Solyss suppressed a smile. They were in a tough situation, and the argument between General Ocaitchi and General Numba had disturbed him. But if Maarkean was calling him, it meant the general had a brilliant plan.

Picking up the headset from his terminal, Solyss keyed himself over to the private channel. "This is *Gallant* actual. Go ahead, sir."

"Solyss, I have an important mission for you," Maarkean said without preamble. That came as no surprise to Solyss. Novastars always got the important missions.

The next bit made him think Maarkean had gone mad. "You are to immediately break off from the fleet and return to Kol. There you are to take on supplies and inform Major Ocaitchi to continue acquiring ships and crew. Then you are to head to the rendezvous in Trepon Sector with all haste. Negotiate a deal for as much assistance from any planet in Trepon as you can and secure Josserand's aid in acquiring control of the *Black Market*."

"I'm sorry, sir, could you repeat your order?" Solyss asked, hoping he had merely misunderstood.

"Go to Trepon. Do whatever is necessary to get aid and to gain control of the *Black Market*. This is imperative, Solyss. We are heavily outnumbered. The fleet is not likely to survive this engagement. We're going to do our best to get as many troops on the ground as we can. But they're going to need space support again when the next battle comes to Sulas. We need the *Black Market*. You and Saracasi are our only hope in maintaining a threat to the Alliance fleet. The Union is counting on you."

Solyss was so taken aback that he could hardly process the whole message. At first, all he heard was that Maarkean was admitting defeat and that he, Solyss Novastar, was being ordered to run away. He would be the first Novastar in the history of the galaxy to flee from a just fight.

But then the rest of the message made its way into his understanding. Maarkean was about to lead the rest of the fleet to a glorious death fighting the Alliance, but it would be to save the army troops. They would land and take control of Sulas. And by sending Solyss off on this mission, Maarkean was ensuring the fleet would be reborn, though it would take months for it to happen.

Solyss had been prepared to make the ultimate sacrifice for the Union. It was the highest honor a Novastar could achieve—dying for the right cause, just as his forebear, Mace, had done against the Kravic. Maarkean was now proving his own honor. He couldn't let that sacrifice be in vain.

"I understand, sir," Solyss said, confidence returning to his voice. "We won't let you down. The *Black Market* will be here before you know it, ready to kick the Alliance out of the sector for good."

"Thank you, Solyss. Good luck," Maarkean said and ended the link.

Solyss stood up, straightening his shoulders to his full height. "Lieutenant Tess."

His executive officer turned from her position behind the helmsman. "Alter course to one five three by three eight. Engines at full burn. Plot a random hyperspace course."

Looking confused, the Camari woman bobbed her eyestalks. "Sir? We're withdrawing? I thought General Numba ordered the fleet to continue to Sulas."

Nodding, Solyss said. "He did. And General Ocaitchi is complying with that order. But we have a new mission. General Ocaitchi will get the army to the surface of Sulas. It will be our job to help them get back off again."

Zeric's mind raced. They were pinned down against the damaged wall surrounding the Alliance weapons battery. This close, the wall-mounted weapons would not be able to target them. They had not yet been able to make headway through and into the base. And a new enemy was at their backs.

He had known that trusting Firek and Ice would be a mistake. Knowing he had been right gave him little comfort. There wouldn't be a lot of time to revel in that satisfaction.

Fortunately, he hadn't been completely unprepared for this. On the comm he said, "Begin Operation Traitor."

Zeric then switched his comm gear over to a new, pre-planned frequency. He had worked this much out with Sigfa before they had departed from Irod. Unfortunately, that was as far as they were able to plan. They hadn't had a lot to work with, thinking Ice might betray them but not having any idea *how*.

"What do you want to do, General?" Sigfa asked over the comm. In the darkness, Zeric couldn't see the lieutenant among the other marines scattered across the wall.

"Well, it looks like Ice has betrayed us, and since the Alliance is no longer shooting into the woods, they're working together," Zeric said, trying to get his mind to think. "But I don't see any other choice. We press forward. Those troop ships are going to be easy targets unless we can take over these guns. Or at least disrupt their operation for a while."

Turning to the marines around him, Zeric shouted. "Grenades!"

Together, several marines pulled grenades from their gear and hurled them through the wall opening. A moment later, several explosions sounded. Zeric paused a few more seconds to ensure all the grenades had gone off, but not all the marines were so patient.

One young Ronid dashed through the opening before Zeric could stop him and took a delayed grenade full force. Zeric cursed the outcome, but he knew that wouldn't be the first casualty today.

As the marines stood back up from the relative safety of the rubble around the wall, fire from behind them started finding targets. Several marines fell, injured or dead. But many others fired back toward the woods, Zeric included.

When it came his turn to go through the wall, Zeric reluctantly turned his gun forward. He would have much preferred to shoot Firek than any of the Alliance soldiers. They were at least upholding their oath to defend the Alliance.

Zeric heard blaster bolts whizzing past his head but didn't feel anything hit him. Even if the Alliance had been tipped off about their attack, they couldn't have had a tight defense set up. Zeric had let Fracsid decide where to set down, which determined which side of the base they attacked from. And the holes made by the rocket attack had been more or less random.

Pushing forward, Zeric shouted for the marines to keep moving. He didn't do a lot of shooting himself. His role was to keep the attack from stalling. Momentarily, he felt glad that Ice had betrayed them. With a hostile enemy behind them, it was less likely anyone would get the idea to turn and run away from the barrage of fire the Alliance was throwing at them.

Once the marines were through the wall, the rain of fire from behind them stopped. That had been his primary reason to keep pushing the attack. They were more exposed out there. Now they just had the Alliance to deal with.

After coming through the wall, they took cover beside a small storage shed. The area they had entered was small. Several structures cut them off from any of the other teams. Zeric had about ten marines with him, and there were just as many Alliance troops facing them. The defensive troops were still focused on trying to set up a heavy repeating blaster mount. Once they finished that, it would be a quick ending.

"Keeping firing!" Zeric shouted. "Concentrate on that repeater mount!"

Beside him, blaster rifle shots filled the air as his marines traded fire with the Alliance defenders. Zeric raised his rifle to add to the fray. The universe around him retreated. The sounds of so much blaster fire in such a confined space overwhelmed his hearing. The odor of burned flesh dominated his sense of smell. But Zeric's conscious mind was aware of none of it. The only things that existed were his rifle and whatever lay at the end of its sight. He concentrated on eliminating that part of the universe.

After what seemed an eternity, the fire died down. Zeric swept his rifle around the small area, looking for new targets. He only found Alliance forces lying bleeding on the ground.

Looking over the troops, Zeric tried to identify who was with him through the darkness. He was disappointed to not see Gu'od among them. Gamaly's warning flashed in the back of his mind, but he ignored it. If he lived through the night, she'd be welcome to kill him.

"Sergeant Ocif!" Zeric said, finally identifying the leader of 2nd Squad. He had to shout to hear himself through his abused eardrums. "Get two marines onto that gun and finish setting it up. Ice is going to be coming through that hole any minute."

Obod Ocif nodded his furry Notha head and directed some marines to get to work. Zeric then sent two to follow the fleeing Alliance guards and ensure no reinforcements came without warning. Once that was done, Zeric tried to figure out where they were within the base.

A quick inspection of the area turned up some clues. He identified the structure they had taken cover behind as housing a garbage bin. They appeared to be in a small alley, probably next to the mess. That meant one of the other nearby buildings would be the barracks. But thanks to the Alliance being on alert, it was probably empty.

"Repeaters ready, sir," Sergeant Ocif called.

Zeric nodded and went over to the two marines who were manning the gun. "Hold that hole, Private. Make any Ice member who tries to come through pay for thinking they can betray us."

The young Braz private's expression was dark and grim. Zeric felt a moment of revulsion that such a look of contempt marred such a young woman's face. But looking back at the marine bodies that lay behind them, he couldn't blame the girl.

"Let's move out, Sergeant," Zeric said and the remaining marines pushed forward.

Coming to an intersection, Zeric faced a choice. To his left lay the command center for the gun battery. Targeting computers, weapon controls, and sensor relays would all be located there. If he had to render the batteries inoperative rather than taking them over, that would be his best place to go.

To his right came gun fire. A battle raged there between marines and Alliance troops. Those marines were pinned between Alliance and Ice. Gu'od could be among those trapped. If he went that way, he could turn the pincer around and pin the Alliance between them.

For every commander, the mission was supposed to come before the lives of any one soldier. Before battle started, a commander had to think about their safety. Once it began, the mission had been decided to be worth risking their lives, and completing the mission became the top priority.

But that was one reason Zeric had never wanted to be an officer. Being part of a squad meant looking out for each other and working to get everyone through a mission alive. Yes, the mission must be accomplished, but that included watching each other's backs.

"This way, Rogues," Zeric said, making his decision.

Chapter 32

"Oh, shit!"

Despite the tension, Maarkean looked across the CIC toward the unprofessional declaration that had come out of Tadashio. The Operations officer had not followed up his declaration with an explanation. Turning back to the tactical display, Maarkean quickly understood.

Sulas' planetary defense batteries had started firing. The barrage lanced up from the surface and tore apart two of the troop transports. Each one would have been carrying close to a thousand army soldiers.

The situation Maarkean found himself in suddenly got much darker, something he wouldn't have thought possible a moment ago. The battle was not going well by any definition he knew, unless you were a member of the Alliance.

Beside him, Lohcja was speaking frantically into his headset. "*Rogue Spirit*, come in. Come in, *Rogue Spirit*."

The Ronid looked up and saw Maarkean watching him. His mandibles drooped slightly. "No response. The sensors show them as dead."

Admiral Numba's flagship and one third of the fleet's capital ships had been bracketed by fire from the Alliance's battle carrier, *Dominance*. With so much interference from weapons fire, sensor jamming, and radiation from destroyed ships, sensor data was unreliable. But Maarkean didn't think the ship was there anymore. If the *Rogue Spirit* was gone, then Admiral Numba was dead, and Maarkean was in charge again.

"*Defiant Glory!*" The comm buzzed with calls from the transports. "The planetary batteries have fired on us. What do we do?"

Maarkean struggled to come up with a plan. Unfortunately, retreating to hyperspace was no longer an option for them. They were cut off by the Alliance forces and too deep into Sulas' gravity well. They were almost literally stuck between a rock and a hard place.

Before Maarkean could answer, the tactical display lit up again with more planet-based weapons fire. He anticipated more destroyed transports and tried to identify the weapons' targets. Maybe he could warn them to maneuver in time. The *Defiant Glory*'s mining sensors were far more sophisticated than anything those transports carried.

To his delight, the new incoming fire found and obliterated an Alliance corvette. A few moments later, another planetary battery opened fire, damaging an Alliance frigate. Intervals of fire from the three batteries began alternating, only the first one targeting the vulnerable transports.

Zeric had come through, after all, though he appeared to have only been 50% successful. Maarkean corrected himself—one battery was not firing, which in this case was the same as a win, so Zeric had been 75% successful. Which, he knew, would turn out to be far better results than he would manage today.

"All ships change course and head toward batteries Alpha and Gamma. Get under their protection and head down to the surface," Maarkean ordered.

The fleet began to shift, but he knew it wouldn't be in time to save all of them. A few thousand soldiers would die to the fire from that ground battery. But it would be small compared to the tens of thousands who now had a safe path to the surface.

As Maarkean watched the tactical map change, he tried to anticipate the Alliance's response to the changing situation.

With one of his few warships already destroyed or disabled, the ground fire would now be the only thing keeping the Alliance fleet at bay. Unfortunately, the large mass of transports would give the Alliance fleet cover to fire from long range.

"Signal all fighters and gunships," Maarkean said. "Have them move in with the fleet. Prepare to engage Alliance fighter craft. They are to cover the transports' landing and then join the forces on the ground. They are not to return to the carriers."

Because there's only one carrier left, he didn't say. And this one probably would not last much longer. Hopefully the fighters would be of some use to Zeric on the ground.

That thought suddenly almost made him laugh. With the destruction of Numba's ship, and soon his own destruction, Zeric would be the senior commander of the military forces. This invasion would now become his responsibility. Zeric would curse his name for dying and leaving that to him.

He'd never really understood gallows humor before now.

"The cruiser *Ordinance* is continuing to advance on the transports," Lohcja noted. "Shouldn't they be keeping away from the ground fire?"

Maarkean shook his head. "Cruisers are primarily designed for ground assault. That includes soaking up some damage from ground fire. They are heavily shielded and armored along one plane. That makes them vulnerable in space battles but a tough SOB in an assault."

If he had needed proof that Alliance reinforcements had arrived from Braz, that cruiser was it. The one cruiser that had been in the sector, the *Entala*, was still undergoing repairs at Ailleroc. The presence of another one could have only come from the rest of the fleet.

"*Liberator*," Maarkean said into the comm to Owrik's frigate. "Move with us toward the cruiser *Ordinance*. Maneuver to get on her ventral side. She'll be vulnerable there. If we can force her to maneuver, we should be able to save some of those transports."

"Acknowledged," Owrik replied.

Davidus had been listening to Maarkean's order and began moving the *Defiant Glory* without waiting for a specific order. There were a lot of Alliance ships in their way, so they might not make it. But at least they would go down trying.

A sudden vibration swept through the deck plating. Maarkean's first thought was that they had been hit by an unseen torpedo. When no reports of hull breeches followed, he looked to Davidus.

The Terran pilot held up his hand, a gesture to wait a moment. Then he said something into his headset before turning and walking from the forward bridge back toward the CIC. "La'ari just reported that the reactor overloaded. We're dead in the water. Running on emergency generators. Shields, weapons, and engines are all down. We have communication, life support, and sensors only."

Saracasi had warned him about this. The *Defiant Glory* had not been designed as a warship. They were seriously overtaxing the reactor with all the added strain of combat. Heavier weapons and shields had not helped that problem.

The reactor had almost failed during their assault on Roc 5. He had thought improvements had been made, but apparently they hadn't been enough to overcome the intensity of this battle.

With a resigned sigh, Maarkean rekeyed the comm. "*Liberator*, our reactor has overloaded. We are out of the fight. If you think you can engage the cruiser, do so. If not, get your ship to the surface."

"Understood, *Defiant Glory*," the response came a few seconds later. "It has been an honor."

Maarkean found it an odd response, since the *Liberator* was not yet unrecoverable. Then he noticed the ship's projected path. As he watched, the captured frigate accelerated to full speed toward the Alliance cruiser.

Belatedly, the cruiser started to change course, but it was too late. Escape pods began flying out from the *Liberator*, but only a few made it out from the *Ordinance* in time. With an impact that Maarkean could only imagine, the two ships collided and both vanished from the tactical display.

Distracted as he was watching the final flight of the *Liberator*, Maarkean did not catch the excited conversation going on around him. Looking away from the display, he cast a curious glance toward Davidus, whose voice he had last heard.

"Two Alliance frigates just moved alongside," the Terran said, his tone neutral. "We will be boarded shortly."

They only had a handful of marines on board. Two frigates would easily overpower his crew. But the idea of surrender did not sit well with him. "All hands, prepare to repel boarders. We won't give up this ship without a fight!"

"The carrier has launched bombers," Arzesaeth reported.

Saracasi could see the information on the tactical display, but Arzesaeth was sticking to the protocol of calling out important information. It was an old military practice, meant to ensure information was understood. It got tedious at times, but Saracasi appreciated the redundancy.

"Well," Saracasi said. "Let's make sure they know what they're up against. Open a channel to the Alliance ships."

Arzesaeth keyed the command and nodded to her. She had no idea what to say that might intimidate the Alliance into backing off. How do you bluff a strong position when you're flying what is potentially a death trap and have no back up?

"Attention, Alliance warships. This the Union warship . . . " Saracasi suddenly realized they had never named the ship.

FX-21 had been the experimental designation the Alliance had given the project. But it was not suitable for a true warship.

A smile crossed her face as she found inspiration within her situation. " . . . *Audacious*. You have entered orbit of a Union world and have taken provocative action. You are ordered to withdraw or we will be forced to open fire."

"Nice name," Arzesaeth whispered beside her. "Though you paused a little too long. Might have ruined the effect."

Saracasi frowned at the Ronid. His commentary was not helpful. But she quietly agreed with him. Lying wasn't her strong suit. Fortunately, she hadn't lied. Just hadn't had anything to back up her order.

"Rebel warship," a reply came a moment later. "This is Rear Admiral Gretaras of Task Force 412. You are in possession of stolen Alliance property. Surrender and prepare to be boarded or it is we who will open fire. You will not get a second warning."

"Well, can't say I didn't see that coming," Saracasi said quietly, gritting her teeth. It would have been so much easier if the Alliance had fallen for her bluff.

"Raise shields. Stand by, targeting systems," Saracasi ordered. They were still outside of optimal weapon range, which gave them some time to power things up. But within moments of her giving the order, the shields were reported to be at full strength. It was one of the perks of the *Audacious'* unique shield system.

Several tense moments passed by. Saracasi watched as they got closer to the Alliance fleet. Twelve PB-107 bombers moved in formation away from the fleet. Their course had them on an intercept trajectory before the bombers were truly into Kol's atmosphere.

Flying with the bombers was TF-412's corvette and two gunships. Together, those ships, along with the bombers' own defense turrets, would provide a blistering defense against any fighter assault. But the *Audacious* wasn't a fighter craft.

"No deviation in course. Entering optimal weapons range," Arzesaeth reported.

Moments later, heavy blaster fire began streaking out from the corvette's single cannon that had a good angle. With the *Audacious* still mostly within dense atmosphere, the weaker cannons from the defense batteries and gunships would lose cohesion and dissipate so as to be worthless weapons.

The blaster bombardment from the corvette streaked down. Saracasi briefly toyed with the idea of just letting the weapon hit uncontested, just to test out the integrity of their shields. But if the result was what she feared, that would be a poor way to start the battle. "Evasive maneuvers."

Saisee, at the helm, began sliding and jinking the frigate. Compared to fighter craft, the movements were unwieldy and slight. But it was enough at this range to throw off the attack. Two of the first three bolts missed by a few hundred meters. The third struck them dead center along the dorsal hull.

Saracasi braced for the impact. Even if the blaster bolt did not impart enough mass to alter the ship's trajectory more than the inertial dampeners could compensate for, there would be a vibration felt from the impact. Except there wasn't.

From Saracasi's perspective, the blaster bolt hadn't happened. No vibrations were felt through the deck. No alarms sounded indicating hull damage. No reports from operations about depleted shield strength.

The ship's specially designed shields had done exactly what the mad genius who had designed them had intended. They had absorbed the blast and replenished themselves in a span of a heartbeat. What would have taken regular shields several minutes to do, these shields had done almost instant-ly.

Looking for confirmation, she turned to Arzesaeth. He nodded, a wide creepy Ronid smile on his face. "Shields un-damaged. No hull damage. Shields remain stable."

"Continue on course. Weapons, stand ready. Lock target onto the corvette," Saracasi said, trying to keep her voice calm. That had merely been the first barrage. More would come.

As they got closer to the corvette, more did come. But like the first wave, Arzesaeth reported no damage. The shots that hit with each barrage would deplete the shields below full strength, but they would regenerate in time for the next barrage to come. The problem with high-power neutron blasters was that the more powerful the blasters were, the longer it took them to recharge.

"Lock all weapons on the corvette's weapon batteries. Full barrage. Fire," Saracasi ordered once they closed to a range she found acceptable.

Arzesaeth relayed the orders to the gunners and then a barrage of blaster bolts streamed toward the corvette. Unlike the corvette, the *Audacious* was a frigate, designed to fight other capital ships. She had more than one blaster cannon.

"First wave, direct hits. Corvette's shields down to 80%. Minimal hull damage," Arzesaeth reported.

"Continue barrage. PD turrets, stand by to target bomb-ers."

The exchange of fire continued for several more minutes. Saracasi watched their reactor output and power transfer system more than she did the tactical display. A single cor-vette might not be able to penetrate their shields, but that didn't mean the whole system wouldn't just blow out on them.

Chavatwor claimed he had solved the problem. The Kowwok engineer was a genius, and Saracasi believed that if anyone in the galaxy could do it, he could. But the ship's original designer had undoubtedly also been brilliant and had failed.

"Alliance frigate moving away from the escort carrier," Arzesaeth said, disrupting the pattern. The frigate had been holding back, guarding the vulnerable carrier craft. Now it was descending toward the atmosphere. Not toward them, however, but toward the UDF shipyards.

"Looks like they're trying to draw us off," Saracasi commented. "Either stay with the bombers or go stop the frigate."

"The bombers can make a bigger boom," Arzesaeth said, his pilot background showing.

"Maybe, but that frigate isn't exactly throwing flower petals," Saracasi said. "What's the status of the corvette's weapons?"

"One neutron blaster and both MKPD batteries are destroyed," Arzesaeth reported. "Both plasma beams are functional."

"Give me three more barrages. Try to take out at least one of those. Then we need to worry about the frigate. The bombers are Jerik's problem."

CHAPTER 33

Zeric's small squad of marines encountered no resistance as they made their way toward the sounds of the firefight. Whatever Alliance troops had fled his breach point had either not come this way, or the troops were too busy fighting to have prepared any roadblocks. Either way, he didn't complain.

Coming around the corner of a building, Zeric saw a collection of more than two dozen Alliance soldiers. They were hunkered down behind emergency barricades. This group had gotten their repeating blaster set up. It was firing away into an area Zeric couldn't see.

With each bing-bing-bing-bing, Zeric imagined another marine dropping dead to the ground. He could see Gu'od's body covered in blaster burns. His mind immediately shifted to the marines safely hiding behind some cover. And then Ice crept up behind them and shot them in the back.

In the distance, ringing off the concrete walls of the Alliance buildings, the sound of repeater fire came from behind them. Ice must have tried to make their way through the wall behind them. The private, whose name Zeric couldn't remember, had engaged them. Almost as soon as the firing started, it stopped again. Either he had driven Ice back, or Ice had gotten through.

Either way, Zeric couldn't afford to wait anymore. Not wanting to give any indication that they were coming, Zeric gave a silent nod to Sergeant Ocif. The Braz nodded in reply. The other marines raised their rifles to a ready position. Letting out a scream, Zeric charged around the corner.

The next few moments passed in a blur for Zeric. He saw every Alliance soldier he shot. He remembered diving down to avoid a blast from one of the soldiers that should have taken off his head. But the whole experience felt distant and insubstantial. His mind had disengaged and his body took over, giving into the battle lust. It was a familiar sensation.

When calm, rational thought returned, Zeric stood over the corpse of the Alliance soldier who had manned the repeater. Bodies lay around him. Not all of them were Alliance.

Surveying the area, Zeric looked to find who the Alliance soldiers had been shooting at. From behind some crates, Sigfa, Gu'od, and a dozen marines emerged. No blaster fire came through the hole in the wall behind them. If Ice was coming, they weren't here yet.

"Lieutenant Neith," Zeric shouted, his ears still ringing from all the weapons fire, "hold this position and prepare a squad to follow me. There were two other breach holes our marines could come through, and Ice has surely come through one of them."

Sigfa acknowledged and then began deploying his marines. Counting the dead, more than half of his platoon was accounted for here. If the rest had stuck together, they would be another formidable group. If they were split up, they might have been overwhelmed.

"Thought your wife might have needed to keep her promise," Zeric said with a smile as Gu'od came up to him.

"And she would have to," Gu'od said, smiling back. Then his smile vanished.

Reaching out, Gu'od pulled Zeric to his left. A burning sensation consumed his shoulder as the Liw'kel pulled him down. As Zeric went down, Gu'od lifted himself up, and used Zeric's body to twist and propel himself over Zeric's head.

Zeric wasn't sure what happened next. The burning in his shoulder was undoubtedly a blaster burn. He had felt enough of those to recognize the sensation. Even with experience, it didn't help him filter it out. Having been used as a catapult and thrown to the ground did not help matters.

"Medic!" he heard Sigfa shout. "Tamarynn, the general's been hit, get up here!"

The redheaded Tamarynn Farr raced up from wherever she had been and dropped down beside Zeric. Two thoughts crossed his mind. The first was that he wished the medic had not left a critically wounded marine to come tend to him. The second was that Tamarynn was too pretty to be on a battlefield. He'd thought that about Gamaly more than once.

That made him remember Gu'od. Struggling against Tamarynn and Sigfa, Zeric sat up, trying to find his friend. Fear overshadowed his pain for a second. Then he saw the Liw'kel standing over a crumpled figure in an Ice uniform.

With a sigh of relief, the pain in his shoulder came flooding back. He growled and pushed Tamarynn away anyway. As much as he wanted to let her treat him, a blaster burn to the shoulder like he had was not lethal, at least not immediately. It had been a grazing shot, nothing more. Worst case, he would end up like Asirzi and have a cybernetic arm.

Ignoring the medic's order to stay down, Zeric forced himself up. He stared at Gu'od as he did. "You moron. I just tell you I'm relieved you haven't gotten yourself killed, and you immediately decide to throw yourself at a guy with a gun? Using me as a slingshot, no less?"

Gu'od shrugged. "I use what's handy. I could have just let him shoot you in the head."

"Better that than deal with your wife."

Zeric stumbled over to Gu'od and the downed Ice figure. As he suspected, once he got a better look he recognized Firek. The Terran was still breathing.

Fighting through the pain, Zeric reached down and grabbed the man. "Was revenge on me worth all this, you bastard?"

Weakly, obviously woozy from the head blow Gu'od had delivered, Firek smiled. "Rather conceited to think that. Revenge against you was just a bonus. Truth was, we just received a better offer than your congress could afford to pay."

Confused, Zeric dropped Firek. When had Ice had the chance to get an offer from the Alliance? They had been cut off while on Irod for the last few months. They had all been aboard ships along with marines during the insertion to Sulas.

Then it hit him. There was a traitor among them. Someone working for the Alliance must have tried to use Ice to ruin the operation. An image of Firek and Davidus talking sprang to mind.

His first thought was to warn Maarkean. Fighting with his comm gear, Zeric called up a channel for the fleet. By this time they should already be on their approach. Zeric was supposed to have control of the bases' weapons. But he would have to settle for the fact that they were not yet firing.

"*Defiant Glory*, this is Rogue One. Come in. Anyone in the Union fleet, please respond," Zeric said and then repeated himself. He got only static in response. "I'm not getting a reply," he growled.

"This base undoubtedly has better communication gear than we do," Gu'od replied.

"Well, then, let's get on with this mission," Zeric said, gritting his teeth through the pain in his shoulder. "Lieutenant, we have a gun battery to capture."

Sigfa nodded and started directing marines forward, leaving a team behind in a defensive formation. Zeric started to follow, but the dual grip of Gu'od and Tamarynn forced him down to a sitting position. Reluctantly, he allowed the medic to treat his injury.

By the time Tamarynn released him, Sigfa's platoon had succeeded in gaining control of the base's central command center. Alliance units were still putting up sporadic resistance around the base, but the main body had been defeated when Zeric had surrounded them. With Firek captured and Ice outnumbered, the fighting spirit of Ice collapsed.

Entering the command center, Zeric called for a status update. Sigfa had already been there long enough to gain access to the comm and sensor tracking stations.

"I've made contact with Major Ki'Li," Sigfa reported. "2nd and 5th Platoons have succeeded in taking their guns. I get no reply from 4th. The major reports that the battery 4th was supposed to capture has fired several shots into our approaching transports. The ships have altered course out of firing range.

"It also appears that an Alliance fleet has appeared in orbit. We've damaged a few of their ships within range, and they are backing off now. Unfortunately, we have been unable to make contact with General Numba on *Rogue Spirit* or General Ocaitchi on *Defiant Glory*. The only navy ship I can reach is the *Cutty Sark*."

Suppressing his concern, Zeric nodded. "Let me talk to Major Relis."

Sigfa handed Zeric the comm, and he said, "Fracsid, this is Rogue One. What's the status of the fleet?"

The comm channel came back full of static—a result of Alliance jamming attempts. "Glad to hear your voice, General. Unfortunately, I don't have good news on that front. The fleets been shattered. *Rogue Spirit* and *Liberator* are confirmed losses. As are a few of my gunships. *Defiant Glory* is still intact but dead in space, surrounded by Alliance ships.

"General Ocaitchi ordered all fighters and gunships to escort the transports down to the surface before we lost contact. He also dispatched *Gallant* before the battle, so at least one of our ships made it out. The Alliance fighters are backing off from the transports now that they're in range of your ground weapons. Our fighters have started setting down at guns Alpha and Gamma."

The news struck Zeric like a rock to the head. Davidus' betrayal had gone far beyond having Ice switch sides; he had tipped the Alliance off and set a trap for them. Now thousands of their comrades were dead, and they were trapped down here without fleet support. At least there was a chance Maarkean was still alive aboard the *Defiant Glory*.

"Sir." The sound from the static-filled comm channel brought Zeric back to the present. "What are your orders? I think I can get my gunships through the Alliance blockade, but if we do, I don't think we'll be able to get back down to you."

Zeric considered the question. The gunships would be incredibly useful down here, but with an entire Alliance fleet in orbit, the area they could fly would be limited to where they were under the protection of his guns. That left a lot of sky.

He glanced at his Liw'kel friend standing beside him. Gu'od's expression was his normal stoic front, but Zeric could tell that there was turmoil behind the façade. Cut off as they were, he would not be able to keep his promise to get Gu'od back to Gamaly in a month.

"Fracsid, can you get a ship to the surface and pick up a passenger?" Zeric asked.

There was a long pause before the response came through. "I can try, sir. But it will be tricky. The longer we wait to try to break free, the tighter the Alliance can close their net."

Before Zeric could say anything else, he felt Gu'od's hand on his uninjured shoulder. Turning, he looked his friend in the eye. Gu'od held his gaze, but Zeric saw a slight quiver in his antennae.

"No. I will not have anyone's lives risked for me. I cannot disrupt the Balance to such a degree for personal needs," Gu'od said, his tone not as decisive as his look implied.

"Are you sure?" Zeric asked.

Gu'od said nothing more in response.

Zeric debated what he should do for his friend. He wanted to be able to get Gu'od back to Gamaly. He knew that on some level, at least, Gu'od wanted him to as well. But with Numba and Maarkean gone, he was now responsible for everyone's lives.

"No, Fracsid. If you can do it safely, get your remaining ships out of here. Join up with Solyss and Saracasi. Figure out a way to break this blockade. And Fracsid, let Congress know that someone betrayed us. I think it was Commander Brieni, but I don't have any proof, and he might not have been the only one. Keep your eyes open."

"Aye, sir. Good luck down there," Fracsid said before breaking the channel.

Zeric collapsed into the chair beside the comm station. He was now in command of this entire army.

"Damn you, Maarkean," Zeric said under his breath.

Two more Alliance marines charged up the stairs to the *Defiant Glory*'s bridge. Crouched behind the main tactical display terminal, Maarkean took aim with his SK-9 and dropped one of them. The blaster bolt hit the marine in the chest, burning through his combat vest. Maarkean had abandoned the stun setting a long time before.

"Any response from engineering?!" he shouted again.

Around him, many of the bridge and CIC crews were already down, wounded, or stunned. Most had not been armed or trained in close quarters fighting. Lohcja crouched beside him and Davidus and Kaars were behind him. Across the CIC, in the forward bridge section, Tadashio and a few more crewers provided a flanking position for the Alliance forces trying to push their way up the stairs.

"None," Kaars reported. "Last reply we got was that La'ari was trying to bring the reactor back online. Marines had moved to defend engineering, but the Alliance was making a heavy push. Power still shows as being offline."

Their one hope of getting out of this was that La'ari could get the reactor functioning. They were far enough from Sulas that they could engage the hyperdrive without the gravity well holding them in real space. With two Alliance frigates docked to them, however, Maarkean wasn't sure what would happen if they tried to jump to hyperspace. The worst case was that all three ships would be torn to shreds, which would be a victory in his mind.

Another wave of Alliance marines charged up the stairs, cutting off his reply to Kaars. Maarkean fired and missed. Blaster bolts flew around him, followed by screams of pain. Before he could aim at the advancing marines again, they were almost on top of him.

Dropping his pistol, Maarkean reacted on instinct. All of his training with Gu'od in the battle techniques of the Ni'jar had started to sink in. With a quick series of blows, he disarmed and then dropped the closest marine. Not pausing a beat, he leapt over the tactical table, tackling another marine to the ground.

Over the next few seconds, Maarkean called upon every bit of strength remaining to him and every technique Gu'od had shown him. Three marines surrounded him, plus the one he had landed on. Pushing against the downed marine, he propelled his legs upward, knocking back one marine's head with a sharp kick.

As he launched himself back up, he pulled the rifle from the downed marine's hands and swung it in an arc. The butt of the weapon hit another marine, causing him to stumble and fall back down the stairs and onto his comrades. That left one marine standing in Maarkean's reach.

Seeing the marine fall down the stairs brought a smile to Maarkean's face, and he momentarily lost focus. Instead of landing elegantly on his feet, ready to launch into another attack, he staggered, falling backward into a computer terminal.

Trying to regain his balance, Maarkean watched the remaining marine raise his rifle. As the marine fired, a flurry of blasts took him in the chest, throwing off his aim. The blaster bolt from the rifle destroyed the terminal behind Maarkean's head.

Lohcja clicked his mandibles at Maarkean in a self-satisfied expression. Nodding at his friend, Maarkean took the chance to dive for cover behind the tactical terminal. Picking up his pistol again, he started looking for another target.

Across the bridge, Tadashio and his team were heavily engaged with a group of Alliance marines. Maarkean couldn't get a clean target on any of them due to the safety railing in the way.

Suddenly, a tingling electric feeling cascaded through Maarkean. The intense familiarity of a stun bolt shut down Maarkean's ability to control his body, and he fell to the floor. Maarkean's mind permitted one final thought: that the stun bolt had hit him from behind.

As the world shrank into darkness, he heard Lohcja exclaim, "Kaa—"

While Saracasi took the *Audacious* toward the Alliance frigate, she watched Jerik lead his squadron of fighters up from the surface of Kol. With the corvette mostly disabled, the bombers had only the gunboats and their own defensive guns for protection. An experienced fighter squadron would have called that easy pickings. But there was little experience among their pilots.

By the time the two groups of crafts had engaged, she was forced to turn her attention to the frigate.

As she watched the projected interception point, she realized she had spent too much time engaging the corvette. They wouldn't intercept the frigate until she already had a firing angle on the shipyard. The Alliance would have enough time to do some damage.

Anxiously, Saracasi tried to will the engines to burn faster. She racked her brain for a quick engineering solution to increase engine power. Or a military tactic her brother had mentioned sometime during her childhood that she could pull out and use for a victory.

Nothing came to mind. There was no way to reach the frigate before it got into firing range of the shipyard. Long-range fire would not force them to alter their course. She could only wait. Or do something completely different.

"Come about, heading two six zero, mark one seven four," Saracasi ordered, eliciting an eyestalk turned in curiosity from Saisee.

"Weapons, lock onto the carrier," she continued, answering none of the curious looks.

So far, she had been playing this battle like a reluctant defender. If she just did the minimal amount necessary to stop the Alliance, she had told herself, she could still throw away the uniform at the end, knowing she had resisted the killer inside her. She had targeted the weapons on the corvette and mostly ignored the bombers.

A barrage from their weapons would have torn a bomber apart, whereas the fighters' attack would destroy them, but likely give the pilots a chance to bail out. In effect, she had kept her weapon on stun.

But stun was not always an effective weapon. Sometimes you had to switch to the lethal setting. Like she had done on Enro. Like she knew she would need to do again in the future. She felt no remorse in her decision. Just sadness that it wasn't a harder decision to make.

"Entering weapons range," Arzesaeth said.

"Fire, full barrage," Saracasi said, her tone neutral.

Carriers, even small escort carriers like this one, were important tools in warfare. They allowed smaller, hyperspace-incapable craft to be brought to where they were needed. Most big ships were vulnerable to concentrated bursts from groups of smaller craft. Their shields would not hold up. And hitting the fighters in return was much more difficult than hitting bigger ships.

But because their primary offensive weapon was their complement of carried craft, once those had been launched, carriers usually were not priority targets. They had little heavy offensive weaponry and were easy to mop up at the conclusion of a battle; after all the ships with the big guns were taken care of.

Nevertheless, carriers almost always had an escort during a battle. If an enemy did decide to go after them, they could lose the battle and still strand a bunch of fighter pilots as well as put at risk a large crew. They were tempting targets to desperate defenders.

The carrier began firing back immediately. Unlike the corvette, she carried more than one heavy neutron blaster cannon. Not as many as the frigate, but enough to cause the *Audacious'* shields to dip each time they were hit. The regeneration kept them strong, but it started to show Saracasi where the line was between complete immunity to fire and a burning hunk of metal.

Their first pass along the carrier's spine resulted in minimal hull damage but almost completely depleted her ventral shields. Saracasi ordered Saisee to swing around for another pass.

"Frigate is changing course!" Arzesaeth exclaimed triumphantly. "They're headed back here. Carrier is shifting to intercept. We'll be in range of both ships in two minutes."

Well, Saracasi thought, her offensive gamble had paid off. The frigate had backed away from the shipyard before it could do too much damage. The bombers were still engaged with Jerik's fighters. Neither side had a clear advantage, but the bombers were unable to line up for an attack run. The shipyard was safe for the moment. Now she just had to deal with two armed Alliance warships at once.

Arzesaeth did not need to inform her when they had entered the effective weapons range for the frigate. The frigate coordinated her fire with the carrier, one ship firing and forcing Saisee to either avoid it or to make a predictable course change directly into the incoming fire from the other ship. This increased the frigate's effective range significantly.

The young Camari did a remarkable job avoiding what blaster bolts he could, but the *Audacious'* shields still took more damage than they ever had before. Each impact put a strain on the regeneration and power transfer system. Saracasi's instincts told her that her ship would not hold up for much longer.

"Concentrate all fire on the carrier's power system," she ordered. "Continuous barrage."

A ship's power system was one of the most heavily protected systems onboard. The deuterium most ships used for fuel was vulnerable to combustion in the oxygen-rich environment inside a ship. But because it was so vital to keeping the reactor running, it had to be protected from an outer hull breach. Do enough damage to the hull leading toward a reactor and there was a chance the barrage would penetrate the hull and ignite the deuterium or just disable the reactor, shutting the rest of the ship down.

It was not a maneuver to make if you wanted to capture a ship alive. Disabling the engines and/or weapons and then boarding a ship was the preferred tactic. But in war, Saracasi thought, you didn't shoot to wound.

Giving the gun batteries a proper angle to maintain a constant stream of fire on the carrier limited Saisee's options for maneuvering. Saracasi watched nervously as the shield display registered an increasing number of hits. Instead of minimal drops in effective rating between each barrage, their shields were getting perilously close to being depleted entirely. Hull damage was starting to get through, though, fortunately, it had so far been minimal.

"That's it!" Arzesaeth shouted. "I'm reading signs of overload and internal explosions!"

"Saisee, get us clear!" Saracasi ordered.

Moving as fast as physics would allow, Saisee pushed the frigate's engines, trying desperately to get clear of the exploding carrier. Exploding ships were one of the most dangerous weapons on a battlefield. Internal explosion from an overloaded fusion reactor or deuterium explosion turned a once-solid ship into a giant flak round. Space filled with high-velocity debris. And here in the upper atmosphere of Kol, even the thin air turned into a deadly compression wave.

As Saisee pushed the engines hard, Saracasi watched the reactor status display, and knew their own overload was about to come. Fortunately, Sheanna down in engineering saw the same thing. "Bridge, engineering. Power distribution system overload. Triggering emergency shutdown."

With a slight flicker of the lights, the ship's main anti-matter reactor shut down. During her previous journey aboard this ship, they had overtaxed the power distribution system running the hyperdrive. It had been luck they had managed to shut the reactor down in time.

One of the first improvements she and Chavatwor had installed was an emergency shut-off switch for the power system. Instead of power surging throughout every system onboard, they each became isolated and ran off a back up capacitor. The power spike then had only one place to go, a power sink on the ventral hull.

"The bypass worked!" Sheanna said over the comm, her voice indicating she hadn't believed it would. "Couple fired circuits, but no damage to any major system. Back up capacitors holding power for now."

"Shields holding but are in minimal maintenance mode," Arzesaeth added. "They're up, but they won't regenerate."

While they were in a far better position than she had found herself in above Roc 5, when an overload had completely shut down the shields, weapons, and most everything else, the regeneration effect was their only benefit. Without it, their shields were significantly weaker than the other frigate's, and they carried less weaponry.

"Well," Saracasi said. "Guess it's time for another bluff."

Arzesaeth gave her a look that indicated his skepticism, but he opened a comm channel to the Alliance frigate. Saracasi took a moment to collect herself, slipping into a short meditation. Then she tried to find all the hostility, menace, confidence, and smugness she had in her.

"Alliance forces, you will receive one more opportunity to withdraw. Your carrier is destroyed, and your corvette is disabled. I have no wish to destroy any more of you. But your cause is hopeless. As you can see, we have so far taken no damage. Your weapons are unable to penetrate our shields," Saracasi said.

To the outside observer, what she said would appear true. Their shields would register at full strength and the hull showed only minimal impact scars. No systems would register as offline. While they could not fire more than a few shots or keep their shields up for more than a few minutes, to the Alliance they would look primed and ready for another round of combat.

In response, the Alliance frigate, corvette, and one gunship—Jerik's squadron had managed to take out one of the gunships themselves—altered course and headed away from Kol. The remaining bombers turned away from the shipyard, on a course to the Alliance base elsewhere on the planet. They released their bombs harmlessly into the desert to reduce their mass and increase their speed.

It took Saracasi a moment to process that they had just won. They had fought off an Alliance taskforce of five ships, destroyed two, and disabled two more. Presumably, they had also scored the first kill of an Alliance flag officer, as Admiral Gretaras had probably been aboard the carrier.

The crew around her cheered, and Saracasi smiled. She had won. The Alliance had been driven back. She'd only had to kill a couple hundred Alliance personnel to do it, and she was okay with that on every level. There was no arguing with the position that the universe had placed her in. She was a warrior.

EPILOGUE

"Here's the final after-action report, Admiral," Commander Dolan said, bringing up the report onto the room's screen. They had been in control of Sulas space for two weeks now. It had taken this long to get the full picture of the results of the battle.

Sartori looked up from the casualty listing she had been reading. She knew almost none of the names on the list, but she still made it a point to read over everyone who died under her command. She would do the same once a list was compiled of the rebel dead. They were rebels, but they were still Alliance citizens.

The large screen Dolan had activated showed statistics about ships damaged or destroyed on both sides. There were numbers of estimated troops that had landed on Sulas and numbers of prisoners captured from onboard the rebel carrier. The screen also showed a 2D map of Sulas and the areas the rebels now controlled. Most of it was empty swampland around the defense batteries they had captured. Another map showed the odd orbits her ships needed to take to avoid coming under fire from those same guns.

All in the all, the operation would be called a success. But to her, it had been a failure. The rebels had had one capital ship escape, along with several gunships, and the vast majority of the transports had delivered their troops safely to the surface of Sulas. They also controlled three defense batteries, which would make clearing them off Sulas more difficult.

But it would not be impossible. With the reinforcements of the Marine Expeditionary Force, she now had thousands of highly trained marines, in addition to the army defense forces already on the planet. She also had undisputed control of three quarters of the Sulas sky.

"I see one of our prisoners was Major Ocaitchi," Sartori said, surprised by this discovery. She would have expected a zealot like Ocaitchi to die rather than allow himself to be captured.

"Aye, Admiral," Dolan confirmed. "His ship turned out to be the one our spy was aboard. We avoided destroying it, and he managed to disable the ship from within."

"Excellent. With Ocaitchi in our hands, we'll be able to put some pressure on the rebels."

"Speaking of our spy, his plan to break free and remain ingrained with the rebels worked. We had to let the carrier escape, but he should have information on their remaining fleet strength in a few weeks. Before we released them, we checked the ship's computer for the location of Irod. Unfortunately, the crew had already managed to destroy their navigational data before we took it, so no record of the location of their secret base remains. We could try interrogations. Ocaitchi will almost certainly have those coordinates," Dolan said.

Sartori frowned. The location of the world of Irod had been a bit of intelligence their spy had been unable to acquire. They knew it was somewhere in the sector, relatively close to Sulas, but not what direction. This sector of the galaxy had a very dense cluster of stars, most of which had only been casually surveyed. She could check them all, but only if she had the resources to dispatch a dozen scout ships for a few months.

"Hold off for now. There might not be much of a rebel fleet left, but they still managed to do repel our task force on Kol. Plus, we still have an operation on Enro to plan. The location of an isolated world is of little consequence," Sartori said. "For now, let us concentrate on trying to remind Major Ocaitchi of his oath to the Alliance. If we can break him, make him remember what it meant to serve us, that will be our best weapon against the rebels."

"Aye, Admiral." Dolan nodded. "The task force commanders are waiting to meet with you."

Sartori sighed. "Very well. I'll join them in a minute."

Dolan nodded and left the room. Sartori sat there alone for a moment. Victory against these rebels was going to take longer than she had originally hoped. Her retirement would undoubtedly have to be postponed even further.

They had lost a few ships to the rebels, mostly due to the incompetence of the mercenaries and the rebels' willingness to make suicide attacks. The reports of the FX-21 appearing to be operational at Kol had her worried. That one ship had driven off an entire task force, coming through the battle without a scratch.

But it was only one ship. If she could turn Ocaitchi back to the Alliance, she might be able to undermine the rebels' will to fight. It could take time, but a few more victories like the one today would show that the Alliance would not surrender to terrorism. The rebels could keep their shipyard on the backwater world of Kol. She would take back the rest of the sector.

Saracasi stood before the airlock onboard Chavatwor's new orbital shipyard. In the three weeks since she had fought off the Alliance task force, it had arrived and the Kowwok shipwright had moved work on all large ships into orbit. This included the repair work being done on the *Audacious.*

She wasn't alone in the airlock chamber. A team of marines led by Asheerah Aru and a medical team led by Dr. Istru waited a short distance away. Beside her, Fracsid Relis and Solyss Novastar stood silently. Up until a short time ago, Saracasi had thought that these two men and their ships had comprised the entirety of the remaining Union fleet. But then the *Defiant Glory* had appeared.

When the carrier jumped into orbit, she had debated simply blowing it away. It did not seem possible that it could have broken free from the Alliance after being captured. Her instincts told her to suspect a trap. Unfortunately, she had held onto hope that her brother was still onboard.

"What do we do if General Ocaitchi isn't there?" Fracsid asked, breaking the silence. "We can't just follow his orders, knowing what we know."

"What exactly do we know?" Solyss said. "General Dustlighter said he thought Commander Brieni was the traitor, but he didn't have any evidence. We can't arrest a man on suspicion."

"But if he is the traitor, and General Ocaitchi isn't here, then he's the senior officer. We can't have him in command of the navy!" Fracsid argued.

"So our choice is to either let a potential Alliance mole lead us, or arrest a man without evidence, just like we're fighting the Alliance for doing?" Saracasi said, exasperation in her tone.

A tone sounded from the airlock, and the light above the door shone green, interrupting their conversation. Saracasi decided that they would just have to hope that her brother was on board and he could decide what to do. He trusted Davidus, but he didn't like the man, so she had no idea what decision he would make.

The airlock door slid open, revealing a dirty brown Kowwok with his left arm in a sling. She recognized the Kowwok as Tadashio, the *Defiant Glory's* operations officer. As she had still been half-expecting a troop of Alliance marines to be on the other side, she breathed a sigh of relief.

"Major, am I glad to see you," Tadashio said, pain evident on his furry face.

"Same here. Now, Specialist, go see Dr. Istru," Saracasi immediately ordered.

"I was told to escort you to the CIC, ma'am."

"We know the way. Get that arm looked at," Saracasi insisted. Based on the quality of the sling Tadashio wore, the medic who had gone with the *Defiant Glory* must be among the injured or dead.

Saracasi stepped aside to let Tadashio through the airlock. Before she could board the ship herself, Asheerah moved forward with two marines and proceeded onto the ship. The Liw'kel marine had wanted to seal off the airlock and storm the ship, but Solyss had insisted she wait further down. He had more confidence than Saracasi did that the ship was still in Union hands.

Following the marines onto the ship, Saracasi walked down the corridor toward the stairwell that led up to the bridge. Several lights were non-functional. There were blaster burn marks on the bulkheads. There had definitely been a firefight aboard.

Emerging onto the bridge, Saracasi found what looked like a scene from a horror story. The metal decks were stained with blood. Computer terminals flickered or were dark. Fortunately, whoever had died up here had been taken away a while ago.

Among all the chaos, Saracasi's wish for a happy ending was crushed when she saw Davidus Brieni standing at the command terminal. Kaars Aerinstar stood beside Davidus, the two Terrans talking quietly. The rest of the bridge crew went about the task of shutting down the ship now that she was docked.

"Commander," Saracasi said, deliberately not using Davidus' honorary title of "captain," "where's General Oca-itchi?" Davidus turned toward her group as they came up the stairs. His expression was dark, worry lines creeping out from his eyes.

"I wish I knew. When we managed to break free and re-take the ship, he and Colonel Cargon were not aboard. For the first day after we were captured, they were imprisoned with me and the other officers. But then the Alliance started taking us each out for interrogation. I never saw them again after they were taken."

Saracasi sighed heavily. That meant her brother was still a captive of the Alliance. But he had survived the battle. That meant he was alive. He had gotten her out of an Alliance prison once, and now she would have to return the favor.

Unfortunately, that would have to wait. For now, she had a hard choice to make.

"Commander Brieni," Saracasi began, "evidence has come to light that the Union was betrayed to the Alliance at Sulas. You have been implicated in this treason. I'm afraid I'm going to have to take you into custody until we can sort everything out."

Her words hung in the air. Davidus just stood there, his cheek quivering, either from exhaustion or anger, Saracasi wasn't sure. He said nothing in response, which surprised her. After a moment, Solyss gestured for Asheerah to come forward and arrest him.

Shrugging off the marines, Davidus straightened his back. He cast an accusatory glare at Saracasi. "Just like your brother, you can't stand being forced to serve under me. Justice will prove me innocent."

As she watched the marines lead Davidus down the stairs, Kaars stepped up beside her and said, "I never would have thought him a traitor."

She ignored the man. Davidus was an arrogant ass, and she couldn't take the chance that he was the traitor, but she wasn't entirely convinced that he was.

"Now what?" Fracsid asked. "With General Ocaitchi a prisoner, General Numba dead, Commander Brieni arrested, and General Dustlighter trapped on Sulas... what do we do now?"

Silence filled the air for an uncomfortable moment, and Saracasi took a deep breath.

"We keep fighting."

ACKNOWLEDGEMENTS

I'd like to take a moment to thank my editor Hilary for her tireless efforts in helping get this book ready under a tight deadline. I also want to thank my wife for her support. Most of the editing stages occurred after our son had been born, and without her effort in giving me time to work, who knows when we would have seen the final product.

ABOUT THE AUTHOR

Wayne currently lives in Houston with his wife, son and dog. He remains a fan of geek culture, board games, video games, fantasy, science fiction and all around silliness.

CONNECT WITH WAYNE

Email
wayne@waynebasta.com

Blog
www.waynebasta.com